Urbis Morpheos

Urbis Morpheos

Stephen Palmer

Introduction by GWYNETH JONES

PS Publishing 2010

Published in June 2010 by PS Publishing Ltd. by arrangement
with the author. All rights reserved by the author.

ISBN
978-1-906301-43-9 (Trade Hardcover)
978-1-906301-44-6 (Traycased Hardcover)

Design & Layout by Michael Smith

Printed in Great Britain by the MPG Books Group,
Bodmin and King's Lynn

PS Publishing Ltd | Grosvenor House | 1 New Road
Hornsea, HU18 1PG | United Kingdom

editor@pspublishing.co.uk | www.pspublishing.co.uk

Introduction

Stephen Palmer's intriguing first novel, *Memory Seed* (1996)—set in a far future where the last human city on Earth is falling victim to a plague of greenery—was quickly recognised as a new phenomenon. This was the birth of "Greenpunk", a hybrid of radical science fiction and Green fantasy, where the anarchic "street" that finds its own uses for new technology (in William Gibson's telling aphorism) is the riotous continuum of organic life itself. In *Memory Seed* the Vegetable Kingdom, instead of being tamed, or destroyed, ignored or exploited, has become the marauding exploiter. Instead of teeming data networks giving anti-biotic "birth" to a bodiless, sentient AI, an arcology of hyper-evolved cellular life cannibalises machine processes, and finally, in a surreal climax, subsumes—just as in Greg Bear's rather more disciplined and straightforward version of this scenario in *Blood Music* (see below)—human intelligence itself.

Other "Greenpunk" titles followed. In *Glass* (1997), closely related to *Memory Seed*, the story of the last city, "Kray", is retold from a different angle. In *Flowercrash* (2002), a female-ordered far-future Utopia, based on botanical information networks (the *"flowers"* of the title), is challenged by masculinist authoritarians. Later novels have moved Stephen Palmer's organic-shamanic nanotech fiction closer to a more conventional near-future SF, rather in the style of Ian MacDonald: as two royal sisters struggle for supremacy in the Ghana of the mid-twenty-second century (*Muezzinland*, 2002); and a legendary underground Tibetan DJ detects alien invasion in ambient trance music (*Hallucinating*, 2004).

Stephen Palmer's new work, *Urbis Morpheos*, marks an emphatic return to his Greenpunk territory, but there have been some important changes since his last adventures in organic-shamanic Wonderland. As before, this is a far future Earth. The action is set loosely "a million years" further down the line from where we are now; and as before, in *Memory Seed*, the world is in the grip of an Ice Age. There is a city, in some sense still "Kray", the *last city*, but even more fragmented and hallucinatory. There's a pair of female human protagonists, Psolilai/psolilai, who dream of each other's exploits and could be the same person. There is a mysterious quest, which will decide the fate of the future. So far, it's the mixture as before. But the struggle between nature and machine has changed shape. Natural ecosystems are on the defensive now, surviving in problematic havens. Manufactured ecosystems are pervasive intruders, barely kept at bay by a constant and laborious kind of fire watch. Yet it's obvious to the reader (though not to all the characters) that these opposing armies, deadly enemies, have moved into close convergence. Weird artificial plants, animals, birds, and many different orders of artificial sentient beings, teem and hybridise as vividly as organic life itself—some of them inimical, many of them potential allies. The female protagonist(s), as in previous novels, are devotees of Gaia, but devotion to Gaia has become a political opinion, rather than a religious conviction or moral imperative—and like all political opinions, subject to realignment. It may be time to think the unthinkable, abandon the ancient wars and declare peace between nature and manufacture.

Urbis Morpheos is a tale of two wildly productive future species, mechanist and organic, grown so close in convergent evolution that they can hardly be distinguished from each other. Stephen Palmer's highly idiosyncratic and personal symbol of their convergence is a *fungal* knowledge interface. If you're in need of information, in this wonderland, your first and best resort is always to eat a psychoactive mushroom of some kind. Nausea and actual vomiting can be safely ignored; if you're afraid the species might be seriously toxic, make an infusion and drink it as tea. A fantastic library, where the leaves of the volumes are mushroom gills, holds edible secrets. Mushrooms that grow out of mushrooms are stores of meta-knowledge; they will provide you with information about the information networks of nature. Needless to say, the experience can be powerfully upsetting, and if you are not already a devotee of the 'shroom, I'm happy to say that *Urbis Morpheos* won't have you rushing to try this risky form of mind-expansion. Yet it's an effective metaphor. Mycorrhizal fungi, standing in the same relation to animals, plants and bacteria as information technology to the mechanist world—parasitic, pervasive and indispensible—close the loop, and complete the reflection.

We have Cyberpunk, we have Steampunk, and though "cyberpunk" was declared dead very shortly after the canonical texts were published, each form has produced a flourishing evolutionary line: hordes of hybridised, cross-fertilised, cannibalised and mashed-up descendants. It's disappointing that the third potent interface proposed in the nine-teen-eighties never really took the critics' or the public's fancy. Greg Bear's *Blood Music* (1984)—wherein a reckless molecular biologist injects himself with artificially-created sentient white blood cells, trig-gering a catastrophic change of being for all life on Earth—seemed at the time an outstanding founding-father. It's still one of the books I confidently offer to virgin readers, curious about science fiction; with very positive results. Kathleen Ann Goonan's "Nanotech Quartet" (*Queen City Jazz, Mississippi Blues, Crescent City Rhapsody, Light Music*) offers a very different but equally demanding nanotech future: but works like these have remained isolated. "Nanotech" is most often spotted lurking in the undergrowth of a genre scenario, a catch-all term for invincible, *amorphous* futuristic technology (not unlike the magic "nanotech" particles in a cosmetic ad).

Perhaps the problem is that tendency towards the amorphous. Fans of "hard" sci-fi will tolerate any amount of weird gadgets, but they prefer situations where 1+1=2, and boundaries are clear. Fans of "Green" future-fantasy prefer to see ancient heroes recalled, and ancient myths replayed; and tend to be allergic to scientific terms. Stephen Palmer's vision, combining the applied science of very, very small machines with a passion for organic futures and organic solu-tions, takes the bold risk of falling between audiences. But the attentive reader will find, buried in the phantasmagoria that is *Urbis Morpheos*, as in all Palmer's Greenpunk fiction, a skeleton of simple genre story-telling. There's a quest, a rebellious hero(ine), her band of unlikely allies; cosy interludes, ferocious violence, and finally, the "unexpected" but inevitable solution—a tale Palmer himself has called (perhaps mischievously) "a fable about recycling". Drama and characters may be subordinate to the world-building, but for the right reader, that won't be a disadvantage. The story is of minor importance. What *Urbis*

Morpheos offers is a vision of mechanist evolution, so often depicted as the enemy of all things "Green", as a "Second Life" as messy, unpredictable and unfathomably interconnected as the real thing.

Gwyneth Jones
March 2010

Urbis Morpheos

PART 1

RAPID EYE MOVEMENT

KNOWLEDGE BECAME WISDOM

For the one-thousandth morning I looked out from the window of my cell to see narcoleptic snow lying heavy upon the ground. But there was no point in imagining escape, since I was two thousand feet up Tall Cliff Steel, with hundreds of identical windows above and below me, each the portal to another cell, and a lone, miserable occupant.

I shared my cell with a drone, a waddling creature shaped like a disk, a product of the manufacturing ecosystem that lived in packs on cold and metallic ground but which could be trained to follow simple orders, like a dog. Guard Psolilai well, it had been told.

I shivered. Bad snow falling fresh from leaden clouds meant winter had arrived.

The day was like any other, grey, chill, with the orders of the wardens in my ears, the smell of stone dust in my nose, darkness surrounding me, no sign of the sun. Chains chafed my wrists as my gang trudged from cells to rockface and back to cells. But tomorrow was a rest day. I would lie on my bunk and consider impending madness.

It was common practice for the chains to be unlocked at the end of each corridor, so that prisoners could walk to their own cells and report to their drones. I trudged alone to my cell — to find a handbag hanging from the doorknob. I looked at it. I picked it up. A movement to my right alerted me to a watcher, and I turned to see a robed woman, old and leaning on a gleaming emerald staff around which a double spiral of silver twisted. For numinous seconds we stared into one another's eyes.

"Trouble at home!" hissed the woman.

I took a step towards the interloper, then watched her duck out of sight. I ran forward to look down the stair well. Nobody.

I shrugged. Oppression bent my back: the bullying atmosphere of the cliff-face prison. There was no point investigating what was most likely a prank.

Inside my cell I spoke my name and identification code to the drone, then stepped into the tiny kitchen, an alcove at the side of the cell, opposite an even smaller closet. I stared at my sink and stove. One spoon, one knife, one cloth. Food was delivered four times a month, good quality, but unvarying: cheese, unleaven bread, nuts, stone jars of water.

When night fell I turned to the handbag, which in my dejection I had not even opened. I sat down and studied it.

It twitched.

I jumped up. The handbag fell out of my lap and dropped to the floor, to emit a resonant ting, as if some delicate instrument inside had chimed the hour. On my hands and knees I examined the bag, sniffing it, checking the weave of the cloth and noticing that it was organic cotton, no fabric of the manufacturing ecosystem. Expensive.

When I opened the handbag by releasing the drawstring at its mouth something leaped out, a thing like a button that landed on my table and hopped across until I cupped my hand over it, at which point it bounced around, stopped, then began emitting a whine. I let it go. It hopped up to the bed, then settled. It was some parasite of the corridor, a scion of the manufacturing ecosystem looking for a mate to help pass on its artificial genes. But the other object was more interesting, a black box in which was set a nuclear furnace, and when I examined it I realised that it was an exotic, probably fished from the far Westside uranium swamps and forced into labour.

My thoughts returned to the figure at the back stair well. No local person; yet how could anybody unauthorised gain access to the cell corridors?

This place froze in winter. I held a source of heat in my hand. The link was clear, yet implausible, for I had no friends with influence enough to help me through frosty days, icy nights. But then my thoughts were interrupted—a knock at the door. The drone emitted a pre-recorded message: "Shroomfynder."

Three years of blandness were lifted from my mind in a moment. With a single motion I dropped the furnace into my pocket and covered the parasite with my coat, before hastening to my window, adopting a casual pose and calling out, "Enter."

In strode a burly man dressed in black, with darting eyes and lips compressed. He surveyed the cell then crossed into the kitchen, where he examined all the organic matter there, the food stains and the food itself, the wooden bowl in the sink, and then the fittings of the closet. The survey took a few minutes. "Any sign of fungi?" he asked.

"No."

"Mould?"

"At this time of year?" I scoffed.

He frowned and departed. So . . . two nights and a day lay clear before me.

I decided to test the furnace in case it was faulty. It worked. Simply by selecting a temperature on the control panel I could make my cell warmer than it had ever been before. That evening I dozed, while the drone pattered around the cell, unable to rest.

—I dream of the Mahandriana, so distant, yet within my grasp. I stand in the haven's foundation level and survey what lies around me. Above all other impressions it smells, and not with pleasant perfume. Under an immense roof the ground is divided into five zones, each flooded with an oily lake into which streams run. The further four lakes are hazy behind dark mist or indistinct from distance and the number of supporting columns, but I can tell from the nearest lake that this water is the source of the rancid smell. The place is gloomy despite luminous globes suspended from the roof, and noisy too, the roof acting as a reverberator. With evening fallen I decide it is best to ascend, leaving the mud, slime and noise for some quieter level.

I approach a woman. "Excuse me, how do we ascend—"

I awoke suddenly. At once I noticed something suspended a yard above me. The parasite had extruded a length of cord to dangle from the ceiling in a fluffy embrace, as if inside cotton wool, where, like an insect, it was metamorphosing. I noticed that it had hung itself in the convection current of warm air above the furnace beside me. I had a headache. The room was too hot!

Midnight, and from the artificial chrysalis a glossy black flier emerged, fluttering around the cell and batting into walls.

The drone fidgeted. That was unusual behaviour. It was then that I recalled the shape, colour and texture of the hopping button and realised that the drone was identical in form, though far larger. What kind of flying machine might emerge if I forced a second metamorphosis? Sharp thoughts, these . . .

Sleep retreated from my mind. I set the furnace to maximum, making the cell uncomfortably hot, forcing me to strip to my vest. Frost on the window outside vanished and there was an odour of rank steam, as if from some foul soup kitchen. But I endured it all and was rewarded with the sight of white froth emerging from the gaps in the drone's armour, which fizzed then set hard as the drone tottered under the table and affixed itself to the underside. A second chrysalis.

I realised that my heart was thumping. With no idea of the timing, I prepared myself.

Inmates were given a set of work clothes. These I laid out, paying attention to the cuffs, piercing holes and tying double lengths of twine to these areas, so that they could be tightened like tourniquets. Sweat made my hands slippery; wet beads tickled their way down my neck and back. I was breathing short and shallow, alert for any sound from the corridor outside. The air above the furnace shimmered.

I laid out my thick shirt and put everything useful upon it: utensils, spare clothes and hat, string, a chair leg that might serve as a club. I tied up the bundle and pulled out the arms: a makeshift backpack.

Then I waited. Night passing . . . listening at the door.

Something was happening inside the cocoon.

Dawn had broken: clear skies. With my ear touching the cocoon I heard scratching, rustling, before something smashed through the case and struck my forehead, sending me tumbling across the floor in a shower of fragments. A single black leg scraped at the table, damp, but spiked and vicious, and I recalled the form of the miniature version, a cross between a wasp and a razor. Now this seemed an insane idea. But I tied my pack around my shoulders, pulled on my outer clothes, tied up all the loose openings, then checked my hat and gloves and wiped the blood from my face.

With a crack the cocoon split, sending debris into the walls with explosive force. The table lifted, then tottered and fell as I came face to face with an autonomous flying machine that seemed constructed of pure obsidian. It had eyes and they stared at me. I shrank back, but this device was a final incarnation not interested in prey; it made for the window. I followed, looking for a place to ride. The thing was six feet long and gloss-finished. Its wings were already drying; they glittered in the half light. With its aerials it smashed the window. Freezing air flooded the cell. I panicked, leaping upon the machine and gripping it with my hands, elbows and knees. The machine bucked and swayed as it forced its front half through the narrow window. There was just enough room for me, my head scraping the lintel.

For the first time I saw what lay below my cell. And in seconds I would be airborne. The bitter wind rasped at my throat and made my eyes water. My nose was running. I screamed and clung tight as the machine made a final effort, flinging itself out.

It could fly. Just.

I realised that this machine was not meant to carry a heavy load. Through half-closed eyes I saw that we were plummeting, the wind roaring past my ears. But then I felt a thrill pass through my body as the wings found a higher mode of vibration, and our path stabilised, before the machine levelled out and I saw that we were making for the perimeter wall of the prison.

Then a snap and a shock through the machine body. Vibrations ceased to my right and the machine dived in that direction, dipping, levelling, then dipping again. Already we were half way down the cliff-face. One wing broken. Much more of this and we would crash within the perimeter wall. Three right legs stuck out to the perpendicular, quite motionless: the left legs spasmed. The right wing was arhythmic. We were dropping fast.

I gave a scream as the perimeter wall approached and I saw we were going to smash into it. I was dead for sure. An automatic response made me relax, and I almost jumped off, but with seconds to go some hunch stopped me. The machine clipped the top of the wall, span out of control in a shower of sparks, and I saw spiralling cliff, wall and ground, before I struck the earth and rolled to a halt.

Bad snow in my mouth, sour as crabapple. I could hear the wailing alarm of the wall, the barking of snow dogs, the cawing of high-altitude rooks. Falling debris and sparks caused the bad snow to hiss in a circle around me.

A gate opened a hundred yards away. Yellow light flooded out, sending the silhouettes of snow dogs leaping over the pristine landscape.

Despite the urgency of my situation, I realised what my priority was. Narcoleptic snow was absorbed through the skin but it was also orally active. I pulled out my flask of water and washed my mouth out. The snow dogs were racing towards me, encouraged by their human owners, who followed, forging their way through the drifts. I would be meat in seconds if I did not escape. I looked at the devastation around me.

The flying machine had spilled its biomechanical guts all around, but its exoskeleton had split into two halves, including a whole upper carapace. With a grunt I leaped into this upper half, which lay upside down like a coracle. Grabbing a leg, I pushed off. The carapace acted as a sled, and in seconds I was sliding down the hill, at first slowly, too slowly, but then faster, until my descent became a frightening rush. I dug the leg into the ground behind me and managed to slow my flight.

A unit of albino rooks followed, their serrated beaks glittering as the sun appeared over the horizon. They flew fast, knowing the snow dogs were already defeated.

I could not balance the need for speed and escape from the rooks with my fear of a chaotic descent and the overturning of the carapace. One of these fates would take me. My natural instincts forced me to slow the carapace. The rooks closed. In a gesture born of desperation I flung the dripping innards of the machine behind me, whereupon the rooks hesitated, dropped, then feasted. I was safe.

My descent continued for an hour. By the time I was at the bottom of the slope my chest and arms felt like lead, my breath came hoarse and my skin felt as if it had been flayed. I was exhausted. Lying back, I allowed myself to come to a halt in the back alley of a row of terraced houses, where the carapace struck a cluster of metal dustbins. I sobbed for a few minutes, then rolled over into a more comfortable position.

The sun shone through fans of iridescent plastic. Indicator buzzers whirred on every wall like an insectoid symphony. Far off, the ululation of a hunting balloon echoed among the black and empty skyscrapers.

I struggled free of my fatigue and looked at the wasteland around me: Urbis Morpheos. I had little food and one weapon. If it started snowing again, I could die.

Speed was essential. I took my bearing from the sun and strode off.

Time distorted, and the day passed quicker than I would have liked, eight hours of struggling along the remains of paths, climbing around collapsed houses, coughing in the steam emitted by rivers of yellow ice. Nothing moved in these gothic streets, except a breeze-blown whisper of bad snow like a skein across the bare expanses ahead. In the sky I saw balloons, one huge dirigible, and, as the sun turned orange, hawks and crows of the natural ecosystem. I soon saw that the birds were following the dirigible, which was an automatic supply vessel making for the northern district of Vita-Hassa, on the edge of the Ice Shield. So I remained alone.

I had walked three or four leagues. Far to go.

But even a single night in the open could prove fatal. Naturally, entering any of the deserted houses around me was impossible — they would be choked with linked machines. Deadly. But I found caves in crumbling chalk walls, where, assailed by the noxious vapours of chemical waters, I tried to sleep.

Outside, the indigo sky turned black. The ring system appeared, pink and cream and white, a structure arcing south to north and sparkling where the objects that formed it struggled for orbital supremacy. To the east rose the moon, and then, like a watchful and cosmic eyeball, the moontoo, its surface tonight as blue as a cornflower.

9

Morning arrived dull. Clouds had leaned in overnight from the south-west and there was a clear threat of bad snow. I checked my cuff and trouser ties, settled my hat on my head and my gloves on my hands, then departed the chalk caves, taking again a heading of south-west. Today I hoped to cover eight leagues.

The first narcoleptic flakes fluttered down from grey skies at noon. My face remained exposed, so I took my rag-cloth and made a mask of it, but after a few hours I realised that chemicals were entering my mouth as the melted substances were absorbed by the cloth. I had to stop, soak the cloth, then wring it dry. So little water remaining. This would impose the limit to my time in the wilderness.

It became ever more difficult to pass along the streets. The drifts were blown by a strengthening wind and I had to reset my mask. It grew dim. By late afternoon, I was struggling.

Hills lay close, but they were an hour away.

I realised that my body was creating heat; I felt warm. I stopped. The wind howled down from the hills. Flakes were melting into my eyes. Not good.

I forged on, part of my mind aware of the danger, the other part seduced by a drowsiness that seemed to rise from my toasted toes.

Sleepy . . .

I shook myself awake. I had walked some distance without noticing the passage of time. Houses lay empty around me; veins of street metal twinkled in the last light of day. The bad snow was heavy. It showered to the ground when I shook myself.

Sleep.

I staggered forward a few paces. Got to keep awake. If I could find shelter from the bad snowstorm I might survive. I breathed out. In. The acid stink of narcolepsy filled my lungs, and, though I was not walking, I wobbled and almost fell over.

Bad snow contained a variety of artificial substances. While one set tried to drown me in sleep another set made my perceptions blur. Were those shapes nearby sheds, or were they distant hills?

Got to rest. Head heavy . . .

I found myself leaning against a grey brick chimney-stack. There was a hole, and like a wounded animal I clambered inside and curled up, as a somnolent blanket was thrown over me by the chemicals in my bloodstream.

Heat suffused my head. A flicker of thought informed me that I was still conscious. I heard the wind battering the chimney in which I sheltered.

Then I felt coldness entering my extremities. I was losing body heat. That meant I was losing life through the interface of cloth and brick. But somehow the warmth in my head kept me drowsy and, despite the vague sense of fear that I felt, a hint only, like a nightmare glimpse in a lovely dream, I was unable to rouse myself. Sleep was all.

Sleep was everything.

And then I was flying through the air. Flying slowly, from a single wing between my shoulder blades. Then I was on a bed, face down — almost — with a musty smell in my nose. The bed rocked.

Something cool upon my face.

With an effort I managed to open my eyes. This was a strange sort of night, close up, malodorous, melting flakes stuck to it.

I leaned back.

My view altered. I sat behind a man and we were moving forward upon a horse. The man was tall, stick thin, and when he turned his head to glance at me from the corner of his eye I saw white skin, a hooked nose and a malformed chin that rose up to meet it. But surely he was a freak at seven feet, more bat than human. He wore a black cloak, his height augmented by a pointed hat. He smelled of smoky old cellars. His boots were slimline kneehighs, with toe ends that curled up into spirals. Rings adorned every finger of his left hand. When he pulled back his hat he loosed a braided ponytail that fell down to the small of his back.

We rode upon a creature made of a substance like dense, yet articulated foam, with a thick bulging neck, white eyes, and a third ear pointing ahead from the centre of its forehead.

I tried to speak. A transparent mask hissed and writhed as it protected me from a return to narcolepsy. I sat up straight, frightened I might fall off. Soon we halted at a cave carved into a bare hillside. Leaving the horse at the cave mouth, the man led me inside, found a dry area, then helped me to lie down. My heart was grateful to bursting so I fumbled inside my improvised backpack for the nuclear furnace, which the man examined then set in the middle of the cave. In minutes the cold winter night was banished. The man pulled the mask off my face and it crumpled into a cellophane ball, which he discarded.

"Who are you?" I asked.

"My name is Gularvhen. I know who you are."

I was for the moment too disorientated to reply; we could quibble over identity later. Eventually I said, "Are you from Theeremere?"

"I am peripatetic."

"You have other homes?"

Gularvhen set his pointed hat upon the ground. "In the main I journey between Theeremere and Vita-Hassa."

"What do you do there?"

"I seek mushrooms from the edge of the Ice Shield."

I nodded. This was an itinerant mycologist, and one bent on profundity, for mushrooms living near the ice would bring knowledge of the deepest physical processes. "You must find travelling so far quite a problem," I remarked.

"There are ways and means," came the reply.

"Are you riding to Theeremere?"

Gularvhen stood up and peered out into the night. "We must journey together until we arrive there. The weather is oscillating between two states, one of tranquil frost and one of rough storm. This implies chaotic underlying patterns. Summer will be short and harsh this year."

I nodded.

"Only the experienced should be out of haven alone," he continued.

I shrugged. My circumstances were exceptional. "Are you old, then?" I asked.

"As old as Gaia," he replied.

Again I nodded. This was a common enough expression amongst the erudite, acknowledging the continuity of life on Earth; but he had said it as if a literal statement.

I asked nothing more.

12

N ext morning we began riding an hour after dawn. I sat behind Gularvhen, a position lacking comfort. He had offered a short introduction to his mount. "This is Hoss. You need not fear him."

The skies remained clear. At noon Gularvhen rose to his full height in the saddle and surveyed the land, before guiding Hoss towards an escarpment of stone. We looked down across the squalor below. Natural grass suggested that the streets here were inimical to manufactured life.

"That stream at the bottom may be worth exploring," said Gularvhen, pointing to a reflective ribbon half-concealed by fallen statues.

We descended into a maze of alleys, expecting nothing but mud and muck at the bottom, but the stream water was transparent enough for me to glimpse stones and weed on the bed.

"The bad snow may not be interacting with the devices of the manufacturing ecosystem here," Gularvhen said. "That would explain the clarity of this water, which is as yet unpolluted." He turned his attention to the stream and gave an exclamation. "Look!"

Floating in the centre of the stream I saw a dozen mushrooms, pale with large caps, trailing hyphae like beards that tugged at the irregularities on the bed and so reduced their speed to a dawdle. These were free-floating aquatic mushrooms, proving that the manufacturing ecosystem had not found a toehold in this district.

"We could learn from them," I said. "Do you have maps of this area?"

"Only parchments a century old," Gularvhen replied. "The landscape and the maps will have lost any similarity decades ago."

I indicated the nearest mushrooms. "Grab a couple."

He waded out and pulled the two smallest mushrooms from the water, disentangling their hyphae and dropping them into the stream so that more fruiting bodies could form. "The river may turn west towards Shohnadwe," he said, "but with luck it will bear south, in which case we would only need to find a raft."

I took one of the mushrooms and examined it for parasites, of which there were none. "Raw?" I said.

"It would be better. Our situation gives me some cause for worry. That is not to say we are lost."

Activated in the mouth, the chemical complexes held within the body of the mushroom would have their most profound effect on the brain. I popped the fungus on my tongue. Bitter, but not inedible.

Hoss approached, opened his mouth and began keening, a sound that started like a thin wail, becoming thicker as new voices were added, to create a complex, almost musical sound. I took a few steps back. I chewed for as long as I could before swallowing. The eerie sound was having an effect on me, making me receptive to the meditative thoughts emerging within my mind. Then the streets around me came into focus as fragments of the knowledge represented by the mushrooms clicked into place; and I knew where I was.

We nodded at one another. "South," we said in unison. I smiled.

Hoss wandered off.

I said, "That was music, wasn't it?"

Gularvhen nodded. "Hoss has six voiceboxes, hence his bulging neck. These enable him to create polyphonic music when the occasion demands."

"But why?"

Gularvhen held up the stalk of the mushroom that he had eaten. "This fungus contained a vast suite of chemical complexes relating to different types of knowedge. To a certain degree, Hoss can select for specific types, maximising the efficacy of the mushroom."

I frowned. "That implies he understands what is going on."

Gularvhen raised his hands in the air, a gesture of nonchalant uncertainty. "Who knows how near the truth that is?"

I glanced at Hoss. No mushrooms grew on him. Of course, he was not necessarily of the natural ecosystem.

Afternoon, and pale sunlight flickered through the narcoleptic snow-clouds. Bad snow—it covered the city of Urbis Morpheos. It fell like vile manna from clouds piling in from the western sea, the city deliquescing under its influence, stone turned to mud, to clay, which was washed away down innumerable storm drains.

Having escaped internal exile, Psolilai now stood Eastside amidst the glistening stacks and gnomons of the riverside district. She was slender, tall, two blue eyes in a freckled face framed by long, red hair. She wore a black leather jacket studded with steel, faded stonewashed jeans, and impractical boots with stiletto heels.

Behind her stood her rescuer. They had travelled a long way to get here, from Tall Cliff Steel to the centre of the city—an escapee and a mycologist, she on foot, he on his bizarre steed. Now, from deserted yards paved with blood-coloured sandstone, she looked down upon the high walls and towers of Theeremere. She heard the distant clanging of autonomous dirigibles.

"There it is," Psolilai said. "The gate leading into the old walled city."

Gularvhen mounted his horse and trotted up to her side. "It is indeed the gate into Theeremere," he said.

"What now?" Psolilai asked.

"Is this where we have a discussion?" Gularvhen replied. He added, "You had better speak first."

Psolilai said, "If in truth you know who I am, you already know enough of the tale of my incarceration."

Gularvhen shrugged. "Perhaps I exaggerated what I knew."

Psolilai looked up at him. Astride Hoss he seemed half in the heavens, like a skyscraper. "All tales are exaggerations of the truth," she said. "I am fair and decent, despite what you have heard."

"You do not know what I have heard."

"I can guess."

"Guessing is for the vague, and you are above that."

For a moment Psolilai found his manner annoying, until she remembered who she was—and looked at herself from his point of view. Now that the riverside district was at hand, her future, and perhaps even her life, were at stake. The bond that she shared with Gularvhen, born in desperation, was young. Eventually she said, "My red hair at least would give me away down there. But Theeremere has plenty of nooks in which to vanish."

"So it has."

"We each have a hold over the other, Gularvhen. I escaped . . . and as for you, the inhabitants of Thee despise those of Ere, where you doubtless have your base. So shall we hold our tongues and make for Ere?"

"It would bring me joy."

"And Hoss?"

"No gate guard questions a nag."

Psolilai nodded and made to walk down the hill before them.

"Wait," said Gularvhen. "One question remains, the matter of your family."

"One sister, an uncle and an aunt."

"Very well. They can be contacted later, when we have concealed ourselves." Gularvhen studied the snow-filled sky, then returned his gaze to the maze of streets before them. "It is late afternoon. The shift at the Sighing Gate will be old, their only thought the warmth and comforts of the guard house on Gramine Lane. We will enter there."

Psolilai bunched her hair up, pulled on a floppy hat. "Come on," she said.

Because the Sighing Gate was set in an eastern wall of Thee, it found itself protected from the worst of the weather. Psolilai noticed little of concern as she stopped just yards from the entrance to survey what lay before her. Bubbling stone dripped like wax down a candle, so that the battlements were round, not square as they had been made.

They looked like rotten old teeth. Three guards sat at their post, old-timers with hair lank under rusting helmets, the passage of Gularvhen and Psolilai exciting not even a glance from them. The pair passed into the walled city.

Immediately, they turned left. The lane before them was narrow, wide enough for two and no more, the buildings to either side leaning like drunkards over a table. Stalactites hung down from eaves, shedding bad snow meltwater. Few people were abroad, those daring the weather dressed in woolly hats and masks, and great cloaks, ignoring their fellows in the lane. Psolilai took the lead as they passed Shroomfynder Court and approached the Emerald Bridge. Some damage had been done to the grass and reeds that covered its length, the grass mottled, though far from dead.

Half way across, Psolilai paused to look west. Through curtains of bad snow she saw the Pillar reaching up into the heavens, its green column sparkling even from this distance, with all the psychic reek of the truly ancient, around it the double spiral of silver that served as a staircase upward.

So they stepped into Rem, and the single-file Indole Lane. They had to press themselves into doorways when they blocked the way. Hoss was disturbed by claustrophobia, harrumphing as he was prodded and pushed by passers-by. With night falling they navigated shadow-strewn lanes by light of window and methane lamp, until, at Analytical-Tendency House, the lane widened and new lanthorns threw off an ochre light. They stole on. At the place where Indole Lane became Salvinorin Lane, Psolilai saw the statue of Amargoidara, Steward Lord of the Analytical Council, upon which she spat—having first ensured nobody would notice her act.

From the statue it was a quick step to the Wool Bridge and the path into Ere. They followed Tryptophane Lane, where many homes had lost entire storeys, as buildings deliquesced beneath bad snow. Where melted stone reached the ground it blocked drains, causing floods and thick lakes like mud—there were boards and planks everywhere, and sheets of sand where the local red rock had disintegrated.

At the end of the lane, Psolilai turned to Gularvhen and said, "Here you must take the lead. I used to live on Sulphur Tuft Passage, but that house is barred to me."

Gularvhen nodded to show he understood. "Folk at the Church of the Parasol Cap have a reputation for kindliness," he observed.

He led the way without further comment. Afraid that she might be recognised, Psolilai hid her face as they pushed their way through the gates and empty stalls of Isatin Lane, pulling down her hat as far as it would go. At their destination, she stopped. What she saw appalled her.

The Church of the Parasol Cap had all but melted. Five storeys remained, stone walls slick with rivulets, the roof a single sheet of deliquescent stone — five storeys grey and gloomy, the remainder of the glorious twenty that had been built a century ago from marble and quartz. Narcoleptic snow drove in from the west; unprotected, the Church had suffered. At ground level there were stays and scaffolding, but it seemed a botched affair, as if true heart had departed the faithful.

Fatigue tugged Psolilai down like a pin to a lodestone. Her feet dragged. Complex chemicals were assembling in her mouth, as the bad snow residue of many days approached levels from which they could deliver their loads of sloth. She felt, because she was home again, that the hour for surrender had arrived. Foul acid breath. Sleep.

One task remained. Inside the Church, Psolilai found herself in dim orange light. "This is my colleague," came Gularvhen's voice.

"My!" A jolly voice. "She looks for all the world as if she has returned from prison."

"For all the world," agreed Gularvhen.

Psolilai retained faculties enough to realise that this conversation was a simple communication procedure, telling her that the Church understood the reason for her presence. She followed Gularvhen up an echoing stairway, looking not left, nor right, nor ahead, except to watch her boots negotiate the steps.

A room. A bed. She slept.

She did not know it, but on the roof a raven hopped from puddle to puddle, searching for a way in.

She dreams that her uncle is dead. She dreams of psolilai Westside, ascending the great white pillar that is Mahandriana, seeking 3Machines: working a gallery of particularly thick soil — on one of the lower levels, where viniculture has been practised for centuries, and where the lowest layers of earth are dense with cabling and networked devices. But it is wrealities that are causing her the worst problems. On nocturnal expeditions she collects wild wrealities, pulling them from decaying technology like puff-balls from pasture. In her room, as dawn breaks through ragged cloud, she will with trembling hands take the wrealities and lick them as if they are sweets, experiencing a rush of meaningless visions, like meteors smashing into her brain from inner space. Meaningless, but addictive—

She woke up.

She gazed at the room in which she lay. It was small, brick and stone and fine cloth tapestries, one window only because this chamber was hidden in the maze of the fifth floor—now the upper floor. Furnished with table, chair and desk; six neon strings following triangular panels down from the centre of the domed roof to provide omnidirectional light. Extremely thick carpet, so those on the floor below would not suspect her presence; an atmosphere of peace on the scent of old roses.

She got out of bed. A note had been pushed under her door, informing her of her uncle's death. She would have to meet her family for the funeral.

Her family . . .

18

The way to the Field of Gaia was broader than most, five yards at least, wider past the Pool of Wrealities and the Shrine of Boletus. Psolilai walked alone, until, on the most exposed corner of Ere, she saw the bloody sward. On the hill at its northern end stood the megaliths that comprised the Circle of Beak and Claw. There, she was due.

Because of historical differences between Thee and Ere, all funerals held at the Field of Gaia required the presence of an officer of the Analytical Council—and there she was, a short woman cloaked and hatted, walking a dozen yards behind two people, Aunt Sukhtaya tall and broad, beside her a wispy figure that had to be Psolilai's sister Ryoursh. Psolilai noticed friends and colleagues of her uncle, two score or more, heads bowed. The land seemed bare, larger than she remembered, and colder.

Through the outer ring of the ancient monument they walked: Psolilai, Aunt Sukhtaya, Ryoursh, side by side. The officer poured civic scorn upon the ceremony then strode off, as Aunt Sukhtaya led her nieces into one of the two inner rings. Under a crimson sheet in the other lay the corpse. For the first time Psolilai and Ryoursh looked at one another. Neither blinked. Then Aunt Sukhtaya gave a groan and walked towards the body. Ryoursh glanced away. Aunt Sukhtaya pulled the sheet aside with a theatrical gesture, then returned to her nieces. The wait began. People glanced at the skies.

The first birds arrived an hour later, flying out of the sun, with beaks blood-mottled and claws extended, the vanguard of the chubby regulars who would appear later when the sun was high and the body open. Screeching, they settled on the corpse and began butchering it. At the first sight of blood Psolilai felt her tears; she studied the eroded forms of the megaliths, that once had boasted laser sharp edges. Ryoursh strolled over and put an arm around her, but Psolilai felt the gesture empty, warmth clothing cold, no flash of connection, nor even recognition. It was a cultural gesture, fit only for outsiders, and like as not designed for them. At that moment Psolilai realised the gulf between them was deep.

Clouds parted as morning wore on. A single plastic vulture landed on one of the outer stones. No titbits today.

Now hawks arrived that gorged every day on human meat, and the consumption of the body began in earnest. This phase allowed those distant from the immediate family to leave, and this they did, until, later, when more clouds rolled in from the west, all who remained were the three women.

Uncle Illuvineya was a tangle of guts and blood and bone, spread thin over the grass. Already what remained was seeping back to Gaia. Ryoursh departed, saying nothing. Lone snowflakes drifting down. Aunt Sukhtaya sighed and wandered around the circles, inner, outer, then inner again, until an orange beam of sunlight shone out from underneath the clouds. Dusk approaching. She hugged Psolilai, wiped her face dry, then departed.

Who amongst the crowd would have realised that Psolilai had escaped Tall Cliff Steel? Probably none. Tales might circulate, but for now they would remain in Ere. In a place this labyrinthine, rumours died without being noticed.

A few fat buzzards remained, hopping over blood and sinew. One pulled out a bone and cast it aside. It looked dark for a bone. Psolilai took a step forward, but from the corner of her eye she saw the plastic vulture extend its wings, then jump off the megalith and glide down. Something made her run. They arrived together, Psolilai grabbing the bone between finger and thumb, the vulture gripping the other end with its beak, screeching its frustration as she stood up and attempted to pull the bone away. The vulture flexed its wings and tried to slap them into her face, but she ducked and yanked at the bone until it was free. With a disconsolate croak the vulture flapped away.

This was no bone. It looked like a scriber. It was an object of antique beauty, opaque tourmaline surrounded by a spiral of bronze. It must have been inside her uncle's body.

The Field of Gaia was of considerable size, the nearest buildings mere shadows across Baeocystin Lane, yet Psolilai felt eyes watched her claim this treasure, eyes of malice. Minds that thought she should not keep it...

She looked around the Field. It was empty, frosted with bad snow, footprints in a single trail. She put the antique object into her inner pocket and walked back to the Church of the Parasol Cap.

It was indeed a scriber. But when she sat at her desk to examine it more closely it twitched in her hand, and she almost dropped it, pushing back against her chair in fright. It was moving her hand. It pulled to the top left corner of the desk, then dropped. She found herself unable to let go. Automatic writing! Words flowed from the scriber, incised into the wood, leaving a trail of shavings and dust so that the curly script was not immediately legible. As her hand performed line after line she blew the debris away, until the device was done and she was able to read the entire script.

'To you, below is described the last stage of exploration that I was able to complete, searching for the truth of the Constructor and the Transmuter on the way to the owl, the Constructor and the Transmuter being gold disks no larger than a hand, identical in every way, yet somehow separate in a fashion that I have been unable to fathom, with the latter long since buried in compressed layers of matter, I know not where or why, and the former, so I believe, lost in the dense environs of the Sonic Forest, south Westside, a place to which I beg you go, before others, less moral than I, reach it first, and perhaps damage Urbis Morpheos beyond hope, for these are profound and extraordinary creations not natural in type, known also to the agens, perhaps to their mallead kin, but known also to others who meddle where they should not.'

Psolilai read this many times before lying on her bed to think; for she too was seeking an owl. That this constituted a last message from her uncle was incredible, the method of transfer too bizarre, and yet it seemed a cry from the heart, *to* somebody, from *him*, warning of people deemed dangerous. And he was no fool. The name of Illuvineya was lauded across Ere and even into the less traditional quarters of Rem. Of course, the Shroomfynders and the Snufflers, the Threadbreakers and the Sporeseekers, and all the civil groups set against the dread of the underground loathed him for his mycological views, doubtless toasting his aerial burial from their dens and inns.

Had Uncle Illuvineya known who would remain inside the Circle of Beak and Claw such thoughts would be plausible, but Psolilai could see no sense in his script, unless the scriber was intended for any person except the dangerous ones. There were deep mysteries here, and Psolilai, who had loved her uncle, albeit from a distance, needed to bring truth to the light.

Through Gularvhen she obtained new clothes, black leather, undecorated but of the best quality, lined with fine wool and stamped with the mark 'Bihara Of Rem', guarenteeing organic hide from the riverside sheds. Unattractive, but tough. Old jeans. New boots, also black, and they were like Gularvhen's except with a stiletto heel. Most important were the rainbow-striped woolly hat and the sparkling scarf, both of which offered a particular type of social invisibility by designating the wearer a simple labourer from neutral Rem. Psolilai slipped out of her old leathers, and dressed.

Another parcel arrived: a belt and a rapier, the former composed of linked quartz toruses, the latter a new weapon complete with a leather holster. Both of these she fitted to her jeans. The final touch was provided by a tattoo box. She clamped the machine first to her left upper arm then to her right, and in half an hour the inking and pain were over; to the left a moon, because she was a woman, a green moontoo as a personal symbol to the right. Thus described, she was done.

A knock on the door. Psolilai opened it, to see a lad dressed in tabard and tights.

He said, "Young lady to see you, ma'am."

"What name does she offer?"

"Ryoursh."

Psolilai grimaced. "Send her up, but confide to her that I seem tired."

"As you say, ma'am."

Psolilai undressed and hid her new clothes, for she did not want her disguise to become known in Ere. She concealed the scriber under a pile of socks, then pulled on a gown. Five minutes later Ryoursh appeared. She looked calm, even relaxed, with Inka, Psolilai's old raven, on her wrist. But the earlier coldness remained as a barrier through which they interacted. "Good evening, sister," she said. "This is the briefest of visits to return your property. Inka led me here."

Psolilai doubted that, but she took the raven, which cawed and jumped to her shoulder. The bird's eyes were sunken, a pale blue nictitating membrane covering the sockets. "What happened to him?"

"Perhaps a fight, or the cruelty of some child."

Psolilai looked again at Inka's damaged eyes. The new membranes were thick, yet they seemed to glow. Otherwise her bird was unchanged.

"I will depart," Ryoursh said, taking a final look around the room. "Your extraordinary journey has left you pale."

This, then, was a point of weakness. Ryoursh knew Psolilai had escaped, and she wanted her sister to realise that. She represented danger.

"Wait," Psolilai said. "Did Uncle Illuvineya know I was coming home?"

"What a strange question," Ryoursh replied, before closing the door.

Evening came. Unsettled, Psolilai wandered the Church, listening to echoes of the storm outside, until she found herself standing before a great glass window in a rear chamber. Bad snow had etched a hundred designs into it, but clear patches remained, and through one she took a peep. Gularvhen's steed Hoss stood outside. The rear yards were natural sanctuaries, laden with fruit and vegetables from spring to autumn—now ruined, brown, damp. Hoss stood on a rotten tree trunk slimy with mould, his head bowed, his whole body limp as if smudged by water, his hooves enlarged and set unmoving on the fungal wood. A scene of wintry dejection.

Psolilai put her ear to the glass and heard a single chord of six voices, constant and gloomy. The music of Hoss.

Next morning a card arrived stamped Rem, requesting the presence of one Lil at the headquarters of the Severance Patrol on Norbaeocystin Lane. Psolilai cursed. Lil was her childhood name; her sister was making trouble. In Theeremere young and old alike were mustered in the struggle against machine linkage, the subterranean bane, and she, despite her situation, was no exception. Ryoursh knew this, and perhaps hoped that the name and face of a former prisoner would drift up to official levels. But the fact that Ryoursh had not squealed meant that someone—Aunt Sukhtaya for instance—was directing affairs. Had her aunt organised the escape from Tall Cliff Steel? It seemed unlikely.

Psolilai pulled on her new leathers, hat and scarf, and departed the Church, arriving in Norbaeocystin Lane, running up the steps of the dark building occupied by the Severance Patrol, then accosting the first clerk that she met, an old man. He looked at her card, then went through his records on a tiny wreality.

"I object to you using such a familiar abbreviation," Psolilai remarked.

The clerk glanced up at her, unimpressed. "What then is your full name?"

"Liltamsa." Irritation made her voice harsh. "Why have I been called here?" she asked.

The clerk frowned. "You jest."

"I am neither of the Severance nor the Isolation class. I should be working with the Assembly of Eye."

The reply was an accusation. "Your registration was made yesterday evening, but I would guess you have seen at least twenty winters."

Psolilai smoothed over the contradiction, saying, "In Rem we work in communities. If my lane elder has not registered me properly, that is a matter for him."

The old man grunted his disapproval. "Improper. Take this note when you next go up to the Eye."

Psolilai took the proffered card and departed. A successful riposte, apart from the fact that she would now have to perform finding-duties once a month. Her mood lightened.

At the Church of the Parasol Cap the lad stopped her. "Ma'am," he said, "you left your door open. I took the liberty of shutting it."

"I didn't leave it open," she replied.

"No matter that it was unlocked, ma'am. You have only been back half an hour and few people are about."

"But..."

Psolilai sprinted up the steps to her chamber. Inside, she pressed her back against the closed door and surveyed the place, allowing her intuitive mind a chance to spot minute changes, a fragment of mud here, dust marks there, perhaps the smell of melting stone from the intruder's boots. But nothing. She checked her possessions. Packs untouched, scriber present, no mark or ruffle on her clothes. The carpet was clean.

She sat at the desk. A fragrance tickled her nose. She bent down to sniff the wood, and her memories were shifted by a new odour, waxy, not unpleasant—oil pastel. She had used them as a child. Now she understood. Somebody so like her even the boy was fooled had come here and taken a rubbing of the writing onto thin paper. Locking the chamber, she clattered down to the ground floor, to find the boy cleaning a meditation room. He looked frightened.

"When did I go up to my room and leave the door open?" she asked him.

"Half an hour ago, ma'am."

"What was I wearing?"

He gestured at her leathers. "An outfit like the one you wore when you first came here. And a mourning hood. The tall mycologist said it was for your uncle."

"Fetch Gularvhen for me."

"Ma'am."

Psolilai remained in the meditation room. When Gularvhen appeared, ducking to pass under the door, she shut it, then gestured him to a couch on the further side of the chamber.

"I need to confide in someone," she began.

He nodded.

"Somebody has this morning impersonated me with the aim of

copying some information provided by Uncle Illuvineya. This information was not, I think, aimed at a specific person, but he did hope it would not reach one or more persons."

"Unnamed?"

"And dangerous."

Gularvhen looked away, as if to think. "Could I see the information?"

Psolilai hesitated. "Do you promise never to pass it on?"

"I promise on the Parasol Cap."

Good enough!

Upstairs, he read the inscription, then said, "We would do well to sand this off. I will ask the boy to perform the task—he is trustworthy. As for the script, it means nothing to a peripatetic mycologist. Your first move should be to the Pool of Wrealities, where difficult questions are more likely to receive an answer."

"I'd better jot this information down," said Psolilai, eyeing a scroll, and an inked quill.

"No," said Gularvhen. "I will, not you." Pulling his book *The Condition* from his pocket he glanced at the inscription, looked at his book, then said, "I think I will memorise it. I will not forget."

25

"All right . . . but you better hadn't."

Gularvhen leaned over the desk and read the inscription a few times. Psolilai nodded as, muttering to himself, he departed.

Tired, she slept.

—she dreams of voices rustling across the surface of her brain. "You are special in some way," one voice says. "Do not deny it. You are the only one I know who has eaten of mushroom and wreality. My next experiment I hope will allow me to accept the wisdom of 3Machines. If so, I have my bridge, for you will be able to ingest wreality wisdom and I that of the mushroom."

"You are mad," psolilai declares, "quite mad. The two ecosystems are forever sundered. And do you seriously expect me to believe you have some altruistic motive for all this?"

"You cannot escape me," the voice says. "I will do as I will."

psolilai sneers, "You are a monster."

"I am a scientist."

"You are a tyrant."

Then a faint whisper. "I am an explorer."
"You are a fool—"

N ext day Psolilai set out for the Pool of Wrealities, a short walk across Muscimol Lane. It lay inside a vast building weeping marble tears. Tolerated by officialdom in Rem, hated by the activists of Thee for whom it represented a prime source of linkage, to Psolilai, as to all in Ere, it stood as a library. She entered it with joy.

The chambers honeycombing the annulus that surrounded the Pool itself were small, tiled and clean, meant for personal preparation, each with a door in from the exterior corridor and a door out to the centre. Psolilai hung her leathers on a hook and donned a cotton robe and a headband to keep the sweat out of her eyes. Already she could smell the sylvan odour of the place. Her boots she swapped for slippers, but her rapier she kept. Raids from Thee were not unknown. So attired, she walked inside the dome.

The Pool itself was not immediately visible, though the steam it generated billowed high to the roof, condensing there and returning to ground level along copper conduits. A swathe of metallic life inter-twined with greenery—palms and lianas and twisting ivy, all bearded with moss—created a screen between Psolilai and the water. Tropical birds screeched high up, fighting over nesting space, while dragonflies buzzed by and smaller insects stridulated. On the ground she saw silver centipedes, sheaves of swaying plastic, and the jeweled cutting-worms that were the single concession to the activists, these devices controlling the inevitable expansion of cables from the Pool to whatever outside might be trying to forge a way in. Such blatant linkage could not be tolerated even in Ere.

She ducked as she passed beneath an arch made through the screen. The Pool was visible as an expanse of water under a complex network of bridges, lianas and scaffolding, that rose above it, more than half its area invisible under such edifices. Banks of mist swirled around. On the opposite side she saw figures, tiny in the distance; around the Pool, people were kneeling at the water's edge, working with the scarlet wrealities. She noticed a clean and grassy section of bank, where she settled.

No wrealities bobbed on the surface, but she could see four under-water, including a three foot globe set with glassy nodules. That was the one. The larger the wreality, the larger the library. She plucked a chromium stem from the spray at her side, bent the top into a hook and pushed it underwater, so that the wreality was caught and she could pull it to the surface. When it sensed air it expanded with a hiss, and a hundred gleaming spikes emerged from its scarlet hide, but childhood experience took charge and Psolilai flipped the wreality over to expose the mass of nodules it was trying to hide. Defeated, the machine relaxed.

She cleared her throat. "Search for ancient devices," she said. "The Constructor and the Transmuter."

From the largest nodule a collection of light-symbols radiated out, translucent blue, green and purple, shimmering like the thinnest silk back-lit by reflections off the water. In form it was an approximation of a human that posed, gestured, and moved its lips when it spoke. "Which first?"

"Wait," said Psolilai, as a thought struck her. "Has anybody else asked you about these devices?"

"No."

Psolilai knew that Uncle Illuvineya must have come here during his own research. No matter. She would never have access to his work and so would have to begin where he had left off. "Continue the search," she said, "the Constructor first," Besides, there were ten thousand wrealities living in this pool, and as many again dwelling in the mud at the bottom, wrealities that had not been searched for centuries. Locating machines that he had questioned would be an impossible task.

Then came her reply. "The Constructor. Too ancient to find its origin, implying fabrication during the final phase of the rise of the manufacturing ecosystem, when evolutionary pressure caused indi-vidual species of artificial life to lose utilitarian qualities. In appearance it is a gold disk, diameter five inches, half an inch thick, engraved with designs that dance before the viewer. Unknown purpose."

Silence. That seemed to be all. "And its resting place?"

"Unknown."

Uncle Illuvineya had got a little further, then. "What about the Transmuter?"

"Identical. Unknown purpose, although different to the Constructor."

"Resting place?"

"Unknown."

Psolilai sat back on the damp ground. Having heard what she had expected to hear, it was time to make other enquiries. "What about links with agens?"

"Agens live outside Theeremere, only they can answer your question."

"Malleads?"

"No links are known."

Psolilai frowned. "What is a mallead?"

"Agens are those conscious entities that evolved from the manufacturing ecosystem into a society. Malleads are creations of that society, also conscious, yet apart, as wrealities stand apart from human beings. Three are thought to remain. Their prime ability is shape-changing."

"Remain?"

"Strife between the two artificial species is described in old texts."

Psolilai nodded. "Thank you." She stood up, stretched, and turned.

Young woman walking towards her, only yards away, rapier outstretched. Psolilai drew her own weapon, blade hissing as it whipped through the air. She leaped forward to disarm her opponent.

"No!" shouted the woman.

Psolilai adopted an attacking stance and thrust out: clashing handles, sharp points flicking past her ear, dancing left, right, ducking, clashing again, meeting the woman face to face with their rapier handles locked together. She pushed away. The woman made a lightning movement and Psolilai watched her weapon fly into the air, cartwheel once, then land point down in the earth.

Psolilai was stunned. "You disarmed me!"

The woman took a few moments to regain her breath, before raising her weapon and replying, "I disarmed you with a fishing rod."

Psolilai stared at what she had thought a rapier, then turned her gaze to the woman: slim, a handsbreadth shorter than she, with the tough skin and tougher clothes of one who lived on the street. Blonde, heart-shaped face, a gaze like a reptile.

"Who are you?" Psolilai asked.

"Your cousin Karakushna."

Her *cousin?*

Karakushna turned to survey the undergrowth surrounding them, then faced Psolilai and said, "Until now there was no point in you knowing of my existence."

"But you weren't at the funeral."

"Mother banished me when I was eleven. I live huddled deep in a Rem community." She grinned. "We learn to fight, to survive, despite the odds . . . "

"'Until now', you said," Psolilai mused. "What changed your mind?"

"Your escape, of course."

Psolilai shrugged. "In fact, I was sprung."

"You're here, that's all that matters." As if to strengthen her position, Karakushna added, "I was the woman who threw a single psilocybe at you when Amargoidara had you marched from the courtroom in Analytical-Tendency House."

"That was a risk."

"Sukhtaya didn't see me because I was in disguise."

"I meant Amargoidara—"

Karakushna snorted. "A plebeian compared to my mother. Of course, she must never know you're here with me."

Psolilai frowned. "But do you know why I'm here?"

"I knew you would come home eventually—and last night I heard the news. Illuvineya's death means only you remain to continue his work."

"What is his work?"

"Banishment excludes me from his house." Karakushna shrugged, then indicated the fishing rod. "This is how we find out more."

Psolilai gazed out over the water. "And he did want someone to know more. He left a message. I know now that it was for you."

Karakushna's eyes misted as, from memory, Psolilai spoke the message of the scriber. They hugged one another. "Though the message may have been for me," Karakushna said, "you must be my eyes and my hands. I can't become known. The work is yours."

Psolilai nodded. She understood. "The fishing rod . . . "

"We can only use it once. Let's do it now."

Karakushna led Psolilai around the Pool, stepping over cables, pushing through undergrowth, then making out over swaying bridges to an island of rushes, which in turn led to a rickety float-way shrouded in mist. They passed others on the way: companies and fellowships, couples sharing mushrooms, intense expressions on the faces of loners questioning scarlet orbs. Sweat soaked into Psolilai's headband, her gown stuck to her back, to her armpits. Thirsty. Tempting to cup a handful of water from the Pool, but it was a soup of nanos and bacteria.

They arrived at an old wooden seat on a mud bank. Steam blocked any view of the distant edge. "Where are we?" asked Psolilai.

"Near the centre of the Pool. I came here a lot as a girl. We're safe for the moment."

"For the moment?"

In reply Karakushna extended the rod so that it was twice as long as before, took a fibre disk from her pocket, attached it to the handle, then from it paid out a length of line. To the end she tied a white wire. "That wire is a piece of new cable I plucked from a shoreside wreality after I saw you come in. It attracts wrealities, you see? They like to join up."

Psolilai nodded, then shivered. "Always wanting linkage," she murmured.

Karakushna cast the bait out into the Pool, then sat on the seat, legs crossed.

"Now we wait," said Psolilai, sitting beside her.

Karakushna nodded. "Keep quiet for a while. Wrealities sense words."

Psolilai tried to imagine how deep the Pool might be, the ghost of an idea forming as to what her cousin was attempting. Hours passed. When the screeching quietened, Psolilai knew that electric birds had responded to the nocturnal burrowing of the myriad cutting-worms, that had in turn reacted to the reduced activity of the wrealities. Night outdoors.

The line jerked. Karakushna leaped up, cursing the pins and needles in her leg, tugging the rod up and winding in the line. Water around the line first swirled, then bubbled as Karakushna hauled in her catch.

Grey mud covered the immense wreality. The water boiled and crashed as it emerged, a globe ten feet across, warty and whiskered as an old soak, metal spines lashing out in all directions. Karakushna struggled to pull it in. And it fought. Psolilai braced herself against the seat and grabbed hold of Karakushna's gown so that her cousin would not be dragged in. Karakushna slipped on the mud, but retained control of the rod, and by winding in the line managed to drag the wreality ashore. Meanwhile the Pool was beginning to foam elsewhere, as thousands of lesser machines sensed the incursion and dived for safety. The Pool of Wrealities would be closed for days . . .

They had one chance now. Alternately gasping for breath and coughing out the anaerobic stench, Karakushna pulled until the nodule mass was uppermost. She held firm her position and the wreality calmed. Water lapped at the mud bank.

"We have some questions," Karakushna said.

Sparkling sheets of light tinted yellow and red radiated up from the nodules, so that a full sized creature appeared before them, its thousand holographic components articulated with sinuous ease, unmistakeable in grace—a felin, scion of the natural ecosystem, evolved over geological periods from some animal lost to time.

"Fascinating," said Psolilai.

"Unexpected," Karakushna decided.

The wreality spoke in a deep voice. "Begin your questions."

Karakushna made a gesture with her hand, indicating that Psolilai's moment had arrived. Psolilai stepped forward and said, "We want to know the purpose of the artifact known as the Constructor."

In reply the wreality thrashed out. Karakushna held firm the line. Drenched, muddied, Psolilai took a few steps back, wondering if they could expect an answer.

After a pause the wreality said, "The Constructor is a device for the direction of the innumerable processes that constitute the manufacturing ecosystem, from the indeterminacy of the quantum level to the ebb and flow of the aeons. Its makers are unknown. No subtlety is lost to it, no flight of sticky cloud nor rush of nano swarm, no clunking metal machine nor even any wreality. It sees all and can move all."

"Where does it lie?"

The wreality's voice grew higher as it replied, "In the centre of the Sonic Forest." Now a wail. "Where the leaves pile up and the humus—"

Snap!

One final effort broke the line.

The wreality sank.

31

As The Information In Her Brain

The sullied streets of Qentheoz stretched on. And this part of Westside stank.

Gularvhen and I crossed some of the most difficult terrain we had yet encountered—tall statues that if touched expelled clouds of biting flies, quicksand pits, bogs that stretched for leagues; and all the debris of the manufacturing ecosystem, the riven stones, sulphurous bricks, the holes and cracks emitting noxious gases. We saw not one sign of sentient life. This was a dread district, sick, rotting, and after only one day we loathed it, and were frightened.

From a tree, I plucked a pear. It smelled delicious. I bit into it and a swarm of black grubs trailing slime spilled out over my hand. The centre had been hollowed out by the larvae. With a scream I dropped the pear, and ran on.

We reached the river that flowed down to Teewemeer. Although less polluted—the water was clear—I could see signs of degradation on its bed, pebbles sheened in coloured slimes, artificial weeds like tongues, alongside a selection of simple natural life, white toads, fat fish, and once a four-legged heron. On the river bank we decided to camp, apprehensive about the day ahead, but pleased that we had found a place we could bear for one night.

A variety of animal sounds reduced our slumber to a minimum: the constant stridulation of insects, yelps and wails from creatures captured as prey, and a howl that rose to a shriek then descended to a bass rumble, five minutes or more, a period I thought would never end. I spent the next hour hoping not to hear the howl again, but just as I dozed off it started, much nearer, a time-stretched cry that, as it dipped towards the threshold of hearing, made the ground vibrate. Then silence. Even the insects responded to this appalling noise, their stridulation just a whisper.

We awoke in dishevelled state, agreeing that we must reach Teewemeer by sunset. On the water we saw a riverboat, and at the rear of the riverboat we saw two naked children.

Gularvhen said to me, "psolilai, go and investigate."

I walked to the riverbank and shouted, "Hello! Are your parents there?"

The children giggled and stared.

I tried again. "Are you going south to Teewemeer?" I pointed downstream to make my intention clear.

The riverboat began to approach the bank. Gularvhen said, "Somebody inside has heard us. If we can convince them of our good intent, I think we should float down to the haven. It would be much quicker."

I agreed. Anything to get off the land.

"Can you find your mummy and daddy?" I called out. Louder, I added, "Is anybody there? We are peaceful travellers."

"They are too young to understand," Gularvhen said, "and anyway may not speak the local language."

"We should board anyway. They're only children."

"But where are their parents?"

When the riverboat touched the bank Gularvhen leaped aboard and made a search of the cabins. "Nobody," he reported. The children stared at him. "Except them," he added. "Come along, jump aboard, and then I will guide Hoss. With luck we will see Teewemeer before dusk. It cannot be more than ten leagues distant."

It seemed that the unfortunate parents of the children had been eaten by beasts. But there were no clothes on board, and I had to use my own spare garments to cover the children. They looked confused.

The riverboat floated out into the middle of the current and began moving downstream. I conducted my own search. To the front of the riverboat were four linked cabins, all empty, to the rear three more, one an engine room, one empty, one damaged, its wooden floor pierced by a hole a yard across, rich red wood revealed, gloom below. Hull space, nothing more. As for the engine, its workings were unclear, but the riverboat was moving faster than the current so I decided it was operational.

When I returned to the front of the riverboat I found Gularvhen and four children. The first two had discarded their clothes. All four stood around Gularvhen, no taller than his knees, staring up at him like puppies.

"Rescue me from these wretched brats!" he said.

"Where did those two come from?"

"I thought you must have woken them from slumber in one of the cabins to the rear."

I shivered. "They were all empty."

"This is something of a family tragedy," said Gularvhen, stepping over the children to approach me. Under his breath he added, "We will have to hand them over when we reach the haven."

I nodded.

Noon passed. Drizzle began to fall. We ate the best of what rations remained to us, then sat on the prow of the boat watching the riverbank pass.

Six children behind us.

I stared at them as they stared at me. The first two, I noticed, were taller than the new arrivals, their faces darker, more cunning. They never smiled, yet I knew they had teeth . . . and then there came a feeling of prickling at the back of my neck as I considered alternative explanations for the existence of the children. As for Gularvhen, his face was pale.

"Let's disembark," I said.

Gularvhen looked at me, at the children, then at the riverbank. "Agreed," he said.

But the task was impossible. No mechanism existed to steer the riverboat, its engine a mass of plates and amorphous lumps resistant to exploration; no rivets, no crevices, no plates or attachments. There was no rudder or wheel. I began to feel anxious. I returned to the prow and studied the river. It was wider now, muddy, the bottom invisible. Swimming across would be difficult, if not impossible.

"I don't like this," I said.

"Nor I, psolilai, nor I . . . look! Another pair of children."

A fourth pair of children appeared from one of the rear doors, blinking in the light, then joining their kin. Eight pairs of staring eyes, and not a cry, not even a whimper.

I noticed a change at the rear of the riverboat. I pointed, my face creasing in disgust. "Look, it's transforming. Like a grub."

"Some kind of red dye in the river."

I sniffed. "Do you smell blood?"

Gularvhen stood to his full height, as if steeling himself. "I will venture a brief examination," he said. "Remain here with Hoss."

I shrank to the horse's side as Gularvhen strode away from the prow, but he stopped after a few paces.

"The riverboat is changing into a worm," he reported. "Thick hide leaking blood. . . ugh! I see two children clambering out of the hole."

I shuddered.

"This is a necrogenic beast," he declared. "The mother is dying and so the illusion is fading. Quick now! Jump, before it is too late."

I turned to scan the water ahead. In the distance I saw the river split into two, revealing a great island, tall, greened, lamps twinkling atop its summit. "Teewemeer!" I cried.

Hoss leaped into the water. Hezoenfor the sparklehawk rose into the sky, his plumage glittering. Gularvhen grabbed his pack, threw it into the river, then jumped. But the nearest two children moved forward, grinned, then extended razor teeth. Petrified, I could only stare.

"psolilai!" Gularvhen cried as he swam away from the riverboat. "Jump!"

The necrogenic worm was sinking as it died. Two children stalking me. . . unable to wrench my gaze away from those eyes. . . fixed to the spot.

Water at my knees. The children licking their lips.

"psolilai!"

Like cobras, the children opened their mouths for the kill. With a scream I jumped backwards and hit the water, shock shattering the illusion. Gasping for air I struggled, turned, then began to swim with the current to the island shore, now just a few hundred yards off. Behind me, the dead worm sank.

Ten children followed me, their little limbs splashing through the water. Seeing them sent adrenalin through my body and I swam like never before, a burst that lasted half a minute, propelling me towards

35

the shore but leaving me exhausted, cold and sinking. Now I drifted to the right, away from the island, but Gularvhen was at my side, and he tugged me away from the current until I felt firm ground at my feet. I saw Hoss drag himself onto the shore. Hardly aware of what I was doing, I found my balance, stood upright and struggled ashore.

I turned. The faces of the children leered at me as they floated by, sinking beneath the surface to leave only bubbles. I stood sobbing on the shore. My body shook. Foul water leaked from my nose. My leathers, jeans and boots were freezing. Sneezing, coughing, spitting water to the ground, I collapsed.

Gularvhen dropped his pack at my side. "We made it," he gasped.

My fit subsiding, I found energy enough to reply, "We did, but only just."

Gularvhen lay back, sighing. After a while he said, "In a moment we will have to find a path to climb. The haven lies on the summit, which is flat. We must go on before we freeze."

I agreed.

"Hoss will carry you," Gularvhen decided. "I have strength enough to walk." With a grimace he squeezed the water from his pointed hat.

With the sun low in the west, we began the ascent. I studied the island as we climbed. It consisted of three great truncated cones, in plan not unlike the three parts of Theeremere, that rose out of the river to flat summits all on a level; the slopes green with natural plants, criss-crossed with paths, but devoid of felins or other beings. As we rose the paths swung about so that their inclines were manageable. The gaps between the three sections remained narrow; a suggestion of bridges spanning ravines when I peered up through the shadows.

After an hour we reached the top, to see a massive arch under which our path led. Gularvhen pointed and said, "There, felins on guard. We are safe."

We approached the gate. Two felins sauntered over, unarmed but wearing cuirasses and greaves of hardened leather. One said, "Halt there. Who are you and what do you want at the Haven of the Moontoo?"

With a theatrical gesture Gularvhen wrung water from his pack and tossed it to the ground. "We have survived the beast of the river," he said. "We are soaked and freezing."

More felins emerged and there was frantic activity. The guard exclaimed, "By Yamajatha! Dismount immediately and come to our hearth. Have you eaten recently? Drunk?"

The arch revealed itself as a gatehouse of brick in which many chambers had been built. I found myself hustled into a room with a fire. Small, furry hands helped me remove my leathers and boots, then my other clothes, a cotton towel offered to keep me warm. A goblet was thrust into my hand and I smelled mulled wine. I drank it all. On a tray by my side I saw food, cakes and bread, peas, apples and leeks all steaming in a thin soup. I ate; Gularvhen too. We said nothing until the pangs of hunger were subdued and we felt warm and dry enough to return to decorum.

An old felin approached me. He was short even for a felin, with pale ginger fur and drooping whiskers. "You have done well to survive the river," he said. "Who are you?"

I replied, "Travellers on our way to Mahandriana. We survived the beast."

"Aha," said the felin, "the riverboat worm. A vicious beast with a talent for illusion made worse by our proximity to Mahandriana. But such is our lot, living so close." The felin touched my hand with his. "I am Murth Yoor, serjeant of this gate." Gently he pulled the towel from my upper arm, to reveal one of my tattoos. "You may enter this haven, but your friend is unmarked. Since you are both strangers he must acquire the moontoo for his person." He glanced at Gularvhen, then added, "A few minutes' work, no more, and there is no pain."

Gularvhen submitted to the process of tattooing, and then, clothes dried, we were free to enter Teewemeer, Murth Yoor our guide.

The gatehouse stood at the west end of a thoroughfare, Serotonyn Street, a narrow passage suitable for felins slender and graceful, but not for human beings, still less for Hoss. We had to squeeze past steps and signs as we walked down the street, the green eyes of a hundred felins shining bright as we passed by. At the edge of the southern ravine we turned left into Ybogayne Lane, the wind blowing up from the depths to ruffle our cloaks, before we reached a bridge like two swan necks fused into a single arch. Clasping the rope guides, we crossed into Tryptophyne Street, following the ravine's edge until Murth Yoor signalled a halt.

37

Pointing to the top of a ziggurat visible behind the houses of the street, he said, "Do you see it? That is the Shrine of the Moontoo, a place revered by felins, since from that point Yamajatha, the provident one, stepped into the heavens having founded this haven. There you can stay, for I own chambers inside."

We thanked him, then continued our walk, following Ysatyn Street until, turning the corner, we saw the ziggurat in its entirety. The lower half was visible as stepped stones behind a curtain of trailing green plants, but the upper half was clear, and there we saw windows, lamps, and felins climbing and descending, using the outside stones as flights of stairs. The summit was set with pillars and elegant towers.

Gularvhen turned to Murth Yoor. "And Hoss?" he said.

"Your mount will be housed to the rear of the ziggurat. His safety is assured."

We entered by means of a tunnel leading off the street, the door low so we had to duck, a task most difficult for Gularvhen. The ziggurat was hollow, stabilised by internal pillars and walls, creating a honeycomb of chambers. And the place was busy. Murth Yoor led us through crowds of felins, countless eyes staring up at us from waist height, before a door was shut to bring peace in a cool corridor.

Echoes in the silence. I could hear my heart beating.

"Is this ziggurat a place of religion?" Gularvhen asked.

Murth Yoor pointed to a chamber containing a dais, upon which was set a scarlet orb. "Here we keep one of our analytical-tendencies," he said. "We do not worship the machines, nor anything else, but we keep dear the memory of Yamajatha, alongside nature, of course."

Climbing several flights of stairs brought us to a pair of chambers whose windows looked out over the southern haven. The rooms were small, undecorated, but comfortable; cushions, couches, low tables on which sat wrinkled fruits and pitchers of spiced water. The rooms were clean and dust free.

"Here you are my guests," said Murth Yoor. "Doubtless you have stayed in other havens, who followed their own rules when it came to civic service."

I nodded. "If you mean unlinking duties . . ."

"It is the same here. You will be asked to sign a register of strangers, to be called upon as circumstances dictate. Although we are insulated from the wilderness because of our position, we are subject to attack from the manufacturing ecosystem."

"We understand," said Gularvhen.

Murth Yoor bowed. "To be frank, I doubt you will be called. Remain here until dusk, when I shall take you to a meal of welcome."

He departed. Gularvhen appraised the room in which we stood, gazing out of the window, then muttering, "Is it they who speak our language, or do we speak theirs?"

I sat on a couch. "We have an accent and use different words, different emphasis . . . but it is our tongue."

Again Gularvhen looked through the window. "It is like being at home," he murmured. With a sharp intake of breath he shrugged, then said, "I will take the other chamber. Sleep is what I require, however brief."

As promised we were invited to supper, in a chamber sited near the ziggurat summit. The walls had been covered with sheets of paper dyed every colour of the rainbow, in the centre a great oval table surrounded by shaped cushions, seats in which sat a number of felins. The air smelled of food and wine. I glanced at Gularvhen. Either these were the luxuries of a corrupt hierarchy, or the felins had overcome the problem of food supply in a restricted area. I remembered then the dense vegetation of the slopes.

Murth Yoor noticed our discomfort. "Yamajatha understood the principle of biodiversity," he explained. "The slopes that we garden, and the yards and plots atop this island, are dedicated to the production of food. It is truth. We are a culture as much of nature as can be managed in Urbis Morpheos."

I nodded, joy in my heart. Gularvhen and I sat on either side of Murth Yoor, glancing at the ten other felins, who had already begun their meal.

"Feel free to choose," said Murth Yoor, indicating the spread. "The only custom we have at table is that of tale telling. You may eat what you like when you like."

I surveyed the bowls steaming all around the table: potatoes, leeks and onions, apples, pears and grapes, goblets and pitchers everywhere filled with a wine the colour of moonlight. On side plates lay rye bread baked black, raw cucumber and olives, and tiny bowls of salt. I decided to enjoy the repast.

Later, the rate of eating was reduced, as the meal reached a conclusion and more wine was poured. "You are our guests," Murth Yoor told me, "so you first must tell a tale."

Embarrassed, I glanced at Gularvhen. "My friend is the better speaker," I mumbled.

Gularvhen laughed. "psolilai exaggerates," he said. He dabbed his lips with a napkin and continued, "But I, riding between districts on mycological quests, hear many tales, one of which I shall now relate. It is a tale from the lost haven of Vallevaess. This haven lay on the plain known as Persellafaer, an ancient land now lost to the aeons, in a time when people and agens lived together, beings from the manufacturing ecosystem, it is said, allowed into havens without even a glance. But my tale concerns four people, Keen Ears, a noble man, his wife Wisdom Tongue, who knew all about finding food in the wilderness, and their young daughter Sunset Hair. The fourth person was Ancient Adviser, a man on the edge of the Vallevaess clan, curt and alone, but valued for his wisdom. Now, the clan had long been pestered by agens, who wanted to know human secrets, in particular of the analytical-tendencies used by Wisdom Tongue's family to survive the perils of the wilderness. So it was that the agens did a dreadful deed. Before Wisdom Tongue's eyes her husband was cut, burned, then killed. The agens threatened to do the same to her if she did not yield up her secrets. In her human fraility, Wisdom Tongue told the agens what they wanted to know. Thus the clan was betrayed. But worse, the clan said Gaia had been betrayed too. Then the agens turned against Vallevaess, and there was battle. Wisdom Tongue was killed. But Ancient Adviser found Sunset Hair and told her, 'I am the only one left who can save you.' He picked her up and smuggled her out of the haven, but agens upon the walls sounded the alarm. 'They saw my pale face in the moonlight,' said Ancient Adviser. So he was chased. A horde of hissing, ticking agens followed him. Now, there was nowhere to run, the wilderness parched and cracked, sending up fumes to the sky. Ancient Adviser said, 'I am tiring, but do not give up hope.' And Sunset Hair replied, 'Gaia will save us.' Just then a glittering hawk flew over their heads. Ancient Adviser ran up to the brow of a hill and watched where it went, hoping to see a natural haven. He saw a great plain of sunlight, reflecting across the wilderness. In a moment he had carried Sunset Hair to this plain,

40

where he stood her up and covered her in metal foil. Also he covered himself. So they escaped, for the agens were unable to see their prey, mirrors in a mirrored land, and passed them by. And when he knew they were safe, Ancient Adviser said, 'May we never be outcasts again,' to which Sunset Hair replied, 'Nobody can be cast out of Gaia.' And Ancient Adviser knew then that Sunset Hair would ever follow Gaia, that is, nature, if only to make restitution for her mother's betrayal, and in the end redeem herself."

The sound of a satisfied murmur passed around the table.

As Gularvhen related this tale I felt emotion stirring within me, at first in my chest, then in my mind, as if some memory long since cooled but now boiling over had been awakened. Two tears fell gentle from my eyes, and then I was weeping. I lifted my leather jacket and covered my head with it, leaning on the table as my body shook; my head in my arms. In this position I remained, until the weeping subsided and I was able to wipe my face, sit upright, then reveal myself.

Silence had fallen. In a weak voice I asked, "Why is Teewemeer called the Haven of the Moontoo?"

"Let me relate the tale," Murth Yoor replied. "The tale of the founding of Teewemeer is the tale of Yamajatha's desire. Seeing the suffering and terror in Urbis Morpheos, Yamajatha, the provident one, pondered the possibility of bringing peace to his city. Leaving the encampment of his birth he wandered far and wide in his search for a new home both elegant and fertile, yet safe, and suitable for his felin kin. At length he discovered an eyot upon a river. But his true desire was for the light of goodness, and in his eyes the best such light was offered by the moon. So Yamajatha decided to reach for the moon. First he raised up a hill, but soon he saw that he did not have enough stone to reach the moon itself. Instead he began building a pyramid atop the hill, the point of which he hoped would pierce the moon, so that its pale fluid dripped down upon the city, and healed it. But this too remained incomplete, for he realised that the moon was too distant. Last of all he built a tower on the flat summit of the pyramid. This tower he forged from the machines of the plain around him. At last he had made a structure from which he could reach the moon. And from it he did leap." Murth Yoor paused, then said, "Alas, Yamajatha felt his desire too hot. It was a leap too far. For the tower itself betrayed him, its mechanical heart corrupt, offering inaccurate measurements. But the truth of Yamajatha's desire remained strong, and that truth manifested in the form of the moontoo, a satellite providing, if not the light he so desired, then a glimmer of it. And so Urbis Morpheos still lacks peace, though we felins have found safety."

The felins around the table lowered their heads, and there was a muttering, the words of which I did not catch.

It was midnight. Gularvhen retired to his room, but Murth Yoor took me aside and said, "Would you wish to see the stars this night?"

"From the top of the ziggurat?" I replied.

"It makes an excellent observatory."

I agreed, and the felin led me to one of the external stairs, which we ascended to reach the summit. We alone had its possession. Across a clear sky all the heavens were laid, rings, moontoo and all.

Murth Yoor pointed at various objects. "There our sibling galaxy, there the brightest star."

"It is wonderful."

"Tonight all four of the visible planets beyond Urbis Morpheos can be seen." He pointed them out. "There the nearest, red Bythoi, there Gyanyerdha, there bright Lyn, and there ringed Vytheendyah, the most distant observable with the naked eye."

I turned to view the structures built on the summit. All but one—a great statue in the form of a horse—were towers. I said, "What are these buildings?"

"Specialised observatories." Murth Yoor pointed to the central tower, black walls sparkling. "From that tower Yamajatha himself leaped."

I gestured towards it with one hand. "May I?"

"Of course."

I entered the tower through a door that shut itself behind me. The structure comprised a single cylinder, its walls glowing, floor and ceiling featureless black, so that for a few moments I felt vertigo. It passed. As my eyes became used to the quality of the light I noticed an arc in the air, a spiral of translucent squares rising from the floor to some unobservable end at the ceiling. The lowest square lay at my feet, a handspan above the floor.

I put one foot upon it, and raised myself with the other.

It held my weight. I was standing above the floor.

The second square lay within easy reach, so I took a step up to it, and it too held my weight. I ascended a dozen steps in this manner, slowly, yet with confidence.

Difficult to see what lay below, the cylindrical form of the tower now a truncated cone, above me the spiral continuing, each step clearer, a faint orb its conclusion. So I ascended, and the tower fell away, became a disk, as I climbed nearer to what I soon saw was the moontoo.

Its face became my visual field, edge to edge. A tesselation covered its surface, imperceptible lower down but now visible. This tesselation was composed of the interlinked forms of a felin face, grey and white fur, luxuriant whiskers, dark, dark eyes. The same face multiplied out across the moontoo.

Changing. Whiskers shrinking, ears from furry pointed to pink and lobed, eyes to blue human; evening-red hair framing a freckled face. My face!

Like ink across paper my image spread, replacing the felin face, until all I could see was a geometry of myself, triangles, hexagons, larger triangles, from the front of my nose to infinity at the edge of the moontoo.

I took a step back—missed my footing.

I turned, twisted my body like a diver, and with grace, legs straight, arms forward, hands to a point, I dropped down, steps blurring, black dot below becoming a circle, the floor of the tower like a midnight pool into which I plunged.

Then and there a single turn spiral of squares—steps above and before me. Clasping the lowest step, lifting myself upon it, then ascending to a black ceiling, through which I broke, to step upon the floor of the tower.

Walls glowing soft around me. Ceiling and floor featureless black. A hint of vertigo.

A door to my side. I opened it and walked through.

Murth Yoor awaited me, leaning against a pillar, a clay pipe in his hand. Scent of tobacco smoke.

"An interesting structure," he remarked.

I took a deep breath. "Steeped in history," I agreed.

43

So this was Mahandriana, Haven of the Owl, Westside. psolilai had reached her destination after a journey of terrors and mystery.

She surveyed what lay around her. Above all other impressions the place smelled, and not with pleasant perfume. Under an immense roof the ground was divided into five zones, each flooded with an oily lake into which rivulets ran. The further four lakes were hazy behind dark mist or indistinct from distance and the number of supporting columns, but she could tell from the nearest lake that this water was the source of the rancid smell. The place was dim despite luminous globes suspended from the roof, and noisy too, the roof acting as a reverberator to the voices of the hundreds of people who milled around her. With evening fallen she decided it was best to ascend, leaving the mud and noise for some quieter level.

She asked a woman, "Excuse me, how do we ascend?"

"There are staircases inside the central column," came the answer. "Are you new? Stay in the lower Teeming Levels, that's my advice, until you become familiar with the haven."

Friendly, but rushed. psolilai waved on her two companions, heading for the nearest column wall, which she could now see was pierced with doors. The staircase inside was wide and crooked, made of the same pale substance that formed the haven, and she wondered if it—if this entire place—had been built in situ, carved and moulded, like wasps make a nest. Scores of people walked up and down the stairs, some carrying items, others leading beasts, some alone, bent on private tasks, others jolly in the company of friends.

The trio ascended a few levels, then Gularvhen chose a door to lead them off the staircase. The gallery before them was so wide psolilai could not see its sides. The roof swept high to an edge, then, like a soft cheese, it drooped. The lower edge was sheer, providing a panoramic view of Urbis Morpheos beyond. Clustered upon this gallery were hundreds of buildings, a haven in miniature, with gardens, alleys, smoking chimneys; lamps like globes on inverted tentacles lighting the scene. Nothing here was straight. Streams ran down crooked passages, to be whisked off the edge by the wind. Even the houses were rickety, built haphazard on uneven ground.

But it was cold in the open air. psolilai shivered. At her side Kirishnaghar said, "Even I want shelter tonight."

psolilai looked up at Kirishnaghar: tall, portly, chubby flesh, wearing sumptuous blue robes and a black hat, a walking-stick in hand. Beard grey and white, combed into two forks. "Shelter, yes," she replied with a sigh. "But where?"

Gularvhen led them down a narrow passage, under an arch, pausing before a dark house of three storeys, illuminated inside by yellow lanthorns. Ramshackle: not a place of inspiration, with its irregular windows and its rickety door.

psolilai read the legend above this door: The Inn of Twilight Ratiocination. She shivered, linked arms with Gularvhen. "Shall we try this inn?" she asked.

"We have nothing to lose. I believe I can smell straw and dung, and that means a stable for Hoss."

"Come on, then." With these half-hearted words psolilai led them inside.

A first impression of warmth, cosy atmosphere, then, as she glanced around the room in which she stood, solid objects—a bar, glasses twinkling, a fire of coals in a grate; deep and comfortable chairs set around wooden tables. A staircase to the left; doors leading behind the bar. It was an inn of peace, no sound of footsteps above, nor even a voice.

"Hello?" she said.

A furry head popped up from behind the bar. A felin.

psolilai stared. "Are you the . . . ?"

High, twanging voice in reply. "The proprietor? Ilyi Koomsy is my name. You wish to stay?"

psolilai hesitated, glancing at Gularvhen, then at Kirishnaghar. "Well . . ."

Gularvhen took a step forward. "What are your rates my good fellow?"

Ilyi Koomsy scampered around the bar, jumping upon a table so that his face was on the same level as theirs. "Rates?" he said. "First a drink! You have travelled a long way. I would be a fraud to leave you standing here, unwatered."

psolilai glanced at Gularvhen, offering him the tiniest shrug of her shoulders. "We accept with alacrity," he replied. "For my part I shall take a glass of brandy. I am the peripatetic mycologist Gularvhen."

"Just a glass of sugarwater for me," said psolilai. "I am psolilai . . . also peripatetic."

Ilyi Koomsy turned to Kirishnaghar. "And our sightless guest?"

"I am not thirsty," Kirishnaghar replied. Silence followed. Lamely he added, "My good fellow."

"My horse stands outside," said Gularvhen, as the felin busied himself behind the bar.

"I will settle him in a stall," Ilyi Koomsy assured him. "Here, take your drinks while I see to his needs."

"Do not feed him," Gularvhen warned. "He is not as ordinary horses."

Ilyi Koomsy ran through one of the doors behind the bar, revealing a glimpse of an untidy kitchen. They stood in silence, sipping their drinks, Kirishnaghar settling himself in the furthest chair so that he was in shadow. Then psolilai heard the stairs creak. An old felin descended. Without a word he walked to the bar and peered through the door, then, as if cold, shut it and wrapped his orange gown around his body, to shuffle forward and study them both.

"I thought I heard voices," he said. His voice quavered, yet it possessed a vibrant note, as if recalling former glories. "May I inspect your unlinking tags?"

They obliged, psolilai disconcerted by his imperious tone.

"Hmmm. And you are staying here?" the felin continued.

"I think so," psolilai replied. "The owner is seeing to our horse."

"That is my son. I am Dyeeth Boolin, proprietor. My son and I keep this inn, and its sibling concern, the Teahouse of Aurorean Eudemonia." He waved one hand towards a window. "You may have seen it on the edge of this gallery."

"The truth is," said psolilai, shaking her head, "we are newly arrived."

Dyeeth Boolin turned to gaze at the fire. "Mmmm. And the moontoo so recently changed." The old felin sat in a chair and was about to speak, but Ilyi Koomsy ran in.

"Father, these people have come to stay with us. We must prepare rooms, discuss rates. They have a remarkable horse."

"Much here is remarkable," Dyeeth Boolin replied. He stood up and made for the stairs. "Ilyi Koomsy," he said, "see to their needs. Waive all charges." He turned to Gularvhen. "Later, I will come down to speak with you. Please be at peace here."

With that he departed. Ilyi Koomsy stood before them and said, "Pay no attention to him. He is a melancholic, taken with fits of sagacity.

Now, your rooms. We have five guest rooms upstairs. My father lives in the garret."

"And yourself?" Gularvhen asked.

"I live with my wives at the Teahouse of Aurorean Eudemonia. You must take breakfast there whenever you can. Free! But supper here."

psolilai was offered first choice of room. At the rear of the inn on the middle floor a short corridor led to a single chamber, small, but comfortable, with a view encompassing the whole open edge, sky and all. "This is perfect," she said.

Gularvhen chose the room over the stable. Kirishnaghar was less fussy. "As long as my room has a window, I will go anywhere," he said.

Later, after they had settled and eaten, Dyeeth Boolin joined them before the fire. He sat with them, but was taken by surprise when Kirishnaghar appeared. "Who are you?" he asked.

"The third member of this company," Kirishnaghar replied.

Dyeeth Boolin began stuffing a clay pipe with weed. "Hmmm. And you too study mycology?"

"I am no mycologist. I have some small skill in illusion."

"You should have introduced yourself when you arrived."

"What are manners," responded Kirishnaghar, "when there is truth?"

psolilai decided to head off any arguments. "We're delighted to be here," she said in a loud voice, "but we are surprised to be staying at your expense."

"A whim, a whim," Dyeeth Boolin replied. "I confess myself intrigued by your motives for travelling. One of you, I would guess, is something of a dreamer."

"You guess well," said psolilai.

Dyeeth Boolin lit his pipe and puffed at it, but made no reply.

"Do you have many strangers staying here?" asked Gularvhen.

"Mostly native to Mahandriana—merchants, scribes, rogues and the like. Sometimes residents of the upper levels stay here. Also wanderers from havens such as Gunnuguedir and Teewemeer."

psolilai asked, "And do you enjoy your work?"

"I am more interested in discussing your motives," Dyeeth Boolin replied. "Yours, psolilai, not those of your companions. You imagine yourself a visionary?"

Not wishing to be rude before her generous host, psolilai was forced to put her wishes aside. "I have placed myself on a certain path," she said. "It is difficult to describe. Yes, I am a visionary, seeking 3Machines. You know that name?"

"Some call 3Machines the owl."

"What do they mean by that?"

Dyeeth Boolin replied, "That is not a question that can be answered at this point in time. So, psolilai. . . you are a utopian, then?"

"A Gaian," psolilai replied.

Dyeeth Boolin nodded, puffing hard on his pipe. "Mmmm. Give me an outline of your vision."

"Well, as a Gaian," psolilai began, "I want to return nature to sole occupancy of the planet. If we don't use our abilities to aid nature, Urbis Morpheos is doomed to a manufactured future . . . endless streets and squares, slums and back alleys."

"Is that so bad a thing?" asked Dyeeth Boolin.

"Of course! The manufacturing ecosystem follows unnatural laws. Ultimately, those laws come from selfish minds, exaggerated over the aeons into the appalling state we face today. My dream is to return to nature. All beings of the natural ecosystem, all plants and animals, are suffering because nature's balance has been lost. I hope to return that balance."

Dyeeth Boolin stood up, strolled to the fire, then turned to face her. His hands fidgeted behind his back. "A commendable stance which I promise with all my heart to support," he said. "But you will never return nature to sole occupancy, as you put it. There is always the question of sentience. Because we felins, like you humans, are conscious, we have the ability to manipulate our environment. We need tools. We need raw materials. Would it not be better to accept a minimum level of use? Given the opportunity to use sustainable resources, we could live with nature and still retain our required level of technology."

psolilai shook her head. "I do not believe so."

Dyeeth Boolin nodded. "Hmmm. Very well. Still, I shall support you. But now I must bring you some news. For the next few days I shall be away. I find I have to visit Teewemeer. Ilyi Koomsy will look after you. Please do not leave my inn for another, for we have much yet to talk about."

48

Gularvhen also stood. "We promise not to leave," he said.

Dyeeth Boolin stood on the first step of the stairs and said, "If you want my advice, try prospecting in the rivers flowing into the haven." With that, he left for his garret.

psolilai retired to her room at midnight, leaving Gularvhen and Kirishnaghar deep in a discussion about the ethics of deception.

Late next morning they braved the fresh, cold air of the plateau to see how the rivers were laid out. There were many, some dark with pollutants, others bubbling streams; clear, populated with minnows. psolilai chose the cleanest. Instructing Kirishnaghar to fetch prospecting pans, she took Gularvhen upstream to examine the land there. The river was shallow, its banks often shingle shores on which algae and water plants grew. She bent down to study this environment, but saw no glitter of metal.

Kirishnaghar returned carrying three pans. "The hills around Mahandriana are the cradle of the haven," he said. "When we arrived we saw the black fog of evening, but every morning a golden mist arises from the ground, to disperse up here. It is symbolic of the diurnal rhythm upon which we all depend." He looked up and down the river. "This is a good site for prospecting."

Now psolilai understood Dyeeth Boolin's concluding remark. They would not be panning for nuggets, but for symbols, for ideas. Enthusiasm took hold of her and she waded into the river, introducing a handful of underwater grit to her pan, sitting on the shore, then swirling the material, allowing the water's flow to separate the numinous from the trite.

"What are we looking for?" asked Gularvhen.

"Ideas, concepts," psolilai replied with a laugh. "A nugget to help us find 3Machines."

So they began their search. Noon arrived, and passed.

"Bring us food and drink from the inn," psolilai instructed Kirishnaghar. "And my hat and scarf, please."

It was late afternoon before psolilai found anything. Beneath the grit and sand she saw a speck of colour, pale blue, but intense, like the sky. She froze. Swirling stopped, the grit concealed all. She began again, and after a few minutes had washed away enough debris for the speck to be visible at the edge of her pan.

"Over here!" she cried. Excitement made her heart beat fast. She knew not what she had discovered, but she recognised the importance of the moment.

Gularvhen peered into her pan. "What is it?" he asked.

"A fragment of a notion," she replied. "Look how deep the colour is against this rusty old pan. The river is washing specks down from the mountains."

"Or they are being attracted by the aura of the haven," said Gularvhen.

"Or both," Kirishnaghar suggested.

"Whatever the reason," psoliai said, "this is what we are looking for."

Gularvhen frowned. "But what do we do with it?"

psolilai shrugged. "Later," she said. "For now, let us find more."

Kirishnaghar offered another thought. "Dyeeth Boolin it was who sent us here. He knows more than he has so far revealed."

Before the light faded psolilai found two more specks, one pink, one olive green. With Gularvhen's mycological tweezers she transfered them into a sample bottle, which she pocketed. Then they strolled back to the haven, happy.

—she dreams of bad snow falling deep, acid reek filling Eastside streets, but now it is accompanied by fog so thick it is in places impossible to see more than an arm's length ahead. And this ochre fog is corrosive. Bad fog.

Whereas bad snow transforms stone into bizarre forms, or just thick treacle that oozes down the walls of buildings, bad fog is more insidious, attacking wood, paper and fabric, transforming them into mats of conglomerate junk. The scale of the haven is reduced: streets hardly wide enough for two to pass, door arches low, windows small, dripping bridges of stone linking upper levels where before just the breeze has blown. Some runnels of stone rise upward, defying gravity, as the substance hierarchies in the bad fog create artificial absorption paths as part of their construction. Everything is black, grey, ochre. Every lane is punctuated with sticky puddles. Many lanthorns remain unlit.

Worse is the effect on people. She steps underneath the arch of the Sage Gate and sees two guards. Their faces are blotchy white. They cast their eyes back down to their board game, as if defeated by the conditions—

She woke up. She remembered her dream, and wondered if it presaged failure ...

Next day the trio walked higher upstream, to a place where a curve in the river made a long expanse of stone-strewn shore. Here, all day, they panned.

It was late afternoon when psolilai found the first large nugget, an elegant curve of buttercup-yellow as large as a thumbnail. Gularvhen examined it. "If this was organic matter," he said, "I would consider it part of an agaricus cap, that of the yellow-stainer."

psolilai looked at her treasure. Mushrooms—of course! "You're correct," she said. "What are these fragments? Concept debris formed under the influence of this extraordinary haven. They are not real objects, they symbolise ideas, and we eat them as we would an ordinary mushroom."

Gularvhen nodded, his eyes flashing. "I do believe you are right," he said. "With Hoss beside us, we have here the crucial resource with which to begin our search."

"We will prospect until Dyeeth Boolin returns," she said, "and then question him. By then we should have enough fragments to use."

They all agreed. With dark fog falling down the hill sides, they returned to the Inn of Twilight Ratiocination, where Ilyi Koomsy fed them a hearty supper.

psolilai was up at dawn. From her window she watched the golden mist rise. It all fitted. Gold mist for dawn, black fog for eve: symbols made real. In her pocket a jumble of ideas. All she had to do was consume enough to let her mind sort things out.

D yeeth Boolin was unwilling to share his thoughts when he return- ed two days later. Puffing on his pipe as they huddled around the fire, he seemed unconcerned about their finds. "They may simply be pieces of a sculpture," he pointed out. "But there is no harm in testing them."

psolilai took out the sample bottle, now filled, in which every frag- ment had been stored. "Do you see that yellow nugget?" she asked. "Gularvhen has identified its curve as characteristic of a particular species of mushroom." She shook the bottle so that it rattled. "This is concept debris. My intention is to brew up a tea with it, then drink it with Hoss nearby."

"Do it now," suggested Dyeeth Boolin.

"Will you join us?"

"I am too old and cynical for such things."

psolilai frowned. "You called us remarkable," she said, "and you waived all fees. I think you know more than you let on."

"My dear, we all know more than we let on."

Gularvhen rose to speak. "Let us brew our tea," he said. "I am impatient to learn what ideas float around this haven."

A cannister of water was placed on a tripod above the coals, and into this psolilai deposited the fragments, Gularvhen adding mint and hibiscus for taste. They waited. Ten minutes later, with steam rising from the cannister, Gularvhen used the coal-grab to remove it, pouring two mugs of the tea. psolilai glanced through the open door behind the bar to see Hoss standing in the yard outside.

She drank her tea of abstract notions.

Music of low bass, tweeting violins, and a single, lovely voice.

Thoughts and images entered her mind—a palace atop Mahandriana.

"The owl is the bringer of dreams," said a voice into her mind's ear. "Yet it is a bird of ill-omen too. And it is the bird of wisdom."

The owl, then, was the key.

With a moan she departed her intertwined thoughts, recognised the common room, the fire, the chairs, people sitting in them.

"3Machines can be found," she breathed.

"Somewhere inside the Owl Palace," Gularvhen said, "atop this haven."

psolilai slept dreamless that night.

She awoke to a quiet inn. Knowing that the others would be breaking their fast at the Teahouse of Aurorean Eudemonia, as they had before, she took her time rising and dressing. She sniffed at her clothes. Sweaty and dirty. Her blue jeans and her jacket were scuffed, but wearable, and her boots were undamaged. But what she wore underneath needed cleaning, and she herself needed a bath. There was no bath at the Inn, just large pitchers into which hot water could be poured.

She went downstairs, where she found Dyeeth Boolin sitting alone, wreathed in weed smoke.

"Good morning," he said. "Will you take a meal at my son's house?"

psolilai assented. "But I need a bath," she said.

Dyeeth Boolin hesitated, as if thinking. "Hmmm. It may be possible." He gestured at the front door. "If you will allow me?"

psolilai followed him down the passage leading to the Teahouse. "I must ask you a question," she said, "and I hope for a plain answer. You can speak plainly."

"I will do my best."

"It was you who suggested we go prospecting."

Dyeeth Boolin nodded. "There is no mystery. Haven't you considered the possibility that you are not the first person to come here seeking 3Machines? I am sensitive to profundity of thought. You intrigue me. That is all."

psolilai smiled and spoke no more on the subject. But she knew there was far more hidden than revealed.

At the Teahouse, Dyeeth Boolin led her along a fence to an arbour, where lay a hole in the pale substance of the haven, and inside that steaming water. "This is a natural hot spring," he explained. "The arbour is enclosed on all sides. Don't undress just yet, I will fetch your breakfast."

psolilai sat beside the pool, looking into the water, which had the milky blue appearance of a spring in which many salts were dissolved. Minutes later, Dyeeth Boolin was back, in his hand a large mug. "This is a nutritious drink," he said.

psolilai was left alone. She slipped into the pool. It was hot, but her skin became used to the temperature, and then it was comfortable. She drank her drink, a thin broth, and relaxed.

Settle Into Still

We stood at the stream of a dozen mushrooms.

Finding a suitable raft was easier than I expected. The previous winter had seen the demise of a great heat exchanger plunged miles into the ground, the vanes of which Gularvhen was able to locate and drag out of the soil, then snap by laying them across boulders and jumping on them. The slab of aerated plastic he chose was twice as long as he was tall, and even had stabilising extrusions underneath. Almost perfect.

Although we did not know exactly where we would end up, we did know we would save a lot of time by allowing the stream to carry us south. Yet it was with trepidation that I stepped on the raft and sat down at its centre, for in more than one sense I was entering new territory. Of particular note were clouds building to the south-west.

With Hoss to the front of the raft and Gularvhen to the rear we pushed off. Our river passage was tolerable. An hour before sunset, Gularvhen threw a hook on a line into the muddy bank, bringing us to a halt; he had spied a suitable copse of stone trees in which we could shelter from what was certain to be a night of bad snow. Disheartened, I looked east to see a yellow moontoo rising into layers of cloud. Around me, the first bad snowflakes were falling.

The stone trees had been much altered by the action of bad snow, their upper branches thinned to skeletons as over time droplets of rock had fallen from them like bullets to the earth. Yet this copse was far safer than open ground. Gularvhen rummaged in his pack and brought out a tarpaulin, the five corners of which he tied to branches.

"Unfortunately this fabric is artificial," he said, "and will have dissolved some more come morning. But it will serve us tonight."

"Do you have a spare blanket?"

He shook his head. "You will sleep poorly even with the action of the nuclear furnace. Exotic devices know they are far from home when they are set to counter a brumal wind."

I did sleep poorly.

Hope faded when morning came. The bad snow looked set in, falling thick from grey clouds that revealed not a hint of anything above them. There would be a queue of low pressure zones waiting to pile in off the western sea, no chance of a break, and although we were within ten leagues of Theeremere the toughest part of our journey now lay ahead.

"I have seen worse," Gularvhen remarked. I derived no comfort from the statement, since I thought it a lie.

We floated on, until the stream became a river that spread into a swamp, a morass of stone and wood, plastic and silicon, jumbled up by the action of innumerable nanos so that the scene spoke of nothing other than decay. Gularvhen stopped the raft as soon as he recognised the danger ahead, and we picked our way to higher ground, avoiding asthma-inducing steams that tried to choke us, elsewhere running from metal mantises. Good fortune meant that none of the district's really dangerous entities caught up with us. But the chase shocked me.

The weather worsened. The wind became strong enough to blow stray flakes through our protective clothing, and again we faced the problem of narcolepsy from melting bad snow. By noon we were sheltering at the foot of a steel skyscraper, unable to continue. Hoss, at least, was unaffected.

The storm subsided at dusk. Exhausted, we had no option but to follow a path around the skyscraper until we found a vertical crack in the metal, inside which we were able to improvise shelter with boulders and the tarpaulin. The furnace helped, but it was beginning to suffer under the excesses of its new environment. I ate the last of my meagre food, a single crust. Gularvhen had dried stocks, but he rationed them. He refused to let me examine the contents of his pack.

Gularvhen became terse to the point of ill manners.

55

—I dream of Kirishnaghar waiting for me. "I have not seen one single person leave or enter the Owl Palace," he says. "However, I have planted the seed Metaxain gave me in debris nearby."

I glance at his blinded eyes. "Debris?" I ask.

"It is like a thin soil composed of rotting organic matter and the like. I suspect the Sky Level has accumulated natural debris over the centuries, which has rotted down in sheltered places to form a soil in which grasses and bushes grow. There is also an animal ecology, birds, insects, rodents and the like, small only because it is windy. The fungal substrate is natural and subject to erosion—"

I awoke, and I wondered: am I the dreamer or the dreamed?

The morning brought furious weather. These were the worst storms for years. In Theeremere I could have watched them from the study window of my house on Sulphur Tuft Passage, but here they were killers. With Hoss unable to forge a clear way through the drifts we had no choice but to stay in our icy shelter. The tarpaulin was ragged at the edges.

Night brought no slackening of the storm.

On the next day the winds died down, but bad snow still fell. "We have completed the main part of the journey," said Gularvhen. "The time has come for us to take a calculated risk. We cannot remain here."

I agreed. "If we use old roof slates to push aside the drifts, we might not become narcoleptic," I said, "or at least not so quickly."

We looked into each other's eyes, nodded once, and so our plan was set.

Hoss helped. We were on foot and he could protect us from squalls with his body, but after a few hours we were tired, and, worse, both of us felt the desperation of the other.

A snap from up ahead.

Two figures strode out from curtains of bad snow, all black, yet ghostly, one with smouldering yellow eyes, the other's frosty blue. They approached with conviction, almost running, as if navigating by unhuman senses. I felt no dread, just numbness, with Gularvhen at my side standing silent having dropped his slates to the ground. The figures approached, their heads turning from side to side as if checking for escape routes. Their lair must be very close for them to venture out in such conditions. Perhaps they had heard sounds, and come to eat.

Hoss made no response as he fixed the newcomers with his pale gaze, third ear twitching.

Nothing to do. Running was pointless.

Both figures stopped a few feet away, giving me the impression that my personal space was being invaded; I took a step back. Silently, they imitated me, freezing me with merciless eyes that lacked pupils but emanated horror through the purity of their colour. Still they said nothing. I felt crushed under something nameless.

"You are Psolilai?" said the one with the jaundiced gaze.

I nodded.

Gularvhen butted in, "I am her friend. We mean no harm."

Both of them turned their heads towards Hoss. "We know what you are," came the reply.

"Don't hurt us," I pleaded.

The yellow-eyed being threw a sack at me. "Inside are clothes free of narcoleptic chemicals," it said. "Wearing them will increase your chances of survival."

I opened the sack to see leather and denim clothes inside. They looked like the sort of clothes I would normally wear; I was disconcerted.

"We are here to assist you," said the blue-eyed being. "Follow us."

Without thought I took a step forward, but Gularvhen grasped my shoulder and spoke up loudly. "How do we know to trust you?" he asked the pair. He hesitated when they offered no reply, then added in a quieter voice, "Did you mean both of us are to follow you?"

Yellow-eyes remarked, "We would break no true bond of friendship."

I felt sufficiently irked to reply, "We met only a few days ago, but he has been true to our common goal."

"Then all is well. Move, now, before more substances seep into your mind."

They were not human. Not quite. Possibly they were agens lacking the sensory augmentation of those sentients of the manufacturing ecosystem. Or possibly not. In my short life, I had seen nothing like them.

But Gularvhen pulled me back when I stepped forward again. "Do you trust them?" he asked me.

I looked up into the grey sky. "I don't trust this weather." With a shake I freed myself from his grip and walked on. Gularvhen mounted Hoss, then followed the track cleared by our rescuers.

So we walked on through the streets, the two beings throwing snow aside to clear a way through the drifts, apparently unaffected by narcolepsy. I noted certain facts: their clothes, black from collar to toe, looked artificial, yet no damage had been done to the fabric, while their faces, tanned but fresh, seemed to repel bad snow as if greased. No humans, these.

Evening arrived and we were led into a cave, familiar to our two guides if their lack of hesitation over the route was anything to go by. Both beings sat against one of the walls, shoulder to shoulder, while I settled myself against the opposite wall, Gularvhen and Hoss next to me. The furnace we placed on the floor. In the gloom, the intensity of the two pairs of eyes increased, until, hypnotised, I saw nothing other than four burning lamps, unshuttered, not even blinking.

Bad snow fell deep next day. But we were close to home, and despite mutable land I recognised the silhouette of nearby hills as morning became afternoon. Theeremere was that dark smudge up ahead.

A new morning, and pale sunlight flickered through narcoleptic snowclouds. The two beings had vanished. I looked down at the new clothes that I wore, and I felt they must carry a hidden meaning.

I heard the distant clanging of autonomous dirigibles.

As they left the Pool of Wrealities, Psolilai hugged her cousin again and asked how they could keep in contact. Karakushna gave her the identities of a number of her public aliases.

Later, Psolilai found that the Church of the Parasol Cap looked like a pincushion.

From the lane outside, she stared in horror. An attack was underway. Rapier in hand she sped forward, prepared to defend what already seemed her home. Innumerable barbs were wriggling into the masonry, the spent ones limp like string, the active ones marked by their thrashing tails. Glass and wood littered the yards and lanes all around, and there were running, shouting people everywhere, some in hand-to-hand combat, others trying to disable the weapons. Several command machines flew around the building—hawks on patrol, releasing clusters of blades. Without doubt this was a co-ordinated attack. Psolilai knew all the adherents of the Parasol Cap and so was able to identify the assailants, but they fought in a particular way, slashing and hacking; cutting, in fact.

Psolilai disarmed several people before reaching the entrance hall. The registrar who had spoken to her when she first arrived was fighting in a corner, elegant as a deer, not so much as a bead of sweat upon his face. Elsewhere, it was tougher. The boy lay unconscious. Then Gularvhen appeared, loaded with blades plucked from the stone, and suddenly Psolilai comprehended the metaphor.

"Cutting!" she cried, running towards him.

"Pardon?" he replied.

"This is Threadbreaker work—cutting, separating. Blade and barb. If we turn all our equipment off they will lose the scent and the attack will falter."

He understood. He ran away, throwing his spasming catch to the ground for others to disable. Psolilai holstered her rapier and ran to the rear of the entrance hall, where steps led down to a cellar. The problem would be the disparate nature of devices here—centralised control unthinkable. Flicking switches off and shouting at machines with speech recognition, she ran through the cellar; satisfied that all the devices were inactive she returned to the fray. She glanced outside. Light beams from the circling command machines were receding. They had noticed and recognised her deed.

It took a further half hour for the human attackers to return to the passages from which they had emerged. By then, the few people injured were in the infirmary. No deaths had been recorded.

The atmosphere began to grow calm.

Midnight, and peace returned.

In a room painted the colour of leaves, drinking cups of spearmint tea, Psolilai and Gularvhen discussed what had happened. For Psolilai there was only one response. "I want to leave Theeremere for a while."

"This is hardly the first attack on the Church of the Parasol Cap," said Gularvhen, his tone indicating that he thought she was exaggerating her problem. "Recall the infamous night of the Black Shroomfynder."

Psolilai shook her head. "Tonight happened because certain peo-ple know I have escaped Tall Cliff Steel. I can't remain here for long, with the chances rising every day that Amargoidara will hear of my return."

"Surely he already knows that you have escaped," Gularvhen pointed out.

"Sprung," Psolilai corrected. "No . . . Amargoidara will assume I have perished in the wilderness, until rumours change his mind."

Gularvhen nodded, but slowly, as if his thoughts were elsewhere.

"Yet I don't know the woman who sprang me," Psolilai continued, "nor why she might have done it."

"Who would want you free?"

Psolilai shrugged, sipping her tea. "Followers of the mushroom. Ere eccentrics. A mysterious benefactor."

After a pause, Gularvhen said, "You will head for the Sonic Forest."

"Of course."

"I could accompany you."

Psolilai thought for a moment, imagining the advantages. "Thank you for the offer."

He smiled.

"Ryoursh could have turned me in," Psolilai mused, "but I think she wants more, much more, and so she has not yet spoken my name to authority."

"You said before that someone might be controlling her."

Psolilai shrugged. "Whatever the truth, I have to speak with Aunt Sukhtaya before I depart . . . but I suspect those two women are pulling in different directions."

"There is nothing more difficult than family," remarked Gularvhen. "Let us make plans, and leave before the moon is new."

Later, it was evening, shadow shrouding all, puddles in the lane reflecting the ring system and a half moontoo, green like a lime. Psolilai found the door to her aunt's house ajar. She heard voices. In silence she listened, hardly breathing. One voice commanding, one emotional: aunt, sister.

Ryoursh was saying, "I told you what I saw when I went to visit her at the Church of the Parasol Cap. Your two got in, didn't they? You have no further use for her now you have the—"

"Cut out these absurd prejudices!" Aunt Sukhtaya answered. "This never was a time for killing. You do not lead me, niece, *never* think that you do."

"I'll do what I need to do—"

"There are many forces above you. My path will be followed and no other—"

"Shhh!"

Psolilai froze—she had been heard! She did not know what to do. There were thumps from inside the house, then Aunt Sukhtaya appeared at the door to say, "Psolilai! So that was you tapping outside. I'm glad you came to see me. Come in, please."

Psolilai managed a smile as she walked inside the house. There was no sign of Ryoursh. They sat awkward and wary in a small, cold lounge.

"So, you are back," said Aunt Sukhtaya.

"Am I forgotten in Theeremere?" Psolilai asked.

"Some people hate you, some love you," Aunt Sukhtaya replied. "Some I suppose will have forgotten you."

"Most of them."

Aunt Sukhtaya's eyes gleamed as she glanced across the room, causing Psolilai to look away. "Soon there may be secret meetings in Ere," she murmured.

In an effort to dismiss this obvious flattery Psolilai replied, "I will not be here to join them," and then regretted it.

Aunt Sukhtaya sat up. "You are leaving Theeremere?"

"Not . . . not immediately."

"You are! Where are you going?"

Psolilai felt intimidated by her aunt's bulk, felt harassed by the intensity of that gaze. Aware that her dissembling was poor, she said, "South perhaps, who knows?"

"You must have a reason for leaving. What important districts lie south? Only the Sonic Forest, south and west."

So tempting to interpret this as deliberate probing, but it seemed an innocent remark. Psolilai's discomfort increased. Trying to end the conversation she said, "I hardly think—"

"There are ancient squares, halls and towers to the south and the east."

"Aunt—"

"The ocean, perhaps?"

Frustrated, Psolilai said, "Perhaps I will leave this haven in order to explore, but my plans are vague."

"You will need transport, niece. I know a place where you might find a vehicle—ah! So your intention *is* to leave Theeremere."

"Please, aunt, my plans are secret."

She was unstoppable. "It is the blue house half way along Grisette Passage, off Tryptamine Lane." Here she named a notorious haunt of collectors and explorers.

Despite her embarrassment, Psolilai realised this could be an important contact. There was only one Hoss, and over long distances he was suitable for a single rider. She felt the time had come to disengage. "I have to leave," she said, "the hour is late."

Aunt Sukhtaya glanced out of the window as if checking the weather. "Go now," she said, "before the Grisette house closes."

Psolilai nodded, planted the briefest kiss on her aunt's cheek, then departed.

She walked down to Bufotenine Lane, but stopped at its end. Thoughts assailed her. Ere grew narrow here, where the river looped out—Grisette Passage was not far away. She would need a vehicle if she was to keep up with Gularvhen riding Hoss, and possessing a vehicle would allow her to leave the haven at her convenience, quickly if her residence at the Church of the Parasol Cap became untenable. Her mind made up, she walked down to Grisette Passage. Afternoon was waning. Bad snow fell light, big flakes fluttering, sticking to buildings. She pulled on her rainbow hat, pushed home the top stud on her leathers, and strode on.

It was half home, half workshop; a single, low door leading into the blue house and its open-plan ground floor, which was crowded with machines, all daubed luminous yellow where communications nodes had been gouged out. Many of these items were familiar to Psolilai—who had in her youth worked in the device fields of the lower slums—but others were mysterious, and some looked advanced, too advanced for amateur collectors on the edge of the law. Wild wrealities, for instance, like small scarlet fruit amongst the dross. There lay a titanium sabre. And this just the material they felt was safe to display.

But it was a bandit quarter so far south, with Rem distant across the river, Thee just a vague threat on the horizon. An old man shuffled down the stairs at the rear of the house, revealing himself to be unkempt and warty, showing two of the worst black eyes she had ever seen. A faint blue gleam from behind these bruises.

"Yes?" Though his voice was querulous, he seemed alert.

"Do you have any machines that might replicate the abilities of a horse?"

"Of a horse . . ." His voice became dull, as if to say, only that?

Psolilai knew she would have to hint at her purpose. "Out haven."

"Ah. A horse would best perform such a role."

Psolilai nodded, then said, "I can't afford a horse, so I hoped you might have something here. Do you know Sukhtaya of Psilocybin Passage? She sent me here." Psolilai felt desperate enough to take a risk. "She will underwrite your loan."

"Hmmm. How far are you going?"

Difficult. "Perhaps fifty leagues."

"Perhaps longer."

"Perhaps shorter. South, for certain."

"Where to?" he asked.

"To the limits of my endurance."

Muttering, he wandered around the room then disappeared through a side door. Psolilai heard a roar, a thrum, and then a smoother roar as a motorcycle appeared outside the front door, old man following. She walked out to examine the machine. It was a chunky, two-wheeled motorcycle with a solar engine, storage bags, even a compass. The wall opposite showed two bilious circles from the machine's dual head-lamps. And she was delighted, for it had been too long since she had ridden a machine like this.

"This is a morphic motorcycle that will adapt to mutable terrain," said the old man. "It runs off photons. You will not be able to ride it through Ere for fear of exciting the passions of robbers, so push it slowly to your home. I will provide a fabric cover against the narcoleptic snow."

"Thank you," said Psolilai. "I am grateful. How well will it fight the action of bad snow?"

"Very well indeed."

He seemed distracted. Psolilai reminded him who her benefactor was, then pushed the machine away. It was a long walk to the Church of the Parasol Cap, but an uneventful one.

Two days passed. A single task awaited Psolilai before she and Gularvhen departed for the Sonic Forest, and that involved Karakushna. As an invisible, her cousin lay beyond reach, but she had mentioned the details of her aliases; an hour of waiting in a Rem lane, then Karakushna appeared like a ghost out of a side passage.

Psolilai described her plans. "Gularvhen and I are going to follow your father's work by travelling to the Sonic Forest. Keep watch over your mother and Ryoursh. They follow some sort of uneasy alliance." She handed over the scriber, saying, "Keep this safe, I trust nobody else with it, and I dare not take it with me."

"What do you hope to achieve?"

"Uncle Illuvineya said that in the wrong hands the Constructor and the Transmuter would damage the owl beyond hope." She glanced up at the glowering sky. "We hope to protect the owl by finding the Constructor and placing it beyond reach."

"And if he was on the track of these artefacts, less moral people might also be."

"You speak the truth."

Karakushna hesitated, then said, "My father was akin to the owl, because he was so wise."

Psolilai nodded. Sorrow took her then, and, for a moment, pity for herself and for her cousin; for all her family. "I have dreamed wisdom," she said, "and I have dreamed the owl. I will find the owl, never fear."

"Wisdom . . . it's just age, you know."

"It is many things."

Karakushna hugged her cousin then melted back into the lanes of Rem.

4

MORE COMPLEX STATES

Gularvhen and I stood at the edge of a forest, but it was no natural
haven. With Qentheoz behind us, the Qavail Forest now barred
our path, a swathe of tangled stone and plastic in which lay our next
destination, Gunnuguedir. I glanced into the sky to see a lone vulture
circling low on blue translucent wings. It had followed us since
Teewemeer.

I turned to Gularvhen. "We must find Gunnuguedir as soon as
possible," I said.

He leaped upon Hoss. "Into the forest," he said. "Together, and swiftly."

So we entered the Qavail Forest, me sitting behind Gularvhen,
Hezoenfor flying ahead to offer Hoss a lead, like a will of the wisp.

The terrain was treacherous. The path we followed ended in a bog
which Hoss had to plough through, knee deep, only to struggle on
the opposite side into an impenetrable layer of polythene, twisted
sheets half a league across tangled between granite roots rising from the
ground like the gnarled hands of buried giants. In places the plastic
thickets were too dense to penetrate and we had no choice but to
retrace our steps and try another route. Lacking a path, we soon
became lost, our only hope the topographic brain of the sparklehawk
fluttering ahead.

After a few hours we rested. "How far is it to Gunnuguedir?" I asked.

Gularvhen raised his gaze to glance at the sparklehawk, which was
preening its mirrored feathers on a branch above him. "If Hezoenfor
does not know, neither do I."

And the forest grew worse. Polystyrene lianas hung down from stone branches, forming curtains impossible to see through, impossible to pass. Once, we managed to dig the damp earth from under such a curtain and pass beneath it, but it was a single exception. Elsewhere stone roots became fences, then walls, many running sealed so that they formed pools, streams, once a lake. These barriers meant that progress was minimal. Each league forward was composed of one to each side and many steps back. Any hope of a straight line was in vain.

Gularvhen stretched his arm out so that Hezoenfor could fly down for a moment. "Hezoenfor is of the natural ecosystem," he said, "evolved over aeons in a glittering environment. We will need Hezoenfor when we continue, for there is no better guide than a sparklehawk."

Evening was falling, so we decided not to risk further travel. With the nuclear furnace for heat and a plastic roof over our heads, we made camp.

I examined my rapier. "We must reach Gunnuguedir soon," I remarked. "This forest is an inferno of nanos." I tapped the rapier handle with a stone and the weapon disintegrated into fragments.

"We will need to protect our packs," said Gularvhen. "Wrap everything manufactured in cotton."

Next morning Hezoenfor again led the way, flying ahead along the clearest stretches, occasionally rising to observe on a larger scale. "Hezoenfor will sense a natural haven," said Gularvhen. His voice was low, grumbling through fatigue. His back was hunched, causing him to bend forward, his boots holed at the front, his hands tense as if from rheumatism. His mood deteriorating. I took the initiative, watching the sparklehawk as best I could from my position behind him.

So a second day passed in Qavail Forest. We made two leagues, no more, and by evening we were dejected, tired, silent. In a cavern of stone and dripping plastic we rested; around the furnace we discussed our plight. No choice but to continue. Better to go around in circles than give up, Hezoenfor our only hope.

The third day dawned wet. The rain was cold, the light dim, the forest a tangle of columns, plastic and pits worse than ever before — fallen walls, stone boulders large as houses, everywhere slippery polythene like white moss. But in the afternoon we spotted a river: faint hope. When we saw Hezoenfor flying upstream and down like a hound seeking scent, we decided to follow the soft and glutinous bank; and then, as the light failed, I saw green up ahead, and a hint of flame.

Exhausted, Gularvhen collapsed into a cradle of polythene. "You go on," he murmured.

Frightened by his plight I struggled down the river bank, until I saw a broad river ahead meeting the one I followed. A rope bridge spanned it, swaying in the wind, trees green and tall on the further bank—natural trees! The flames were lanthorns. A ladder gave me access to the bridge, which swung free, tied between two trees. I crossed the bridge to the half way point then called out, "Hello? Is anybody there?"

A stroke of lightning, then thunder, but no reply. I carried on, using the rope to pull myself along, my legs as heavy as stone. Then a dark shadow emerged from a shelter, which I saw was a treehouse built between branches—the shadow a man in green armour.

A challenge. "Haryak! Skish tsa grafrey!"

There was no chance of describing ourselves to this man. I approached hands out and empty, to suggest goodwill. "Do you speak . . . ?"

He did not.

I looked back into the artificial forest to see if Gularvhen was visible, but the cradle was hidden. I pointed, mimicked an injured person, then walked back along the bridge waving the man on. In response he clicked his fingers at the treehouse and a second man emerged; they spoke, and the newcomer followed me.

Here was a man of insight. Seeing Gularvhen, he picked him up, slung him over his shoulder and without a glance at me returned to the rope bridge, where he crossed and entered the treehouse. Noticing that Hoss wanted to follow, I led the horse across the bridge. But I felt uncomfortable, for I wanted to tell the men why Gularvhen had collapsed, and I wanted to tell them that we were heading for Mahandriana.

The man offered me a mug of hot liquid. I accepted it; sour tea, which I drank.

Although it was almost dark, the men came to a decision. One lifted Gularvhen and descended along a ramp to the forest floor. I followed, Hoss at my side, the other man remaining at his post. The man put Gularvhen on Hoss' back. Flames in glass boxes lit a path, which we followed. The mud squelched beneath our boots. Cold and dejected, I followed my guide. There was no sign of the sparklehawk.

An hour passed before I knew Gunnuguedir was close—there was a break in the trees, a valley ahead, the smell of smoke, of animals, of human habitation. Before me, the valley was filled with lamps.

The man turned to face me. "Gunnuguedir," he said.

I tried to smile.

I walked down into the haven with the man at my side. The houses were massive, lower floors of stone supporting towering wooden levels, windows diamond glass, lanthorns everywhere. The streets were muddy; the rain continued. A few people stopped to gape at Hoss, but mostly they were too involved in their own thoughts to notice me, their faces hidden beneath wide hoods.

The man led me to a building upon a narrow lane. I tied Hoss outside then followed him in, to find two women and two men sitting in a room warmed by a log fire. All five spoke in their own tongue, before one, an elderly man, helped carry Gularvhen to a chamber with a bed, where he was left to sleep. I felt alone like never before.

They offered me a room, quiet, clean, with a strong bolt on the inside. Having checked Hoss, I decided to sleep. There were coal embers in the grate, a creaky bed, water in a glass, and a dog asleep before the fire, which I decided to leave. I locked myself in, and, weeping, laid my head down to sleep.

I awoke in the middle of the night. Half an hour passed with no return to slumber, so I decided to take the night air. Like a brisk shadow the dog hopped out when I opened the front door, which I was pleased at, since I had felt uneasy at its presence. Outside, the street was empty and silent—drizzle ceased, a few sections of the ring system visible between ragged moonlit wrack. Then my fatigue returned. Gularvhen was still asleep, so I returned to my room, hesitating when I felt the dog whisk by me; but the animal lay twitching on the rug, its eyes shut, so I decided to leave it.

Next day, while Gularvhen recovered from his exhaustion, I rode Hoss through the streets. Glancing into the sky, I noticed that the rings seemed to have acquired a bright spot. This in itself was not unusual—once every few generations the entire system became a war zone for machines, turning night into day. But the moontoo seemed to have moved closer, which was odd. From my vantage point in a square, I watched.

I soon realised that the moontoo was moving towards Urbis Morpheos. It was like a pearl the colour of summer sky, its glow reflecting off the rings as it passed near them then descended towards the upper atmosphere. Soon it was twice as big as the moon. Ice crystal clouds began to condense, so high they formed streamers arranged in concentric circles that expanded and brightened with the motion of the moontoo, until watching it was like travelling into a cosmic vortex.

Other people had noticed the display. Everyone peered upwards.

Gouts of yellow flame emerged from the moontoo, and then a shower of black motes, that moved as if in zero gravity, arced, then fell towards Urbis Morpheos like a dark waterfall. But they did not fall in one direction, they expanded evenly and grew larger. The shower was coming our way. No lateral motion at all . . .

I did not know whether to ride back to the house or watch in awe. Some of the locals were running, but others stared. Anyway, it was too late. By the time I had thought about the consequences of staying outside the shower filled half the sky. Now there were screams. Hoss remained calm, looking upward in curiosity.

I regretted my decision when the first black mote struck. They had looked pretty in the air, but in fact they were charred missiles the size of a house. The first one hit the artificial forest adjoining Gunnuguedir. Flash of yellow light, silent pause, then the shock wave and a roll of thunder. In seconds both the forest and the haven were being pulverised.

It was then that I turned Hoss around and galloped for shelter. Through the air I could feel each thud, each shockwave, ten, twenty, too many to count: screams and crashing, and everywhere the sight of smoke columns rising. I could smell burning wood and plastic.

People crashing into Hoss as I hurried back to the house.

People trying to get water to fires.

Pandemonium.

Then the shower stopped, an abrupt cessation that left only the noise of panic and of crumbling houses. Far off, plastics burning in the artificial forest sent plumes of black smoke to the sky, that merged on the wind to create clouds of dark ash. At the house, all was well; the nearest missile had struck many streets away. With night closing in I could see a few fires from my window, and I congratulated myself on escaping.

Next morning there was grief on the streets. Clearly some people had died. I indicated in sign-language to the owners of the house that we would be departing, and, leaving a recovered Gularvhen to his breakfast, I adopted a sombre face and rode Hoss around the haven.

And then I saw one of the missiles.

It was not what I had imagined. No lump of charred debris, this was a still-smoking shape almost aerodynamic, its pointed nose buried deep in the earth, lumps and channels set along the raked-back body, and what appeared to be feet at the upper end. I stared. It was the work of a moment to turn my head and view the missile upside down. Quite clearly the image of a felin.

I sat back on Hoss, my thoughts whirling, memories returning me to the climb on the ziggurat. I approached the charred object. No doubt. This was a felin shape, rock perhaps, metal, or even plastic, but unmistakeable in form; the delicate feet and hands, the inquisitive face half buried in the ground.

I had to find another one! I rode on. An hour later I had seen five similar objects.

I did not know what to think. The link was clear, yet obscure also; it could not be doubted but it made no sense. What had I done during that climb into space? In truth I had considered the event a hallucination. I laughed for the madness of it.

But then I noticed that the charring produced by the missile's flight through the atmosphere had been modified, turning the colour from shiny black to mottled grey. Nothing to excite me there, but then I caught sight of growth around the chin of the object, and when I knelt down to look I saw that the mottling was in fact a mixture of green on grey, here extended into a lump, elsewhere more like powder. I could not be sure, but it looked fungal. It could not be lichen or plant based material, algae or slime. Nothing grew so quickly except spores on organics. I stood up, took a step back, and realised that what had exploded out of the moontoo was a substance of nature. Before better judgement could stop me I scraped off a lump and placed it inside a specimen tube, which I dropped into my pocket, glancing around as if I had stolen it.

So ... I lay on my bed, the tube glinting—I held it inches away from my eyes to study the sample inside. A lone test lay before me. Knowing that Hoss stood only a few yards around the corner of the house, I opened my window to its fullest extent then returned to my bed.

I dropped the lump into a goblet of water, and, once it had dissolved, I drank.

Faint music, tribal lore in rhythm and flute, overscored by celestial voices in a minor key, leading to one last thought before the rush of wisdom. I had indeed ingested a mould.

And the moontoo? Created by a person living today, a variable satellite acting as a gateway, visible only to those with sight deep enough to see. Three colours. I shook my head, heard chittering outside—nocturnal animals—and distant human voices. The clink of glasses, the thud of shutters being closed. Nothing more from Hoss.

I sat up. Knowledge of the moontoo lay within me, and I knew I would never forget it.

In Mahandriana, psolilai began considering her plans. They had arranged for Ilyi Koomsy to take them to the nearest unlinking station, which lay on the level above the Inn. Pushing through the crowds on the stairs they ascended, then followed their felin guide into a narrow gallery with a vent at the end. In this claustrophobic space psolilai felt for the first time a sense of density that, outside, she had been less aware of. She thumped a pale wall with her hands. This was fungal material, yet it felt and looked like porcelain. She tried to imagine the weight of the haven. Impossible. No wonder the lower levels were squashed.

Registration took a few minutes, and then they were free to go. She struck up a conversation with Ilyi Koomsy as they returned. "We were told that 3Machines leads alone," she said.

"Yes! She teases wisdom from the analytical-tendencies and broadcasts it to us all."

"Where are the analytical-tendencies exactly?"

"Inside the Owl Palace. Five orbs! How lucky to have such work."

Disturbed by what she had so far gleaned, psolilai said, "3Machines keeps all five analytical-tendencies in the Owl Palace?"

"Where else?"

psolilai cast her mind back to the havens that she had known. In every case analytical-tendencies had been distributed according to locality, operated by council, group or regime. She had never heard of solitary use. Too dangerous.

"The levels of Mahandriana," she said. "How are they divided?"

"There are four," replied Ilyi Koomsy. "You and I can go anywhere in the Teeming Levels and in the Adverse Levels above us. On top lie the Complex Levels, and somewhere at the summit is the Sky Level, where lies the Owl Palace. Within each set of levels there are thousands of galleries, caverns, and the like. Explore! You will be entranced by variety!"

"I am more concerned about the Analyticate here," she said. "I have never heard of a haven in which the analytical-tendencies were gathered up and kept together. It is macabre . . . perilous."

Ilyi Koomsy snorted. "Only if you don't trust your leader," he pointed out.

"How often does 3Machines appear?"

"Never. She is too busy analysing. Besides, she is a renowned sybarite."

psolilai made no reply.

Gularvhen joined them, to tell Ilyi Koomsy, "Analytical-tendencies work by their own laws. Those who use them do not control them, rather they listen and sift. If what you say is true, it marks a shift so deep psolilai was more or less bound to query your received wisdom."

But Ilyi Koomsy was not convinced. "You will find that everything is strange in this haven," he said. "And now! Back at the Teahouse. Wheat cakes and honey?"

psolilai took Gularvhen aside later that day. "These people are fools," she said. "A leader who never appears, with access to all the analytical-tendencies, uprooted and forced into one building? It is nothing but folly."

"I agree," Gularvhen replied, "yet we are naught but foreigners in a strange culture. We are in no position to question years of tradition."

"Yes we are," psolilai insisted. "Analytical-tendencies are wrealities dressed up, they are scions of the manufacturing ecosystem, and as such they work against us, and against nature. I will not let tradition block my way."

Gularvhen nodded, chin in hand. "Our path has some steep slopes ahead," he observed.

Later, agitated by what she had learned, psolilai departed the Teahouse alone, leaving the others to return to the Inn. She wanted to go up.

The Teeming Levels were sixty in number; she climbed high before reaching a barrier. On an empty level she found a cluster of men wearing dark cloaks pinned with jasper owls, and she guessed that they were agents of the Analyticate. They stood guarding a row of double doors.

Lifts. This was the system of transport between the Teeming and Adverse Levels. She approached the men and said, "I wish to ascend, please."

"Tag?"

psolilai had strung her wooden identity tag around her neck. Upon showing it she was escorted to the nearest doors, there to wait alongside others for the lift to arrive. The lift itself was white, irregular, corners rounded, lit by a selection of mishapen lamps. At the lowest gallery of the Adverse Levels she got out and began exploring.

She soon realised why these levels had acquired their name. Unlike the Teeming Levels, buildings here were larger and fewer, giving the wind a better run through the galleries and tunnels; and they were higher. Gusts threatened to blow her off her feet. There was no sign of gardens, none of the imported topsoil that marked lower levels, and the buildings were graceful, serpentine, as if sculpted by erosion, in some cases stretching without break from gallery floor to ceiling, like plastic pillars.

psolilai was quite alone. She stopped before a rounded building occupying the centre of a gallery. One door led in. She read the affixed label: The Library of Dri. NO EATING INSIDE THE LIBRARY.

She had spent a few hours wandering. Now she felt it was time to rest.

The library door was unlocked. In a hallway she paused, taking in her surroundings; silence, dust, a strong musty smell overlaid with something richer, earthy like autumn. She noticed that the dust on the floor was unmarked by footprints. A single door ahead. When she opened this door she saw what the Library of Dri contained—like no books she had ever seen.

One chamber filled the building, domed roof, pale walls, lamps hanging down on cables. But before her stood row upon row of . . . not books, but what? The smell was intense, the atmosphere damp, the floor slick and patterned with slime. Everything grey or black. And these bulky volumes before her were book shaped, but surely not books.

She crossed to the nearest row of shelves, from which she took a volume. Its cover was so wet she almost dropped it; she looked around, as if for a librarian coming to chastise her, but only the echo of her gasp disturbed the peace.

Being so wet, the volume was difficult to open. She rested it in the crook of her arm and opened the cover, to see a blank, grey, moist page. The others were similar, all irregular, in differing tones of grey. No page contained writing, nor was the volume titled. She replaced it. Taking another, also untitled, she found the same thing, though here the leaves were paler, tinted yellow. But neither letters nor numbers. Ten volumes she tried, coloured white, brown, grey, black and yellow, irregular pages all, and no clue as to the library's purpose. She walked along every row; spines without titles. Nor were the walls marked.

A hissing sound. She stood still, sure she had set off some alarm. The hiss became a swish. Sensation of cold on her head, and she crouched, glanced up, to see a mist of water falling from nozzles in the ceiling.

Deliberately, the library was being moistened.

She decided to leave before the conundrum began annoying her. But as she did she saw, amongst the monochrome volumes, one of scarlet hue. She walked over, plucked it from the shelf and opened it. Scarlet pages inside, unmarked, damp. She frowned, replacing the volume. Outside, she stood in thought before the door, then strode to the edge of the gallery, where a gale blew in. Sheltering in the lee of a stalactite she washed her hands in a pool of water, removing the scarlet stain, before returning to the Inn of Twilight Ratiocination.

"Tomorrow, tomorrow," Gularvhen insisted, as she demanded he follow her back.

The pair left for the Adverse Levels after breakfast at the Teahouse, psolilai enthusiastic to arrive, Gularvhen lagging behind as he took in sights new to him. But in the library hallway he stopped short, as if against an invisible wall, his eyes closed, breathing deep. "Mushrooms," he said.

The fragrance of autumn. She should have recognised it.

"A great number of mushrooms," he added.

She led him into the main chamber, where, for the first time in her experience, he laughed out loud, long and loud, rocking back and forth until his pointed hat fell off.

"What is it?" she asked.

"Now I understand the label on the front door," he said, wiping his eyes. "Truly this is a unique place. Do you not feel the potential of this library?" He strode forward to pick a volume at random, opening it and gesturing with his free hand at the pages inside. "The gills of mushrooms, doubtless collected over the centuries from many sources." He replaced the volume and took another, waving at its yellow pages. "Gills and more gills," he exclaimed. "These volumes are beyond value. They contain leaves of history, kept damp to preserve them, for if they dried they would crumble to dust."

"Then this library is not meant to be used?"

"Probably a ruse of the Analyticate," he replied. "But we must eat here. We must feast, psolilai."

She looked around, expecting company. "Now?"

"Before we are caught."

psolilai hesitated, unwilling to take risks so soon after arriving at the haven. "But these are unlikely to be free," she said. "What if we are caught?"

Gularvhen shook his head. "Is this not a library? Most likely these gills are from mushrooms growing in the lands surrounding Mahandriana."

"What is the point of acquiring random knowledge? The mushrooms these gills were taken from could have grown on anything." psolilai shook her head and took a few steps away from him.

"Try a few," Gularvhen insisted. "There is no such thing as too much wisdom. Try one at least, if only to use this unique resource as it was meant to be used."

75

Somehow, despite her apprehension, the thought of acting against the Analyticate tipped the balance. Knowing he had overcome her resistance, Gularvhen collected two of the smaller volumes and sat down in the centre of the chamber, where psolilai joined him.

"We shall ignore the sign outside," he said.

"Just one gill for me," psolilai replied.

"The main door is kept unlocked," Gularvhen observed. "This must be a public library, whatever its social status. I do not think we are in danger."

psolilai glanced at the lamps above. "I hope we're not being watched."

Gularvhen handed her one of the volumes. "Eat," he said.

She examined the book's pages. There were twenty, fat semicircular gills bound in a slimy grey hide. Now that she knew what they were, the thought of writing on them seemed sacrilegious. Shrugging, she tore off a corner and stuffed it into her mouth. Chewed. Bitter taste, worse than cinchona bark, but she chewed more, then swallowed. Then lay back.

To feel wisdom kicking in, ancient memory revealed through chemical hierarchies, acting in the cerebellum, as if a dream.

Eyes closed. Sense of understanding: of rock and stone and erosion and sedimentation and fossils and the long, long, slow, slow march of geological time.

Mushroom growing fragile on desolate rock . . .

Her clothes were drenched and she sat shivering in a puddle.

In moments she understood. The nozzles had let down a rarefied pool of water so that the entire chamber was in mist. She ran out of the library to find Gularvhen sitting outside, and soon they were descending to the Teeming Levels, discussing the wisdom that they had acquired.

—That night she dreams of her other self, of Psolilai, and of a fat man who steps forward when a tall agen says, "Sithy, nerfy."

Psolilai just stares. The fat man stops a few yards away.

"Furghurth!"

One of the boils on his neck bursts, spattering fluid across Psolilai's face. She screams and crouches down. He kneels, and two further boils burst, again splattering her. Now she runs. But he runs too. And he is fast, far faster than a fat man should be. But he never touches her. His limbs sound like skreeking metal. As she stumbles down a path, he follows, losing his shift, boils bursting at every step. When she trips and falls, he stops, leans over, and every last boil bursts, like liquid fireworks, so that her clothes are drenched—

A nightmare! psolilai found that she had wrapped herself in sheets, like a corpse awaiting the grave.

Next day she discovered that Kirishnaghar had not been wasting his time. "This evening," he told her, "as the sun descends behind the mountains, I will show you something."

"What is it?" she asked.

"I would prefer you to tell me," he replied.

Dusk, and Kirishnaghar led them to a small gallery on the western curve of the haven, a few levels above the Inn, where, alone at the edge and wrapped against the biting wind, they sat down to enjoy the view. With the disappearance of the sun, the plateau before them was thrown into shadow.

"Watch the sky," said Kirishnaghar.

psolilai followed his instructions. "I see only a lark," she said.

He craned his neck to look up the side of the haven. "Is it out already? There! That is no lark, observe its fat body, its stubby wings."

"An owl," said Gularvhen.

"Not just any owl," replied Kirishnaghar. "Watch closely."

psolilai watched as the owl approached the haven. "Scarlet . . ." she breathed.

"Indeed," Kirishnaghar replied. "A scarlet owl—probably some device of the manufacturing ecosystem. I noticed it yesterday. I think it emerged from the open air level at the summit. It is a wreality."

psolilai agreed. But wrealities were never owl shaped. "We need to learn more of the Analyticate," she said. "Something feels wrong here, and the people cannot see it."

"Or they like it," muttered Gularvhen.

psolilai grimaced as she considered the unethical political system. "We need to return the owl to the people," she decided.

Gularvhen nodded, but without enthusiasm. "By finding 3Mach-ines?" he asked.

psolilai ignored the question. "I'm going up to the Sky Level," she said. "You return to the Inn and question the felins. Kirishnaghar, you come with me." With that, she turned and strode to the rear of the gallery.

psolilai and Kirishnaghar ascended side by side, forging a way through the crowds then using the lifts to reach the Adverse Levels. Finding the nearest staircase they continued, but soon psolilai was out of breath. "This is defence enough," she said. "No wonder everybody lives on the Teeming Levels."

"You will climb one hundred and twenty levels before you reach the summit," Kirishnaghar observed. "Do you wish to stop now?"

She shook her head.

But they were stopped at the next barrier, one hundred levels above ground, where the staircases ended and a single gallery opened out, its edges filled with balloons jostling in the wind. These were the mode of transport between the Adverse and the Complex Levels. And here they reached the end of their climb.

psolilai was told, "Only residents acknowledged by the Analyticate have access to the balloons."

"Such as who?"

"Agents of the Analyticate, senior sages and scholars, civil officials. Not you. Besides, I see from your unlinking tag that you are foreign. At least a decade's residence would be necessary before you could be considered."

"That's unfair," said psolilai.

"It is how we live," came the reply.

psolilai fretted. "But what is there above us? Why must people be denied?"

"Many houses, many wonders. None for you."

5

Simultaneously Altering

Amargoidara, Steward Lord of the Analytical Council, sought the owl, but he sought it for the wrong reasons—he was selfish. I cannot stand selfishness. And so I told the people of Theeremere the truth, that their leader was striving for himself alone. In doing this deed I fashioned the enmity between myself and Amargoidara. But it was necessary. I sacrificed, but I was no martyr, for my intention was to be a constant thorn in the side of officialdom. Some people have called me courageous.

I walked along the dust-shrouded corridors of Analytical Tendency House—cobweb-strewn, the haunt of real spiders and of artificial ones—to arrive early at my chamber. No other scribes were in. The sun had only just peeked over the ragged horizon. I was nervous, knowing that if my deed was noticed I would be captured. I had slept little the night before, dreaming of terrible trials in ghastly chambers. But they were ready for me; they had already detected my betrayal! The night's duration had seemed stretched for me, but for them, preparing my trial, it must have seemed short.

A man I did not recognise stood in my chamber, waiting for me. He said, "Psolilai? Scribe to the Steward Lord?"

I nodded. He walked towards me.

I was taken to the place of adjudication, a large chamber of white-washed walls and black wooden furniture. There were moths everywhere, eating into the fabric, which in places was little more than foam. I smelled disinfectant and hot metal, and many sweaty bodies.

Everybody was present, including all five of the Analytical Council. Fenneoca the Analytic Logistician, swarthy lump of a man, hatted, wrinkled skin unshaven, smoking a neverending cheroot. The felin Kyoory Fye, tiny compared to Fenneoca, ginger complexion, red hair, blue eyes, and long, white whiskers. He was the Analytic Reificiary. Next to him Zethezdial, Analytic Justiciary, old, bald, caked with make-up to disguise his poxed skin. The powerful bulk of Analytic Serjeant Neogogg, also bald but with copper-tinted flesh, muscles rippling under his skin-tight grey plastic suit. And there, slightly apart, Amargoidara. Tall, lean, greybeard, slow movements but lightning-fast mind. He wore a mask that transmitted his state of mind, for it was not permitted that his inner self be revealed via his face to the ordinary citizens of the haven.

Here was the centre of political power in Theeremere, anti-nature all of them, anti-mushroom and pro-manufacturing, working in Rem but scorning the place to live in Thee, each man hazy behind rumour and whisper, which they encouraged to give their detractors a harder task. What immorality they achieved was unknown, but it was assumed, even expected, Neogogg attacking women, Fenneoca the sadist gambler, Zethezdial in the pay of all four anti-fungal secret societies.

I stared at them, numb to their inhumanity, for in my mind I had long since cast them into the realm of the unnecessary.

There were others present, officials of the court, technicians, interpreters of the manufacturing ecosystem, also Aunt Sukhtaya, and Ryoursh sitting with dandies who must be Threadbreakers or Snufflers; and rows of people who just seemed to be an audience. Not a jury, that was certain.

Amargoidara stood up and walked towards a plinth, upon which lay an object beneath a cloth. Amargoidara pulled the cloth away to reveal a scarlet globe a yard across—one of the three analytical-tendencies that formed the foundation of the triple split haven. His voice hissed from behind the mask, which now showed an angry face. "This analytical-tendency tells us how to live in our world," he declared. "It is a specialised wreality, assembling historical knowledge, then giving us advice." The frown on the mask grew deeper. "It is not to be ignored. No other source of knowledge is superior since it accumulates human knowledge. But this analytical-tendency, and indeed the other two, have been ignored by one person."

I let my expression remain neutral, unsure of the purpose of this session. Best not to let them know what I was thinking.

Sad face on the mask. "It is always unfortunate when our moral sources are ignored, and, worse, when an alternative theory is put forward." Now Amargoidara turned so that the face mask gazed upon me. "You have defied the rule of the Analytical Council. We exist to transfer the immensity of human wisdom, accumulated in the analytical-tendencies over uncounted aeons, to you — for your benefit. Like a brat you ignored us."

I knew that my sentence was about to be pronounced.

Return of the angry face. "For this ill deed we exile you from the hope of this haven, in a wilderness place cold and high. To Tall Cliff Steel you will be taken, there to live for the rest of your days. We estimate ten to fifteen thousand of those."

I said nothing.

"Do you have anything to say?" Amargoidara asked me.

My mind went blank. Shock. Then an official was at my side. He slapped something white across my mouth. It stung. I lifted one arm, assuming that the gag would come off, but it did not because my fingernails could find no edge.

"Do you have anything to say?" Amargoidara repeated, his mask acquiring a leer.

The tape was stuck to my mouth. It was aerated, I noticed.

"Oh, yes," said Amargoidara, "you can breathe through it. You will be wearing it for some days."

I shook my head as two tears fell from the corners of my eyes. I was led away, and I wished more than anything in the world that I could relive this moment, if only in a dream, and so, somehow, turn my fate from bad to good. As I walked towards the exit of the chamber I noticed in the crowd a young woman with tears in her eyes, which fell just like mine from her eyes' corners. She threw a mushroom in my direction, but then was lost in the press of people shouting at me. Yet the symbolic freight of that mushroom meant much to me, because it showed me that I was not alone.

I knew I had support.

But I was no victim. Life — courage, determination, vision — burned within me. I was already contemplating escape. I sought the owl, since

I hoped the wisdom of the bird of dreams would help me forge a better manufacturing: I sought the owl hoping to find a mode of construction that would not ruin Urbis Morpheos. So I planned escape.

A few days later the dirigible carrying me to the northern districts landed in the exercise yard of Tall Cliff Steel, and I realised that escape would be impossible.

They left Theeremere through the Sage Gate, Psolilai on the morphic motorcycle, armed with her rapier and wearing her leathers, rainbow hat and scarf, blind Inka on her shoulder: Gularvhen riding Hoss, wearing his usual coat and pointed hat, a mirrored hawk called Hezoenfor upon his wrist. The packs on their backs were crammed full.

"This is a bike that can adapt to any terrain," Psolilai explained, "and with you on Hoss we should make the Sonic Forest in a se'night."

"Hezoenfor has been an occasional companion of mine for years," replied Gularvhen, "a sparklehawk that evolved in a reflective environment in the tranquil districts between Bitah-Sui and Phistipristin." He studied her attire. "I see you keep to your disguise."

"Natural garments deteriorate slower in bad snow. Why do you wear that hat?"

"To make me appear taller."

From the Sage Gate they followed an overground tunnel of branches that had sprung up to scavenge manufactured oddments dropped by those arriving at and departing Theeremere. The tunnel was an accretion of dendritic machines, which had over the aeons acquired self-organising properties. Small lamps lit their way, winking on and off as they passed, while groups of metal voles cleared up debris. After a league, this tunnel disintegrated. Hezoenfor took the opportunity to survey the land, before returning to Gularvhen's wrist.

No rivers led south-west from Theeremere because the land rose into a district of dense terraced housing, so they were forced to pick their way through a patchwork of devastated slums. For a few leagues rusting iron lanes allowed them to pass through copses of hardened plastic, but then they stumbled across a great valley of activity laid transverse across their way. Hundreds of yards underground seams of ore lay, and an ecology of machines was mining it, complex devices at the bottom, spotted scarlet with wrealities, smaller machines devoted to metal purification and parts manufacture higher up, at the top, where Psolilai and Gularvhen stood, a range of trading machines bringing in raw materials from other districts. The ground was invisible below this ant-like activity; no chance of crossing it, so they had to go around. The stink was nauseating, smoke and fumes on the wind, sour with pollution.

So the trek continued. Skies stayed frosty clear. On the sixth day they found a newborn volcano. It had risen from a courtyard of brown clinker, spewing out transparent tech-globes like soap bubbles, that rose, inflated and burst, mutating into a hundred aerial machines that dropped, then flew lazily to the ground, or glided off on thermals to meet and mate with other devices. A small community of travelling agens attracted to the site worshipped on the slopes, but when they heard the thrum of the morphic motorcycle they dispersed.

Afternoon on the seventh day, and they reached an escarpment from which they could see for leagues, ahead a blur of green laid horizon to horizon, set lush and inviting between skyscraper stacks and massive black pylons.

"The Sonic Forest," said Gularvhen. "I will let Hezoenfor seek food."

He launched the sparklehawk into the air, whereupon it flew straight for the Sonic Forest. With the sun low, it reflected light like a chromium shard, allowing Psolilai to track its progress as if following the darting course of a will o'the wisp. It flew for leagues along the Forest edge before returning.

Gularvhen examined its beak. "It has not caught anything," he said, "but its easy flight means we can assume the Sonic Forest is a natural haven."

Psolilai was for a few moments struck by the beauty ahead of her. She could smell the Sonic Forest on the air rising up the escarpment wall; woody, peaty, rich organic. Sudden emotion made her choke. Parts of Theeremere were green like this, but to find a natural haven was rare.

A path—stepped in those places where other denizens of the land had passed—led down to the basin in which the Sonic Forest grew. In the pale mud Psolilai saw footprints: smooth agen feet unshod, the pad-prints of many animals, and something large, whose seven-clawed feet had sunk deep. The tyres of the morphic motorcycle spread wide as Psolilai steered it down the incline. Hoss followed, picking his fastidious way one step at a time.

There was a sluggish river at the bottom of the escarpment, the mead of which constituted a zone of natural and manufactured mixing. Grass overwhelmed slate slabs, which oozed plastic, that in turn solidified into pits that became the home of plants. However it was the green Forest that held sway.

And now Psolilai could hear it. On the westerly breeze she caught a tinkling sound, as of a thousand wind-chimes, occasionally a deeper clang, once a subsonic boom. Hoss too could hear something, his third ear twitching in all directions, the expression on his face alert, even excited.

One final being of the manufactured ecosystem appeared as they rode across the mead. Gularvhen pointed to a column of soft lights, and, approaching, they saw it was a galithien, one of the sentient artificial species most rare, a tree of thought-sculpted gallium arsenide with roots that spread for leagues. This was a tall one, in form like a silver birch, with blue, green and violet lights in its bark that glowed like nebulae. Fragments of gold flake lay strewn upon the earth, remnants of some sacred ritual performed by travelling agens.

So they moved to the eaves of the Forest. Hoss' middle ear never stopped twitching as he strove to hear music in the sounds that now dominated, but Gularvhen was unable, or unwilling, to report any conclusion. However it was clear to Psolilai that the random symphonies of sound meant something to Hoss.

Passing beneath the first trees, they halted. Psolilai said, "The Sonic Forest is large—twenty leagues across. Shall we follow a path to see where it takes us?"

"As long as we do not deviate too far from a south-westerly course, yes. Watch the movement of your compass."

Psolilai nodded. They were heading for the centre of the Forest.

With their way a tangle of briar and tree root, mud and twisting path, Hoss was restrained to a walk, but Psolilai was able to adjust the infinitely variable gears of the morphic motorcycle, and so neither stall nor fall off. The cool air turned frigid as the green canopy blocked light and heat from the sun, yet Psolilai felt refreshed, as if enjoying a shower. She understood that arboreal pheromones were stimulating her brain.

There were many mushrooms here. Tempted to stop, she slowed the motorcycle to a dawdle, but there were too many species in too many locations for her to make sense of their distribution. Still, their abundance was encouraging.

Soon the light became too bad for them to navigate the winding way, so they found a glade off the path in which they could rest. It was carpeted with redbells and ferns; a paradise. Through a hole in the canopy Psolilai could see early stars, the edge of the ring system, and, coming into view from the east, both crescent moon and yellow moontoo. A tinkling symphony accompanied this moment of pure joy.

"Imagine the whole world like this," said Gularvhen.

"Yes," Psolilai breathed. "Unending beauty..."

Inka hopped upon a log, while Gularvhen threw his sparklehawk to the air, dismounted, then settled Hoss at the edge of the clearing. They sat in the middle, opening their packs to reveal the food inside, locating and setting up the nuclear furnace then toasting the night's bread on it, which they ate with apples, late tomatoes, and honey. They drank water flavoured with lotus petals.

Sleep came easy on sonic drifts.

—breathing short and shallow, searching a grubby wall for signs of imminent mushroom germination. Nothing. Then she is standing in golden light. And there! Something dark expands from the wall, thin like a cord with a lump on top. She chases it, but it dances like a punctured balloon. Just seconds to go. With the first gaps appearing in the mist she manages to grab the cap and stuff it into her mouth. Clear air around her, gooey blue slime all over her hands.

psolilai lies on the damp ground and awaits wisdom—

She woke up. After breakfast they returned to the path, which ended in a tangle of undergrowth, no exit obvious, and rather than retrace their steps, which they considered a retrograde move, they decided the path must continue behind the undergrowth. Leading Hoss and pushing the morphic motorcycle, they struggled on for hours. The path did not continue and they knew they were lost. Worse, dusk was approaching.

"What do we do now?" asked Psolilai.

"There are no maps of the Sonic Forest," Gularvhen observed. "I would try one of the local mushrooms, but it seems to me that the knowledge I would acquire would not be related to geography or suchlike. It would concern loftier concepts."

"Is there anything else we could do?"

Gularvhen looked up at the canopy. Bass booms had accompanied the shimmering ambience all day, as if warning of thunderstorms. The sonic flurry seemed deeper, more complex, with a hundred chaotic themes sounding in parallel. Not deafening, it nonetheless filled the sensorium. As for Hoss, he was now adding his own polyphonic themes to the noise.

"Should we push on?" Psolilai asked. "There's still a few minutes of light left."

"There seems no other choice. But is Inka disturbed?"

The raven was flapping his wings, his claws digging into Psolilai's shoulder through the leather. She patted his head, trying to calm him, but without warning he jumped and flew off. Psolilai tried to grab a foot, but she missed.

"He'll fly away!" she cried. "He's blind!"

Frustration showed in Gularvhen's face as he watched the bird ascend.

"Can't you get Hezoenfor to follow?" Psolilai cried.

Gularvhen shook his head. "A sparklehawk can only fly during the day."

In despair Psolilai watched the tiny black dot in the sky as it rose, then vanished. "This was a bad move," she said, sitting heavily on the ground and clasping her head in her hands. "We should have gone back to hunt for the main path."

Gularvhen, upset also, said nothing.

Night falling.

A man at the edge of the glade, white robes pale in the moonlight, flowing beard, long hair pushed behind protruding ears, a blindfold across his eyes. In the gloom he looked like marble.

Psolilai jerked out of half-sleep. "Who's there?" she mumbled.

Gularvhen also woke.

With exaggerated movements the stranger turned his head from side to side, as if locating a sound source. "My name is unimportant," he said, his voice deep, cutting through the ambient noise. "Where are you headed?"

"We're lost."

"The path continues eight hundred and fifty yards due south."

"We are making for the centre of the Sonic Forest," said Gularvhen. "Do you know which way to go?"

"Head south-west. All paths focus."

With that he was gone, vanishing into the dark between trees. In Psolilai's mind the encounter seemed to have lasted just seconds.

"Who was that?" she asked.

"Some denizen of this place," Gularvhen replied, "navigating by sound alone."

The remainder of the night passed in peace.

N ext morning Psolilai awoke to see a shape on a nearby log. "Inka!" She leaped to her feet and walked over to stroke the bird. "We have had a lucky escape," she said. "He seems undamaged."

Gularvhen's face showed his relief at this news.

87

"He must have flown off for food," Psolilai continued. "I've got nothing fresh for him. Perhaps we could try to trap something here."

"Better to give him scraps of your food," said Gularvhen. "We do not wish to disturb the ecological balance of the Forest."

"How was he able to fly back?"

Gularvhen considered. "They do have an excellent sense of smell— and hearing, of course."

Taking his advice, Psolilai tried to feed Inka scraps of bread, but the bird was not interested, hopping onto her shoulder, fluffing out his feathers, then lowering his head as if for sleep. They found the main path, then spent the day covering ground. By dusk they reckoned they had progressed five leagues—perhaps ten remaining. The weather held out, sunny and chill.

Another day passed, and another. They found themselves ascending a gentle slope, moss all around, the trees different from those of the periphery, thick, ancient, the heart of the place, the path still narrow but almost straight, as if made with a purpose in mind. They knew they were approaching their goal. At a wide clearing they rested. Here sunlight flooded down unhindered by leaves; grass up to their knees made hay where it died, rotting logs at the edges, berry sprays billowing in from hawthorn and rose. Dandelion seeds floating like fluff.

"We are near the centre of the Sonic Forest," Gularvhen mused. "The time has come for us to narrow our field of view."

"What do you mean?"

"We have reached the point where further travel is pointless. The heart of this place could be leagues across. We sit in it now. Therefore we have to use alternative means if we are to achieve our goal."

Psolilai looked around the glade. She had been expecting to see some clue indicating the resting place of the Constructor, but as yet nothing had suggested itself. "What means do you have in mind?" she asked.

"The Forest is a natural haven filled with mushrooms of many species. We must acquire their knowledge if we are to peer inside the moss, if we are to look under the roots of the trees."

Psolilai shivered. "Don't say that."

He laughed. "The Constructor may be buried. Become used to the idea."

Psolilai looked away, disturbed by this subterranean image.

But Gularvhen regretted what he had said, for he then added, "There will be no linkage with other devices, this place being natural. Do not worry, the Constructor will be inviolate."

Psolilai looked up at his pale, crooked face, and smiled. "You're the mycologist. Gather a crop."

With Hoss in attendance Gularvhen walked around the glade, bending over to pluck mushrooms from old logs and tree stumps, and from the ground itself, so that he looked like a black stork locating food. Hoss blew chords and trills at each collection. Psolilai, watching, was struck by their intuitive partnership, by the link between Hoss and fungi, and it occurred to her that there might be a way of discovering the creature's true nature, despite the lack of mushrooms growing on him . . .

Gularvhen returned to the centre of the glade. Hoss whistled and Gularvhen looked up. At the same time Psolilai's attention was caught by a movement in the air above the glade. Aerial mushrooms. Gularvhen whipped out a net, extended the handle, and plucked one from the air.

"Now we have a complete haul," he said.

"Show me."

He spread out a spare shirt and placed the mushrooms upon it. "This is the aerial mushroom. These are from the earth itself, with their thousands of hyphae like nets. The former will bring knowledge of topography, the latter of geology. These darker fungi I collected from decaying wood and other plant material, and they will give us knowledge of the Sonic Forest itself, for example, any anomalies."

So the order of the knowledge they were to acquire could be sequenced, they decided to chew raw the aerial mushroom and those growing in the earth, but to make tea from the others, so that, because the chemical complexes of the darker fungi would be absorbed more slowly through the stomach, their knowledge would arrive later. In this way they hoped first to learn the large scale secrets of the Sonic Forest then its intimate details.

The mycelium of the aerial mushroom was almost tasteless, but the spherical earth fungi were foul, tasting of dank soil, rotting matter. Psolilai pinched her nose shut to try and reduce the impact of the flavour, but she had to chew long and well to channel the chemicals into her bloodstream as fast as possible. Anyway, her ears popped. Grit grated against her teeth. Meanwhile Gularvlien, who seemed unaffected, even enjoying the taste, boiled a can of water over the furnace. Soon he had tea brewing, brown, dilute, unappetising. Psolilai resolved to gulp it down.

By now the first nausea was gone; a feeling of euphoria washed over her. Her perceptions were changing too, the sound of the leaves and branches becoming less random, almost musical, as she began to detect the structure beneath the chaos. Individual notes became glowing motes whisking through the Forest, symphonies to rainbows in a kind of synaesthesia. Hoss created ethereal music.

They drank their tea. A second wave of nausea hit her, but it passed in moments, and she was left to sit back against a mossy log and let her surroundings seep into her brain.

Which they did. An immense panorama of artificial memory began to coalesce in her mind as the music Hoss produced turned from fragile to noble. She became aware of the age of the Sonic Forest, hundreds of thousands of years, how it had changed under evolutionary pressure through multiple selves, in time rather than over space, and so, although alone, achieved a kind of sentience. Those multiple selves constituted a society. Temporal perspective spread, Psolilai was able to comprehend the character of the Sonic Forest, and because there was identity there existed a name: Xain.

Knowledge became wisdom as the information in her brain settled into still more complex states, simultaneously altering the organisation of her neurons, as dream knowledge approached permanent memory. Dream knowledge was resonant, created by culture, by magic, but it could coalesce into wisdom: cerebellum to frontal cortex. A dream was another's reality: all was a whole. Dream was the method, wisdom the goal, the dreamer—seeker. Urbis Morpheos—ruined. Hope synthesized from leaves, from creatures, from Gaia.

She understood that in the Sonic Forest every sound, every swish of leaf against leaf, of twig upon twig, was akin to a neurotransmitter event, the whole building up in layers from such sensory data into symbol groups that coalesced at length into self-awareness. A miracle of nature brought about on the geological time scale.

She saw nothing now of night sky or day, just greyness above, the blurring of time.

Recalling her former, individual self she looked at Gularvhen, and with him at her side she walked through mossy mounds, under low branches, leaping across streams, over briar tangles. There lay the Constructor, static in the flow of time; on the diurnal scale, gold heavy, gleaming. She disentangled it from a peaty embrace.

In joy they returned to the clearing, and then, through a maze of paths fuzzy at the edges, they strolled to the edge of the Forest.

Psolilai in agony.

She looked out over the mead to be assailed by incoherence, pain, clashing sound of rock over rock, the smell of death, of acid.

Glancing behind her brought relief.

They lay as two panting individuals, noise around them turning to music as the solace of sonic complexity returned to soothe them. It was difficult to speak, since that communication returned them to their former mode of existence, before the glorious memories of the Sonic Forest.

Gularvhen said, "We have been seduced by this haven."

Psolilai agreed. "The city . . . the outside world . . . I can't bear it."

"We must forget what we have learned!"

"How? It's impossible."

"Our knowledge is fresh, like dream knowledge. Very few dreams are remembered after waking—in my case, only one. We have to destroy this dream."

Psolilai understood. The mushroom complexes existed as reverberant electro-chemical cycles in the cerebellum, not yet made permanent in the neuron nets of the frontal cortex. Little time remained, however. Inability to forget their wisdom would make the Sonic Forest their prison.

"How?" she repeated, her voice a wail. "Must I forget psolilai too? I haven't found her yet!"

"The galithien," Gularvhen gasped.

"How?" Her voice now a murmur.

Gularvhen struggled to peer out of the Forest, his body trembling in pain. Looking back at her he said, "It lives out there, perceiving the world over millennia through its roots. We have to speak with it."

Psolilai felt herself drifting away. "You do it," she said.

She watched his efforts through half closed eyes. Crawling through the frosty grass he passed under the eaves of the Forest and reached the mead, where, now on his belly, he pulled himself toward the galithien. The screens upon its bole glowed bright, recognising his presence.

"Help us!" he cried. "We must forget."

You have acquired knowledge of the Sonic Forest which you must forget? The message scrolled itself across rough bark.

"Yes!"

Alongside you is one able to immerse himself in extended time. With you inside the Sonic Forest he must sing, and loud, becoming an irritant symbol in the audio architecture of the Sonic Forest. Only then will the Sonic Forest change to reject that symbol, as if to forget a nightmare. When your seduced minds also reject it, you will briefly return to your former selves, and then you have your one chance to escape.

"But how will I tell Hoss all that?"

I will inform him.

"How?"

He will hear my voice through his piezoelectric hooves.

91

"Hoss has piezoelectric hooves?"

Not yet.

Gularvhen had no energy left to continue the conversation, dragging himself back to the forest eaves like a trampled insect about to curl up and die. Psolilai could feel the reality of Urbis Morpheos scratching like a steel file against her senses. "Hurry up!" she said.

"Hoss already knows," Gularvhen replied.

They turned to look at the horse. Psolilai was able to match movement in the thick neck with new sounds that were at first unpleasant, hideous like a nightmare, but which as the Sonic Forest became less of a blur before her eyes changed to resemble music, and finally became a descending sequence of chords. She was back in the real world now. Xain was gone, Gularvhen standing at her side. Grabbing Hoss he ran forward, Psolilai following with Inka in one hand, the handlebar of the morphic motorcycle in the other. Pushing and stumbling, they ran under the eaves of the Sonic Forest and into open land.

Psolilai found herself uncertain of what had happened. One memory remained, faint, dark. Acting upon it, she put her hand in her pocket and drew out a golden disk.

"We succeeded," she said.

"Yes," Gularvhen murmured. "I'm trying to remember how."

Psolilai put a hand upon his arm. "Don't," she warned.

Exhausted, they camped by the river at the bottom of the escarpment. It was frosty cold weather, with only the furnace to warm them, no shelter except low bushes, the wind rising from the west and promising bad snow. Examining the Constructor, Psolilai saw sigils engraved upon it that changed according to the viewing angle, so that it was impossible to see anything for more than a few seconds—the effect one like a reading glass speeding over gold-plated script. Heavy enough to tire her arm muscles, it also weighed on her conscience. Should she own it, let alone wield it?

Night, and time to perform a test, now that Gularvhen slept. She remembered Hoss standing on a rotting log at the back of the Church of the Parasol Cap, just as he stood now, as if asleep. A fungal link existed, she knew. From her pack she chose a knife, no longer than her index finger, but sharp as a razor. She crept up to Hoss. He seemed to have sunk a little into the earth, his hooves like suction pads connecting with the land, and seeing this Psolilai felt sure her guess was correct. She sliced into his spongy flesh. It separated, no resistance. She felt the blade hit something hard, perhaps a bone, but she cut again to make a wedge. When she lifted it out she glimpsed dark bones. The flesh knitted together like a time-lapse healing, but Psolilai held a slice in her hand.

It was the same colour and consistency from the surface down, no skin nor any hint of vessels or organs. Though her mouth was dry she stuffed the flesh in, chewed, then, with difficulty, swallowed.

Now she was wide awake. She awaited enlightenment.

It came slowly and without the usual symptoms, no nausea, intensification of colour and sound, nor sense of floating above the ground. She understood that Gaia's fungal ecology, from moulds and yeasts, through truffles and morels, to boletus, mushrooms and toadstools, and the larger, more frightening growths that swamped dead trees, were all aspects of nature, a global system of storage and transfer, a repository, and yet also an ocean, and a shower of rain.

No knowledge of Hoss, however.

The immensity of this system overwhelmed her and for a moment she caught a glimpse of the scale of the planet, before her mind was returned to spores, individual fungi; to the taste of them. Yet she also wondered what had brought the fungal ecology into existence. Returned to the real world, she studied Hoss. She had expected to gain knowledge of him from the unicellular organisms that she felt must be part of his body, but instead she had peered through a window upon nature. Hoss then was special, and so must Gularvhen be.

She dozed until dawn.

—psolilai says, "The people of this haven are part of my calling, if only because they will experiment first with what I offer. And it is my nature to orate."

Another voice: "Then we must reach the Owl Palace as soon as possible, absurd though that is. If agens live there, ah, we will have a dreadful struggle—"

Clouds building from the west, billowing up, falling, growing dark with bad snow and ice. A deep depression moving in behind stacked weather fronts. Psolilai understood that the psolilai of whom she dreamed was as driven as her, as prone to obsession, as brave, as flawed. But psolilai was no leather-clad biker, and that disappointed her. Who was real? Who dreamed the other? If she found the owl, would that provide an answer?

They departed the Sonic Forest.

The morphic motorcycle broke down late that afternoon. Crossing a concrete yard Psolilai heard a wheeze, then a choke, before the machine slowed and stopped. She put one foot on the ground to avoid falling over. Inka hopped away while she looked at the machine's incomprehensible mechanics.

Gularvhen surveyed the sky, now cloud covered. "This is bad timing," he said. "We are six days from Theeremere."

In desperation Psolilai withdrew the Constructor to wave it, then stroke it over the machine, but instead of repair only a mechanical shudder was produced. Sighing, she sat back. "I can't just leave it," she said. "Aunt Sukhtaya was my bond on this loan."

"You may have to face her."

A sudden image of her aunt's furious face. Psolilai shivered. "No, there must be a way of making it work. Perhaps the light collectors are covered with dirt."

But nothing she tried made the machine's engine start, though she noticed its yellow headlamps were as bright as ever. With the light failing, Gularvhen said, "We will push it to shelter, rest for the night, then decide what to do tomorrow."

To this Psolilai agreed. Nearby they found a cluster of derricks over which polythene strands had been excreted by passing technobeasts; a kind of cave. No life inside, natural or artificial. With the first flakes of bad snow falling they set up the furnace, opened their packs and made themselves as comfortable as possible. Howling wind kept Psolilai from true sleep.

She greeted dawn in poor mood, made worse by the refusal of the morphic motorcycle to start. In the end she kicked it and walked off, allowing herself to be pulled upon Hoss so that the journey could continue. She covered her mouth and nose as best she could to reduce the chance of narcolepsy. Dread of Aunt Sukhtaya filled her mind.

That day the Constructor seemed to smoulder in her pocket. She had no idea how to use it, but her thoughts whirled around it like bad snow in a vortex, until she began to wonder if the weather itself, or at least what it carried, could be altered. But she did not know enough about using the artifact.

"Gularvhen?"

"Yes?"

"Where does bad snow come from?"

"From the nearer western seas. Moisture picked up in those seas contains the substances that combine to form suites of bad chemicals."

Psolilai pondered her new idea. "Do you think I might use the Constructor to alter the composition of the bad snow, so that it becomes natural again? Then I could save Theeremere from melting away."

"Not impossible," he replied.

"It probably is," Psolilai muttered.

"Nothing is impossible that can be conceived. The only impossible things are those no mind may imagine."

Psolilai pictured a Theeremere free of destruction, and it felt good. The seed of another idea was born in her mind, its soil the ruinous snow that swirled about them . . .

Evening, and they found a copse of stone trees shaped like tables, under which shelter was possible; open one side, closed on the other. Bad snow could not fall through the fused roof, though it drifted in on a strengthening wind.

Some hours after dusk Psolilai saw a shadow on the hill outside, accompanied by flickering lights. At first she thought it a trick of the night, but when she noticed it again, this time nearer, she woke Gularvhen. Too late—the creature was upon them. Like a giant it roared as it lumbered up to the copse, two saucer eyes burning yellow, clawed, fanged, rags flapping around its limbs, too big to move with any speed but surely able to pick up a human being. Grotesquely, it sniffed the air then dropped down upon hands and knees, as if searching. Psolilai clung to Gularvhen. Hoss pressed himself against the rear of their shelter.

It sniffed again, then dragged one black hand across its nose. A rumble of a voice: "Give me the Constructor."

They ventured no answer.

The giant stuck its head through the opening in the copse and repeated, "Give . . . me . . . the . . . Constructor."

Gularvhen stood up. "How do you know I've got it?"

In reply the giant uttered a screech and thrust out one arm, feeling for them. This was more than Psolilai could bear. Screaming, she ran to the back of the shelter and cowered behind Hoss. There was an inexplicable rush of air, a groan as of metal grinding, and then the giant was beside them, crouching over so that the shelter was filled with its body. Gularvhen had been bowled over, and he also shivered at the rear of the shelter.

"Give me the Constructor!"

The voice was deep enough to make the ground tremble. But Gularvhen leaped forward, and, though he was half the height of the giant, he shouted, "Begone, uncanny ogre!"

It seethed with rage, fumes emanating from its mouth and nostrils. Sparks flickered from claw tip to claw tip. "I know you have it here. Give it to me."

"How do you know?"

"Because twice you ask me how I know."

"Then you are no beast," Gularvhen shouted, "for you can reason!"

The giant struck him aside, leaned down and put its face near Psolilai. "Give me the Constructor."

Psolilai was pressed against stone by the force of its presence, her hand stealing into her pocket to pull out the golden disk. But instead of offering it up she threw it to Gularvhen, who caught it in one outstretched hand. She could not defend it: he might. But before he could move, the giant's tongue shot out—a silver tube—and the artifact was lost. Tongue passed it to hand, which held it up in triumph.

Psolilai stared. The giant's hand and wrist were changing. Needles emerged from dark skin to curl out, then return and clasp the Constructor, so that after a minute it was sheathed in writhing tendrils. The effect was of submersion. Fingers changed so that the hand was but a club.

"It is incorporating the Constructor," Gularvhen gasped.

Psolilai understood. The giant was a machine of the manufacturing ecosystem and it wanted the power of the Constructor within its corpus.

Pulling her rapier from its sheath, she stood up and took a step forward, though she knew her fear would betray her. The giant paid her no attention.

Then there was flapping at her eyes, and loud cawing. She ducked, raising her free hand to slap away her attacker. "Inka!" she shouted. "Get away!"

The raven was trying to distract her, maybe disable her, his beak and claws stabbing her face. Gularvhen tried to catch him. Psolilai ducked and rolled, then stood beside the giant. With a thrust and a flick she cut the tendrils surrounding the Constructor, so that the device dropped to the floor. She did not think about what she was doing: she just acted, as if in self-defence. Inka screeched and flew again at her face. The giant let out a roar.

"Go for the eyes!" Gularvhen shouted.

Psolilai felt hope. She was emboldened. She dodged a blow, then struck out for the giant's eyes, hitting its face just beside its nose. There was a sound as of glass chimes smashing, and the giant retreated. Knocking Inka back with one hand, she stepped forward and struck again.

Then the giant was outside. Inka dropped to the floor. Silence. A black shadow poured itself down the hill, liquid, yet jerking as if broken, to the sound of rattling metal.

Psolilai picked up the Constructor and dropped it into her pocket. She would have sworn that Inka watched her do it.

"We have had a miraculous escape," said Gularvhen.

Psolilai nodded. Delayed emotion made her tremble. She sat upon the cold earth and looked down at her boots.

"We must keep watch alternately," he added.

Inka seemed to withdraw into himself, huddled up against a stone.

Bad snow was their obstacle during the days that followed. It never stopped. Every night they washed their absorbent clothes then hung them over the furnace, so that the chemical load released by melting bad snow was reduced to a minimum. Psolilai felt time pass as pure fatigue. Mornings, she could hardly wake. Her nose was blocked, her mouth ulcerated. White patches on her skin. Her leathers stank.

Exhausted . . .

Light was poor from dawn to dusk under dense clouds, and nights were black. Without the compass on the morphic motorcycle they had to navigate by guesswork, using landmarks noticed on the journey out. Though they tried to keep out the bad snow with face masks, Psolilai found the days turning grey, as did the nights, the boundary between them becoming less clear as slow narcolepsy overtook her. Her bloodstream was carrying a more concentrated load of substances and some of these would soon combine within her body. Her liver would be unable to cope with these poisons and her kidneys might fail. Her urine was orange.

And then they came across the valley of the ore-machines. Heartened, they made a last effort, to find an iron lane, and then the tunnel. As dusk arrived, so did the Sage Gate.

They were home.

THE ORGANISATION OF HER NEURONS

Psolilai dreams orange lights. "Over there, Kirishnaghar," she says, grasping his shoulder. "Land beside the lanthorns."

"It appears to be the haven of Umadraish," says Kirishnaghar, though he sounds uncertain. "We had better land outside the haven, then discover what manner of people live there."

"Don't bother with that," Psolilai replies, "you're from this land, so you can lead us."

"Set the dirigible down inside the haven," Gularvhen adds.

"I am not of that haven," Kirishnaghar insists. "Despite your enthusiasm, we will land outside. The shamen of Shohnadwe are aloof, even threatening."

Psolilai thinks this unhelpful. "You don't seem threatening," she remarks —

I awoke with Kirishnaghar's cold face vanishing from my mind. It was dawn, and soon we had broken camp. As we followed the path leading towards Mahandriana I saw ahead of us a toy balloon, left, I thought, by some careless child. But Gularvhen was cautious. He picked up the toy, examined it, then nodded to himself. He smiled, but he seemed troubled. He glanced at me. "What do you see?" he asked me.

I shrugged, in no mood for games. "An abandoned toy. Shouldn't we carry on?"

Gularvhen placed one hand across the faint blue lamps of the toy, then said, "Now what do you see?"

Horror struck me dumb. I watched as Gularvhen threw the toy to the earth. It expanded, growing as if some invisible person was blowing it up.

I whispered, "A second balloon!"

"Yes," said Gularvhen, "for this is one of the three malleads."

I turned to face the balloon. "Reveal yourself," I commanded.

Balloon shape became human shape, a portly man, chubby flesh, wearing sumptuous blue robes and a black hat, a walking-stick in hand. Beard grey and white, combed into two forks; tall, noble, yet through his face expressing fear and shame. I reminded myself that this was not a human being, not with glowing blue eyes so stark. This was a shape-shifting machine.

"You have a tale to tell," I prompted.

Kirishnaghar nodded. "I will tell my tale," he said, "and it will be truth, since I am unmasked. Yes, there are three malleads, and my kin-of-deed was Voaranazne of the yellow eyes, who with me rescued you and Gularvhen from death in bad snow—on the orders of Sukhtaya. Voaranazne it was who stole the Constructor from you that night in Eoshoomah."

I nodded. I had dreamed all that.

Kirishnaghar continued, "Later there came a parting. Voaranazne decided to keep the Constructor, merging it as best he could with his corpus. He was easily seduced by power. I was shut out. When you challenged him in the garden of the Pool of Wrealities, the power of the Constructor was invoked and it returned to the Transmuter. Of course, there is a terrible consequence for yourself . . ." Kirishnaghar sighed and concluded, "Then I arrived hoping to put everything to rights, but the agen appeared and we—"

"That was no agen," I interrupted, "that was my sister Ryoursh, who wanted me for her own reasons."

"At the time," Kirishnaghar insisted, "it was an unknown agen clean out of the dark, and so we fled. Since that time Voaranazne and I have worked against one another, Voaranazne with Sukhtaya, I a lone agent hoping for . . ." But Kirishnaghar left what he hoped for unspoken.

I began walking along the path, gesturing for Gularvhen and Kirishnaghar to follow me—I was impatient for Mahandriana. "Speak on," I urged the mallead.

"I do not ask for favours," Kirishnaghar said, "but I do ask that you hear me out."

"Such was my intention," I replied, draining all feeling from my voice. "You have yet to explain why you follow us, for instance."

Kirishnaghar replied, "Two factions have emerged. One is composed of Sukhtaya and Voaranazne, a faction occasionally aided by your sister, though of late she has followed her own course. This faction may be in contact with the third mallead, but, although we two worked for Sukhtaya, we were unable to verify any contact with Auzarshere of the green eyes. As for the second faction, it is composed of yourself, Gularvhen, and, I hope, myself. Truly I have parted from my erstwhile kin. Voaranazne is now my opponent."

I responded, "What does Aunt Sukhtaya want?" As I asked the question I visualised a fiend behind me, always on my trail. At that moment I hated my family.

Kirishnaghar replied, "She wants access to the Constructor and the Transmuter, and she will do anything to win those two artifacts."

I nodded. Uncle Illuvineya, I suspected, had stood in her way.

"You follow a natural path," Kirishnaghar continued. "Your opponents are besotted with the principles of manufacturing, which have ruined Urbis Morpheos."

I nodded. "That I believe," I said. "I am seeking 3Machines in Mahandriana, for when I have 3Machines I have the wisdom necessary to aid nature."

Gularvhen asked me, "Where do you think wisdom comes from?"

"From nature," I replied. "3Machines will divulge accumulated wisdom . . . how nature was before the rise of the manufacturing ecosystem, how this planet could be . . . "

There was silence for some time.

"I have one last thing to say," said Kirishnaghar. "I wish to apologise to you both for the deceits I practiced upon you. I followed the wrong road."

Neither of us made a reply. We continued up the forest path. I noticed the grey ghosts of ancient buildings amidst the trees, set amidst piles of rubble and rusting shards. Early afternoon passed, and then ahead, at the top of a ridge, I saw a building, and movement. People.

Gularvhen halted Hoss. "There is a station ahead," he said.

"Carry on," I replied.

A marvellous sight awaited us at the top of the path. A panorama of ridges lay before us, gorges too deep to see into, twenty at least lying parallel east to west, but crossed by a single cable that stretched from ridge to ridge, fading into distant smog. This cable carried a number of vehicles that moved on wheels, ridge to ridge, thus crossing the impassable landscape.

A young woman approached us, dressed in green cloak and breeches, tall and confident, with the air of a well-fed and happy individual. Her blonde hair shone in the sunlight. There was no sign of any weapon about her person.

"We bid you good afternoon," said Gularvhen, in his most formal tones.

"Welcome," she replied, looking us up and down. "I am Pereptihin, Lieutenant of the Company of Sentries. Have you come to enter Mahandriana?"

She spoke our language without difficulty, almost without accent; perhaps a hint of a nasal slur. I stepped forward to reply, "I am the dreamer psolilai, this is the peripatetic mycologist Gularvhen, and here stands Kirishnaghar, noted land-ranger."

Pereptihin gestured for us to follow her into the station. It was a stone building of considerable bulk, its upper parts devoted to the machinery that held the cable, below that a number of offices in which green-clad men and women worked. There was no sign of other guests. As I entered the building I heard faint music, which at first I thought came from Hoss, standing outside.

Pereptihin smiled and said, "You hear the music of a string quartet. Let me take you to the loading platform."

We climbed a set of external steps. On a broad platform I saw an empty cablecar and, sitting apart, four instrumentalists playing a music that trilled and wove itself through a variety of themes and counterpoints.

Pereptihin explained. "This is the Quartet Line. It carries visitors and residents alike, in and out of Mahandriana."

"Are there no other routes?" I asked.

"Not if you value your life. The terrain of Urbis Morpheos is tortuous here, deadly in many places. The Quartet Line works on the principle of attraction and repulsion—opposites attract, likes repel. Each cablecar carries a string quartet playing elegant music, and this music is repelled by that of the stationary quartet you see playing here. But it is also attracted to the music of another quartet situated at the end of the line. Their music is dissonant and unpleasant. The net result of the repulsion here and attraction over there is a propulsive force sufficient to move the cablecar to its destination."

"And if you wish to travel here from Mahandriana?"

"A cablecar is used upon which plays a quartet making dissonant music."

Gularvhen asked, "How can this system possibly generate propulsion?"

Pereptihin turned to him with a smile. "You stand close to Mahandriana."

He nodded once.

Pereptihin led us indoors. "The process of registration is simple," she said. "In half an hour you will be on your way."

We sat down at a desk, Pereptihin opposite us, papers spread before her, a quill in her left hand. She asked us to spell our names, then said, "You travel as a group?"

I nodded. Pereptihin scratched marks on the sheet before her.

"What is your purpose here?"

I had already prepared the gist of an answer. "I am a visionary," I said, "and I have come here to research my dreams. That is our sole reason for travelling. These two men are my colleagues."

Pereptihin wrote several sentences, then pushed the sheet towards me. "Would you all sign at the bottom, please?"

I did so, then passed on the sheet. Pereptihin next gave me another sheet of paper. "These are standard guides to the lodging houses and inns of Mahandriana. You will at first find the haven rather confusing, since it is so large. Also, certain levels have restricted access—but these are usually the upper levels, for example that on which 3Machines lives."

"3Machines?"

"Our Elder Analyst, who resides in the Owl Palace."

Gularvhen queried this. "She analyses alone?"

Pereptihin nodded. "She has access to conclusions drawn by the analytical-tendencies, which she then disseminates according to her wisdom. Now then, our last task is to arrange the varieties of unlinking you will undertake. psolilai, you first."

Like a nervous child I cleared my throat, leaned forward, and said, "I am most familiar with what is often called the Severance Patrol."

"Cutters?"

"Yes."

"Then you I will place in the Fracture Division."

Pereptihin turned to Gularvhen, raising her eyebrows to indicate that she was ready for his information. He said, "As a peripatetic I am unused to unlinking duties, but when I do perform them I work in the Legion of Scry."

Pereptihin's face lit up. "That is the equivalent of our Company of Sentries. We two are akin!"

Gularvhen's lips twisted a fraction. "After a fashion," he said.

Pereptihin turned to Kirishnaghar. "And you?"

"I am best suited to detecting duties," said Kirishnaghar. "My blindness means my other senses are immoderately sensitive."

"Then you will unlink for the Company of Surveyors. It is unfortunate that you all have different skills, since you will be called at different times. I regret this."

I made an airy gesture. "We're used to it," I said.

Pereptihin then issued us with fingers of varnished wood. "Don't lose these, they are unlinking tags, summarising your details. Issuing replacements causes me a nuisance. Many people wear them around their necks or on their wrists. Within one month you must present yourself at the nearest unlinking station, and there register for work." Pereptihin smiled, then added, "It is not so bad. Expect to be called no more than twenty to thirty times a year."

I let out a gasp. "Twenty to thirty?"

"You think that excessive? Mahandriana is a strange haven that as yet you know nothing about. Unlinking is a vital civic duty and we take it seriously."

"What is the penalty for failing to perform unlinking duties?" asked Gularvhen.

"Expulsion."

"Who would perform such a task?"

Pereptihin replied, "The Analyticate has agents civil and covert. Behave well, and they will not even notice you."

"Will these agents be able to speak our language?" I asked.

"The people of Mahandriana speak all tongues."

With that, we were led up to the platform and into a waiting cablecar. From some lower office a quartet of musicians appeared, taking their seats at the rear of the cablecar then setting up stands on which they placed sheets of musical notation: one viol player, two cellists, a basso cello. They began their first tune, as did the stationary quartet. Sitting at the front of the cablecar I felt a jolt as the vehicle began to move, and then we were hanging in mid-air, a gorge below us.

The sun dipped westward into a swathe of red clouds. It was cold, no barrier halting the wind from whipping through the cablecar. Gularvhen placed Hezoenfor on an enclosing rail, then pulled tight his scarf, gloves, and his pointed hat. In the sky the first hint of the ring system appeared. Eastward the moontoo glowing emerald green. A scene chill, but glorious.

The music trilled on. The cablecar took an hour to reach its destination, which was a station on the side of a hill. We heard the dissonant music of the attractive quartet, watched the frantic movements of the musicians' bows over their pock-marked instruments, then disembarked, showing our wooden tags to a green-clad woman, then walking to a board on a post. It read: Mahandriana 1/3 league.

I turned to Gularvhen and grinned. We decided to walk the final steps, Gularvhen leading Hoss, the sparklehawk upon its saddle, Kirishnaghar beside me. Through charred and narrow streets we followed our road as it twisted from shadow to shadow, then flattened to follow a ledge around the hill; to our right a deep ravine, to our left the walls and buttresses of skyscrapers stained orange by the setting sun. We walked the road alone. Puddles were ice-edged, and our breath plumed. First stars in the sky.

Excitement built up inside me as the minutes passed. I scoured the streets ahead for my first glimpse of the Haven of the Owl, but every turn revealed only passage ways, yards, dead trees silhouetted against the indigo sky. Then the buildings fell away to our right, and I saw Mahandriana. I stood awestruck.

It was a single column of white, layer upon layer melting over one another, honeycombed with countless galleries, windows, ledges and balconies, built up through a thousand yards to its summit, which, so high, faded into dark mist rolling down from the surrounding slopes.

Gularvhen choked. "It is a fungus! It is one great fungus."

From a ledge a few yards ahead I was able to view the entire structure. It stood on a plateau nestling between three smoke-stained hills,
its lowest levels compressed by the weight of those above, with the very
lowest level a tracery of arches and columns marking entrances and
exits. No order existed in the construction. Some levels were like frozen
wax on a candle, dripping down to merge with lower layers, while on
some upper levels external balconies stretched out with dizzying reach.

Ten thousand people lived here. I could see lanthorns in every hole,
every space, upon every gallery, marking rooms and chambers carved
into the substance of the fungus. These lamps twinkled as people
walked in front of them. At the bottom there were also many people,
tiny like ants at this distance, treading a number of paths laid dark
against the ground.

I looked at Gularvhen, and we both burst into laughter. "What
species would you say it was?" I asked.

"Boletus? Gyroporus? More likely something unique, without a
name."

We walked on. A series of steps led down to the plateau. Dark mist
descended, until, when we were but a hundred yards from the haven,
the whole structure was cloaked. For a few seconds we froze. But the
mist subsided as if absorbed by the ground, and we were able to look up
and see the great column silhouetted against the night sky, layer upon
layer of lamps spiralling up, as if echoing the constellations.

O ne evening, as psolilai ate supper, she felt sudden nausea, discomfort
around her chest, her belly—and then she was sick, quick and
painful, making her cough. A mess before her, yet it was dry, pale, like
a miniature bush of thorns.

Gularvhen picked it up and studied it in the light of the common
room lamp. "You have regurgitated a pellet," he observed.

psolilai said nothing as she recovered from her experience. The taste
of blood in her mouth. She lay down, put her head on her arm and
closed her eyes.

Gularvhen talked to himself. "It seems to me that this pellet contains
the bones of things indigestible to you, rejected, as it were. Here a

tracery of metal, sharp like a weapon, here a piece of plastic, here a ball of scarlet wire. This bit of steel looks like a rifle, this bit like a barred window." He paused. "Here a scrap of tin, and here a bit of glass. Most curious. I will keep it for analysis later on."

psolilai hardly heard him. All she wanted was her bed.

—a layer of grey cloud tinged purple, top and bottom unnaturally flat, yet billowing here and there into fluffy curves. It does not move as do ordinary clouds, motionless before the western wind. Psolilai watches for movement, hoping for a glimpse of zri, but all she sees are streamers of water vapour whipping across the aerial land, like sand over desert. The zri must be hidden within.

"How do we land?" she asks Kirishnaghar.

"Being one of the seven conscious races of the manufacturing ecosystem," he replies, "the zri have their own peculiar customs, passed on over the generations. This particular culture is unlike any of the Great Circular Ocean, the heartland of the zri. They allow no alien machines upon Thymosfa. You jump—"

She awoke at dawn next morning. At the Teahouse of Aurorean Eudemonia she took breakfast with Gularvhen and Ilyi Koomsy, who had a message for her, a single tile on which two black lines had been drawn. "The symbol of the Fracture Division," he explained. "This token means you must perform unlinking today."

psolilai accepted the token with equanimity. At the unlinking station she announced her presence, whereupon she was introduced to the couple who with her would form a team. The first was a woman of athletic build, Cuanatola, who described herself as a scholar of wrealities; quiet, restrained even, but not impolite. The second was a man the same height as psolilai, somewhat slack of limb, but handsome, his blonde hair curling under a floppy hat, twinkling blue eyes around which laughter lines ran deep, skin free of boils or marks. He smiled, then bowed and introduced himself. "I'm Metaxain," he said. His voice was rich, musical, and then she found out why. "I'm a singer and viol player of the lower Teeming Levels. And you are?"

psolilai introduced herself, then added, "I'm a visionary."

Cuanatola asked, "You seek learning, like me?"

psolilai nodded. "Other people call me a visionary," she explained. Because that sounded pretentious she added, "I don't call myself that."

"But you don't mind repeating what other people say," Cuanatola remarked.

psolilai shrugged and looked away.

Taking their instructions for the day, they departed the unlinking station. psolilai asked Cuanatola, "Do I sound . . . new?"

"Oh, don't worry about me," Cuanatola replied with a smile. "Half the population of the Teeming Levels are from other havens. Don't feel bad—you add to an already cosmopolitan mix."

"But how is it that we can all understand one another?"

Metaxain stepped beside her, saying, "It's in the air we breathe. Mahandriana is the Haven of the Owl. To a greater or lesser extent we're all scholars here."

"The air we breathe?" queried psolilai.

"Spores. That's how Mahandriana influences the districts around it, and that's how it influences us—dreams themselves can be reified here. There's no haven like Mahandriana in all Urbis Morpheos."

They reached their workplace, a gallery laid out for the production of vegetables. Alongside a team from the Company of Surveyors they worked through the soil, cutting out wires and cables that had invaded from the plateau, separating autonomous devices of metal and plastic, later discovering a hive of silicon bees, then a cluster of wrealities like stones in the earth. All this manufactured material they incinerated, except the wrealities, which were collected for examination by agents of the Analyticate. The bee hive was connected by cables to a master hive in which they found a director bee larger than psolilai's hand. Metaxain smashed it with a hammer, leaving the other team to destroy its den.

At the end of the day they prepared to leave the gallery. Metaxain approached psolilai and said, "You must come to the Divan Inn, where I live and work, and take supper with me."

psolilai shook her head. Food was scarce. "I would never take another person's meal," she said. "My own supper awaits me at the Inn of Twilight Ratiocination."

Metaxain shrugged. "Food is in short supply," he said, "but water isn't. Come and drink with me, while my company plays music to the gathered throng."

psolilai was persuaded. Against her loftier wishes she was attracted to him, and flattered that he had approached her. She had never considered her scarecrow figure and freckled face attractive to men. So she smiled, and they left the gallery together.

The Divan Inn lay only two levels above the ground. Here the populace were loud and numerous, the inn a shamble of wooden alcoves, dusty lamps, and the couches from which it took its name. Metaxain led psolilai to a reserved alcove, in which they sat, chatting, until he was required to play music with his company. They were a trio, the others a lutenist and a flautist. They played, and the people danced.

Later he returned to the alcove. psolilai complimented him on his dextrous viol playing, then pointed to a man in scarlet costume who had intrigued her all evening. "Who's that?" she asked.

"The notorious political troubadour Ma—you must have heard of him and his antics."

"But scarlet?"

"The colour of wrealities," Metaxain explained. "Ma is an apologist for the Analyticate. He wanders from inn to inn promulgating his theories. Personally I can't stand him, though some of the locals dote on him."

psolilai looked again at Ma. With his dark hair, flashing eyes and bright clothes he drew attention. His voice was loud; arguing a group of drinkers, he overwhelmed them. psolilai decided that she disliked him.

But he could hold his audience: he was a demagogue. Sensing that people were watching him, he began a speech. "Thought, my friends, is the blood of this haven." He tapped his forehead with a forefinger. "We must cultivate pure thought. We must find a clarity that is so devastating we can live by it for ten thousand years. And where do we find clarity uncluttered by the sensuality of the mundane world? Only in those scarlet epitomes of thought that the most noble of us are permitted to touch, with trembling hands."

Hearing this, psolilai clambered upon the table before her and shouted, "This is all nonsense!"

Ma turned to stare at her, his expression surprised.

psolilai found herself standing before a hundred upturned faces. The room hubbub receded and she could hear goblets clinking against one another. "This is all nonsense," she repeated. For some moments she let them quieten, then wait, so that their attention was fixed upon her alone. "Are we to believe a doctrine," she continued, "which so constrains the human mind that it forbids us even sensation? Are we to live in a black robe before we are laid out to be consumed by the vultures? For this is the truth of Ma's position." The thrill of it! Her heart racing. Lowering her voice just enough for them to notice, she spoke on. "To you, that may sound extreme. But listen to me. Of what are you made? Are you simply a brain? Imagine yourself in a dark room, with thick, thick tapestries on the walls absorbing all sound, and you dressed in a suit that covers all your skin. A black robe. What are you then? You are nothing without your senses. Your senses support your mind, they are the foundation of your mind, you cannot think, cannot feel, cannot imagine or create without your senses." She placed both hands at her temples. "You are not conscious without your senses. The myth of rational analysis is just that. A myth. To divorce abstract thinking from the truth of the senses is to live in a world that does not exist and never will, for we cannot divorce thought from sensation. They are entwined, like root and soil. Therefore I say to you, believe Ma, believe that a just and humane doctrine can devolve from isolated thought in a scarlet box, and you live in a world promised only, a world that can never come about. Forget purity, forget clarity. Revel in your human senses and be alive."

She got down from the table, sat, and took a sip of the sugarwater in her goblet. The hubbub returned. No other response from the locals, but she knew from their expressions that she had made her mark. As for Ma, he was angry, if his face was anything to go by.

Metaxain put a hand on her arm. "Well done," he said. "So you're an orator."

psolilai grunted.

Metaxain leaned towards her. "I'm a shaman."

"Which animal do you follow?"

Metaxain hesitated before answering, "I'm a shaman of trees. Do you want to know my dream? It's to plant a tree in the Owl Palace, just to bring something of the natural world to that place."

Entranced by these words, psolilai moved so that their faces were close. "What is this Owl Palace?" she asked.

He whispered his reply. "3Machines resides there, living the life of the benevolent sage, sifting the icy thoughts of the analytical-tendencies. Sometimes she presides over wild festivities . . . though I've never met anybody who's been to one of those festivals. Still, it can't be right that she's allowed to live unwatched up there."

psolilai nodded. "It's inhumane . . . but tell me, have you ever heard of the Library of Dri?"

Metaxain shook his head.

psolilai sat back, disappointed. She had hoped to learn more from Metaxain. When he tried to hold her hand, she shook him off.

When she departed the Divan Inn an hour later a few people clapped, Metaxain leading the applause, but the majority did not even see her go. Yet the face of Ma remained in her mind. Something about him provoked her.

Later, she mentioned all this to Gularvhen. "We have seen," he remarked, "a number of scarlet objects of late. I agree that something here is wrong, but I cannot decide what it is. The people seem happy with their leader and her methods, and we cannot doubt that her analyses are sent down to the Teeming Levels. Ultimately, though, we are powerless without knowledge of 3Machines."

"Have you noticed how few political executives there are here?"

He nodded, but made no further comment.

Thinking on this conversation, psolilai talked with Kirishnaghar in his room. "I have an idea," she said, "but it requires help from somebody."

"And that would be me?" he replied at once.

Stung, psolilai frowned. "Well, we need to get through to the Sky Level—"

"And investigate the Owl Palace? Already I keep watch, every day at dawn . . . "

"You didn't tell us about your plans," she protested.

"My watch remains incomplete."

Suddenly she let out all her sarcasm. "And what have you discovered so far?"

He seemed unconcerned by her new mood. "That the Owl Palace is sealed off from the Sky Level, that nobody goes in or out of it, that agents arrive every day and pile wrealities around the walls. Those wrealities then decay, as if the knowledge they contain is sucked in by the Palace. A curious beast lives on the top level, a scarlet hog."

psolilai sat back. This was honest reporting, she had no doubt, and she found her thoughts drawn again to the Analyticate. "Are we being led to a conclusion?" she murmured. "Local people believe 3Machines has gathered all five analytical-tendencies to her bosom, though they have not a scrap of evidence. The sharper-eyed—perhaps those with foreign eyes who see things in a different light—notice wrealities in odd shapes. There should be five analytical-tendencies in this haven. Yet there are four levels."

"Unless the Owl Palace itself constitutes a level. It is from a nest in a wall that the scarlet owl emerges, a nest I have examined, to find no other egress."

"Yes . . . it may be a discrete level. We are missing an analytical-tendency, then. We have seen a scarlet owl, a scarlet hog, a scarlet book, and Ma, a fool. My guess is that one more exists in the Complex Levels." She glanced away, then returned her gaze to him. "You must have found access to the balloons that move people between the Adverse and Complex Levels," she said. "You must therefore be able to transport me up to the Complex Levels."

"You are correct. But you would have to rely on luck to find anything there. The book in the Library of Dri, though not concealed, is hardly as obvious as Ma."

psolilai shook her head. "This last object will be called Han, An, or simply A. Here is my plan. Once I have found this object I will risk a taste of it. If I am convinced that it is a wreality, we have our answer. 3Machines manipulates the analytical-tendencies by sleight of hand— in which case this entire haven is linked up in a way people here do not suspect. If it is not a wreality, then she does indeed keep all five in the Owl Palace."

"Why not simply taste the book in the Library?"

"I am looking for coherence. I need to see an object in the Complex Levels. I need to understand 3Machine's cunning. There may be other veils to push aside before we discover the truth."

Kirishnaghar nodded. "You are correct," he said.

psolilai's plan was set for two days hence. Kirishnaghar was able to infiltrate the balloon throng some hours after midnight—an easy task for one such as him—and on the edge of the gallery await psolilai. She crept around the gallery walls next day, dodging the balloons and their mooring posts, then clambering into the basket readied for her. In minutes she was airborne, following another balloon to the landing platform of the gallery above, the Complex Levels spread out before her.

No officials awaited her—Kirishnaghar had predicted this—and so she was free to move. The levels lacked houses and soil, but had over time been decorated with murals, elsewhere with incised patterns. A convoluted structure meant that the wind was baffled by the outer galleries and did not reach those of the interior. Before long she saw a young woman strolling along a tunnel. Feigning haste, she said, "I urgently seek Han . . . or is it An? Do you know of it?"

"Han?" came the reply.

"I was told it lay in a building," psolilai improvised.

The woman's expression changed. "You must mean the Brain of Han at the Museum." She pointed down the tunnel and gave directions, which psolilai followed, to arrive at a smooth dome, streaked blue and green and set with a plaque naming it as the Museum of Han. Inside, all was dusty, and like the Library of Dri there was no sign of recent visitors. psolilai soon found what she had been looking for.

It lay in a transparent case, a scarlet brain immersed in water, lit from one side by a single lamp to highlight its folds—an object that made psolilai feel queasy. She removed the lid, then tested the water with one finger: ice cold. She stood back, arms folded, considering her options. This was by far the riskiest part of her plan. There was a dream she recalled . . . almost falling to her death in the delirium produced by ingesting artificial knowledge; and although that was impossible here, there was no guessing what damage nonhuman knowledge could do. Still, she had to take a chance; her new plan demanded that act.

She took a few deep breaths, scraped the surface of the Brain of Han with a fingernail, then lay down. Then she sucked her finger.

Nothing.

Her body went limp with relief. They were fakes, then, designed to entangle the curious and the resourceful, or perhaps to divert their insight. She pondered what she had learned. All five objects symbolised knowledge in some way—doubtless another of 3Machine's traps: a political theorist, a brain, a library, an owl and a hog. There would be other wanderers like her in other inns, other people wondering what all

113

this meant, but very few of them would know that wrealities were orally active, and while folk tales sometimes described scarlet as a poisonous colour, she had never heard stories offering a more sophisticated view. Very few people therefore could acquire the understanding that she now possessed. A direct assault on the Owl Palace was, she realised, the only way forward.

Kirishnaghar would have to stake it out. She returned to the Inn of Twilight Ratiocination, where she described what she had learned.

Dyeeth Boolin gave them all a warning. "You risk your lives trying to enter the Owl Palace. It is meant only for 3Machines. Not even her closest agents enter."

In frustration, psolilai said, "How do they communicate with her?"

"Who knows? There must be a way. Perhaps 3Machines shouts through very thin walls. Be cautious, my dear. Your demise would be quick, and nobody would come to watch over your body. Nobody would even know."

psolilai sighed and looked away. She understood the weight of these words. So far they had been lucky.

Dyeeth Boolin said, "Mahandriana has existed for aeons, and the Owl Palace is a building unlike anything you have encountered before."

psolilai tried to control the anger she felt, but she was too frustrated to keep her feelings to herself. "How do you know?" she shouted.

"I have lived in Urbis Morpheos for a long, long time."

PART 2

WAKENING

7

AS DREAM KNOWLEDGE

Bad snow, acid moist air, the Church of the Parasol Cap a shelter, though its roof and outer walls were now wafer thin. Dark days passing like a month of evenings.

Psolilai toyed with the Constructor, trying to make it work, hoping for something, anything, but it remained enigmatic and she gained no insight. Fear of losing the artefact made her nervous, and she decided the Constructor was best kept outside the Church. She thought of Karakushna. Later, she visited her cousin's lane community, had a hurried conversation in a doorway, and handed the Constructor over, describing it in loose terms only in case Karakushna was tempted. Afraid, her cousin promised never even to remove it from its velvet bag.

But with the Constructor no longer in her possession, all she could think of was that idea she had mentioned to Gularvhen: Do you think I might use the Constructor to alter the composition of the bad snow, so that it becomes natural again?

She needed to know the answer to that question.

The boy told her of a message that he had received; her aunt wanted a meeting. Psolilai grimaced, trying not to think of Aunt Sukhtaya and Ryoursh. She had signed herself off unlinking duties before leaving the haven; if her sister heard of her return, she would have to continue them. For the moment she needed time and space, with no disturbance.

The message was repeated the following morning, and Psolilai had no option but to return to Psilocybin Lane. Sitting demure in the claustrophobic study she began with an innocent, "You wanted me, Aunt Sukhtaya?"

"That Church of the Parasol Cap is an unsuitable residence for you. There is a suite of rooms free here, why don't you move in?"

An unexpected angle. "I don't think I could so soon after Uncle Illuvineya's death."

"I would enjoy the company."

A single glance allowed Psolilai to discern the bulk and force of her aunt, then realise that this idea had to be killed without delay. "It's out of the question," she said. "I would be shamed under my uncle's memory."

Aunt Sukhtaya sniffed. "You are different to your sister."

That sounded like a threat. "Yes, we are different women," Psolilai temporised, before deciding to attack. "I'm sure you see much more of Ryoursh than I do. It would be unseemly for me to stay under the same roof."

Prickly talk ended. Aunt Sukhtaya settled herself in her chair and said, "Tell me about your journey."

"The bad snow was—"

"The rumour from the Church is that you went to the Sonic Forest."

This halted Psolilai. A quite blatant strike. Anger made her fidget. She replied in a cold voice, "So you have an agent there?"

"Agents."

"Then I have no need to describe where I went."

Aunt Sukhtaya smiled. "They keep watch for me, reporting the movements of people in whom I have an interest."

That might be true, but the threat was clear, and Psolilai knew she would now have to fight—it was almost a condition of her freedom in Theeremere. A month of gesturing was over. Looking her aunt in the eye she said, "Only a very strong woman could have escaped the harshest prison—"

"Do you consider yourself a strong woman?" Aunt Sukhtaya interrupted.

Psolilai's mind was drawn back to her chamber at the Church of the Parasol Cap, to recent events there, and she felt sure now that the forces Karakushna said swirled around them swirled also around the Constructor. It was the focus of all this. She stood up. "I don't want to argue with you, Aunt Sukhtaya—"

"This was no argument!" came the instant reply. "You are unsettled after your journey. I should have waited, but there is nobody to look after you."

Psolilai hated this fake concern more than the threats. "I'll keep in touch," she said as she walked towards the door. "Besides, I have Gularvhen to watch over me."

"He is a monster! Beware of him!"

Psolilai stared at her aunt, then hurried away. Returning to her chamber, she first stood by the door, sniffing the air and studying the carpet, before stepping in. Her guess was that somebody had been here again. Time to seek evidence. Creeping around the chamber, examining every object, every item of clothing flung to the floor, checking the windows, the latches, even the layers of snow on the sills outside: nothing there. But there were some clues, a line of dust-free wood where an object had been touched, mud traces by the door . . . the niggling feeling that objects had been moved. The boy had not been on duty outside.

Psolilai descended to the ground floor to find him. Reliable lad, this, with good eyes and ears. "Has anybody been here to visit me?" she asked.

"No, ma'am."

She smiled. "And I haven't been here."

He shook his head.

She sought out Gularvhen. They drank rosehip tea in her chamber, he balanced on a chair with his legs crossed, she relaxing on the couch. "Somebody took a rubbing of the scriber inscription," she said, "and I think that person came here again today to see what they could find."

"At least the Constructor is in Rem."

Strange. "How did you know that?"

"You told me."

"I did not."

He uncrossed and recrossed his legs. "You must have."

Psolilai put the point aside. "This person has skill enough to evade detection."

"There are many strange beings in our world."

She stood up. "I'm worried. I think I'll visit Karakushna. In Rem."

His face betrayed no emotion, but he murmured, "Already the artefact causes difficulties."

"What do you mean?"

"It is an object of the manufacturing ecosystem."

Psolilai dismissed this remark with an airy gesture as she made for the door. "That doesn't imply it is bad." She recalled her idea for solving the problem of bad snow. "I believe it could be used for good."

The boy stood upright as she walked past him.

She glanced down and said, "Ensure he leaves my room and shuts the door."

"Yes, ma'am."

Out now in Isatin Lane, bad snow fluttering, a few lamps fading pale into the night, buildings to either side rising as high as fir trees. The lane was cold and empty, stone sticking to her boot heels like mud; doors locked tight, shutters shut. A moan through the haven as the west wind probed deep. The gates would be icy tonight. Then Psolilai came to the junction of Tryptophane Lane and Bufotenine Lane, and saw a figure lit by a nearby lanthorn, high on a roof with the wind whipping loose clothes, hair flowing free, bulky and powerful. Aunt Sukhtaya. In her right hand she held a gold disk. Triumph emanating from her.

Then Aunt Sukhtaya jumped down behind the building.

Psolilai was left in shock. Her first thought was to give chase and retrieve the Constructor, but she knew her aunt was too strong for her. Her next thought was for the safety of her cousin. She ran down Tryptophane Lane and crossed the Wool Bridge into Rem. Through gaps and over obstacles she ran, until her breath came hoarse. Off Norbaeocystin Lane lay the winding Blewits Lane, and the shared houses of her cousin's community.

"I'm looking for Khamoskaya," she blurted to a girl in the passage, using her cousin's local name.

The girl pointed at a door, then ran off. Psolilai opened the door and entered a hall, where she saw a guard. "Khamoskaya?" she gasped.

The guard was disconcerted by her appearance and refused to let her pass, but then a door opened and three people walked out, two old men and Karakushna, who ran forward, pushing the guard aside in her haste.

"Trouble?" she asked Psolilai, clutching her with bony hands.

Psolilai bent over to ease the stitch in her side and regain her breath. She looked up to say, "Sukhtaya has the. . . you know!"

"She has it?"

Psolilai hugged her cousin. "You're alive. Did she come here?"

Karakushna laughed, shaking her head. "Never in a decade would she find me, I'm buried far too deep, and she knows none of my names."

Now Psolilai stood upright. "But she had the Constructor in her hand and she was laughing at me."

"Are you sure? Where?"

Psolilai recalled the scene she had witnessed, undoubtedly her aunt, the golden disk correctly sized, coloured. "She jumped down off the roof and vanished."

In reply Karakushna opened an ottoman and pulled out a heavy coat, boots, hat and scarf, wrapping herself against the bad snow in moments. "Quickly," she said, "this needs investigating." From the inner pocket of her coat she withdrew the velvet bag, which she handed to Psolilai.

They stepped out into Blewits Lane. Bad snow whistled down the passage, and as one they pulled close their face scarves. They ran down to Norbaeocystin Lane. Psolilai, leading, paused to peer left and right. She froze. Something far right, black shadow menacing.

Two black shadows. She reached out to grip Karakushna's arm. Whatever they were, the creatures had seen two scared women and were approaching fast.

"What are they?" Karakushna whispered.

Psolilai knew without question that she was the object of interest. "A trap was laid so that I would lead people to your door," she said. Dread fell upon her as she realised her mistake. The shapeshifters! And Karakushna was unarmed. She took a step forward, then unsheathed and raised her rapier.

Bad snow fell fast, flakes heavy as hail.

There was a panting noise, as of wheezing smokers, and the two shadows became visible—an ape creature with wide shoulders and huge hands, yellow eyes glaring, the other hunched and skinny, hooded faceless, sabre claws visible from the ends of its sleeves. The larger creature pulled a shoe-scraper from a doorway, bent it and discarded it. Psolilai understood the threat. The tip of her rapier wavered.

The creatures approached. Bad snow splatted over cobbles. Visibility decreasing by the second. The leading creature hesitated, to peer into the sky.

Psolilai took out the Constructor. It gleamed gold, sigils flickering.

And the weather changed.

Two vortexes plunged down from clouds heavy as dark cushions, to quest with spinning tips and find the two creatures. Precipitation became ordered—constructed—so that the showers achieved mathematical complexity, winding themselves around the pair, encrusting them, hardening as they froze, stopping the creatures from retaliating. All they could do was jump and crash into walls like drunkards.

The slender creature was the first to escape. As Norbaeocystin Lane became a blizzard of bad ice it sliced open its frost prison with claws alone and ran away, stumbling, once falling, picking itself up to disappear around a corner. Two vortexes became one. The mathematics altered. Enraged, the fat creature tried to free itself from the storm, thrashing about as if attacked by a swarm of bees, until it too realised escape through flight was the only option. An astonished Psolilai watched it lumber off.

The storm desisted. Clouds rose. Bad snow fell in fluttering flakes, and the maddened beast-howl of the wind subsided. Psolilai held the Constructor between her thumb and forefinger, in front of her face, excluding all else, so that for vertiginous moments she felt as if she was falling into a pool of sunlight.

"Is this what the Constructor can do?" she asked. "Can it change the form of the manufacturing ecosystem even on the small scale? Take a phenomenon like snow and build something new, at will?"

"Why did it work?" Karakushna asked.

"I don't know. I think it had begun before I took it out of my pocket."

People were opening their doors to peer out into the night. "We'd better get back to my house," Karakushna decided, taking Psolilai by the arm and pulling her into Blewits Lane.

Later, in a small room owned by Karakushna, they sat down and drank ginger tea, hands around mugs for warmth. Psolilai said, "I've seen those bilious eyes before, in a giant that attacked me and Gularvhen when we returned from the Sonic Forest."

"What beast is it?"

Psolilai did not answer. "And perhaps once before," she continued, "when Gularvhen and I were rescued in bad snow not far from Theeremere."

Karakushna too was pondering events. "And you say you saw Sukhtaya earlier, holding the Constructor?"

"A ruse, with the purpose of leading those two creatures to the true position of the Constructor. All they had to do was follow my impulsive flight."

"Then it wasn't her on the roof."

"A simulacrum. And now I recall the simulacrum of me that walked one day into my chamber at the Church of the Parasol Cap, fooling even the boy at my door . . . a mourning hood concealing its eyes."

Karakushna frowned. "Shape-changer?"

Psolilai nodded. "If so," she said, "I feel again the immense forces that you described swirling around us. Only three malleads are known to exist—the agens persecute them. Yet what is the connection to Aunt Sukhtaya?"

"It runs deep," Karakushna opined. She stretched out her hand, palm up, and added, "Don't worry, I won't use the Constructor."

Psolilai nodded, handing it over. "Hide it elsewhere, never again in this house."

"There are many holes in Rcm."

Leaving Karakushna's house by a secret exit, Psolilai returned to her chamber at the Church of the Parasol Cap. All was quiet. She lay awake on her bed, thinking. This night she had changed the quality of bad snow falling on Theeremere. Suppose that feat could be repeated on a much larger scale?

Understand, then create. The Constructor, responding to her knowledge, or perhaps to an earlier conversation with Gularvhen, had created meaningful change. It could happen again. It was what she wanted. She knew the science of precipitation in cold weather, how water became snow on the breeze. If she could come to know the character of weather patterns over the aeons, how nature changed with changes solar and terrestrial, then by the same process she might be able to stop bad snow forever.

She leaped off her bed. Time to discuss the matter with Gularvhen. With Inka clutching her wrist, she made for his quarters.

He was less enthusiastic. "If the Constructor responds to your knowledge," he said, "then your knowledge must become wisdom. To rescue Theeremere you must acquire deep understanding of the cycles of nature, how weather changes over the aeons, how the natural ecosystem is supported by the planet, how the bad substances of the manufacturing ecosystem become involved."

"Wisdom," Psolilai mused. "You're a mycologist. There must be mushrooms somewhere . . ."

"Indeed," he replied in a warmer voice, "there are the vast mushrooms of the Ice Shield. Some regions at the edge of the Shield are composed of innumerable layers, ice made from compacted snow that fell fifty thousand years ago, or more. Mushrooms there would contain deep knowledge."

"But you regularly travel to Vita-Hassa. We must go there, together — now!"

He shook his head. "Never in winter. Hoss would not manage it, nor I."

Despite his reluctance, Psolilai felt inspired by her idea. "We have to make the attempt. If we can find those mushrooms, acquire their knowledge, then with the Constructor I could work a miracle that would last an age."

"Perhaps next year."

"No! Now. We could ascend above the bad snow, so that it wouldn't affect us."

"A dirigible, then," said Gularvhen, doubtfully. "But the season is long gone in which balloons leave their groves and journey across the skies."

"A balloon . . ."

Gularvhen sat up. "There are many further difficulties. Those living in Vita-Hassa tend to hibernate through the awful winter. Also, in seasonal latitudes the winter of the natural ecosystem is the summer of the manufacturing ecosystem. Even as I speak, strange and deadly beings stalk the icy corridors of that haven. The time for our journey is months away, when spring returns to Urbis Morpheos."

Psolilai stroked Inka's feathers as she considered his reservations. At length she said, "You told me nothing was impossible that could be conceived. I've decided on this. I want to go now. What better time of year than when the worst of the bad snow is upon us?"

He smiled. "Your emotion does you credit."

"Then it is agreed."

He pondered this forthright declaration. When he stood up and bade her good night, she knew he had been won over.

A day passed, then another; morning dull with bad sleet. Psolilai walked towards Muscimol Lane hoping to find out how the Pool of Wrealities fared, but she got no further than the beginning of the thoroughfare. Aunt Sukhtaya stopped her.

"Good morning, niece. I wondered if you had returned the morphic motorcycle?"

Psolilai looked away, forseeing the difficulty ahead. "It did not manage the journey back," she said. "Its engine failed. We did our best, but it was too heavy to push."

A face of stone before her. Aunt Sukhtaya nodded once, then said, "Very well. But what will you use now?"

"Aunt?"

The subsequent laugh seemed genuine—certainly it had zest. "Come, niece, you cannot imply I am so foolish as to think your journeying complete?"

Psolilai felt like a girl before her matron. "Who knows what I'll do next?" she managed, aware how feeble this reply was.

Aunt Sukhtaya did not flinch. "If you cannot ride, you must fly. That is what others do at this time of year."

"Fly, yes." Psolilai cursed to herself, aware once again of her aunt's ability for teasing words, even hints out of her. "But only a madwoman would fly through a storm of bad snow," she added, trying to rescue herself.

"Most of the intellectual nobility in Theeremere own balloons, myself included."

This casual remark, spoken with disdain, caused Psolilai's heart to skip. Immediately she saw the danger—this balloon a possession of her aunt—but her need was great, greater than her fear.

"It is a single grey dirigible moored in the Quartz Park," her aunt concluded. "Examine it sometime, if you will."

With that, Aunt Sukhtaya walked away. Psolilai watched until she was out of view.

The dilemma was tough. She suspected her aunt of subterfuge, this casual meeting probably engineered, having all the signs of a ploy, but access to a dirigible was tempting beyond the possibilities of restraint. First, she must view it.

The Quartz Park lay in western Thee beside the Possible Bridge, a natural bowl in which thousands of milky stalagmites rose up, sculpted from a natural silica outcrop by bad snow. In recent centuries, environmental changes causing worse bad snow had twisted these columns into ever more macabre shapes, flattening some, raising others above the height of buildings. The place was home to an ecology of benign machine species, notably balloons, fabricated in groves at the edge of the Park. To this haunt of the mechanical Psolilai went, ill at ease with the gloomy Thee atmosphere, thankful that so few locals were abroad.

She explored the Park until she spotted a lone dirigible attached to a quartz crystal; bulbous, made of grey fabric, with two yellow anti-fog lamps on its lower surface, a single hawser of steel its bond. The basket underneath was large, with a canvas roof and private cubicles to the rear. Its condition was good. Psolilai looked it over, deciding that it was suitable.

Back at the Church of the Parasol Cap she sought Gularvhen. "I bring good news," she said.

"That is always welcome."

"In the Quartz Park I've seen a dirigible suitable for the journey to Vita-Hassa."

His face expressed surprise.

"It will be ideal," Psolilai continued. "It belongs to a friend of my late uncle's, met at the funeral—he chanced upon me in the street yesterday. Shall we go and view it?"

After a hesitation, Gularvhen replied, "I suppose there would be no harm."

Having examined the dirigible, the pair returned to Psolilai's chamber. She sensed his reluctance to make a decision. "Do such machines frighten you?" she ventured.

"Not at all. When I was a lad I guarded the door of a woman who flew away on a balloon, so I am familiar with the concept."

"Are you afraid of flying itself?"

"No."

"Then what?" she asked.

"It is the timing of the journey. I would prefer to wait."

"I won't wait."

He shrugged. "Then our path is set."

Psolilai smiled. It was agreed.

After another pause for thought he said, "The main problem will be provisions, since we face a round trip of three hundred leagues. There is little enough food for the winter, especially here in Ere, where there is no civil guard or official headquarters to guarantee supply. If we simply take food that is meant to tide ordinary citizens over until spring, we will be pilloried."

"Why not take the provisions we would have anyway?"

"We could try. It is the principle, however. Shortages after midwinter might be blamed on us, especially as we will not be present for un-linking duties."

Psolilai gestured at the room around her. "Is there no store here?"

He nodded. "But it is controlled by the registrar. I will have to convince him of our need."

"Pretend there might be advantages for the Church in our mission."

Haughtily, Gularvhen replied, "There will be no need to distort the truth."

Psolilai fretted as she waited, checking her room for clues to inter-lopers; walking in circles. In a meditation room she tried to relax, but the soft music there irritated her and she returned to her chamber. The lad she deliberately ignored. One of the neon strings was dead, and standing on a chair she repaired it, just for something to do.

Gularvhen returned an hour later, in his hand a lunar calendar, which he consulted before saying, "We should aim to leave the day after tomorrow."

Psolilai clapped her hands together, and her smile turned to laughter. "This is the right thing to do," she said, "I know it is."

"Chance may yet overturn us."

She hardly heard him. "What about the manufactured side of the knowledge I require?" she mused. "It's not only sea and the weather that delivers bad snow."

"There are people we might ask in Vita-Hassa," Gularvhen replied. "For now, think more of the Ice Shield and what it represents."

Unwilling to see her aunt again, Psolilai had the boy deliver a note exp-laining that the offer of the dirigible was accepted. He returned it annotated: 'Very well, you may use the balloon as you see fit, your Aunt S.'

Departure morning arrived. The Constructor nestled in her pocket. Knowing this would be a more complex journey than that to the Sonic Forest, she decided not to take Inka, but her raven refused to be parted from her wrist when she made to leave her chamber for the last time. Blinded, he had become insecure. She called the boy in, and he held the bird while she prised free first one foot, then the other. Inka flapped his wings into their faces. Instructing the boy to hold the bird until she had gone, she departed.

Gularvhen awaited by the front door—and not alone.

"You're taking Hoss?" Psolilai asked, unable to conceal her astonishment.

"Of course. We always journey together."

"Will he board the dirigible?"

Gularvhen seemed surprised by these questions. "If we find mushrooms on the Ice Shield, we will need his music."

Psolilai decided not to probe further. Through sparse bad snow they walked Tryptophane Lane, then Serotonin Lane up to the Possible Bridge, and into the Quartz Park. Sunny moments caused the whole area to glitter.

Gularvhen pointed to the dirigible. "Who is that man in the basket?"

Somebody there—a stranger. "I don't know," Psolilai said, as her heart sank.

They approached. The newcomer was tall, though still a foot shorter than Gularvhen, fat, and dressed in thick blue robes and a black hat. He operated the guys and rods of the basket with confidence. When he saw them he paused, then returned to his work.

"Excuse me," Psolilai said, "but you are in our dirigible."

He had a curious gaze that soon became a stare, unblinking brown eyes that looked wrong, lower lashes too lush. Psolilai found herself glancing away, as if embarrassed.

"Do not worry," he said, "I am your pilot. I wear the sensory augmenting eyelid paintings of a Shohnadwe shaman. Welcome aboard. I'm Kirishnaghar."

Psolilai stood still, silent, listening as Gularvhen took a deep breath, released it, then also kept his peace. Eventually she said, "I don't think we're meant to have a pilot."

"You cannot fly without me."

Unable to mention the dirigible's true owner, Psolilai found herself trapped. She wondered if her voice sounded too cheerful when she said, "Then we will have to take you on, Kirishnaghar. Do you have your own supplies?"

Expecting a negative answer, she was surprised when he replied, "I'm from Uothoomah on the far western coast. No shaman of my haven eats when bad winter snows kill." And he patted his stout body. Fattened over the summer, Psolilai guessed. She shuddered. It was difficult to look at his face because his eyes were shut. The eyelid paintings were lifeless.

"Shall we ascend?" he asked her.

Psolilai looked at Gularvhen, still uncertain. "What a strange accent he has," she remarked, "being from the land of Shohnadwe."

He answered, "I have encountered it on many occasions, and it is good to hear again."

So she had her reply. In a confident voice she told Kirishnaghar, "You may take us to Vita-Hassa."

It was impossible to decipher the movements of his hands as he made the dirigible rise; they were like coded signals, elegant, precise. But the machine rose smoothly into the showers of bad snow, and soon they were hanging over Thee, drifting towards the northern loop of the river. Psolilai pulled down her undershirt at her waist and wrists, tightening the studs on her leathers—it was getting colder. She pulled a second hat over her rainbow one. Gularvhen steadied his pointed hat against the wind. Hoss looked bored.

A distinctly acid odour marked their passage through the lower cloudbase, until they rose through the layer and saw above them higher clouds, and above that a brushing of cirrus. A circular rainbow lay around a fuzzy moon.

The dirigible began to pick up speed, until Kirishnaghar estimated they were moving at two leagues per hour. Mental calculation suggested three days before sighting Vita-Hassa. Crows began to follow them, and then hawks, attracted by the crows. The hawks began to harry the weaker birds so that a din of squawking and cawing was set up. Psolilai looked at the panorama around her to see far off a single hunting balloon, and, further still, a hint of the metal cliff in which she had been exiled. But they would skirt that range, flying to the east; no danger.

The first day passed. Night found only Kirishnaghar and Hoss awake in the basket. Next morning they passed Tall Cliff Steel, and Psolilai felt a knot of fear in her chest. A wasteland of slums stretched below them, icy, inhospitable, but marked by black domes where self-organising machines of the manufacturing ecosystem mined, refined, and constructed. Shattered streets radiating from these domes marked the routes of newborn devices. Later, something distant—specks glinting on the horizon, like gigantic mirrors—came into view, and for a few moments Gularvhen looked sad, and sighed.

Morning of the third day, and Psolilai noticed something new on the southern horizon. First it was a mote, then a blob, an aerial vehicle approaching, smaller than the dirigible, with more verve, a canvas slung low underneath in which supine figures could be seen. Bothering neither with navigation lamps nor a proper basket, it seemed a machine of the wilderness.

Then the vehicle was close enough for faces to be visible.

"Agens!" Gularvhen cried.

An agitated Kirishnaghar said, "We must move on before those vile

machines engage with us. I will make full speed."

Just the tone of his voice made Psolilai shiver. The new balloon closed, so that she was able to see crystal whiskers on the faces of some agens, above others swarms of luminous flies attracted to their oily fragrance. These were typical agens, then. She stared, never having been so close.

"What do they want?" Gularvhen asked himself.

Kirishnaghar's fear became brittle anger. "They will attack us. We must get away before it is too late. Crouch down, do not let them know you are interested in them."

Psolilai knelt down, but then peeped over the edge of the basket. There was a flash, a snap, then a spray of liquid over her.

"Are you hurt?" Gularvhen asked, leaping to her side.

Psolilai felt nothing. "It's just water," she said.

Kirishnaghar flattened himself against the opposite side of the basket. "Make sure," he said. "Check any non-natural clothes."

Psolilai congratulated herself on wearing no artificial fabrics, but then she saw Gularvhen's face change. "What?" she said.

"Your ear-rings!"

In two moments the ear-rings were off and lying in one hand. They were made of silver and silicon. They expanded and became frothy factories, creating tiny insect devices that flashed red as they flew away on some bizarre migration of the manufacturing ecosystem. Ten seconds, and her jewelry was gone.

"Nanofluid," Kirishnaghar declared, "not water."

Gularvhen jumped upright, glancing across at the agens. "But they are already moving away," he said.

Psolilai also looked out, then sank to the base of the basket. The attack, it seemed, was over. "They went for me," she said. "Are they really going away?"

"Departing, yes," Gularvhen replied. "But to make so brief an attack is pointless. Doubtless they will return."

Kirishnaghar agreed. "The important thing is to lose them. Vita-Hassa is only hours away. I will steer a circuitous course so they do not know where we land."

They left him to his task. Gularvhen checked Psolilai's face for allergic rashes, but the liquid had used itself up in the manufacture of the flashing devices. "What is nanofluid?" she asked.

"Juice of the huge vat machines that roam equatorial plains," he replied.

Kirishnaghar added, "Travelling agen tribes concentrate it by evaporating off the water, then drink it as part of their drive to transform the raw materials of Urbis Morpheos. It leaks from sacs between their legs, so that every footprint they leave makes some contribution to the diversity of the manufacturing ecosystem."

"We should not be so quick to condemn agens," Gularvhen warned. "Their cultures vary, just as those of people vary."

"Aren't they all meant to be very religious?" asked Psolilai.

"Religion," spat Kirishnaghar.

Psolilai was shocked. The irreligious were rare. The majority might hold sacred neither the Church of the Parasol Cap nor the Shrine of Boletus, but they all trod the unstated path of Analytical-Tendency. Earlier Kirishnaghar had claimed to be a shaman: surely he was a shaman of something?

Curse her ignorance! She knew nothing of Eoshoomah, her neighbouring land. She felt ashamed.

Further hours passed as they flew north. The agens vanished. Now Psolilai could see the edge of the Ice Shield, and then, later, upon a word from Gularvhen, she saw too the pinnacles, steps and halls of Vita-Hassa, features she had missed through their camouflage. Immense yards filled with still and silent trees lay around these buttresses of ice, but every yard was empty of people. Vita-Hassa was a white haven, sprinkled with frosted green nature.

Approached Permanent Memory

Psolilai knew that her mission was to ascend to the Owl Palace. There she would find 3Machines, there she would find wisdom. But she struggled for some time before devising a plan to approach the Owl Palace. Talking to Metaxain, she put forward her idea, as they sat taking supper at the Inn of Twilight Ratiocination. "Surely it must be possible to claim the wisdom of the haven itself?" she asked. "If we ate the white fungal substrate . . ."

Metaxain shook his head. "Don't think that hasn't been tried before. The substrate has a low entheogenic quotient because it's so large—by the time you'd eaten enough to receive any wisdom, accumulated toxins would have killed you. There are a number of cases documenting fatality if you're interested."

psolilai was not to be put off. "This haven must contain knowledge."

Gularvhen offered his thoughts. "There is one possibility," he murmured. "The relevant chemical complexes within the white substrate may not be orally active."

Again Metaxain shook his head. "Many people have made up saturated solutions to bind into open wounds, but without effect."

"Please allow me to finish," said Gularvhen, holding up one hand. "If the chemical complexes of the substrate are tryptamine based, then we would need to ingest them alongside a monoamine oxidase inhibitor, in part to enhance the mildness of the knowledge, in part to make them orally active. The only problem is that plants containing such chemicals most often grow alongside the tryptamine-containing fungi, and such is not the case here."

"It's a beginning," said psolilai, though she was doubtful.

Metaxain's face took on an excited expression. "As a shaman of trees," he said, "I could perhaps provide the missing link. There are ways of encouraging a forest to grow."

psolilai was puzzled. "Are there?"

He made no reply, gazing with defocussed eyes at the far wall. Dyeeth Boolin, who had been smoking weed beside the fire, took the opportunity to speak. "One metaphysical difficulty awaits you, my dear. No mushroom provides knowledge of itself, rather it speaks of that part of nature to which it is connected. You would need to ingest metafungi growing on the substrate, since only they would speak of what they were connected to."

"That is not necessarily true," said Gularvhen. "If the Owl Palace is conceptually separate from this haven, we will glean some vital clue concerning it. But I agree, if it is part of the whole then we will learn nothing."

So they were left with one option: trees. Metaxain, however, was not expansive when it came to describing his methods, until psolilai realised that he was disconcerted by her friends; he hardly knew them. She took him to her room, where he spoke without restraint. "I did not exaggerate when I described myself as a shaman of trees," he said. "It's from trees that my knowledge comes—no contact with the animal world. I only eat mushrooms growing on trees. Please don't think I was being rude to your friends, but 3Machines, who dotes on wrealities, is no friend of nature, so I keep my beliefs to myself."

psolilai nodded. "I also have experience of those who rule through the manufacturing ecosystem," she said. "Tall Cliff Steel . . ."

He smiled. "I don't mind telling you that you're the best Gaian I know."

Delighted at hearing this, psolilai returned the compliment. "And you're one of the most intriguing," she murmured. "But I have dreamed of the shamen of Shohnadwe, and I know how they live. If we let you work alone, would you make a forest for us?"

"I'll do it if you want me to."

Flattered once again, psolilai felt her face become hot. She glanced away, murmuring, "I do want you to."

Later, when Metaxain had departed, psolilai summarised their conversation then added, "He will help us take the next step forward."

"Mmmm, but is he trustworthy?" asked Dyeeth Boolin.

"Oh, yes," psolilai said, lightly. "So many of our remarks have been without words."

At once Gularvhen took his notebook *The Condition* from his pocket, and jotted a short note in it.

"Let us hope Metaxain can be trusted," said Dyeeth Boolin. The old felin seemed vexed. "One of the great triumphs of the manufacturing ecosystem is its ability to mimic natural life. Think of the agens, machines in human form, think of the many metallic species we find during unlinking, ants, bees, and the like. Think of the kelzinzi, bobbing up and down by the shore like so much seaweed."

"That illustrates nature's morphological splendour," Gularvhen suggested.

But psolilai felt cross. "Your point?" she asked Dyeeth Boolin.

"Let us hope the forest your charming young acquaintance intends to conjure from the ground is natural, not some artefact of doom. If I know anything about the manufacturing ecosystem it is its power of temptation." He turned away, puffing at his pipe then stretching his furry feet before the fire.

psolilai looked at Gularvhen and Kirishnaghar, shrugged, then retired to bed.

The golden mist next morning rose from an annulus of trees, and although psolilai had already witnessed the ability of Mahandriana to conjure solidity from thought she was nonetheless impressed by the size and convincing appearance of the forest, green and damp, alive with birdsong, the outer edge of the ring only a quarter of a league distant. A gap remained between the haven and the inner edge of the forest in which people milled. They did not seem much bothered by the apparition; they had seen it all before.

psolilai, however, was entranced. With Kirishnaghar watching the Owl Palace and Dyeeth Boolin unlinking, she decided to explore the forest with Metaxain, accompanied by Gularvhen on Hoss. Immediately she felt on familiar ground—briar and leaf litter, paths edged with mud, here a glade of redbells and ferns, there a deep cluster of birch, above her the sun shining green through the flickering canopy. They walked on. Distances seemed to shift. Though they kept the sun to their left, there was no end to the forest . . .

In a large glade they rested. Here the grass grew tall, rotting logs at the edge of the clearing, hawthorn and briar rose dangling in.

"There are mushrooms here," said Gularvhen. "The trees are mostly beech, supporting a population of russula mushrooms from which I will be able to locate the position of the vine we require."

Hoss blew sweet music as Gularvhen ate a mushroom raw. He turned like a weathervane in a storm, spinning around to locate the nearest vine then vanishing into the trees. Within minutes he had returned, a length of woody rope in his hand.

"From the bark of this plant we will extract our monoamine oxidase inhibitor," he explained, "and then we may see what secrets the haven conceals."

They prepared to depart. psolilai felt torn. "Will this forest fade?" she asked Metaxain.

"When the dark fog falls down from the mountains," he replied in a sad voice.

"You go back to the Inn and prepare the chemicals," psolilai told Gularvhen. "I want to stay here awhile."

Gularvhen rode away. Hand in hand, psolilai and Metaxain walked through the forest, until the sun set and darkness like ink fell over them, and they were left looking up at the haven, the moon and the stars.

At the Inn, all was quiet. Kirishnaghar reported neither visitor nor departure from the Owl Palace, Dyeeth Boolin and his son were asleep in their chairs, while Gularvhen was purifying his chemicals. But soon all was ready. From a baroque excrescence in the passage outside they cracked off a piece of haven substrate, which they carved with a knife to produce shavings suitable for eating.

"We will all eat," Gularvhen said. "Knowledge can be elusive."

"Not me," said Metaxain.

Ilyi Koomsy awoke from twitching slumber. "I will try," he said.

Gularvhen prepared three portions, then opened a window at the rear of the Inn so that the music of Hoss could flow in on the chilly night air. psolilai crunched her shavings. They were like charcoal. She drank the chemical infusion, ate some more, then lay back in her chair, closed her eyes and awaited her dream.

Soft music of a hundred trills floating across her, like tentacles of smoke. An underlying basso cello note; hint of a whispering choir.

Refracted impressions of the planet, white and grey, as if seen through the curtain of a waterfall.

Of the intricacy of nature.

Of small voles and daisies, of great ocean currents spanning half the globe.

Of weather.

And a hint of the mountains, hard rock and never-melting ice, unforgiving, solid, yet splintering and fragmenting to create soil.

The music ceased.

A single note of the choir, then the crackling of the fire.

Gularvhen spoke first. "I feel cleansed," he said, "because I have touched nature."

"I also," Ilyi Koomsy reported. "A brief glimpse of something so . . . whole."

psolilai said, "I learned nothing of this haven, but I did catch a faint vision of the mountains around the plateau. My feeling is that the Owl Palace is part of the haven."

Gularvhen nodded, then, sighing, sank back into his chair. "A regrettable failure."

psolilai shook her head. "Not at all," she announced. "We now have a method of infiltrating the Owl Palace."

"My trees?" Metaxain said.

She nodded. "Suppose we plant trees on the Sky Level? Metaxain could make a wood there, through which we could creep until we reached the Owl Palace. Then we could storm it, or tunnel our way in."

"There may be a more subtle method," said Metaxain. "If I plant a single tree it's less likely to be noticed or interfered with, for the Sky Level can't be large."

"It is not," Kirishnaghar confirmed.

"If I let it grow over a period of days," Metaxain continued, "or even months, we're more likely to succeed—a tree can perform miracles that people can't."

"There is something in that!" Ilyi Koomsy agreed. "The Elder Analyst will never let you storm her Palace. Slow and subtle is the way."

"Perhaps you are right," said psolilai.

"A tree, then," said Metaxain. "A silver birch, pale and graceful in the breeze. And upon that tree a fungus will grow..."

They all agreed to this plan, as did Dyeeth Boolin when he woke up.

psolilai retired to her room, pleased with the day's work, but as the night progressed she found it impossible to sleep. For an hour she gazed out of her window, watching vermin crawl up and down the rooves of nearby houses, until she could stand it no more and she wrapped herself in a cloak and departed the Inn. Until dawn she prowled the streets. She met nobody. At dawn, she felt tired. At the Teahouse of Aurorean Eudemonia she considered taking an early breakfast, for she could hear Ilyi Koomsy clattering pans, but then fatigue took her and she returned to the Inn. There, she slept until late afternoon.

She was in no mood for Metaxain's charming nothings, so she sent him away soon after he arrived to take supper. Frustration plagued her. She wanted progress, but nature was slow. Metaxain had not even planted a seed yet.

Again, she found sleep impossible at night. Hunched in a chair by her window she watched the gallery's nocturnal life, brooding, irritable, trapped in her room, or so it seemed; and again, some hours after midnight, she took to the streets, looking for something that her mind could not grasp.

After a third night she found herself soothed. Day was irritating, night cool and pleasant. Nocturnal life suited her whims. But that evening, as she awaited the last minutes of twilight, she heard the strains of a viol in the yard below her window, which she opened, to see Metaxain serenading her. For a few moments she appreciated the gesture. Then he sang a song of slumber. From the window sill she took a pot, which she threw, and although he ducked it grazed his head. He ran off.

The night she spent wandering galleries, returning to sleep at dawn.

She found Kirishnaghar waiting for her, ready to update his observations. "Agents of the Analyticate arrive with wheelbarrows full of wrealities," he said, "but I have not seen one single person leave or enter the Owl Palace. However, I have planted the seed Metaxain gave me in debris nearby."

psolilai glanced at his blinded eyes. "Debris?" she asked.

"It is like a thin soil composed of rotting organic matter and the like. I suspect the Sky Level has accumulated natural debris over the

138

centuries, which has rotted down in sheltered places to form a soil in which grasses and bushes grow. There is also an animal ecology, birds, insects, rodents and the like, small only because it is windy. The fungal substrate is natural and subject to erosion."

psolilai nodded. "Keep watching."

Gularvhen had little to offer. "We must wait," he counselled, "until the silver birch is grown. Those parts touching, or even infiltrating, the Owl Palace foundations will provide us with knowledge."

psolilai grinned. "I know something of fungi," she said. "Muscimol provides, so Helwelusa told me in a dream. Before long a fly agaric will appear upon our silver birch, but because the tree is part symbolic, living on the substrate, the fungus will bring knowledge apprehended by the silver birch to our minds when we eat it. Then we should come to understand the Owl Palace, and find a place to enter it."

"I believe this to be our only chance," Gularvhen agreed.

"Do you think it will work?" Kirishnaghar asked.

Gularvhen nodded. "An optimist, me."

139

Noise woke her. It was dusk. In the common room below she heard mens' voices, one rough, almost demanding, speaking to Dyccth Boolin as if he were a menial. When Ilyi Koomsy spoke he was silenced with a single word.

She felt drowsy. She lay quiet, hoping the interlopers would depart, but then she heard boots heavy on the stairs and that rough voice again. "I want her now! Don't stop me."

Somebody was coming for her. In panic she leaped out of bed and pulled on her leathers and boots, before, with a single blow, the door was burst open. Before her stood a brute of a man: dark cloak, jasper owl. Without hesitation she turned and ran to her window, where she clambered out onto the roof. The man gave chase, but he was too slow to grab her.

He barked at his colleague, "After her!"

psolilai watched as a second man began climbing out of the window, short, wiry, also wearing the garb of the Analyticate. She crawled a few yards up the roof and shouted, "What do you want?"

He did not answer. He had the cunning, his colleague the force.

With the wind whipping around her, psolilai climbed higher, until she saw the chimney stack atop the roof, to which she made, holding on to a chimney as she turned round to face her pursuer. He followed, slower, taking more care than she had. It occurred to her then that all she needed to do was fly away.

The man spoke. "I will restrain you, then allow you to inch back down to the window. Do not move suddenly."

"Eh?" psolilai whispered, adding in a louder voice, "Why do you want me?"

He did not even consider the question, as from his pocket he produced a cord. "Just stand still," he said.

psolilai looked at the sprawling rooves around her, and, somehow, they were *her* rooves. Momentary image of her gliding in silence across them. The air blew around her body as if encouraging her, and she let go of the chimney. It felt good. Freedom. Balance shifting as she crouched. With a leap she extended her wings and soared into the air: smashing into something, tumbling, crashing over an edge, long drop as her body span limbs trailing, then . . .

Hit the ground.

Nothing else . . .

psolilai sensed a different environment.

A curious odour like new plastic, a hum that she both heard and felt through her back, for she was lying on a cold surface. She tried to wake up.

Red glow before her eyes. She opened them, to see light.

She raised her head to examine her surroundings. She lay in a cubic chamber, pale walls glowing, to one side a ledge upon which wrealities lay. A figure in one corner. She tried to move, but pain in her legs and her back stopped her.

The figure walked forward: a tall man dressed in a silvery robe, short sleeved and caught at his neck with a jasper owl; clean-shaven, young, yet with something of a leer in his expression. "Do not move," he said, his voice deep, quite reassuring.

Then psolilai recalled the roof and the chimney.

"You have sustained injuries," the man continued, "and for a while you will be in pain."

"Injuries?"

"Severe bruising to the back and right leg, ligament damage, many abrasions. Lucky for you no broken bones."

"Broken . . . ?" psolilai whispered.

"The men said you landed in a hydroponic pool."

psolilai recalled the food pond behind Dyeeth Boolin's kitchen. "Yes," she said.

"You should not have avoided them."

"Do you lead them? They came to attack me."

"To capture you," the man corrected.

"Who are you?"

"I am Dezisserine. I am in charge of you."

psolilai let her head fall back. She said, "So I'm in an infirmary."

"You are in my custody—"

"I've done nothing wrong."

Dezisserine did not answer as he pulled a seat close to where psolilai lay. "That is for us to say," he replied, after a pause. He sat delicately, like a cat. "The Analyticate has been watching you for some time. We are interested in you. Ma tells us you are proud."

In a resigned voice she replied, "I venture to suggest that his reporting of me may be biased."

"Ma reported your speech word for word. Besides, Han and Dri also report your credentials. So, psolilai, you have eaten many mushrooms, no?"

That was a strange question, and it hinted that her interrogator might not be as he appeared. She tried to concentrate on nuances of his behaviour. She answered, "We've all eaten some."

His face creased with glee. "As I suspected. Good."

Something vile here, something she had met before, yet could not place, his face too clean, his eyes inhuman bright, as if he was a zealot in lamb's clothing.

And then it all made sense. She said, "You are an agen."

The briefest pause, as if for the flash of a machine curse, before a reply. "You are correct."

"But you don't look like one."

"How many agens with whiskers, or trailing luminous flies, do you think the Company of Sentries allows on the Quartet Line? Very many, do you think?"

He . . . no, it . . .

The tone in its voice suggested the casual brutality of a machine. psolilai began to tremble, for she realised that its admission of agen status implied she would never be able to broadcast the fact to others. "Why did you capture me?" she asked.

It sat back, then gestured at the scarlet jellies on the ledge. "Wrealities. Have you ever wondered how they came to be?"

"I love nature too much to consider such horrible things."

Dezisserine stood up, towering over her. "I am immune to character attack. Confine yourself to facts."

psolilai said nothing.

Dezisserine continued, "Wrealities store, they think, they operate, they communicate with sentient beings. Analytical-tendencies are wrealities that specialise in history. It is through one mighty analysis, so far lasting a decade, that I have come to realise the relationship between wrealities and mushrooms."

"There is no relation!" psolilai cried out.

"Listen first to what I have to say. We know through historical analysis that a million years ago Gaian mushrooms were rare in Urbis Morpheos, and certainly had few, or even none, of the properties they have now. I believe they evolved to counter the existence of wrealities, which constitute a species manufactured by human beings. It is even possible they evolved in response to the coming of the manufacturing ecosystem."

"Nonsense," psolilai said. "Evolution is not teleological."

"That is true. But I view the evolution of wrealities and mushrooms much as I view the evolution of, say, the eagle and the hare. For each improvement in one there comes an improvement in the other, and so on, never ending. But the question I have always asked is this. Why do my species have no access to the knowledge of mushrooms?"

psolilai uttered a derisive grunt. "You would not know what to do with it."

Dezisserine leaned over her. "Ah, but I would like to learn, and one of the ways I can do that is to see how people react when they ingest wrealities."

Now psolilai was terrified. "You are going to experiment on me?"

"You are the perfect subject. One who has eaten of the mushroom but also knows the feel of wreality wisdom."

"I don't!" psolilai protested.

"Do not lie, psolilai, it wastes time. I know of what you dream. And I await you, Eastside."

psolilai shrank back.

"But I do not want people going mad in Mahandriana," Dezisserine continued. "You see, the Brain of Han is covered in a plastic film too thin to see. For the same reason the scarlet book in the Library of Dri is inert. But ah . . . the five have their uses!"

psolilai stared in horror at the flat walls around her. No curves. "Am I in the Owl Palace?" she whispered.

"You are in the Complex Levels," Dezisserine replied. Again the agen leaned over her. "I need to know exactly what knowledge mushrooms are offering people like you, so that I can devise a strategy for dealing with that knowledge."

psolilai said, "You are insane. And so is 3Machines—I suppose this is all her doing."

Dezisserine walked away. "We all follow the lead of the Elder Analyst," it said. "You will, too."

psolilai replied without thought, "Never."

From the ledge Dezisserine took an object like a beetle, before returning to stand at her side. "There are three ways of ingesting the chemical complexes in a wreality," it said, "through the nasal mucosa, eating, and direct injection into the bloodstream. I prefer the latter method since it allows me to control the dose."

It put the beetle on her wrist. The device skittered towards her elbow, then stopped. Four legs emerged to grip tight her skin.

Dezisserine said, "So we are ready for the first experiment."

psolilai tried to pull the beetle off, but the pain was too great for her to follow the action through. Breathing fast and shallow she lay back, aware that she was in a hopeless position. "No," she breathed. "Please, no."

"Inject," Dezisserine said.

For some seconds psolilai stared at the white ceiling, before a number of dark motes emerged in the centre of her vision, elongating into lines, that shot past her as if she was moving forward at speed; many more motes forming ahead. Then the lines became slabs, washes of colour, until she felt she was hurtling into oblivion. Speed blurred the colours into formless haze. A jolt, a sensation of nausea as if from a punch in the face, and she was hanging in a bath of scintillating fragments, like a turbid pool where every flake was a number. Drowning, unable to find a surface, no sense of gravity. Taste of metal in her mouth making a shiver run up her spine.

The pool began to strike her mind, flickering white to grey to blue at random, each change a thump in the teeth. She felt bruised by chaos. Her paddling motion made no sense. Giving up, she floated like a doll.

A sensation of yellow light above her, glowing behind curtains of numbers, and she tried to move towards it. With a stuttering motion she approached, each jump forward an affront to her senses, until, as the glow resolved into a sphere, she found stability.

She also found gold. It was an oblate sphere, at first gleaming and smooth, rougher as she approached, until she saw that its entire surface was patterned. She felt attracted to it. Heads without bodies were entering the sphere in single file from the right, and something like heads were emerging on the opposite side. psolilai tried to focus her bruised eyes, but the glittering sequence of random illumination made it impossible to see detail. She tried to get nearer, the attraction like magnetism, impossible to avoid. Now those surface patterns also looked like heads, arranged in a geometric array.

It was as if an infinite line of agen heads was being sucked in by the sphere, then ejected. Closer still; a rustle of whispers inside her skull. Transfer Station Gold.

Even a smell of gold, sharp and old, like cinders. The smell made the sphere even more attractive to her. Emboldened, she swam through the pool of numbers, until the golden wall stretched across her field of view. Like masks, a thousand agen faces peered out.

One agen cried, "You have been injected with wreality to make you aware of our entity, but it is not for you. Keep away! If you enter it, you will die forever."

On the word die psolilai felt her mind change. Cold, ashen, tired. The gold tarnished, the faces sad. "Die?" she said.

"You are human, not meant for this. In minutes you will die, when Transfer Station Gold drags you in. Fly away! Fly away to mushroom land!"

"Die?" she repeated.

"Yes!" the agen screamed. "For you are human and you have no soul!"

"No soul," psolilai agreed.

"Do not come nearer. Go quickly!"

But psolilai felt weak. The effort of returning to the white cube was too much. "Transfer Station Gold is dragging me in," she said, her voice a monotone.

"No! Your mind will starve your brain of oxygen if it believes it is dying!"

psolilai felt little tugs drawing her closer to the surface of faces. Seven agens now composed her entire field of view. In vain the vocal agen tried blowing at her, as if to drive her away.

"Join in, join in," it urged the other agens, and they also blew. psolilai felt a cold breeze pushing her away from the sphere.

She resisted. "I want to come in," she pleaded. Her lips were so numb she could hardly understand what she said.

In reply the agens blew harder. psolilai had nothing on which to grip. Like rags she drifted away, until the faces became patterns, then points. She turned to face an ungolden deep of numbers, like ocean. That too felt like death.

A glimpse of blackness. Night sky. As she drifted towards it she felt stronger, more human, and she began to see detail behind the departing veils of numbers. Lines of scarlet, blobs, and pulsating ganglions lilac sheened. Here lay a world of wrealities, a network of lines spread out before her, and she like a master strategist, able to pick and choose between them, to use them as if they were her own. The dread of the environment that she had been forced into departed, and she felt power.

Along the wreality network thousands of birds flew straight and true, each one mauve fading to silver, with beaks like hooks that pierced plates set into the wrealities, pulling them out then transferring them to others. Every wreality line was frantic with activity. And in the distance, almost invisible, like a mountain pale behind morning mist, she saw an owl so large it seemed that it was a mountain, silent and massive, a silhouette of the most delicate lilac hue.

She glided over the wrealities to see images and writing incised on the plates, so that the corridor of scarlet across which she flew became a bouncing river of information. She banked, stalled and descended when she saw a row of wrealities whose plates carried images of her

145

face. These she hovered above, as the birds squawked and swerved past her.

It was indeed herself. She grasped the connection between this place and the cubic cell in which she had been injected. Furious, she reached down to pull out every plate, throwing them so that they flew spinning into the ocean of numbers. She did not cease until every face had gone. Then, exhausted, she fell back: floating.

The wreality world faded, to be replaced by whiteness.

Back in the cell. Her mouth was stuck together by some vile fluid, acid like bile. Her head ached. But she was able to sit up and look around.

She was alone. Tempting to crush the wrealities, but intuition told her that she had succeeded in erasing herself from their memories. Best not to risk an alarm.

She found herself active, able to stand and move, though her body was full of dull bruise pain. She walked to the cell door and pushed it open. There was a corridor outside. An agen strode past her: neither whiskers nor luminous flies. In disguise, then, like Dezisserine. One of his colleagues. She watched until it vanished around a corner. It had ignored her.

Yet it must have seen her. Though she was unsteady on her feet she walked down the corridor, expecting Dezisserine at any second, expecting to hear its voice give some patronising command. But that voice did not come. For ten minutes she wandered the maze of corridors, seeing nobody, until she chanced upon a room into which she glanced as she walked by. Dezisserine was there, talking to another agen. It saw her, it ignored her, and she walked on.

It struck her then that Dezisserine would never let its victim escape. Something had happened to blind the agen to her existence. Now escape was urgent, and a shudder of fear passed through her as she realised how her life was balanced, how all might change if she happened to meet a human agent of the Analyticate. She ran until she found a door that looked different to the others. Three agens stood there, but they too ignored her. With the sweat cold on her skin, she was able to slip by and depart the secret chambers, to enter some freezing gallery of the Complex Levels.

Now where? Her only means of departure was the balloons on the lowest level. When she arrived she was able to join three others in a flight down one level, where the Analyticate agents ignored her as they checked those ascending. She was free.

She did not feel free. Her trauma was too great for her to feel secure. The horror of finding beings of the manufacturing ecosystem deep within the haven, like a nest of wasps . . .

Hurrying down the staircases she felt her strength returning. Recuperation in the lift, and then another set of stairs to the level of the Inn; soon she stood at its front door. For a minute she listened. No sign of danger. She walked in.

Immediately she was surrounded, Dyeeth Boolin the nearest, crying, "psolilai, you have returned!"

Then Gularvhen leaped out of his chair. "psolilai! I know it is you!"

And Kirishnaghar. "We thought you dead for certain."

psolilai walked behind the bar and poured herself a glass of brandy. "It is me, and I have survived . . . but I don't know what I've survived."

Dyeeth Boolin was padding her with two furry hands, testing the consistency of her flesh to assure himself that she was no illusion. "My dear! Tell us about it."

She did. They were as nonplussed as she, and as shocked that agens were concealed inside the haven. Kirishnaghar pointed out the conn- ection between the erasure of her images and the agens' inability to perceive her, but beyond that he was unable to elaborate.

Gularvhen stroked his chin with one hand. "Dezisserine must be the public face of a secret research cell," he mused, "else why would it disguise itself with such accuracy as a human? Dezisserine therefore is a real danger."

Kirishnaghar grunted, shaking his head. "Vile," was all he would say.

For some time they sat quiet, digesting what they had heard, psolilai going over her escape time and time again, recalling the glimmer in Dezisserine's eyes when she walked past its room, comparing that expression to the leer she had seen upon first regaining consciousness in the white cell. They seemed the faces of two different beings. Was it possible that these agens, who must weave fabulous camouflages to survive inside the haven, were somehow managed, even controlled by the wrealities?

It was morning. On such thoughts, she slept.

DREAM KNOWLEDGE WAS RESONANT

Vita-Hassa was ice laid upon wire. Vast white balconies curled up natural pillars attached to the edge of the Ice Shield. Where there had been glacier movement halls were excavated or destroyed, steps created, towers built or smashed. It was a haven too complex to map, changing from year to year.

The dirigible landed in a yard near an ice wall. Hoar-limned trees intensified the silence, no breeze blowing, no swishing of branches, just the occasional crack reverberating across the yards as some chunk of ice moved, or split. Everything was blue or white. Psolilai walked across the frosty sward to run her gloved hand over the ice wall. A hundred levels above her showed windows, balconies. The top was out of sight. Peering into the ice she saw twisted hanks of wire leading up from the ground, coiling like the DNA of the place. Deeper, and hardly visible, lay thicker cabling, mysterious behind translucence. This was indeed a place of opposites, part natural haven, part construction of the manufacturing ecosystem, a composite structure that people could never control.

"I will locate an entrance," said Gularvhen.

Psolilai glanced over at Kirishnaghar, who was preparing to leave the dirigible. "You're coming?" she asked him.

His permanent stare locked into her gaze as he replied, "I have no intention of staying here, to be eaten by blue-wolves or shredded by machines."

"Follow me!" Gularvhen called, his voice echoing between ice wall and yard.

Psolilai trotted up to Gularvhen and asked, "Do you know anyone here?"

"I visit this haven most years," he replied, "but my particular friends will like as not be hibernating. This encapsulates our problem. The winter denizens of Vita-Hassa are rarely human."

At a tunnel entrance they halted. Psolilai heard the echoes of their footsteps reverberating down a shiny ice corridor. She shivered. Something about this place, its chill, its aura of malevolent machinery...

"Your primary sense here is hearing," said Gularvhen. "Sound travels. Listen for grating, clanking sounds, anything sudden. Soft sounds will be human or felin. Residents here are trained from childhood never to make unexpected noise."

Thus warned they entered the haven. It was much colder than Psolilai expected. No sun, no heat of machinery, just ice on walls and ground, and a chill that penetrated her clothes. She stopped to put on an extra coat. Light was provided by irregular patches of neon flickering behind ice sheets.

"People live here?" she asked.

In a soft voice Gularvhen replied, "In the upper levels, where conditions are better. These are the automatic levels—quiet!"

Silence: except for distant clinking, as of metal plates, and then Psolilai saw a line of mantis machines walking single file through the crossroads ahead. The machines disappeared from view, and she breathed again.

"We need to find some stairs," Gularvhen said. "This whole zone has changed since I was last here."

He found a staircase nearby. Hoss found the long climb difficult, but he persisted. At the top of the staircase a chamber led off, and Gularvhen led them inside.

"Here are some of the residents," he said, "good local citizens all."

Psolilai looked around. In wall niches scores of people lay huddled up in layers of wool and fur, only noses and closed eyes visible, while icicles hung from the ceiling, and puddles of frozen breath marked the floor. All hibernating, all white skinned.

"When will they awake?" she asked Gularvhen.

"Come spring."

"Or earlier," said a deep voice. Psolilai jumped as a figure dropped from the niche to her left. It was a man. He shook himself, brushed the debris off the thick coat that he wore, then stood upright. He was young, bearded, with black hair and small eyes.

"Good day," he said. His accent was thick, but melodious. "I am glad to discover that you have benign motives."

"Who are you?" Gularvhen asked.

"Khi-Zadassva of the Lunette Watch."

Gularvhen strode forward and clasped the man, so that his face was squeezed against Gularvhen's chest. "I know your brother," he said. "I am Gularvhen, peripatetic mycologist."

"Well met!" said Khi-Zadassva.

"How many of you decided against hibernation this year?"

Khi-Zadassva replied, "A score, maybe more."

Gularvhen turned to Psolilai to say, "One in five hundred of the population. You appreciate now the risk."

"Why are you here?" Khi-Zadassva asked.

"We have a task in which you might be of some assistance," Gularvhen replied. "But first, please take us up to more comfortable levels."

They continued the ascent, Khi-Zadassva leading, Kirishnaghar trailing. The higher levels were not so chill and there were pockets of pale green where hydroponic tanks grew food crops, but everywhere they saw ice, whether as icicles, sheets, or frozen bootsteps. Then Khi-Zadassva led them into a chamber whose roof and farther wall were a single span of ice, shot through with bare wire gleaming against light from a low, orange sun; the other walls bare rock. A scene of wonder that made Psolilai gasp.

They were taken to a stone table, under which lay food stores. Soon a meal of dried fruit and biscuits was ready, accompanied by wine.

"Your task, then," Khi-Zadassva prompted.

"Reports from explorers suggest immense mushrooms grow inch by inch under the weight of the Ice Shield," Gularvhen explained. "Parts of the Shield are ancient, layer upon layer of compacted snow. The wisdom of such mushrooms would be valuable, telling us of the processes that drive and change the weather over geological time periods. Psolilai and I require such wisdom."

Khi-Zadassva nodded. "I have heard of such mushrooms, but never seen one. However I know where to begin any search. I could be your guide."

"We would be most grateful."

Khi-Zadassva pushed plates of food in their direction. "Tomorrow we start. Soon, I will show you sleeping chambers. Your horse, Gularvhen?"

"Hoss remains with me."

Later they were shown a cluster of tiny caves opening out from a side corridor, all of them protected by oval doors made from scrap wood. Neither cold nor warm, the caves were furnished with rickety wooden beds upon which musty blankets lay. Psolilai saw that the doors were well equipped with locks.

Khi-Zadassva noticed her interest. "In case of attack," he explained. "Lately I have seen phalanxes of razor machines mounted on miniature tanks, cutting wires and attempting to set up their own territory. Also a lone mechanical beast with a haunting cry. I have seen only its shadow, tall, slender, with hooks for claws and sabre teeth."

"Why does anybody live here?" asked Psolilai.

"There is nowhere else to go."

"You could move south."

"Bitah-Sui is the district of our birth, and this is its only haven. Where else in Urbis Morpheos would we be welcome?"

Psolilai was left in her room. With nothing else to do she made herself as comfortable as the meagre resources allowed. Without natural light she had no idea of passing time, and so she dozed.

Abruptly she woke—a sound outside her door like two rusty plates forced over one another. In her bed she shivered, sitting bolt upright and clutching the blankets. Shadows enfolded her, a single lightstick by her side. The thin screech sounded again; then rattling at her door. Unable to breathe, to swallow. The cry sounded a third time, and then there was a receding clip-clop, as of tin feet. The thing was gone.

She found that sleep had deserted her. Later there was a knock at the door and a cheery, "Honey cakes in the ice room!"

At breakfast she said, "A wailing beast kept me awake."

Khi-Zadassva nodded. "Harmless," he said, "as long as you don't smell its cyanide breath."

An hour later they departed for the Ice Shield. A bridge led over a gorge between the Shield, which here formed a cliff, and the upper levels of the haven; made of wood and rope, its panels were corrugated to stop people slipping. The wind howled through the gaps. Gularvhen and Hoss crossed without difficulty, but Psolilai was taken by vertigo and had to be encouraged by Khi-Zadassva. Kirishnaghar said nothing. His artificial stare disconcerted Khi-Zadassva so much the two men never conversed.

Above them the moontoo rode high, emerald green in a clear blue sky. Ahead lay fields white to the horizon. Khi-Zadassva issued all but Kirishnaghar with mirrored spectacles.

"Where do we begin our search?" asked Gularvhen.

Khi-Zadassva led them out onto the ice. He pointed right and said, "That scored river of ice is the glacier Mon-Yayot. Ahead lies an associated ice field." He turned and said, "But if we climb those hills to the left we will reach areas where the snow has fallen undisturbed for aeons. If there are any ancient mushrooms to be found, they will be there."

"Will we get far today?" Psolilai asked.

"As long as we can return to Vita-Hassa by dusk, we shall be safe."

So they began their trek. The hills were not steep, but there was little respite; slopes rose one after the other, endless ascent through soft snow or treacherous ice. Psolilai found her stomach and calf muscles aching. Khi-Zadassva offered them mulled wine fortified with stimulants to help them cope.

An hour after noon they came upon a natural bowl. Khi-Zadassva called a halt. "This is a suitable zone," he said. "Look at the topography, the smoothness of the ice. If we all search here we might locate something."

Gularvhen warned them, "This will not be an easy task. We are seeking a mushroom with a cap five thousand yards across. Look for what appear to be regular flaws in the ice."

Not knowing what to do, Psolilai waited for Gularvhen and Khi-Zadassva to begin the search. She glanced across at Kirishnaghar, who was standing beside Hoss; he also was waiting. Then Gularvhen bent over and began casting about for signs, while Khi-Zadassva adopted a crouched posture, scrabbling in the snow every few feet. Psolilai copied them, looking as best she could through recent snow to the translucent ice below. She saw patterns, but they were stress flaws, cracks, the occasional burrow made by a lunar hare.

Then Gularvhen stood to his full height and gave a cry. "Hola!" They all ran over. He indicated the ice at his feet and said, "I think I have found something. Do you see that sheet of chevrons fading into the ice?"

Psolilai scraped snow away to look closer. There was indeed a layer of brown chevrons extending towards the furthest slope, perhaps a yard below the surface, disappearing into opaque regions. "I think you're right," she said, excitement coursing through her.

Khi-Zadassva produced a tube from his pocket. "An energy source," he explained. "I will melt the opaque top layer to improve visibility into the translucent regions of ice."

Walking backwards toward the slope he pointed the device down and waved it from side to side, so that the surface melted, then refroze transparent, allowing them a better view. Psolilai was thrilled to see the marks continue, changing into squares here, lines elsewhere, brown, occasionally black, but all linked to form one structure.

"This is it," she said, awestruck. She stood here on a mushroom cap that would take over two hours to walk around. "How do we dig it out?"

"This is our next difficulty," Gularvhen said.

For a while he alone moved, surveying the mushroom cap, kneeling to peer down, resting his chin in his hand as he thought, then walking on. After an hour he returned to say, "It is beyond we three. I do not see a way forward."

"The manufacturing ecosystem has produced many local species," said Khi-Zadassva, "some of whom chip ice. It might be possible to use such a device."

"Use?"

Khi-Zadassva glanced in the direction of his haven. "Possibly trick or coerce."

"Can't we just dig a hole and pull some of the cap out?" Psolilai asked.

Gularvhen shook his head. "The ice is supporting a rarefied body, one that has grown for perhaps the last twenty thousand years. We will need to concentrate a small amount of mushroom from a large volume of ice."

"For the moment," Khi-Zadassva assured them, "do not worry. We will return to the haven and enjoy a merry meal."

But that evening the merry meal turned serious when Khi-Zadassva described the ice-chipping species he had in mind. "We call them blade beasts. They are machines devoted to the cutting of the thicker cables. They are bipedal like us, composed entirely of blades, with a thin body of white plastic. Their eyes are cameras on stalks. They are very dangerous." Conversationally, he added, "They evolved a million years ago from the smaller razor machines."

"This suggests we should not risk annoying one," said Gularvhen.

"For locals, there are methods. Blade beasts can be trained by a courageous handler."

He meant himself. Psolilai decided not to take a role in this part of the task.

N ext day they began searching for a blade beast. It meant descending to the lower levels. Khi-Zadassva carried sheaves of cabling over one shoulder—bait and reward. For some hours they trudged ice tunnels, listening for metallic noise, stopping when they heard something likely, then carrying on. They happened across a family of silver millipedes, a few more mantis machines, but nothing with blades, until a frustrated Khi-Zadassva decided to descend to the lowest levels, where the cold made their breath plume and crystallise. Now he advised them to have weapons at hand. He walked quietly, speaking only when necessary, alert for attack.

The first surprise came from a wall tentacle that stretched out to coil around Khi-Zadassva, until Psolilai slashed it with her rapier; tinkling fragments dropped to the floor. At once other devices formed groups in order to seek vengeance—wheeled miners, serpentine lengths of autonomous plastic, a swarm of arachnids with eyes like saucers—but the trio was able to beat them off, or simply run elsewhere.

"It is only a matter of time before something really nasty comes our way," Khi-Zadassva remarked. "I feel insecure down here."

This comment did nothing for Psolilai's state of mind, given that Khi-Zadassva was a citizen of the haven. But then there was a thump, a series of clinks and a flash of neon ahead.

"Quiet!" came the order.

From a side tunnel a blade beast emerged, tall as Gularvhen, shiny chrome with a pale stick body, a hundred blades twirling from every joint, each limb a blade, each hand and foot, every finger, every toe; the most hideous thing Psolilai had ever seen. Endoscopic cameras growing from the lump that was its head quested this way and that as the machine appraised its company.

Khi-Zadassva threw a few cables to the floor. With its foot blades clinking against the stone, the beast stepped forward and sliced what it could see, pushing the strands into neat piles. Khi-Zadassva threw down some more, then a third pile, until, when the beast stood close, he pulled out a bag and squirted something over its head.

"We may speak now," Khi-Zadassva said. "I have sprayed it with oil containing mating hormones, confusing it, so that it thinks its autumn has come. Now it will follow us onto the Shield, where it will begin mating preparations."

"Cutting the ice," Psolilai guessed.

"Exactly."

So they returned to the bowl where the mushroom lay. Noon had long gone when they arrived, all of them tired and tetchy. Psolilai watched as Gularvhen set up the equipment he had collected from Khi-Zadassva; solar furnace and tripod, evaporating glasses, implements and a timer. Meanwhile the blade beast was cutting chunks of ice where Khi-Zadassva had laid more cables, emitting a mournful whistle as it dug.

155

Gularvhen began rescuing chunks of ice that contained fragments of the mushroom cap. Now the ice was out in the open, Psolilai saw that the cap was indeed rarefied, each chevron connected to others by the finest hyphae, the whole a structure that would collapse like wet paper without supporting ice. Intrigued, she watched, standing next to Huss, who also watched. The blade beast had already excavated hundreds of blocks of ice, but all that had emerged from the end of the glassware was a brown film. She waited as Gularvhen continued the refining process. Far away, on the lip of the bowl, Kirishnaghar observed all.

During the afternoon the film became a layer, then a damp mess in the final glass beaker. With the sun setting behind low cirrus they decided it was time to call a halt. They returned to Vita-Hassa, their precious cargo in an airtight container.

"We must eat this now," Gularvhen decided. "All mushroom flesh decays quickly, this more so."

"I will leave you to your meal," Khi-Zadassva said. "Call me if you have any requirements."

Gularvhen led Psolilai to her own chamber, where, with Hoss already inside, he shut and locked the door. Psolilai imagined the Constructor burning hot in her pocket, though she knew it was not; no smell of singed fabric. Apprehension made her nerves twinge as Gularvhen prepared the mushroom flesh. The first strains of music emerged from the multiple voicebox of Hoss, and familiarity with his style suggested to Psolilai that the ethereal tone he adopted would continue, helping them to acquire profound knowledge. They ate the mealy flesh raw, with only water to help it down. It was difficult to chew, like eating cardboard soaked in puddles.

And wisdom came.

The mushroom grew from a single microscopic spore released thirty three thousand years ago at the end of the last interglacial, its diameter increasing at a rate of six inches per year. It represented ever more sophisticated knowledge over those accumulating aeons, acquired from the layers of snow that fell, were compressed, then told their tale; more profound knowledge by far than any ordinary mushroom because of leisurely growth and unrestricted size. As the layers deepened, it expanded, remaining near the surface.

It told of the western sea, of how warm water flowed up from equatorial zones, to warm Shohnadwe and all lands east, then sink, cold, dense, salty, and return south as the other half of a convection current. Sometimes this conveyor was on, sometimes off, and this was one variable of the weather crossing Urbis Morpheos.

It told of the water cycle, vapour rising off the sea, clouds seeded by acid droplets formed from gas emitted by oceanic algae, clouds moving in fronts across the sea, across the land, rising cooling, raining down. Water flowing down the gravitational well, from spring to brook to river to ocean, to begin the cycle again.

It told too of the rotation of Gaia, of the precession of the angle of inclination, and the effect this had on the amount of energy reaching the surface. Of the slow changes in the geometry of Gaia's elliptical orbit.

Also it told of variations in the sun's output, which fluctuated.

From the amount, type and composition of the fallen snow knowledge was acquired of all these variables, which could then be analysed for patterns and placed into a whole. This whole was nature's variation, and it told of everything affecting Theeremere.

The knowledge in all its profundity came to Psolilai's mind as the last chords of Hoss' eerie music faded into silence, whereupon she opened her eyes, looked around, and returned herself to the real world by the simple act of recalling where she was. Nothing so deep and dense had ever been brought to her by a mushroom. For time unmarked she gazed at the wall opposite, thinking of aeons, of weather, of this hint of the greater scale of nature, waiting for time and chemicals to condense an unforgettable memory in her frontal cortex.

The knowledge was awesome in its beauty. In a sense, her mind was not equipped to deal with it. She struggled for a while to make her mind somehow larger, so that it could contain the entirety of this knowledge, but it was too much for her. Yet she had more than just a flavour of grandeur, she had grand wisdom, and with that the Constructor could work.

"We were not meant to know all this," sighed Gularvhen.

"I know enough," Psolilai declared. "I may not know nature's cycles from the inside, as I know my own feelings or memories, but I know enough."

Gularvhen nodded. "You sound certain of yourself."

"The manufacturing ecosystem can be controlled. Destroying it is not an option."

"Is it not?" Gularvhen asked.

Psolilai shook her head, then continued, "We'll head for Shohnadwe shores next, where the western ocean meets our great city. And at that junction I will use the Constructor to rescue Theeremere from oblivion."

They departed the cave and later spoke to Khi-Zadassva about the insight they had gained.

He had advice to offer them. "If you are visiting western Shohnadwe, particularly the coast, you will encounter the zri, the sentient clouds. Your knowledge is only of nature. Bad snow has roots in the manufacturing ecosystem."

Gularvhen replied, "Our intention is to travel via Thymosfa, the aerial land of the zri, where we will ask how substances migrate from ocean to cloud, what those substances are, their relative concentrations and so forth. We will talk with the zri." He turned to face Psolilai. "Then you will stand upon the coast and work your miracle. We will return to Theeremere to view the results."

Khi-Zadassva wiped a tear from one eye. "In summer, when the supply dirigibles come once again, I will listen for talk of changes in the weather, and I will think of you."

10

CREATED BY CULTURE

When Metaxain suggested that psolilai accompany him to the Divan Inn, she refused. "I don't want to meet Ma again," she explained.

"He won't be there," Metaxain insisted. "He visits a different place each day, never returning within the year. Anyway, I heard he's gone up to the Adverse Levels. You'll be safe."

"I would rather not."

"Then the Black Moth Inn."

psolilai hesitated, then said, "Very well."

The Black Moth Inn was large and busy, close to the bottom of the Teeming Levels. They drank while listening to a number of individuals making predictions of weather for the forthcoming year. psolilai listened with growing frustration, until she was impelled to action. She stood up, took her goblet and smacked a spoon into it, silencing the crowd. Everybody turned to look at her.

"Predictions," she said. "Can you make predictions without facts?" She pointed at one of the men. "You. What facts do you base your predictions on?"

He chuckled. "Drink on, my lass."

"You have no answer," psolilai said.

"I have," one of the other locals called out. "Ain't nothing wrong with telling weather from the sky, is there?"

"My point is this," said psolilai, hopping up on her table. "Your facts are local. Nothing wrong with that. But imagine a bigger scene. Imagine the weather for the entirety of Urbis Morpheos."

The man laughed. "You're mad. We don't need to know so much weather."

"But you do. Do you think Mahandriana is a micro-climate? It is not. All is linked. In the western ocean a gigantic current once flowed up from warm waters at the equator, taking the chill off Shohnadwe, Bitah-Sui and Phistipristin, and districts further east. Today that current does not flow and our lands freeze. This is made worse by the aeon of ice that we have entered. Now do you see? Forecast the weather over Mahandriana, yes, but do not consider it anything other than local guesswork. We need vision! We need to expand our thoughts into the bigger scene, discover how our weathers are linked by taking in more of the world. And then . . . my friends, then we will be entitled to call our sayings predictions."

Muted applause rippled across the crowd. They waited to see if she had anything more to say, but when she stepped down from the table they returned to their drinks and their conversations. The men who had been predicting spoke amongst themselves, nodding to each other, eyeing her, not as if she was a threat but out of curiosity. Then one of them pushed through the throng to sit at her table. He said, "You were the lass that spoke up the Divan, weren't you?"

"I was," psolilai confirmed.

He sat back. "Well that's strange. Folk there thought you mad, but I quite like you. You got a voice, lass." With that, he departed.

Metaxain smiled at her. "You have indeed got a voice," he said, taking her hand in his. "And you are becoming wisdom."

psolilai kissed his fingers. She felt a thrill run through her body, but she could not tell if it was from Metaxain's touch or from the knowledge that she was having an effect upon the people of this haven.

There was bad news from Dyeeth Boolin when they returned to the Inn of Twilight Ratiocination. "The agents of the Analyticate came to capture you again," he told psolilai. "I think for the moment it would be better if you stayed more often with Ilyi Koomsy."

psolilai agreed to this. "Find me cosmetics," she said. "I have disguised myself as a man in the past and I can do it again if necessary. For the moment, I should be safe. But if I could permanently erase myself from records in the haven wrealities . . ."

"I doubt that is possible," Dyeeth Boolin replied. "For now, my dear, we will help you, but I suspect more difficult times lie ahead. Your public speaking is at odds with your need for secrecy."

"I know," psolilai said. "But I can't help it. I have too much to say, and it won't stay inside me. Metaxain said I'm becoming wise."

"That is not quite what he said," murmured Gularvhen.

Dyeeth Boolin declared, "Then we must reach the Owl Palace as soon as possible, absurd though that is. I am in favour of the expedition."

psolilai turned to Kirishnaghar, who was seated by the fire. "How is our tree growing?" she asked.

"Slowly, but well enough."

psolilai considered all that she had heard. "I believe the aura of this haven is helping me speak," she said. "Possibly it can sense my presence."

Dyeeth Boolin took a puff at his pipe, then said, "That is possible."

Later that evening Gularvhen took psolilai away, leading her in silence to the Library of Dri. There was nobody about, and psolilai felt unsettled. She asked Gularvhen, "Why have you brought me here?"

"I want you to sleep amongst these books," he replied. "We may acquire useful knowledge when you wake."

"You mean from a dream?"

161

"Of course. Dream knowledge is real knowledge, that is not in doubt. What is in question is how that knowledge relates to the Constructor and the Translator, and thus to the owl."

psolilai shivered at the thought of the two artefacts. She said, "You believe the mushrooms here may help me."

Gularvhen nodded. "Their spores, to be accurate." He smiled. "I like to be accurate . . . but sleep, now."

"I don't feel sleepy."

Gularvhen nodded. "Then I will tell you a story."

psolilai sat on the floor, settling herself against one of the rows of shelves. "Go on then," she said, a half-smile upon her face.

"Once upon a time," said Gularvhen, "there was a young woman called Psolilai—"

"Wait!" psolilai interrupted. "I know her—"

"Shush!" Gularvhen hissed. "Let me continue, please. Now, one day Psolilai was inside Analytical-Tendency House in Theeremere, the Haven of the Three Machines, when she was told that she was suspected of leaking secret information. She was taken by guards to a cell, where she was left for some time. She tried to find mushrooms on the walls, in order to obtain information, but there were none. Then, much later, she was taken to a chamber of adjudication, a place of whitewashed walls and black wooden furniture. There were moths everywhere, eating into the fabric, which in places was little more than foam. She could smell disinfectant and hot metal, and many sweaty bodies. Then Amargoidara, the Steward Lord of the Analytical Council, stood up and walked towards a plinth, upon which lay an object beneath a cloth. Amargoidara pulled the cloth away to reveal a scarlet globe a yard across—one of the three analytical-tendencies that formed the foundation of the triple split district. His voice hissed from behind the mask, which now showed an angry face. 'This analytical-tendency tells us how to live in our world,' he declared. 'It is a specialised wreality, assembling historical knowledge, then giving us advice.' The frown on the mask grew deeper. 'It is not to be ignored. No other source of knowledge is superior since it accumulates human knowledge. But this analytical-tendency, and indeed the other two, have been ignored by one person.' Psolilai let her expression remain neutral, unsure of the purpose of the session—she did not want to let them know what she was thinking. There was a sad face on the mask when Amargoidara continued, 'It is always unfortunate when our moral sources are ignored, and, worse, when an alternative theory is put forward.' Now Amargoidara turned so that the mask gazed upon her. 'You have defied the rule of the Analytical Council. We exist to transfer the immensity of human wisdom, accumulated in the analytical-tendencies over uncounted aeons, to you—for your benefit. Like a brat you ignored us.' Psolilai knew that her sentence was about to be pronounced. Then came the return of the angry face. 'For this ill deed,' Amargoidara said, 'we exile you from the hope of this haven, in a wilderness place cold and high. To Tall Cliff Steel you will be taken, there to live for the rest of your days. We estimate ten to fifteen thousand of those.' Psolilai said nothing. 'Do you have anything to say?' Amargoidara asked her. Psolilai did not reply. Then an official was at her side. He slapped a sticky white gag across her mouth, which stung—she lifted one arm, assuming that the gag would come off, but it did not, because her fingernails could find no edge. 'Do you have anything to say?' Amargoidara repeated, his mask acquiring a leer. Psolilai noticed then that the gag was aerated. 'Oh, yes,' said Amargoidara, 'you can breathe through it. You will be wearing it for some days.' Poor Psolilai shook her head as two tears fell from the corners of her eyes."

—Psolilai was led away, and she wished more than anything in the world that she could relive this moment, even if only in a dream, and so, somehow, turn her fate from bad to good. As she walked towards the exit of the chamber, she noticed in the crowd a young woman with tears in her eyes, that fell just like hers from her eyes' corners. This woman threw a scriber at her, which Psolilai caught.

The scriber was an object of antique beauty, opaque tourmaline surrounded by a sheath of bronze. But it was sharp. A single, vital thought flashed through Psolilai's mind. A weapon! She leaped over a wooden rail and ran along to the dais where Amargoidara stood, so fast that nobody could stop her. She glanced back. The nearest guard was a dozen yards away. She turned, raised the scriber, and stabbed Amargoidara's mask.

There came a sound so terrible it threw her backwards, like a bolt of electricity; mingled shriek and electronic wail. Amargoidara fell to the ground as though a myriad mechanical parts were disintegrating inside him, and when the mask peeled away from his face it exposed a visage of snarling fury, with eyes of—

psolilai woke up to find Gularvhen staring at her. "What colour were his eyes?" he demanded. "What *colour* were his *eyes?*"

psolilai stuttered an answer. "Emerald . . . as emerald as the moontoo."

Gularvhen stood up. He towered above her, an expression of shock on his face, but this soon changed to one of triumph. "So!" he said. "So . . ."

As psolilai looked at Gularvhen, he bent down to kneel at her side, then placed a mirror in front of her, a mirror in the shape of a single feather. She could see her face. Two mushrooms had grown from the sides of her skull above her ears.

Gularvhen said, "You look for all the world like an owl, with your round, staring eyes and your sunset hair entangled around those two mushrooms like ear-tufts."

psolilai pulled aside her hair, to see that the mushrooms were exquisite. One was pale, with a pink cap and dense dark gills, its flesh scored with the finest lines, like corrugation. The other was darker, green tinted and shaggy, with a smaller number of chunky gills, white and slimy; it smelled of hay in soft meadows, of summer. The stems and bases of both mushrooms were clean.

Gularvhen picked them off her, the thumbs and forefingers of his hands like a pair of pincers. "These, I take," he said. He glanced at her, then added, "Being, as I am, the mycologist."

psolilai was too dazed to argue. The last thing she saw was Gularvhen running at the nearest shelf of books and passing right through, as if he were nothing more than a phantom.

11

BY MAGIC

Four days hence was Kirishnaghar's estimate of their time of arrival at Thymosfa. He stared out through his eyelid paintings into worsening weather, bad snow cumulus forming on the western horizon. He said little. He ate nothing, keeping to his starvation routine. Some inner tension was mounting within him.

Psolilai was glad that the trip to Thymosfa was underway. She wanted it over and done, so she could use the Constructor. But without full knowledge the ancient artefact was useless.

They drove into the westerly wind, though the dirigible motors hardly changed their pace, Kirishnaghar making an adjustment here, a hand signal there—standing proud when the first flakes of bad snow hit the basket, while the others covered themselves and lay out of the way. Three days and four nights passed. The showers turned into storms, then abated as the dirigible crossed into Shohnadwe. They passed through it all, signalling their way with the two yellow anti-fog lamps.

They reached the coast and saw the sea, heavy beneath red evening glow. "There is Thymosfa!" Kirishnaghar shouted.

Psolilai saw a layer of grey cloud tinged purple, top and bottom unnaturally flat, yet billowing here and there into fluffy curves. It did not move as did ordinary clouds, motionless before the western wind. She watched for movement, hoping for a glimpse of zri, but all she saw were streamers of water vapour whipping across the aerial land, like sand over desert. The zri must be hidden within.

"How do we land?" she asked.

Kirishnaghar replied, "Because the zri are one of the seven conscious races of the manufacturing ecosystem they have their own

peculiar customs, passed on over the generations, like ours. This particular culture is unlike any other—they allow no alien machines upon
Thymosfa. You jump down."

"Jump?" queried Gularvhen.

"You mean off the dirigible?" said Psolilai.

"I speak truth. Below Thymosfa lies my own district."

Psolilai laughed. "I will never attempt it."

"Nor I," said Gularvhen.

"The zri are not barbarians," Kirishnaghar insisted. "All we have to
do is locate the gravitational pillow that the technological zealots of
their kind have set up. It exists as a blemish in Gaia's gravitational
field."

Psolilai and Gularvhen looked at one another.

"Those are their mores," Kirishnaghar said, as if wearying of the
conversation. "You must respect their culture."

"How does this pillow work?" asked Gularvhen.

"As a column of variable gravity. Once inside, you float down to the
surface of Thymosfa like a dandelion seed."

Gularvhen frowned. "And have you tried this?"

"I have seen it done," Kirishnaghar returned.

"You will jump first," Psolilai told him.

"I will not jump at all," Kirishnaghar stated. "The dirigible must be
controlled while you two wander Thymosfa. Later on, I will have to
direct it to the right spot below, ready for your departure."

All this sounded suspicious to Psolilai. Standing behind Hoss in a
quiet corner to the rear of the basket, she whispered to Gularvhen,
"The zri themselves are machines, albeit conscious, so why do they
allow nothing of the manufacturing ecosystem upon Thymosfa?"

"Cultural quirk—on my travels I have heard similar tales. But we
must speak with the zri, for only they can tell us of the substances that
pass above and below Thymosfa in storms of bad snow."

"I can't jump down into air," Psolilai declared.

"Imagine how difficult Hoss will find it."

"You're taking him?"

Gularvhen replied, "How many times will you ask that question?"

Psolilai ground her teeth together and glanced back at Kirishnaghar.
"You and Hoss will go first," she said.

Gularvhen's manner became dignified. "As you wish."

Psolilai returned to Kirishnaghar. "Very well," she said, keeping her tone blunt. "Position us at the gravitational pillow. I will be going last."

Kirishnaghar nodded and turned to alter the course of the dirigible.

Psolilai stood at the edge of the basket while Gularvhen packed his pointed hat away and emptied his pockets. The dirigible bucked and bounced as it reached the side of the gravitational blemish. Gularvhen crouched, then leaped—a black spider in the air, circling down, sleeves flapping, sluggish, arms and legs outstretched. Hoss followed, wholly without fear, stretching his legs out from his body so that his profile gave more resistance. Together, the pair spiralled downward.

"Now you," Kirishnaghar said. There was a certain satisfaction in his voice.

Psolilai did not bother to reply or even to look at him, as with eyes shut she launched herself over the side.

Very much like floating. The air was a rose-scented pool, warm, billowing by, not tearing at her hair or her clothes. Something pushed up at her, opposing gravity, something like a vast hand. She opened her eyes. Below her lay purple, red and grey fields: wispy trees like reeds, bubbling ponds, temples and towers of wool. Nothing green. Across this heavenly landscape blew real clouds, obscuring features then revealing them damp and clean.

Below her, Gularvhen pulled in his legs, attaining a vertical posture. With a jolt he landed on his feet. Psolilai did likewise. She found herself grinning from exhilaration. "That wasn't so bad! I can do it once more when we return to the dirigible."

Gularvhen nodded, then checked Hoss for bruises. "We have all survived unscathed," he said. "Let us locate the zri."

They walked away from Thymosfa's fluffy edge. The ground was warm and tacky, and soon their clothes were wet. Shreds of cloud blew through and across them—they would lose sight of one another for a few seconds, before the biting wind revealed all. Realising that she would soon become cold, Psolilai shrugged a cape around her shoulders, then pulled on a hat and a pair of gloves.

"Follow me," said Gularvhen.

"Wait," she called back. Something approaching, trailing white threads . . .

Gularvhen turned towards her, then looked in the same direction. "A group of aerial mushrooms," he said.

"Do you want to investigate?" Psolilai asked.

He shook his head. "We would learn little of use in our present circumstances."

Psolilai watched as the aerial mushrooms floated by, their hyphae sticking to the ground, reducing their speed. They were dark, indicating that they had absorbed dust. On a whim she reached out to grab one as it sailed past her face . . . a small white button on one side, cap split in a few places, gills.

"This one is budding," she said.

Gularvhen walked over, knelt down to make observation easier, then frowned and leaned back amazed. "Fungi growing upon fungi?" he said.

Psolilai looked closer. "It must be a baby."

He took the aerial mushroom and studied it. "Look more closely," he said. "The aerial fruiting body is dark, its gills adnexed, with glittering scales and a smooth margin." He sniffed. "It has an odour of nuts. But the other is pale, smooth margined, with decurrent gills that have a ruddy hue. The flesh is firm, unlike the loose flesh of the other. Clearly it is a different species."

Psolilai shrugged. A feeling here of discovery, but she remained uncertain. "So?" she said.

For a few minutes he ignored her, positioning himself so that he could grab every aerial mushroom in the group as the trailing members passed by, plucking the small fungi, releasing the others, bounding across the yielding land to await the next, and the next. Hoss followed, blowing single trumpet chords. After a few minutes the pair returned. In a bag Gularvhen had collected nine mushrooms.

"Are they unusual?" Psolilai asked.

He indicated that they should sit. "Unique in my experience," he replied. "Do you not comprehend? Mushrooms dispense nature's wisdom—they comprise a natural ecology across the planet. But these mushrooms we found growing upon fungi of a different species. Logic suggests they should provide knowledge of the knowledge system itself."

Now Psolilai understood. "How fascinating!"

Gularvhen turned to watch the receding mushrooms, then studied those in the bag. "These nine are metafungi. We must be careful.

Because we cannot guess their potency we shall brew tea from them, rather than eat them raw." He paused, again gazing east. "Why should they appear at this time? There lies a mystery I did not dream of. But perhaps they have simply come here to greet us."

Worried about his musings, Psolilai set up the can and heater as they had in the Sonic Forest, while he laid the mushrooms out side by side, muttering under his breath as if to sleeping babes. He caressed them with the back of his fingers, testing their texture, examining their hyphae, which were delicate as cobwebs, poking their gills, plucking one gill only—fingernails like pincers—and smelling it.

"I have never come across this species in my life," he said.

Psolilai regarded him. An otherworldly gleam in his eye reminded her of the boy at the Church of the Parasol Cap, whose eyes twinkled when he thought important people were paying him attention. Here, Gularvhen was tense, thrilled. Like a boy.

"You must take care," Psolilai said. "They might be poisonous."

"The era of poisonous fungi is long departed," he replied.

Psolilai felt overwhelmed by this remark, so assured, yet so extraordinary. She wiped tears from her eyes.

"You weep not for sadness but for joy," said Gularvhen, without looking up.

In silence she watched his preparations, as tenderly he dropped the mushrooms into the boiling water. He turned down the heat. "Now we wait five minutes."

No word was spoken during this period. Then Gularvhen stirred his long limbs, swirled the fluid in the can and poured it into two mugs, one of which he handed to Psolilai. An odour arose from the brew redolent of spring spaces, of dew, of morning. . . tugging at her memories, fleeting glimpses pale green, of nature. Hoss began to create music: drifting chords, rich, reedy, almost heavy in timbre. She drank.

Knowledge arrived in her brain, half remembered dream, images returning; deja-vu. Return to her mental landscape. She realised that the fungal ecology, from yeasts and moulds, through morels and truffles, to mushrooms, toadstools and boletus, to all the larger, more frightening growths that swamped dead vegetation, were aspects of nature, a global system of memory and inspiration, a repository, yet also a rock, and a hint of the soil that rock would become.

169

The understanding of process receded. Cold, damp face, tired body. The bitter taste of mushroom tea on the back of her tongue.

The music faded into sighing breeze. She bit her lip. She had acquired this wisdom already. And Hoss moved his head, so that one pale eye was fixed upon her.

They discussed what they had learned as they headed for the interior of Thymosfa, but Psolilai, immersed in her own memories, said as little as possible, hoping Gularvhen would not take her reticence personally. But he seemed happy, talking more to himself than to her.

They knew the zri were close when strange sounds began to infiltrate the moaning wind, voices almost, deep and bassy, speaking half words that slipped in and out of understanding. From the pale and fluffy trees ahead emerged a pillow of grey, the hint of a human face in its centre, floating down towards them.

"Visitors," said a basso voice.

Psolilai reminded herself that this was a machine copying human interaction. Yet the welcome rang true. "Hello," she replied, giving their names, then adding, "We have come to Thymosfa for knowledge. Are there any here understanding the chemical load of bad snow?"

"Who wants to know?"

Psolilai stood forward. "I do."

"I can tell you," said the zri. By now it was only yards away, a creature of foaming chemicals laced with innumerable nerve-nets, which bored into the electronic substrate of Thymosfa from end to end. Much of Thymosfa was these conscious machines.

Psolilai said, "Tell me of the chemicals that rise from the western sea and impregnate snow flakes."

"Ocean is a pit of pollution," said the zri, "and although its capacity is immense, it is finite. Within its every current lie substances that cannot be degraded by natural means. These substances are products of the manufacturing ecosystem—they exist on the metaphoric level. They attack according to status, carrying information, so that they can transform according to purpose, utility, or even artistic whim. Self-organising, they are now too powerful for nature. On the water cycle they hitch a ride, arising from ocean, making landfall, dropping out of clouds."

"Do they drop on you?"

"From their perspective, Thymosfa is low-lying—no rain on us. We tweak gravity so that it is thus."

"How?" asked Psolilai.

"Gravity is merely one of four forces. Like time, of which it is the sibling, it is nothing to fear."

Psolilai nodded.

"We zri do not exist wholly in the macroscopic world. Our perceptions are other."

Gularvhen stepped up to stand beside Psolilai. "Do you have the knowledge you require?" he asked her.

"I think so," she replied.

"Then we can return to the dirigible."

"I will accompany you," said the zri.

Like mist over vellum the zri floated beside them as they returned to the edge of the aerial land. It spoke more of the chemicals that had organised themselves in the ocean, of their groupings, of how they used nanos as sources of energy. By the time they reached the gravitational disturbance, or sculpture as the zri called it, Psolilai's head was filled with names and equations.

Already the dirigible was in sight, Kirishnaghar manoeuvring it so that it lay below the exit zone, which Psolilai could see from the way wisps of cloud moved around it. This long and hallucinatory tube would return her to the dirigible. But she felt more afraid than she had before. Below her lay an expanse of Shohnadwe, the dirigible tiny like a dark spot; the scene worse because cloud between Thymosfa and dirigible accentuated the drop. "I can't do it," she said. "It would be like throwing myself off a mountain."

"It is longer than the way before," Gularvhen admitted, "but the method is exactly the same."

"And we will have to float into the basket. Before, it was just flopping down onto fluffy ground."

"A matter of thrusting out legs or arms, as I did before."

Psolilai felt her limbs grow weak as fright took hold. "I'm not sure I can do it," she repeated.

"Hoss and I will go first," said Gularvhen. "Watch us descend."

"It will be gentle and pleasant," said the zri. "I myself will adjust the relative intensity of the sculpture so that you float through the air like a down feather."

"Thank you," said Psolilai.

Before she knew it, Gularvhen had stepped out into the air. He descended as if sinking into quicksand, smiling up at her. Hoss followed. She knelt at the edge of the zone, but still could not find enough courage to let herself drop. Then the ground shifted and she realised she was sinking. Nothing to hold on to. But she was not falling fast.

The zri face peered down at her and said, "Goodbye."

No chance to make a reply.

The extended descent continued. Gularvhen and Hoss were ahead by a hundred yards or so. Then she noticed a flash to her right. She twisted and saw from the corner of her eye a silhouette heading towards her, fast and slight. The evening sun blinded her—fields of red upon darkness all she could see. But with one hand shielding her eyes she recognised the balloon of the agens.

It was too late to make any adjustment to her fall, the zri out of earshot, almost out of sight, Gularvhen far below. A minute later she saw the agens themselves, clustered at the front of their balloon, staring forward, their crystal whiskers glinting in the light; eager agens ready to act. Psolilai twisted in the air to find a better position from which to defend herself, but motion in this treacle gravity was too strange for her to make any progress. She rolled and tumbled like a dead leaf. The agens closed. Now they were no more than a hundred yards away.

Gularvhen saw them. He shouted, "Come on, Psolilai! You are almost there!"

But the gravitational field was set. Psolilai tried to swim, to dive, but the speed of her descent was fixed. Below her, Kirishnaghar, who had also seen the danger, manoeuvred the dirigible so that he was below their line of descent.

Psolilai faced a hopeless task. When the agens were within shouting distance she yelled, "Go away, leave me alone!"

They acted as soon as she spoke. Using catapults they fired missiles at her, the first few missing, before one hit. The missiles were sticky, attaching themselves to her leathers. With the dirigible still a hundred yards below her she found herself carrying a dozen irregular objects, inert, yet heavy with the menace of transformation, of attack. She tried to pull them off, but they stuck tight, and as the agen balloon passed within a few yards of her a clear fluid spurted out of nozzles at its side.

She wriggled, but it was impossible to escape the attack. Horrified, she watched the liquid transform the clinging objects into shining tools: blades, hooks, pincers and borers. A sudden mental image of her body torn apart by this fiendish arsenal.

"Help!" she screamed.

She looked down to see Gularvhen and Hoss reach out for the dirigible basket and climb in, Gularvhen first, then Hoss, aided by the two men. The agens were retreating, staring at her, transfixed. She whimpered, twisted and tried to brush the fluid off, but like jelly it clumped and covered the objects, until the process of creation was complete, the fluid was consumed, and a shower of metal implements dropped from her to fall like nightmare confetti. She wriggled, turned, pulled herself towards the dirigible by reaching out for one of the fog lamps. She could have sworn it blinked. But then she was rolling down one side, reaching out for Gularvhen's hand, being pulled into the basket.

Gasping for breath, she got to her feet and looked out. The agens were already flying away. This time her clothes and her jewelry were untouched.

"Why do they attack so?" asked Kirishnaghar.

Psolilai shrugged, too shaken to reply.

Gularvhen watched the leisurely retreat. "It was not necessarily an attack," he observed. "The event was similar to the earlier one, when a manufactured fluid transformed artificial objects. This time they supplied the objects, but the principle is identical."

"Whatever it was," Psolilai said, "they want me to suffer."

Gularvhen looked Psolilai up and down. "My feeling is that they know exactly what they are doing."

"I do not," Psolilai replied, annoyed.

Silence.

With brisk hand signals Kirishnaghar altered the dirigible controls. "We will fly low," he declared, "and I will seek out a landing site in Shohnadwe. Then you can complete your task."

Psolilai studied the sky. Clouds building. But the thrill that passed through her body was tempered with apprehension.

173

12

BUT IT COULD COALESCE INTO WISDOM

psolilai stalked the haven every night, deep in thought, for she found that nocturnal existence helped her to think. She loved the gloom, but now daybreak was coming, Mahandriana standing grey against the pink glow of dawn, and she walked towards the nearest staircase arch. She needed warmth, a dry bed.

"Good morning," said a voice behind her.

She turned to see Dezisscrine.

The agen continued, "I have been watching you ever since my men happened to mention your speech at the Black Moth Inn. You are a Gaian, then?"

psolilai kept quiet. It appeared that her hypothesis was correct: the agen knew little or nothing of her because she had pulled her own records from the wreality representations. She needed to know more about this powerful tactic.

"Are you listening to me?" Dezisserine asked. "I know nature provides well for certain people. You like mushrooms, no?"

"You jest."

"Listen to what I have to say, psolilai. My men—my human men—tell me we have captured you before. I have checked my plans. I suspect you to have performed some cunning deed in your attempt to thwart me, but I will continue. I will have my information."

"Information," psolilai scoffed. "What you need is knowledge, and from that wisdom."

"Then I will have my wisdom, if I have to squeeze it myself from your brains."

psolilai turned. She felt sure enough of herself to say, "I will speak

174

with you this evening. I'm too tired to argue now, I've been up all night. Meet me at the Black Moth Inn—if, agen, you dare."

And it made no reply. She had the upper hand! In its desire for knowledge it had to bow to her. She felt power, then, a strength that before had eluded her.

Sleeping during the day, she returned with Metaxain to the Black Moth Inn that evening, but Dezisserine was not among the throng. They drank and watched the crowds. psolilai found herself disappointed, but then she strolled outside, to see the agen standing in the shadow of a side door. It stepped forward.

"I am glad to see you," it said.

"I thought you had not arrived."

"You did not expect me to mix with the masses, did you?"

psolilai felt some of her bile return. "I suppose that would be a little risky for one such as you. I can't be the only one who has guessed."

"Others know."

psolilai muttered a curse to herself, then said, "What happened to them, I wonder?"

Dezisserine sat on a window sill beside her. "Join me," it said, patting the ledge at its side. She did, letting her legs dangle above the ground.

"Are you an agent of the Analyticate?" she asked.

"I am an agen of the Analyticate," it answered. "A rather different thing."

"Then we are opposed."

"Not necessarily—"

psolilai interrupted, "But you told me you wanted to develop a strategy to deal with nature—"

"Patience! I have completed stage one of a process, injecting you. My records are lost, however, and I am having to cope with . . . amnesia."

"You cannot expect me to care."

"But consider the possibilities," Dezisserine insisted. "It seems that a bridge may exist between the natural and the manufactured worlds. That intrigues you, no? I want to develop a strategy that means neither world can dominate the other. The natural world may be in the ascendant, whereas through others, agens for example, the manufactured world hopes for dominance. If I can make both sides see the other, what then?"

psolilai felt no enthusiasm. "How can I trust a being who works for the Analyticate, captures its victims and injects them against their will?"

"I work for nobody. I work for communication, for a time when you will be able to appreciate wrealities, and I a mushroom."

"It will never happen."

"It already is. Can you guess what I injected you with? A mixture of wreality and the fungal substrate of this haven. You felt the effects, you know them. I can guess them because of the discrepancy between my experience and that of others. So, psolilai, what about it?"

psolilai shook her head and looked away. "Nature is not in the ascendant, and you know it. This is all lies and tricks."

"Either way it is time to move on to the next stage."

psolilai, who had been tapping her feet against the wall, froze. "What do you mean by that?"

"You are special in some way. Do not deny it. You are the only one I know who has eaten of mushroom and wreality. My next experiment I hope will allow me to accept the wisdom of nature. If so, I have my bridge, for you will be able to ingest wreality wisdom and I that of the mushroom."

176

"You are mad," psolilai declared, "quite mad. The two ecosystems are forever sundered. And do you seriously expect me to believe you have some altruistic motive for all this? You are a creature of 3Machines and nothing more. Now don't trouble me again."

Dezisserine jumped off the sill. "You cannot escape me," it said. "I will do as I will."

psolilai sneered, "You are a monster."

"I am a scientist."

"You are a tyrant."

Dezisserine strolled into the shadows of the passage beside the Inn. Then a faint whisper. "I am an explorer."

"You are a fool."

Laughter in reply, chilling laughter that babbled then faded, leaving psolilai sweating cold on the window sill. She jumped off and ran into the Black Moth Inn, but then decided to return to the upper levels, for she wanted to prowl some of the galleries she had not yet seen. No agents lay in wait at the Inn of Twilight Ratiocination, where Gularvhen was yawning, a goblet of mulled wine on the table beside him.

She chatted to him for half an hour, then let him retire. And then she was out, and free.

There was chaos at the Inn of Twilight Ratiocination next morning. Meeting Dyeeth Boolin on the stairs, psolilai asked, "What's all the commotion?"

"Somebody has stolen Hoss."

Immediately psolilai ran around to the stable, where she found Kirishnaghar by the door, and Gularvhen inside, his back turned to her.

"What happened?" she asked Kirishnaghar.

In reply he gestured at Gularvhen. psolilai entered the stable, aware that Gularvhen's shoulders were shaking. He was weeping. She hugged him as best she could, her head on his chest, saying nothing. He would shake for a few moments, go quiet, then start again.

At length he was able to mutter, "My beautiful Hoss has gone."

"We'll find him," psolilai said, blindly optimistic.

Gularvhen made no reply. But then a thought occurred to her, and she was struck dumb while its implications formed in her mind. "I know who did it," she said. "Dezisserine. That agen is experimenting with people. It wants to acquire mushroom knowledge. It must know about Hoss."

Gularvhen turned his damp and flushed face to her. "Dezisserine?"

"We can save the day. We have to find the agen's chambers—especially the cell in which I was injected. If only I could return to the lines of wrealities and pluck out the images of Hoss . . ."

Dyeeth Boolin spoke from the doorway. "So you are not averse to using artificial means when the need arises," he observed.

Angered, psolilai turned to face him. "Gularvhen is upset. That's no way to talk."

"Is it not, my dear?"

"I don't think you're being very helpful," psolilai complained. "This is not the time for petty moral arguments."

Dyeeth Boolin's insouciant look told her what he thought of that.

After a pause for thought psolilai said, "Very well, we will use natural means. Shamen can call upon nature to provide them with knowledge.

We will ask my good friend Metaxain. Stay here, all of you. I shall return shortly."

Gularvhen reached out to grasp her arm. "Thank you," he said.

psolilai ran down staircases to the Divan Inn, where she found Metaxain emerging from a drunken slumber. Dragging him back to the Inn she took him to the stable and explained the problem. "We will give you mushrooms plucked from trees, then you must use arboreal knowledge to follow Dezisserine's track."

"There are very few trees so high," Metaxain pointed out.

"We have to try," she insisted.

"Well, I won't need mushrooms. A good Westside aura is all I need."

psolilai said, "This stable is where Hoss was housed. I think he will have been taken up to the Complex Levels. Try and sense which route the thief took."

Metaxain looked uncertain.

"We must try," psolilai urged, glancing at Dyeeth Boolin. "If you fail, we will try other ways. But Hoss must be returned."

He seemed flustered by her intensity. For a minute he wandered around the stable, as if taking the air, before he walked outside and began brushing his fingers against the various trees of the garden.

"Go inside now," psolilai ordered the others.

Led by Gularvhen, they trooped off, Ilyi Koomsy bringing up the rear. A minute later a starling appeared on the gable end of the roof, and psolilai knew it was the mallead. She scowled up at the bird.

"I feel something," Metaxain announced.

She ran over and clasped him about the waist. "What?" she asked. "Do you see Hoss?"

He was in a light trance. "I feel through the roots of trees on this level . . . I feel two of them, the horse and . . . "

"Yes? Yes?"

"Another being who seems distant to my senses . . . can't quite feel it . . . they're ascending side by side . . . up and up . . . I'm losing them—"

"No! Concentrate, Metaxain. I'll support you."

His eyes closed and his head drooped, so that his chin was upon his chest. "They're in the Adverse Levels . . . now the Complex. Few roots here . . . Ah! My silver birch. I have them! I see the place."

psolilai hugged him, then kissed him when he opened his eyes.

He took a deep breath. "You were right," he whispered. "The agen stole him."

"That agen," psolilai declared, "has a plan that we must stop." She hesitated, looked him up and down. "Did you feel all that without . . . " She was not sure how to phrase it. ". . . without drums or mushrooms or anything?"

He appeared embarrassed. "It was only a mild trance," he explained.

They returned to the Inn. psolilai clapped her hands together and announced, "I am going to bed now, but tonight at dusk we will assemble a search party. Me, Metaxain, Gularvhen and Kirishnaghar. You felins had better stay here in case more agents of the Analyticate arrive. Kirishnaghar, ignore the Sky Level today and explore the Complex Levels as best you can. You will be our guide. But you will need to be in position by the hour before dusk."

He made a shallow bow. "Very well, psolilai."

"Any questions?"

None. They watched in silence as she climbed the stairs. As she sank into sleep she heard their voices, speaking low, as if in secret parley.

Dusk, and they ate a light supper of fried vegetables and honey before preparing their equipment and leaving the Inn. In a melancholic voice Dyeeth Boolin wished them good fortune. "Hmmm, I do not suppose you will have much luck," he remarked.

They climbed to the balloon gallery without difficulty, spotting the blue fog lamps of their own balloon, hurrying over, then flying up to the Complex Levels. psolilai gestured at the galleries around her. "I don't suppose you saw Dezisserine today?" she asked the mallead.

He shook his head.

psolilai turned to Metaxain. "Then we follow you," she said, adding, "Kirishnaghar, let us know if Metaxain leads us into areas you think dangerous."

"There is no safe area here," Kirishnaghar replied. "The Analyticate shields these galleries from the populace with good reason."

Gularvhen grunted, "If we knew what that reason was we might progress."

"Nonsense," psolilai retorted. "I myself explored some of these galleries when looking for the Brain of Han."

Gularvhen tutted to himself, then muttered, "She has an answer for everything."

psolilai ignored him. Metaxain led them into a narrow tunnel from which small stalactites hung, before they entered a large, pale cavern. It was devoid of features. "There is much space up here," Metaxain murmured.

"Lead on," said psolilai.

There was nobody about. Unchallenged, they wandered corridors and galleries for half an hour before Metaxain slowed, then stopped. "Here is familiar," he said, closing his eyes. "The agen brought Hoss here." He opened his eyes and pointed to the mouth of a tunnel, narrow, but high. "Through there," he said. "It leads to the chambers of the agen."

psolilai cast her mind back to events following her incarceration in the cell of Dezisserine. "I think this is one of the galleries I ran through after my escape," she said. "Did Dezisserine lead Hoss down that tunnel?"

Metaxain nodded.

psolilai turned to the mallead. "Scout the tunnel," she said. "If you see Hoss, return at once."

They huddled in an alcove while Kirishnaghar was away. Ten anxious minutes passed. psolilai heard the wind howling through distant galleries, felt a thrum in the substrate of the haven through her feet. She heard no voices. Then she blinked, and Kirishnaghar stood before her.

"I have seen both Hoss and Dezisserine," came the report.

Gularvhen stifled a cry of hope.

"Where?" psolilai asked.

"There is a long, narrow chamber set with open windows, in which I saw them."

"How does Hoss look?" asked Gularvhen, worry plain on his face.

"Exactly as before. The agen was at peace. I saw no signs of anxiety. All you have to do now is wait for the agen to leave. The windows are large, and I believe Hoss could squeeze out."

"We have no time to wait," said psolilai. "Besides, I have to speak with Dezisserine."

"I cannot go," said Kirishnaghar. "Some agens . . . they can smell one such as me."

psolilai nodded. "I will go with Metaxain," she said. "If you hear me cry like a screech owl, run away, for that will be the signal for danger. Otherwise, await us here."

Gularvhen grabbed her wrist. "Would it not be safer to watch and wait? Dezisserine may capture you again."

"He will not," psolilai replied, confidently. "We two have passed that stage."

With that, psolilai led Metaxain to the chamber described by Kirishnaghar. At the first window she surveyed the ground before her. The agen was studying vials of liquid, sitting on a chair, Hoss quiet, head bowed, standing at the far wall. A hundred wrealities lay on shelves, while on tables in the centre of the chamber lay devices damp and scarlet-stained, as if signalling the aftermath of a post-mortem. psolilai shivered. She squeezed Metaxain's hand, kissed him on the cheek, then leaped through the window.

"Dezisserine," she called.

The agen turned without haste, as if unconcerned. "psolilai," it responded, looking up and down the chamber. "What are you doing here?"

"I have come to claim Hoss, who you stole."

"On your own? I think not."

psolilai bit her tongue. She could hardly say that she was not alone. "You are a vile sort," she said, striding over to Hoss, who raised his head and fixed her with one white eye. "What have you done to him?"

"Nothing. I have listened to his music."

psolilai stroked Hoss, confirming to her satisfaction that he was unmarked. "You do not understand music," she said, putting all the scorn that she felt into her voice.

Dezisserine stood. "Your inability to see the truth of this matter becomes irksome," it said. "I hope to acquire natural wisdom, thanks to the music of Hoss, who I suspect is able to select for various types of knowledge."

psolilai felt that something she held dear was being invaded. "You can't," she exclaimed. "It's impossible!"

"Face facts," came the response. "Nature is not beholden to you. Nature is available to all those with the desire, perhaps with the vision to see. I am one such."

"You are a base machine," she retorted.

"I am a conscious entity with morals and ethical purpose. The fact that you do not approve of my methods is irrelevant. You, of all people, should appreciate the need for diversity."

"There is diversity and there is perversity," psolilai retorted. "You are unnatural. You cannot appreciate nature's wisdom."

Dezisserine pointed to the vials on the table before him. "These contain mixtures of wreality and haven substrate. Hoss understands this. Buoyed on his music I hope to receive my first natural thoughts, faint, yes, and ephemeral—but if I succeed, my case is proven. Now all I have to do is decide which of these is the best mixture to use."

"You are a monster," whispered psolilai.

"I am a shaman," it replied.

Shocked by this statement psolilai took a step backwards, too appalled to speak. This was sacrilege. She said, "I have seen real shamen. They are a noble school, supporting nature, working against the predations of the manufacturing ecosystem. You cannot possibly claim kinship."

"But what is a shaman?" Dezisserine answered. "One able to use secret and intricate methods to achieve ecstasy and oneness with the environment. Our environment is bipolar, natural and manufactured. So it will always be. My achievement is to build a bridge where before there was an abyss."

"You? A shaman?"

"There are two types amongst agens, those called assemblers and those called metamorphosers. Shamen agens are rare, but they exist, feeling their way along the interstices between wreality and machine, intoxicated on wreality juice."

A voice from behind psolilai. "Dezisserine, are you an assembler or a metamorphoser?"

psolilai span around to see Metaxain standing at the window.

Again, the agen seemed unconcerned. It replied, "I am neither. That is why I have been able to conceive of and follow this line of research."

"You are a mutant," psolilai said, "neither whiskered nor with flies."

"I am no mutant. But I am exceedingly rare. Just as you are, no?"

psolilai said nothing. Events were speeding out of control. Metaxain hopped through the window and strode up to stand beside her. In a calm, clear voice he said, "I'm a shaman. Are you like me?"

The agen stared at him as if engaging in telepathic evaluation. "Not like you," it said. "But perhaps like the shamen of Shohnadwe." It turned its head to look at psolilai. "Of whom I know something, if not so much as you."

psolilai felt afraid. She felt tarnished by what this creature had said. With nothing to say, she kept silent.

"What would the people of Mahandriana say if they knew an agen ruled them?" Metaxain asked. "You're banned from this haven. Your place is the wilderness of Urbis Morpheos."

"I rule nobody," Dezisserine replied. As if tired, it sat in its chair. "Let me tell you two something," it continued. "When your company arrived here a change passed across Mahandriana. Analytical knowledge stopped falling down from the Owl Palace—"

"Analytical knowledge?" psolilai interjected. "There is no such thing! Where are the wrealities to disseminate this knowledge to the people? Where the council?"

"Shhh," Metaxain said, putting his arm around her shoulder.

"Knowledge falls," continued the agen in a cold voice. "It comes on clouds of spores, psolilai. Spores are the means by which Mahandriana exerts its unique effect on all sentient creatures within its sphere of influence. But the spores have stopped. The analyses of 3Machines have stopped. You will be wondering why? As do I. There is change afoot in Mahandriana, and I believe it has something to do with your company." A gesture towards Hoss. "There stands one possible reason, a being the like of which we have never seen before. Or perhaps it is you, Metaxain, or you, psolilai. But I know nothing either of 3Machines or of rulership. I am a shaman, independent, an outcast from my tribe, forced to live alone on wits and little else. This is my home and I want to know why it is changing. Now you understand more, perhaps."

"But who is 3Machines?" Metaxain asked. "A human woman?"

"So I believe," Dezisserine replied.

psolilai heard the ambiguity of this answer, and she felt sick at the sight of the agen. She turned to look into Metaxain's eyes. She felt like crying.

Metaxain shrugged. "Perhaps Dezisserine is correct," he said.

psolilai felt betrayed, and yet she knew her feeling had little foundation. But she had to deny that fact for a while longer. She could not stop her opposition to Dezisserine. So she whispered, "You too?"

Metaxain glanced at the agen. "Like it says, we must face facts."

psolilai shook her head. "Fetch Hoss," she said. "We're leaving."

Metaxain walked over to where the horse stood. Dezisserine followed for a few paces, then stopped, its back turned to psolilai. She glanced at the vials. Temptation. She took four of them, one between each pair of fingers on her right hand so they would not clink together, then wrapped them in a kerchief and put them in her pocket.

From the other end of the chamber Metaxain said, "I don't think he wants to come."

Dezisserine turned to face psolilai. "You see? He has not been maltreated."

"Only stolen," she replied in a wounded voice. "You said you were an agen of the Analyticate. That's why you stole him."

"I follow the general tenets of analytical-tendency, that is all. It does not mean I support 3Machine's methods."

psolilai cursed under her breath. Her face twisted. "You have an answer for everything!" she yelled.

"Take the horse," the agen replied. "My experiments are complete—I have many recordings. When I reach my conclusion my men will come to escort you back here . . . wherever you happen to be staying."

"Your men will not lay a finger on me," psolilai replied.

And so they left. Dezisserine sat in its chair as if content, watching Hoss clamber over the window and out into the tunnel. They hurried away. psolilai felt her anger returning, and when they reached the alcove she said nothing, letting Metaxain lead them back and do all the explaining.

That night she prowled the galleries around the Inn of Twilight Ratiocination, alert for motion in the shadows, paranoid almost, aware that any human men and women here might be agents of the Analyticate. 3Machines had to be exposed. Grow, silver birch, grow!

Time seemed short to her. Dezisserine had said that something was wrong in the Owl Palace. What could that be? Well . . . she had unlinking skills, she had marvellous eyesight and she loved the night, so she could collect wrealities and suck out their juice . . .

Two goals, then: to erase herself from Dezisserine's wrealities and to discover what was wrong with the analytical-tendencies. She fingered the four vials in her pocket. They represented potential.

A day passed of unrestful slumber. Her mind was too active for sleep. That night she ignored supper and departed for the lower galleries, where, solitary like a wraith, she collected wrealities from soft earth. She knew wild wrealities had a special destination, not incinerated like the rest of the manufactured debris, instead transported to the Owl Palace. These would not arrive at that destination.

Another day passed. She ignored her friends, refused to speak to Metaxain when he arrived at the Inn. Alone in her room, night fallen, she took one of the vials and studied the rosy fluid inside.

She opened the top. It smelled of brand new plastic.

Indecision took her. Aware that she was using artificial methods, she despised herself for being tempted, but she had to discover the hidden truths of the haven. She tipped the liquid to her mouth, then cursed and stoppered the vial. Then opened it again. She did not know what to do. These samples might not be orally active. She went to her door and locked it, then returned to her bed.

She drank the liquid in one go, coughing when it seared her throat.

Hazy seconds passed. The effect, if any, would be slower than before, since then Dezisserine had injected her.

She waited.

Then she felt her mind slip.

A number of dark motes emerging in the centre of her vision, elongating into lines . . .

Moving forward at speed, more motes forming ahead . . .

Lines become slabs, washes of colour, hurtling into oblivion, speed blurring colours into formless haze . . .

Hanging in a bath of scintillating fragments, a turbid pool where every flake is a number, drowning, unable to find a surface, no sense of gravity, taste of metal in her mouth making a shiver run up her spine . . .

The pool striking her mind, flicking white to grey to blue at random, each change a thump in the teeth . . .

185

Turning, to face a deep ocean of numbers . . .

A glimpse of blackness, drifting towards it, detail visible behind departing veils of numbers, lines of scarlet, blobs, and pulsating ganglions lilac sheened . . .

She had arrived!

The trip was possible.

Power!

There was the distant owl, there the lines of wrealities forming a network, there the hook-billed birds flying in frantic motion.

And she like a master strategist, able to pick and choose. . .

psolilai began her work. She flew low over the oscillating plates emerging from the ganglions, stopping when she saw her own face, sinking down, pulling out the plates with fingers like talons, discarding them, then moving on to the next one. In this way she erased herself from the networks. It did not take long.

But discovering hidden truths was more difficult. She looked for the Owl Palace, she looked for the scarlet hog and its owl kin, she looked for sources that might charge spores with analyses, she even looked for Dezisserine, but she found nothing. And then her sense of motion began to falter, as another reality imposed itself.

Exhausted, falling back . . .

Floating . . .

This world fading to be replaced by . . .

A dark ceiling. psolilai awoke, or seemed to, her eyes focussing with difficulty on the room around her. She remembered that she was at the Inn of Twilight Ratiocination.

Three vials left. But it occurred to her as she lay on her bed that she might be able to synthesize her own fluid. She knew of monoamine oxidase inhibitors, she collected wrealities, she could collect samples of haven substrate. Therefore she had access to great power.

She grinned. Perhaps wrealities were not so bad.

13

CEREBELLUM TO FRONTAL CORTEX

T he weather became unpleasant. The dirigible made south-west on
blustery winds, taking them along the coast and into the ancient
district of Shohnadwe. Kirishnaghar was unable to see the ground most
of the time and had to navigate by guesswork. After much fruitless
cursing he decided to risk a descent under the cloudbase; he required
navigation points, hints if nothing else. He promised it would be safe.
They flew at a height of a few hundred yards as bad snow whirled
around them.

Gularvhen pointed and cried out, "There, through the storm, a
cluster of orange lanthorns. Can you see?"

Psolilai saw the lights. "Over there, Kirishnaghar," she said, grasping
his shoulder. "Land beside the lanthorns."

"It appears to be the haven of Umadraish," said Kirishnaghar,
though he sounded uncertain. "We had better land outside the haven,
then discover what manner of people live there."

"Don't bother with that," Psolilai replied, "you're from this land, so
you can lead us."

"Set the dirigible down inside the haven," Gularvhen added.

"I am not of that haven," Kirishnaghar insisted. "Despite your enthusiasm, we will land outside. The shamen of Shohnadwe are aloof, even
threatening."

Psolilai thought this unhelpful. "You don't seem threatening," she
remarked.

His tone cooled further. "You will require a translator if you are to
progress with your task."

"You mean we will require—"

"I mean you."

Impasse. Psolilai glanced at Gularvhen, before saying, "There seems to be a difficulty."

Gularvhen looked steadily into her eyes. "We will land," he said, "then you and I, and Kirishnaghar if he so wishes, will walk into Umadraish. I foresee no danger. And some folk here will speak our tongue."

Psolilai agreed to this plan with a single nod of her head.

Landing at the edge of a nanoactive bog, they dragged the basket away from the slime before its active constituents used the dirigible as raw material. After this, Psolilai found herself in a foul temper. Gularvhen mounted Hoss and rode off towards the lanthorns, now visible as a collection a few thousand strong lining a natural bowl. Quite a large haven. Kirishnaghar did not follow. Psolilai stomped across the squelching ground, following the path of the horse, which she knew would be a safe route through the charred and splintered slum terraces. She said nothing, nor turned to look back. Gloom surrounded her.

188 Night fell as they reached the edge of the haven. Psolilai was able to pick out buildings, streets and squares, all lit by the ubiquitous lanthorns, which shone fiery through settling mist. There came a murmur of voices on the breeze, and a yeasty smell suggesting ale-houses.

Psolilai shrugged. "So they're human here," she muttered. "We'll find shelter, then tomorrow I will use the Constructor. Then perhaps we can fly out of this appalling weather."

The haven was extensive. Streets broad, buildings low, bushes and trees growing free, moss on the doorsteps and under the eaves, a place that Psolilai found generated peace within her through the strength of its natural aura. Bad snow shed by sharply angled rooves. Yet she saw no defences, no wall or river, nor armoured citizens tramping the streets to root out manufactured decay. The smell of burning incense emanated from many houses and she heard relaxed voices, even music, plaintive ballads sung to harp and fretless lute.

Heavy bootsteps sounded ahead, and a figure emerged from the mist. Psolilai stopped under a lanthorn, then took a few steps ahead of Hoss.

"Greetings," she said. "How fares the haven of Umadraish?"

It was a woman, tall, wrapped well, looking at her with curiosity. She replied in a language Psolilai had never heard before. Glancing up at Gularvhen she said, "We shall have to find a translator—as Kirishnaghar suggested."

"Indeed we shall."

The woman approached and offered Psolilai a metal tag that she took from around her neck. Then she walked on. Psolilai examined the tag, which on one side was engraved with letters unfamiliar to her, a curvaceous script that looked handmade. "Can you read this?" she said, handing the tag to Gularvhen.

"These first three characters are numbers. I wonder if this is an address?"

"Why would it be an address?"

"The woman must have considered it useful to us, otherwise there would be little point in surrendering it. She understood that we were outsiders."

"Then what do we do?" asked Psolilai.

"Show this tag to people as we make for the centre of the haven."

Gularvhen's theory was correct. The third man who saw the tag smiled broadly, examined their clothes, their hands, and then Hoss, laughed once, then gestured for them to follow him. He led them along a street lit orange by a hundred lanthorns, a thoroughfare along which many people walked. Psolilai was struck by their relaxed manner—none of the tension of Theeremere. Some stopped to stare at Gularvhen and Hoss, but most were too drunk or wrapped up in their own affairs to notice strangers. Eventually the man stopped by a house and opened the front door. Psolilai compared the tag with the writing over the door of the house. Identical.

Gularvhen dismounted, and they entered. It seemed to be an open house, though not an inn. Half a dozen people sat in a common room before a fire of incense coals; fragrance of burning gum. The oldest man stood up when he noticed the newcomers, his joints clacking.

"Hello . . . you're not from Aishiscooh, are you?" he said as he approached.

Psolilai could smell alcohol on his breath. "No," she gushed, "and thank you very much for coming forward. We're not from Aishiscooh, or this haven, either."

The old man frowned. "This is Aishiscooh."

Psolilai had assumed that she was in the haven of Umadraish. "I see!" she said, embarrassed.

Gularvhen walked forward and said, "Good evening—to all of you who understand me."

Psolilai showed the old man the tag. "Ah," he said, "I know who gave you that. A kind gesture. She saw you adrift in this haven and helped you come here."

Psolilai smiled, gave a small laugh. She felt uneasy. "Why does she wear her own address around her neck?" She knew she was blushing, now.

The old man said something in his own tongue that made his friends laugh. Suddenly the atmosphere changed. A relaxation, the others generating a subliminal hum of chatter, tumblers clinking.

The old man took them to one side. "This is in fact the house of her lover," he explained. "Tags like this are a common gift amongst the romantically inclined. So, you're from Theeremere. What can we do to make you comfortable?"

"We thought this was Umadraish," Psolilai said.

He shook his head. "That haven lies twenty leagues away, down a long road lined with concrete statues. This is Aishiscooh. I am Helwelusa."

They all sat on a couch. "First," Psolilai said, "I must thank you again for taking us in. This is my companion Gularvhen. His horse is outside."

"Tied to a tree," Gularvhen added. "Will he be safe?"

"Of course. Here we respect all things fungal."

Gularvhen jerked back as if electrically shocked, and Psolilai, though she had guessed a little of the nature of Hoss, nonetheless found herself stunned. Silence settled over them. She froze, unable to speak.

Helwelusa seemed unconcerned, saying, "I smell your horse on your clothes."

Psolilai decided to ignore the moment. In a rush she said, "We're here on a special task, that I plan to undertake on the Shohnadwe coast, perhaps tomorrow, if the weather... oh, the weather doesn't matter. Really, all we need is shelter for the night, perhaps some food if that's possible."

Helwelusa said, "Here you are far from the coast, twelve leagues as the mind flies. You'd be better off walking up to Eoshoomah, twenty leagues north-east."

So they had been blown off course, away from the coast. Concerned, Psolilai glanced at Gularvhen. Why had Kirishnaghar made so many mistakes in his navigation? It was as if he was as new to Shohnadwe as they were.

Gularvhen said, "Psolilai, you need to be at the coast. We should reach Eoshoomah tomorrow in the dirigible."

Psolilai bit her lower lip. "What of Kirishnaghar?"

"We will leave him tonight. He has made his choice."

With their plan agreed they were shown a room containing bunk beds, in which they made themselves comfortable. Outside, the storm crashed on.

Next morning they discovered that Kirishnaghar's choice was to fly away.

At the nanoactive bog Psolilai and Gularvhen cast about for clues, watched by Helwelusa, but all they found was the score in the slime caused by their landing. Frustration overwhelmed Psolilai, and she struck the ground with a stick, before throwing it into the nearest pool.

191

Helwelusa approached her. "Your companion has unexpectedly departed?"

"Yes," Psolilai replied. "But why?"

Gularvhen said, "I confess I see no motive other than blithe whim."

"I knew he would cause trouble the second I saw him," muttered Psolilai. Guilt consumed her. Gularvhen still did not know who owned the dirigible . . .

Helwelusa led them away, taking one arm each in his own arms. "This isn't a disaster," he said in a cheery voice. "I myself will guide you to Eoshoomah. It's only a two day walk."

Psolilai tried to sound grateful. "But what then? Here, we are seventy leagues from Theeremere, with Midwinter only days away."

"There are methods," Helwelusa said. "Allow me the luxury of taking pity upon you both! We shamen are sighted folk. We understand."

But Psolilai could not suppress her bitterness. "I want to understand what happened last night beside the bog."

Helwelusa chuckled. "Not a difficult task."

Gularvhen was interested. "How would you accomplish it?"

"A brief shamanic flight into the recesses of nature."

"I should like to see that."

Helwelusa shook his head. "You would only see from the outside."

"For me, that is sometimes enough."

Helwelusa gave Gularvhen a penetrating glance. "In that case," he said.

They returned to the common room, which now lay empty, bathed in the musky after-scent of dying coals. Helwelusa hobbled away, then returned with a tray upon which were set bowls of food; soup, greens, bread so fresh it steamed, and a whole range of sweet fruits glazed in honey. Nothing like this existed in starving Theeremere.

"You live well," Psolilai remarked.

"Nature provides," Helwelusa answered.

He left them to their meal, then, later, returned with a small box. Sitting opposite them at table he opened it, to reveal toadstools set upright in wooden collars, their caps vermilion with white patches.

"I suspected you would use that species," said Gularvhen.

"Did you?"

Gularvhen nodded. "A peripatetic mycologist, me."

Helwelusa took one toadstool and sniffed it. "Muscimol provides," he whispered. Then he shot them both a glance and indicated chairs with a twitch of his head. "Sit still a while," he said.

They followed his instruction. Psolilai watched him, but she also watched Gularvhen, sure his reactions would be illuminating. Helwelusa bit off, then chewed part of the toadstool cap, before sitting head bowed for half an hour. The silent house creaked. Fading coals hissed in the grate. Psolilai began to feel drowsy.

Sudden rattling sounds. Helwelusa had taken a moon drum from the wall, its circular frame covered tight with yellow animal skin, two bobbles on strings flying in unison. With this instrument he made a rat-tat-tat rhythm that facilitated his expansion into trance. Sounds half sung, half grunted emerged from his mouth as he hopped from foot to foot. Brief minutes passed, and then he sagged, dropped the drum, sat back in his chair. Asleep, maybe. Psolilai sat quiet. Gularvhen had watched all with unwavering concentration, and he also made no move.

At length Helwelusa shifted, raised his head, noticed them. "Above the bog," he said, "I see a great balloon that thumps into the ground, splattering mud. There are people in mist that swirls. Animals come and animals go. My kin are widely scattered, and I am alone . . ."

After a respectful pause Psolilai said, "In which direction did the dirigible fly off?"

"No balloon leaves the bog," Helwelusa replied. "I am the lynx. My sight is perfect. There are comings and goings, a badger, slithering things that are not good to eat . . . and a pair of dire wolves with startling eyes."

"But there must have been—"

Gularvhen raised his hand for silence. He told Psolilai, "The lynx is the totemic animal of the shamen of Aishiscooh. We cannot doubt its sincerity."

Helwelusa nodded. "Balloon comes, yes, but no balloon flies away."

A puzzle, then; but now it was time for rest. Psolilai passed a peaceful night in her bunk, Gularvhen dozing below, with his feet dangling off the foot of the bed and his head rammed against the wall.

193

On the following morning Helwelusa made them breakfast, and then they were out in the streets, out of the haven, heading north-east.

The road was bitter and narrow, often blocked by collapsed houses— haunted by blue mantis machines that they fought off with loud shouting. From the grimy chimneys of those houses still standing came chemical smokes, as the autonomous machines inside them created vile works. Everywhere they smelled sulphurous burning: acid rain turned brick into sand. The pavements were rivers of black muck.

On the evening of the second day they reached Eoshoomah. Westerly winds buffeted them, driving blizzards of bad snow, that on several occasions forced them into temporary halts. The sea was rough. Artificial land to either side of the road heaved with construction, as the bad snow found suitable raw materials and built it into cathedrals of plastic, stone and metal, or deconstructed devices created by other means and reforged them as plains of gleaming steel dotted with plastic trees streamlined against the weather. A morass of manufacture reaching beyond the horizon.

Eoshoomah: streets winding down a steep hill, thick-walled houses set in groups, linked by lane and bridge, a smell of wild garlic, ivy swallowing posts and stones. A harbour. Like Aishiscooh, orange lanthorns were common here. There was bad snow damage, many houses covered in glutinous stone, but the effects were milder than those of Theeremere. However the citizens of this place were not averse to technology, for they used metal communication lines, vehicles like air horses, powered utensils; a mixture Psolilai found confusing.

Helwelusa led them to an isolated house, dark, imposing, surrounded by a garden of dead wood and tree stumps upon which a variety of fungi grew. Gularvhen smiled as he walked through. In the house lived some of the local shamen, one of whom was called Rhaingorol.

"He speaks your tongue," Helwelusa explained after the introductions. "He will look after you during your stay here."

Rhaingorol was also an old man, not so active as Helwelusa and with a sharper, less accommodating temper. However his manners were impeccable. When he heard that they only intended staying a night he said, "Then all is well. You may sleep here. Tomorrow the weather will be foul, and we shall have cakes and camomile tea."

Psolilai glanced at Gularvhen. "I will be on the coast," she said, "but thank you for your offer."

Morning came: fierce winds howling around the house, a sense of foreboding. The bad snow had passed on, but the westerlies were bitter. Psolilai felt sick with anxiety. Until noon they waited, but seeing no improvement in the weather they decided to go outside with the Constructor.

On a map they had been shown a lane leading down to cliffs, a path they followed until, sheltering beside a rock, they could see all the land around them, the sea, the shore, snow-shrouded hills rising up inland. Psolilai brought out the Constructor and looked deep into its surface. The sigils were there, arcane and linked into complex zones of line and intersection. The colour was there, but there was something else, a sheen, perhaps a glitter, that made the artefact seem ready for its deed. The owl, she felt, was within reach. Almost without thought she held the Constructor up in her right hand, the other pressed against naked rock, as if for balance.

"I want this to work," she told herself.

What changed first? Perhaps something invisible to human eye, some constellation of nanos and substances, a simple beginning that through the laws of chaos spiralled into something far greater; or yet a conversion, a regression, a series of reactions against the universal law of entropy forced by the power of the Constructor. Or something beyond the human mind. In Psolilai's eye, a new softness of snow indicated first that something was happening, a hint hardly tangible, yet evident in the way each flake fell; nothing dank now against the air, slapping upon the ground. Real snow; and somehow she knew this was how snow could be. Missing its manufactured freight.

Clouds changing too, thinning, lightening, breaking to show blue, eventually the sun. The sun rose quick, arcing upward, reaching zenith, a long slide into evening, all followed by Psolilai's entranced eyes. All over in minutes.

Sound of an electric sigh, polyphony from a thousand tones, gradually louder, rich, intense, metallic music without rhythm.

And the landscape. The random collage of metal and plastic, device and machine acquired a spattering of brown that spread like blood stains, up hill, through snow and water, encrusted black at the edges, each new section linking up with others so that it all turned brown. Decaying or dead, yet without the sorrow and majesty of natural death; this the failure of something, not its demise. The array of base chemicals built up by the manufacturing ecosystem to exploit the environment was fallen like a pack of cards.

Beside her Gularvhen stood as statue, a black form, cloak blurred, his crooked face raised to the skies, expression a mixture of wonder and fear. Hoss just a smear of ochre with eyes pure white and hooves scintillating from electrostatic current.

Then the world stopped spinning around her, red sun glowing on the horizon, dipping into the sea, a semicircle, a segment, a green flash: dusk. Grey stained cirrus far, far away, turning purple, black. The sea mirrored the luminous sky, like mercury, before fading to sombre grey.

It seemed to Psolilai that she had witnessed a small rebirth of nature, pulling shutters off the face of Gaia.

She shook herself free of reverie. Hoss trotted over to Gularvhen, to nuzzle his shoulder. Gularvhen's clothes showed a patina of dew. It was cold.

She looked across the land in evening's last light. The manufactured crust was indeed brown and failed, chill and lumpy. A moon in clear skies often revealed plains of metal in the fields, but now all was dull, as if burned. Nothing bright or new. This change had been wrought by the Constructor, of that she was sure.

"We have succeeded," she told Gularvhen. "The underlying processes of the manufacturing ecosystem have been altered. Every district east of this place will feel the effects of a new snow."

"Do you believe that is the truth?"

She took a deep breath. "Yes. I'm hungry. Shall we return to the shamen?"

He nodded. "Doubtless supper will be ready."

But Rhaingorol was not so accommodating when they returned. The other shamen gave them unkind glances, and two left the room. Psolilai was anxious to smooth over any problems. "Have we upset your kin?" she asked Rhaingorol.

"We sense a shift in the land," he replied, grumpily. "You strangers must be responsible for it."

Psolilai felt sure enough of her ground to take a stance. "I have not touched nature," she said. "All I did was roll back the manufacturing ecosystem, make a strike against it. Nature will be enhanced, not hurt. There is nothing to worry about."

But Rhaingorol was not impressed with this explanation. They ate a meal of leek soup and bread then retired to the rooms set aside for them. Psolilai's room was a cold chamber, undecorated, furnished with bed and table, one enamelled bowl with soap and a jug of water. She fretted before finding sleep, worrying that she had made some catastrophic error with the Constructor . . .

Waking quickly. Not dreaming.

Somebody in the room.

It was too dark to see. Yet some sense told her she was not alone. The softest hint of breathing at the foot of her bed. She trembled beneath the sheets, unable to move, knowing she should jump up and cry out, or light a lamp. Instead she did nothing.

Then she felt movement at her feet where her clothes lay rumpled. An automatic reaction made her pull her legs up, and then she jumped up and shouted, "Who's that?"

There was a snarl, a flash of gold. She pressed herself against the wall as a shadow bounded towards the door. Another flash of gold, then two yellow lights that winked in and out of existence for the duration of a heartbeat. Something changed in her mind, made her feel anger, the need for action. She leaped out of bed and ran towards the door. Looking left down the corridor outside she saw a bushy tail disappearing into the gloom at the nearest corner. She grabbed her coat, flung it over her shoulders and gave chase, but the beast had already run out through an open door, leaving only freezing air and a trail of footprints.

Rhaingorol appeared from a side door. "What was that?" he asked.

"A thief," she replied. She ran back to her room and lit a lamp, then checked her clothes. The golden artefact remained. She searched the rest of the room, but nothing had been disturbed. Sitting on the edge of her bed she reviewed what had happened, then took out the disk again. When she looked at it edge-on she could see it was half as thick as before.

Two figures at her door, Gularvhen and Rhaingorol.

"What has happened here?" Gularvhen asked her.

"I'm not sure."

She studied the disk. The two surfaces were unchanged, but, although the device felt just as heavy, it was without doubt half as thick.

"The thief was a dire wolf," said Rhaingorol. "I saw its footprints by the door, and I smell its oily coat in the air of this room."

"A wolf?" said Gularvhen.

"Would you be so good as to leave us for a moment?" Psolilai asked Rhaingorol.

He nodded. "I will secure the house."

Gularvhen walked into the room, shutting the door and standing before her. "You have something to confess," he said.

"Yes," Psolilai admitted. "The dirigible . . . I lied about it. Truly, I am sorry. It belongs to Aunt Sukhtaya. The more I consider this whole trip, the more I wonder if there has been a shape-changer in our company."

He sat beside her. "One of the three malleads?"

She nodded. "The one with the smouldering yellow eyes. I saw them flicker as it stole . . . but what did it steal? The Constructor? Part of it?"

"I have no doubt that Sukhtaya is behind much of our difficulty, but thinking back even further I recall the two beings who rescued us from bad snow near Theeremere. Could they have been malleads?"

"Not impossible."

Gularvhen nodded, the ghost of a smile on his lips.

"Kirishnaghar is no local shaman," Psolilai continued. "The eyelid technology was a ruse to conceal the intensity of his gaze. His haven doesn't exist . . . he's a machine—of course he wouldn't want to eat in front of us. Of course!" She struck the bed beside her.

"Yet there remains one problem," said Gularvhen. "If we accept the connection between Sukhtaya, malleads and ourselves, we imply that she knew you were on your way south having been sprung from Tall Cliff Steel."

"Then she must have done it."

Gularvhen shook one finger in the air. "Not necessarily. She has agents, informers. And other citizens of Theeremere might benefit from your release."

"Who? The cloaked woman with the silver spiral staff?"

"I do not know yet."

Psolilai sighed. "More likely this is all due to Aunt Sukhtaya. I wonder what she wants."

"It can only be the Constructor."

Psolilai nodded. "Suppose my uncle was hiding his research from her? Suppose they were a couple at odds?"

"She is a stern woman, that is certain."

To this, Psolilai could find no reply.

She managed to sleep for a few hours before dawn. Rhaingorol offered them a meagre breakfast. "You will be leaving soon?" he asked.

"Today," Psolilai confirmed.

"Have you seen outside?"

They had not. Psolilai walked to the nearest window and looked out. Dark sky heavy with snow, flakes already falling thick, black clouds building on the horizon; now she knew why the room was so dim. The land outside the haven was heaving, brown fields crisping under the new snow, objects and devices emerging from beneath the ground like animals from their lairs.

"It's just the last throes of the manufacturing ecosystem in this region," she said, though she wondered if the opposite was true. Gularvhen made no comment.

"How will you beat this weather?" Rhaingorol asked. "Theeremere is sixty leagues away."

That would be tricky. Psolilai glanced at Gularvhen as she searched for an answer.

Rhaingorol struck the ground with his stick, as if in disgust. "Well, there are methods," he said. "We would not have you die in some wilderness hole for lack of help."

"Gularvhen has Hoss," Psolilai said, trying to appear conciliatory.

"Hoss will be running behind you both," Rhaingorol retorted. "This afternoon I will send you on your way. Until then, feel free to enjoy your last hours here."

Psolilai returned to her room, packed her few belongings, then walked to the door through which the wolf had entered, trying to follow the muddy footprints along the path in the fungus garden. They soon ran out, or became one with the earth. Frustrated, she walked to the further edge of the garden to examine some spectacular orange fungi growing on a tree trunk. Snow fell. Yet it did not feel bad. Was it? She was disappointed that the weather alterations caused yesterday had ceased overnight. Perhaps that sunny clearing had in fact been the normal passage of a cold front. . .

Sounds behind her. Gularvhen probably. She turned to explain more, but it was not him. Agens: six in number, in front of them a human being unlike any she had seen before.

He was a man, fat and bald, dressed in a shift, but it was his skin that made her stare, for it was covered with white boils, the shiny surfaces of which indicated how stretched they were from pressure inside. His eyes were quite blank. The agens were of varying heights, their faces marked with a median axis—almost a scar—but lacking crystal whiskers. Every one however trailed a cloud of luminous flies. With their slanting eyes and silent mouths they emanated dread. Psolilai took steps backwards, then felt the fence against her back.

The fat man stepped forward when the tallest agen said, "Sithy, nerfy."

Psolilai just stared. He stopped a few yards away.

"Furghurth!"

One of the boils on his neck burst, spattering fluid across Psolilai's face. She screamed and crouched down. He knelt, and two further boils burst, again splattering her. Now she ran. But he ran too. And he was fast, far faster than a fat man should have been. Yet he never touched her. His limbs sounded like skreeking metal. As she stumbled down the path, he followed, losing his shift, boils bursting at every step. When she tripped and fell he stopped, leaned over, and every last boil burst, like liquid fireworks, so that her clothes were drenched.

He fell at her side. His body twitched.

Psolilai, who had been wearing her usual clothes, saw that although the vile fluid was not affecting the black leather, every stud and button was being consumed. The boils were nano factories. Nearby, the agens watched, incomprehensible expressions upon their faces. The horror inside her made her limbs too heavy to move. Breathing short and sharp, struck dumb, she watched the body at her side jerk then split asunder, to release a hundred autonomous machines that scurried back to the agens, where they were picked up, petted, then carried away. Stench of blood and oil at her side. She took one glance, saw skin without bones, retched and ran to the house.

Inside, she found she was shaking so much she could not sit properly. Gularvhen settled her on a couch. Rhaingorol looked concerned. She could not speak except to utter, not from her throat but from her stomach, the word, "Agens."

Rhaingorol nodded. "Agens inside a haven is very bad news."

Time passed. Hot spicy drink in her mouth, nutmeg and alcohol. She began to feel safe, then cold; then full bladder. When she returned she felt better, though drained. She explained what had happened. Gularvhen and Rhaingorol discussed the matter, while Psolilai, replaying events before her mind's eye, finished her drink, then placed the empty glass on the table before her.

"We must depart," Gularvhen decided. "This district has become too dangerous."

Psolilai nodded. "Too dangerous for me," she agreed.

"The agens made no attack," Gularvhen told her. "They do not threaten your life at all, or so it seems to me. Yet their purpose, I confess, is obscure. All we can do is try to understand their motives, but as yet we do not have enough facts to even stitch a hypothesis together."

"That doesn't cheer me."

Gularvhen became brisk, lifting their packs from the floor. "Rhaingorol has explained his plan to me," he said. "Follow us, Psolilai, and at dawn tomorrow we will be standing before the Sage Gate of Theeremere."

Without reply, Psolilai took Gularvhen's hand and allowed herself to be led out of the house. They followed the path to the harbour, then strode up to the east side of the haven. There, they rested. Rhaingorol brought out his toadstool box and from it extracted two vermilion-and-white caps, which he offered one each to them with a flask of water.

"The totemic animal of this haven is the ounce," he said. "To see, hear and run as the ounce we need to surrender ourselves to a Gaian impulse. Eat and drink, then hear the rhythm that I begin. Together we will open our selves, see further, hear clearer, feel the snow upon our pads, and then I will send you off on your journey east. You shall not tire. You shall not be caught, for the ounce is caught by no other animal. Come dawn, the familiar dankness of Theeremere will stand before you. Then you must rest, until you feel ready to enter your home haven."

Psolilai nodded. The shamanic ritual she was about to experience would be similar to that undertaken by Helwelusa when he searched the nanoactive bog. She felt no fear: slight exhilaration.

She nibbled at the toadstool, sipped water, then took a larger mouthful, ate and ate, until the cap was consumed and all the water drunk. It tasted little; hints of mouldy bread. Rat-tat-tat drum rhythm permeating her dizzy consciousness, looking up to see the shaman's face changing, white fur dark spotted, yellow eyes, sharp teeth, whiskers twitching. The ounce. Gularvhen sat upon the ground, transforming, and she followed suit. The world changed. More sound, different light, a sense of her mind expanding to cover a larger area, or at least be aware of it. She felt the breeze on her fur, a big wet tongue in her mouth, claws. Her eyes were low to the ground. She sniffed, and a riot of scent told her who and what had walked here before.

The other ounce was longer than she, darker. A horse behind him. A third ounce looked across land where the sun lay to the right. She knew they had to run over there, run fast, to reach the dank place.

So they ran. Land sped under their paws as they climbed the hills to the rear of the human place, pausing on a hilltop to survey the ground ahead. It smelled wrong. Brown patches interspersed with white, black, spots of green next to clear rivers. They ran on, pounding the earth, their backs flexing with each stride, maintaining the shamanic rhythm that echoed in their heads. Its source lay far away, now.

Sun dying behind them, red light grazing new snow. Clouds clearing, and an evening smell. Birds twittering: not prey. No time for prey. They need to find the dank place by dawn.

And so night came. Big white moon in the sky between drifting, ragged clouds. No snow until tomorrow. Spot of blue moving through the heavens. Big pale path arcing left to right.

Smells changed as they sped on, smoke on a local breeze, wet green things, odour of plastic forest. To the east they saw flashing red lights, spitting fiery sparks, flurries of motion around these centres that smelled wrong and did not move like people. Once, they caught the trail of another ounce, a northerly trail, but their haste was too great to permit investigation. Other animal smells they ignored too, big dogs, lynx, carrion birds with beaks that snipped flesh.

West lay tall mountains, icy streams bubbling down. They paused to drink, the water running chill down their gullets and into their pot bellies, before they were running again, mouths open, breathing and flexing and striding in harmony.

Snow became deeper. They had to twist their path to run around drifts.

A glow ahead as the sky faded black to grey. Signs of a broad river, of its scummy smell. Pause to listen for birds, ducks; some bloody morsel. Here the snow was too deep to leap over and in places they had to double back, not running so fast now, but some subliminal smell telling them they were almost home.

Low shadow ahead against the glowing sky. Something big lying in the triple curve of a river, deep fog, wrong smell.

They had arrived at the dank place.

Time for rest. Dawn was breaking. The horse cantered away.

She and the other ounce buried themselves in the side of a snow drift as fatigue overtook them, their fur damp but insulating, their pads raw from the pounding they had received, their blood surging and their hearts pumping. Some time passed before their bodies relaxed. Licking their fur and paws, scratching their ears, they lay down to sleep.

It remained cold, but in sleep they felt nothing.

When Psolilai woke she was able to see a section of Theeremere through the entrance to the snow cave. A pall of fog lay over the haven, only the Sage Gate and the western wall visible. Snow fell from low cloud, no sign of the sun. It was evening dim.

She glanced over to see how Gularvhen fared. So far, she had not moved. When she saw what surrounded him she sat up, and so struck her own cage.

Gularvhen was wrapped in a metal exoskeleton, four limbs and a long body, tendrils of decaying plastic dropping from the tubular framework. Rust already ate into the structure's joints. She saw steel claws lying on the damp earth where they had been shed. And something else . . . this piece of precision machinery was crimson coated, larger nodules forming a skin; wild wrealities taking advantage of an expired device.

She refocussed her eyes to look at the exoskeleton in which she was wrapped. This was what had allowed her to run sixty leagues in a day. Realising that what she had thought a Gaian purity was augmented by the use of machinery, she felt admiration for the shamen of Shohnadwe.

203

Ephemeral fragment of a dream, a voice in her head: "Would it not be better to accept a minimum level of use? Given the opportunity to use sustainable resources, we could live with nature and still retain our required level of technology."

"Yes!" Psolilai replied. She shook her head, blinked, then wriggled free of the exoskeleton and crawled over to wake Gularvhen.

He stretched, then opened his eyes.

"We have arrived," she told him. Then she glanced outside and added, "But it doesn't look promising. The air smells acid, and thick fog covers the haven. Are you ready to discover what we have done?"

"I am ready to discover what you have done."

14

A Dream Was Another's Reality

It was dead of night, and psolilai had been out hunting. But now she had returned to the Inn of Twilight Ratiocination. She crept through vegetation surrounding the hydroponic ponds, but was appalled to see two thickset men guarding the rear door of the Inn. Guessing they were agents of Dezisserine here to stop her seeing her friends she crept along dark passages between the old houses beside the Inn, to see one man leaning against the front door, a mug of ale in his hand. Frustration made her curse under her breath. Too many problems hung over her: the mystery of 3Machines, Dezisserine's games, and further off, like the threat of a storm, her other, dream-self.

She dared not force an entry into the Inn. Far too risky.

Dawn was near. She descended to the ground level and wandered the outer arches of the haven, wondering if it might be possible for Metaxain to create a permanent copse in which she could make camp. Then she dismissed the idea as ridiculous. She, living like a hermit in the cold outdoors? A leader like her deserved the best, and she was not getting it.

Golden tendrils rising out of the ground, symbol of dawn made real by the power of the haven. Within a minute she could see nothing except shining sky and mist. Something tickling her leg. She turned, bent down, to see a foggy silhouette rising up out of the substrate itself, a narrow, curling stem and a lump on the end that even as she watched became a cap. A mushroom cap. But already the symbolic mist was lifting, the mushroom six feet high, its cap as big as her head and too high to reach. She tried to grasp the stem, but it was just a shadow, phantasm departing, now gone, and she clawing transparent air.

It must be a metafungus if it grew off the substrate. She became excited. But Mahandriana's mists of bright dawn and tenebrous dusk lasted little more than a minute. The spores of mushrooms such as she had just seen must germinate, grow and produce fruiting bodies within that time. Eating them, therefore, would be a difficult task.

She waited for dusk with some impatience, watching people come and go as they collected water from streams and harvested the meagre resources of the plateau, all the time hoping Metaxain or Gularvhen would intuit where she was and come to keep her company, or even rescue her. She dozed for much of the day. At last there came a hint of black fog rolling down the slopes. Before she knew it, she was amid it. But this time it was too dark to see.

The black fog sank into the ground like ink. She cursed. People glanced at her, and she knew they thought her mad. She was left standing solitary in the light of moon and moontoo.

The Inn of Twilight Ratiocination was still guarded, the Teahouse empty, so she made for the Divan Inn, where she managed to convince the innkeeper that Metaxain would pay for her supper and a mattress on which to lie. But she could not sleep. She felt anger at Dezisserine's men, and she knew that, despite the risk, she would soon have to send a message to her friends. She swore freely—such an ignominious episode.

Half an hour before dawn she departed the inn without a word to the innkeeper. She returned to the outer edge of the substrate, where she had seen the metafungus.

She waited.

Again the hint of a yellow glow in the soil. Her breath began to come short and shallow as she searched the grubby wall for signs of imminent germination. Nothing. Then she was standing in golden light. And there! Something dark expanding from the wall, thin like a cord with a lump on top. She chased it, but it danced like a punctured balloon. Just seconds to go. With the first gap appearing in the mist she managed to grab the decaying cap and stuff it into her mouth. Clear air around her, gooey blue slime all over her hands. She lay on the damp ground and awaited wisdom.

It came.

She understood that the two mists of day and night were one, the corpus of an ancient zri living alone here, mimicking the coming of the sun, then its departure, responding to its gravity, for all zri were sensitive to the ebb and flow of gravity, representing as sculpture the unimaginable sensations derived from their microscopic sense organs. Then came a realisation: the ephemeral metafungus divulged knowledge of gravity despite the fact that the zri was a machine. Here, in the Haven of the Owl, a mushroom could appreciate the symbol of gravity offered by the ebb and flow of the zri.

A wonderful symbiosis that quite took her by surprise. Was, then, her scorn of manufacturing inappropriate?

She wandered from dirty lake to dirty lake, following a dozen well-trodden paths, until she had returned to the real world with a settled mind. She walked to the Divan Inn, where, in a quiet corner, she drank sugarwater. But she was recognised. And she was popular. The locals liked her now, and they pressed ale and even delicacies upon her, until she was embarrassed by their attention. They wanted to hear her speak.

She stood up and shouted, "Time."

Confusion at this, for it was still early evening. No bell had been rung. The crowd quietened, and many turned in their seats to face her. Brief sense of how much they appreciated her in this place.

"Time," she repeated. "How many of us have a sense of true time? How many of us have sat on a shore and watched the tide come in, then go out again, from dawn to dusk? But no. These are the Teeming Levels, aren't they? Here we rush about, running from library to library, from inn to inn, from one colleague to another in our haste to learn whatever we came here to learn. My friends, we are losing our sense of time, and because of that we are losing our sense of nature." A murmur at this. psolilai continued, "And we all love nature, don't we? That is why we set up havens to protect us from the artifice of the wilderness."

They seemed confused.

"Imagine this," said psolilai. "Imagine going out onto the plateau at dusk and watching the stars wheel across the heavens, until the sun rises in the east and it is light again. Can you imagine that?"

"Yeah," someone shouted, "but why bother?"

General laughter, but she pressed on. "I will tell you why we must bother. We must bother because if we are to become authentic human beings, if we are to reach out from our havens and touch the intimate heart of nature, we must appreciate nature as nature is, not as we would wish. Nature exists on a time scale unimaginable to us, but we can make the effort to meet nature half way by slowing down, by watching nature in action over extended periods of time. It is a kind of meditation. Yes, it is quite serious! But if we miss this crucial aspect of nature we miss our full potential. Now, let me expand on what I just said. We can all imagine watching the tide come in and out in response to the motion of the moon, but can we imagine a year? Can we really imagine a full year? Have we watched one bush break out in buds in spring, go green in summer, then die back through autumn and winter? Have we watched it intently?" No replies. "Friends, I beg you all, go out and plant saplings. Watch them grow from year to year — just the one that is personal to you — and in doing so gain a better sense of the passing of nature's time, for if you do, if you plant your own seed and watch it grow to a mature tree, you will have come just that little bit closer to nature. And that . . . that my friends is something we must all do." She paused. "Do you see now what I mean? If we receive a better impression of nature's time we could perhaps make that leap of the imagination and conceive time outside our own experience. We will each of us live for half a century or so. We will all die. But what does nature do in a thousand years? In ten thousand? My friends, ten thousand years from now the western ocean current may return, and our lands, from Nihindra to Bitah-Sui, Hirhoadiog and lands to the east, will grow warm again. The Ice Shield may retreat. We have to imagine such time scales. We have to, for if we do not we miss the majesty of nature."

207

Silence fell.

Then somebody began clapping, and a wave of applause rang through the inn, making psolilai smile as she took a swig of her sugar-water; both embarrassed and full of joy. People came up to her and thumped her on the back, brought her drinks, asked her when and where she was speaking next. Many asked her what species of tree they should plant, and these queries she referred to Metaxain.

Exciting times. A groundswell was building.

Then a presence at her side, and she turned to see Metaxain himself. She hugged him, so pleased was she to see a face she recognised.

"We've been watching for your return," he said. "Men still lurk around the Inn of Twilight Ratiocination, but this time they're not going away."

"Soon I will be lost," psolilai sighed in reply, "the day I am called for unlinking and I fail to turn up. Dezisserine will manipulate the timetable so that I am caught out."

"Not necessarily. We believe Dezisserine's men are unrelated to those directing the process of unlinking, perhaps even unrelated to the Analyticate. For the moment we must watch and wait. The time is approaching when we make our move on the Owl Palace. For now, we'll hide you again at the Teahouse of Aurorean Eudemonia."

"Dezisserine is a fiend. It will find me if it wants to."

"Its plans have flaws," Metaxain insisted. "We've got a chance yet."

psolilai sighed again. Patience was what she needed.

Or perhaps more power.

15

ALL WAS A WHOLE

Theeremere had changed—for the worse. Bad snow fell deep, its acid reek filling the lanes of the haven, but now it was accompanied by fog so thick it was in places impossible to see more than an arm's length ahead. And this ochre fog was corrosive. Bad fog.

Bad snow transformed stone into bizarre forms, or just into thick treacle that oozed down the walls of buildings: bad fog was more insidious, attacking wood, paper and fabric, transforming them into mats of conglomerate junk. The scale of the haven was reduced: streets hardly wide enough for two to pass, door arches low, windows small, dripping bridges of stone linking upper levels where before just the breeze had blown. Some runnels of stone rose upward, defying gravity, as the substance hierarchies in the bad fog created artificial absorption paths as part of their construction. Everything was black, grey, ochre. Every lane was punctuated with sticky puddles. Many lanthorns remained unlit.

Worse was the effect on people. When Psolilai stepped beneath the arch of the Sage Gate, she saw two guards. Their faces were blotchy white. They cast their eyes back down to their board game as if defeated by the conditions.

So Psolilai walked through the Sage Gate, Gularvhen at her side. Another guard looked up, then nudged his colleague, and she thought she heard him say, "Isn't that . . . ?"

She did not wait for any reply. In moments she was concealed by banks of bad fog. But the incident frightened her. Certain people knew she had left Theeremere, and perhaps they had guessed her intentions.

Quickly, the pair walked down Ibogaine Lane then crossed the Wool Bridge. The bad fog dulled sounds, yet reverberated them; it left sourness in the mouth, roughened the throat, sent its tendrils around every object and into every building. With delicate and careful steps—the river lay to their right—they made along Tryptophane Lane. Moving away from the river, the bad fog cleared a little.

The Church of the Parasol Cap had changed. For some seconds Psolilai thought she saw before her an actual fungus, so tall was the building and so extended its lunate roof. Surely an illusion. But the combination of bad snow and bad fog had transformed the place, the lower floors bent inside a warped bole, the upper floors squeezed and heightened into a cylinder.

"Did I do this?" she said.

"We will have to check the timing," Gularvhen replied. "It seems a lot for a day and a quarter."

Inside, they met the registrar.

"What has happened here?" Gularvhen asked.

"Bad fog," the registrar replied with a shrug. "It came yesterday afternoon. The haven has creaked and groaned ever since—these appalling fumes perform construction work. Many of our upper chambers are unusable. I believe the main attack is over, but now a more subtle work begins, chemicals changing function and form. They rise from the river on brown palls, then seep out into the atmosphere. A terrible day."

The pair climbed to Psolilai's chamber, the spiral staircase just wide enough for them to pass, each step twice as high as before. Ceilings were twenty feet high or more, the whole building stretched upward and given a bulbous cap.

At her door, the boy waited. He looked at them, then told Psolilai, "The Church has changed quite a bit, ma'am. Hope you aren't too inconvenienced." With a bow, he opened the door for them.

Inside, Psolilai discussed what had happened with Gularvhen. She felt sure she was to blame. "The timing is perfect, isn't it? I changed the manufacturing ecosystem. I thought nature peeped through the mask of machines and debris. What went wrong?"

"Possibly your vision of the deed you wished to perform was flawed," Gularvhen replied. "For my part, I can scarcely believe that you have made the situation worse. Soon the lanes will be impassable and this haven will be fit only for midgets and the unusually athletic ... for a non-human race, it would seem."

Shock was passing already. Psolilai felt tears upon her face. "I didn't mean to make it worse," she said.

"You did not mean that," Gularvhen agreed, in a voice she could hardly hear.

Psolilai knew that by daring to use the Constructor she had manifested a hubris that had resulted in further destruction of her home haven. It had all gone wrong. The vision was incomplete, the ambition misplaced.

Then she became angry. The sincerity of her hope, of her attempt to change something for the good, had been thwarted by the enormity of what she and every other moral being faced: an ecosystem of such size and complexity it was a twin to nature, a vile twin. She had been proud in her desire to change the manufacturing ecosystem, yet that was no deliberate pride, rather one accidental, for she was tiny and the manufacturing ecosystem was vast, and now she understood that fact.

"It can't be done," she murmured. "The manufacturing ecosystem covers Urbis Morpheos. How could I have fooled myself into trying to make a difference?"

"Do not be downhearted. The existence of the future means we are at least offered hope."

Furious with herself, she slapped her hands on the arms of her chair. "Aunt Sukhtaya has much to answer for. I think I shall visit her."

Gularvhen said, "Is that wise?"

Coldly Psolilai replied, "Wise or not, I shall do it."

Psilocybin Lane was wrapped in bad fog. Night seeped down from an invisible sky. Against the pall she wore a face mask, her leathers pulled tight, only her eyes unprotected, and they smarted raw. She did not bother to check for lanthorns inside her aunt's house, hammering on the door then on the shutters. The door opened; tall crack of light, a silhouette behind. Psolilai pushed forward and said, "It's only me."

She was inside the house. Aunt Sukhtaya was surprised. Nonetheless the door was shut and Psolilai was led into the study; paper peeling off the walls, the very air stained ochre. Like wary beasts the two women sat in opposite chairs.

"I'm shocked that you show your face here, niece," came the first remark.

Psolilai bridled at this. "Here? You mean Theeremere?"

"Today has been a nightmare. Look at my skin, pale patches like mould."

"You're blaming me?"

"I know what you have done," said Aunt Sukhtaya. "My advice to you is not to wander this haven, unless you feel you ought to be lynched for the catastrophe you have caused. Should your sister catch you . . ."

Psolilai felt a first touch of fear. "She knows I'm here?"

"It cannot be long before she finds out. Her agents are everywhere."

This was not what Psolilai expected to hear. "Is . . . ?"

"Is Amargoidara looking for you? Is that what you were going to ask? Who knows? He leads this haven, he has the best agents of all."

"And the best lies," Psolilai spat.

"That is a matter of opinion."

Psolilai felt crushed. She sat back in her chair. Realisation of the consequences of her deed was beginning to sink in. Bad fog suffocating her . . .

"So, you know what I have done," she mused.

Her aunt said nothing.

Psolilai glanced up through her lashes. "You know about the Constructor. Kirishnaghar is your man, isn't he, your mallead?"

"The Constructor never made it back here. You have unleashed a monster upon us. A mallead took it for his own. He will try to integrate it within his corpus."

Psolilai recalled the attack inside the stone copse, when the giant attempted to incorporate the artefact into his hand. Her aunt spoke true. "Was this then your reason for springing me from prison?" she asked. "To have me wander Urbis Morpheos on a mission to drop the Constructor into your hands?"

Aunt Sukhtaya never laughed. She shrugged her shoulders, chortled, a sound like a drain gurgling. "Me, spring you? Never in a hundred years."

"Then who did?"

"My best guess is that your sister did it."

Psolilai let her head tip forward, so that she gazed at the floor.

"Let me tell you a tale," said Aunt Sukhtaya. "One night last summer a strange old woman arrived at my door asking for you. She was heavily robed, carrying a blue staff around which silver twisted. Ryoursh was here too. We let this woman in and explained to her your situation. She listened carefully, then departed. Ryoursh followed, and so discovered where she went. The Pillar. When Ryoursh returned, her eyes burned. She is jealous, niece, she hates you and she envies you. That one visit turned sibling foes into enemies. I believe Ryoursh sprang you from Tall Cliff Steel in order to make real her fantasies of vengeance."

Psolilai said, "You say Ryoursh has agents. So she ranks high in some militaristic Thee patrol, with no reason to envy any special links I may have."

"She hates you, niece. Jealousy gnaws until it is sated."

Dismissively, Psolilai said, "Then perhaps she should climb the Pillar and demand an audience with this woman."

"Much easier to deal with you."

To this, Psolilai had no answer. Nobody had ever reached the top of the Pillar—if indeed it had a top. Her aunt had a point. She stood up and said, "I will leave you now. I doubt I will return to this house, having heard so much of your feelings. Goodbye."

"Goodbye, niece, but it is not for the last time."

Probably a threat. Psolilai ignored it.

It was the thought of malleads stalking haven lanes that most disturbed her; when she returned to the Church of the Parasol Cap she found herself unable to settle. A hundred thoughts whirled through her mind: where Ryoursh might be, where Kirishnaghar and the other mallead, and behind all that the realisation that her deed had been both puny and a failure. She took the Constructor from her pocket and looked at it. Moments passed; tempting to throw it into the river. She returned it to her pocket and sought Gularvhen.

"I'm going out into the haven," she said. "I have to discover what I've done."

Gularvhen glanced out of a window into the night sky. "Is it not time for sleep?"

"I can't sleep."

He raised himself to his full height and replied, "Leaving the Church alone is perilous, especially for you. I will accompany you."

Psolilai vacillated for a moment—she felt a need for solitude—but then agreed. She had no desire to die.

Away from the river the bad fog was more a pall of dirty mist, tendrils rising up from manhole covers and gutters to poke themselves through doors and windows. North and east, pale towers and buckled rooves showed through an ochre blanket. Psolilai pulled tight her clothes and hat, tied a mask over her nose and mouth, then led Gularvhen out into Isatin Lane.

Gularvhen paused. "I am sure," he said, "that this haven is being remodelled to suit a nonhuman race . . ."

Psolilai said nothing. Her thoughts focussed on malleads.

They made south towards the garden surrounding the Pool of Wrealities, which they entered with stealth. No sign of Karakushna, of course. Like as not her cousin was safe in bed.

"What is that?" Gularvhen hissed, pointing ahead.

They stood amongst sparse thickets of gorse, damp grass below their feet. Psolilai studied what lay before her—high walls surrounding this natural zone, mist drifting lethargic. Then she saw a shadow move.

"That's big," she said.

From an alcove a monster appeared. It was as tall as Gularvhen, barrel chested, long armed, two dripping fangs and scimitar claws; skin filthy green, warty and wrinkled. Two yellow eyes glaring like fog lamps. Though she guessed this to be the mallead who had stolen the golden disk, Psolilai felt no fear, only righteous determination sourced in her own failure. As the monster shambled towards them she took the remaining disk from her pocket and held it high, so that its gleam illuminated the garden, and the eyes before her turned from yellow to gold.

It halted. Knees buckling, head lowered, claws scything across one another as its hands convulsed; the sound of knives on a whetstone. Psolilai stood firm. The monster took a deep breath and a step forward, then stopped again. From its pot belly a noise began, a scream half mechanical half liquid, something inside moving, the monster sagging, looking down, clutching its abdomen, then with its claws cutting into itself to reveal first a glimmer, then shining gold. Psolilai knew now that

214

here was the mallead who had robbed her in that dark Shohnadwe night. It was the giant too, and perhaps other forms with whom they had travelled.

The monster's flesh warped and tore as the golden artefact emerged. Sparks popped like crackling fat, white green blue; then deeper organs blew with snaps and loops of flame dancing around the wound. A groan, a tear, and then all trace of gold departed the monster, and Psolilai felt her hand grow hot and heavy.

She looked at the artefact. It had regained its former thickness. She glanced at Gularvhen and said, "Two sides of the same coin."

"Indeed," he replied. "The owl is close, and soon it will be within your grasp. You have failed, Psolilai, and in a spectacular way. Now is the time to find true wisdom, to find a point in your life from which you can spring, like a diver, into truth and goodness. I believe you can do this. More . . . I believe that you will."

Psolilai had no time to reply. The monster stuffed flesh back into its abdomen and with movements like knitting resealed itself. There was a clunk, then a rattle. It grew taller, thicker, and its claws glowed like hot metal. It advanced.

A roaring sound, and clanking from the left. From an arch a second creature emerged, also tall, but cloaked and hooded, fumes wafting from the seams in its garb. It breathed like a blast furnace. The inner lining of its hood glowed blue.

Psolilai drew her rapier as she wondered how to run away.

The monsters were now close enough to smell, one like burning plastic, the other rotten as the bottom of the river. No chance of winning a fight: yet how could they escape a wolf, a bird? Then a third figure emerged from a different alcove, no taller than Psolilai, black cloak and hood, walking swiftly to stop the monsters in their tracks. The figure stopped. So did the monsters. The hood was flung back to reveal a pale head and whiskers.

It happened too quick for Psolilai to follow, perhaps two rockets launching from the ground where the monsters stood, glittering tracks remaining, then bright stars in the sky, one bilious, one frosty, before they became glowing lines that headed south like fading fireworks.

Psolilai stared at the new figure. It turned, hands on hips, then ran off.

"Come back!" Psolilai yelled.

She was ignored.

She turned to Gularvhen. "First the agens attack me, then they rescue me."

"Our rescuer did not move like an agen," he remarked.

The same thought had occurred to Psolilai. "We must suppose it was not of the manufacturing ecosystem."

"The malleads are offspring of the agens. Their twisted relationship alone is perhaps enough to frighten a mallead."

"Who knows?" muttered Psolilai.

"Was that your cousin, then?"

Psolilai shook her head. "Karakushna would have made herself known to me."

Gularvhen stroked his chin. "Somebody from your family appeared just now."

Psolilai shivered. She shivered because she agreed. "Let's return to the Church," she said. "The artefact is whole . . . a slight redemption."

Gularvhen said nothing, but there was scorn in his expression.

216

Psolilai returned again to the notion of disguise. Her position in Theeremere was insecure, black leathers and a rainbow hat no longer enough. Through the boy she obtained a new wig, clothes, and a bag of cosmetic oddments. She sat before her mirror. Using brushes, she gave herself a shadow on her cheeks and chin, then settled a moustache upon her lip, that flopped to either side of her mouth before curling out. Rather theatrical, she thought. The dark wig completed the look. Over her clothes she pulled loose workman's attire, which she dirtied with mud from her boots. Now she was a man.

It seemed desperate, but people in the haven, not least Ryoursh, knew she was back. Her life was in danger. Just one mistake and she would be returned to internal exile—perhaps even to live the life of a blinkered one. Death would be preferable to that fate.

One task remained. She needed to discover who had rescued her in the garden of the Pool of Wrealities. Karakushna was the least unlikely.

In Rem she walked up Ibogaine Lane, making for the lane community of her cousin. Through the thickest of the fog she had to pat alley walls, as she stumbled along the riverside; she stepped arms out-stretched through lanes that were in places hardly wide enough to squeeze through. Her boots became heavy, glutinous stone accumulating on their soles. Then she was in Blewits Lane, approaching the house of her cousin.

Black flag hanging down from the lintel. Shocked, Psolilai halted, looking up and down the passage for other visitors. But there was nobody. Rem was silent, every sound muffled by bad fog. The black flag unsettled her, and she began to fret.

Inside the house the silence was more intense, noise absorbed by furnishings, exquisite tapestries dulled, even disintegrated by the pall. There was nobody about, and she had to open a few doors before she found two old men, swirling whiskey around their glasses in desolate silence.

"I was looking for Karakushna," she whispered.

The men glanced at each another. One got to his feet, pushing himself out of his chair, joints cracking, then walking to a cabinet, from which he took a jewel. Psolilai recognised it as Karakushna's topaz brooch.

It was she who had died.

Her cousin was gone.

The other man cleared the phlegm from his throat, then spoke. "The bad fog got her," he said. "She always had a bit of a weak chest, you see, comes from living so close to the river, like she did as a kid. She used to trawl the bottom for aquatic devices, you know, sell 'em cheap to whoever would buy. She loved water." His eyes misted. "Nice girl. Tragic she's off to the Field of Gaia. We'll all go to the funeral of course, but I wonder who else will turn up?"

The standing man looked down at the yellow gem in his hand, shrugged, then handed it to Psolilai. He sank back into his chair to take a sip of whiskey and gaze at the hearth.

Without a word Psolilai turned and ran from the house, closing the door, taking a few steps into the passage, halting to lean against a wall. She had done this. *She* had killed her own cousin. She wanted to pull out the brooch pin and stab it into her chest.

She had hoped for so much with Karakushna. They had become friends upon meeting. They both fought against adversity. Now all that potential was gone.

217

As tears rolled down her face and her breathing turned to sobbing she could not help but imagine this death, choking in bad fog down some alley, probably alone, and all because she had tried to make things better with the Constructor. She looked up at the few buildings in sight, saw their filthy walls. Theeremere was doomed either to melt into the river or become a place unfit for human beings.

All because of her. The owl she sought was not a bird of wisdom, it was a fake. It was foolishness, it was myopia. For some time she wept, bereft, hating and fearing her family, her fellow citizens, except perhaps Gularvhen, who at least stood by her side. She slumped to the ground, caring nothing for the cold, the damp.

And so she sat, cold and miserable in a dark alley, alone as never before, wondering what power could return beauty to Theeremere, to Urbis Morpheos. Surely there was something, surely something could be dreamed.

Nothing. No inspiration came to her.

She got to her feet, walked to the end of the passage and stood in the middle of Norbaeocystin Lane. Here in the centre of Rem she could see ochre haven around her and dark sky above. With bad fog hugging lower contours, the moon and the moontoo were visible, the ring system, and the brighter stars.

From the north she heard a faint honking. She turned to look. A flock of artificial avians was gliding towards her, following the river south to the sea, where, fuel empty, they would embed themselves in the beach and decay into a hundred useless items. These items would struggle north, reform with others to swap artificial genes, and so complete a circle.

In a flash Psolilai grasped this mockery of a natural cycle. Anger returned. From her pocket she took the Constructor. She studied it. Ancient artifact of the manufacturing ecosystem, it could never be used to help nature; at best it might be neutral. Only something natural could help nature. She turned to face the avians swooping low over the haven, and with a mighty effort threw the Constructor at the leading machine; it bent its swan neck low, caught and swallowed it. Flew on. The flock followed. Their honking sound receded, vanished, and Psolilai felt whole again.

She returned to the Church of the Parasol Cap, where she sought out Gularvhen. He stood alone in the meditation room. She told him

of her thoughts, concluding, "The owl feels close. I still need to locate it."

"You must locate the owl," Gularvhen agreed.

"I feel lost. Where could such an undertaking happen?"

He nodded, then scratched his unshaven cheek. "In Mahandriana,
which is the Haven of the Owl. There is no other place."

Psolilai laughed, for this was the home of her dream self. "But I live
here, in the Haven of the Three Machines."

Gularvhen strolled across to a window, hands behind his back, to
peer out into the bad fog below. "Tomorrow a cool front will cross Urbis
Morpheos, blowing away some of this fog. Get you down to the furthest
garden of the Church, and there meditate on nature, with nature all
around you. Soon you will ascend from Theeremere, perhaps never to
return."

Psolilai nodded. She walked upstairs to her room. At the top she
slowed, made each footstep silent.

The boy was there.

From some mystical space between plaster wall and other reality
Gularvhen appeared, or an older simulacrum, fading from ghost to
man, bending down like a black stork to pick up the boy in one easy
gesture, then look at him, his face torn between love and sorrow. The
boy's expression was one of peace. He had been reading a note. He
tossed it to the floor. Gularvhen turned, he and the boy fading into
nothing more substantial than motes of light, that decayed red to ash
like sparks from a bonfire.

Psolilai was left facing emptiness, just the scrap of paper on the floor.

She picked it up. It read: 'The time has come for your dream to end.
Come, now, with me, on a journey in the real world.'

She dropped the note into her pocket. Something about its tone,
about its melancholy profundity, reached out to her.

Her room was empty: of people, of warmth, of the energy of life.
Without the boy she felt unprotected. These felt like final days.

She sighed, and wondered what would become of her. Perhaps the
time had indeed come for her haven days to end.

The ground at the bottom of the garden was evergreen, shot through
with dead branches, fungi and leaf litter in piles on the grass. Bad

snow drifts had been cleared by the Church lads, bad fog drifting in thin curtains, dispersed by the breeze. Clouds thick above her, but holding back their bad snow.

She chose an enclosed space in which to sit, protected to the west by a yew hedge, to the north by laurel, the other sides open; south a bed of old roses, east a carpet of translucent mushrooms just starting to glow for the day. Above her soughed the leaves of an evergreen plane, forming a ceiling. She sat on cushions. Drink to her left, a miniature stove to her right. The air hardly moved through her outdoor study, and soon it lost its chill.

Tears. She felt again the loss of Karakushna. She decided she would go to the funeral on the Field of Gaia.

And joy. She felt that she had passed through a time of fear and ignorance, to emerge, shaken and battered, but knowing in which direction to walk.

A certain amount of contentment. Gularvhen would be at her side, and he was a wise man.

A figure emerged from the black iron gate in the wall behind the rose bed, dressed in cloak and hood, carrying a tray on which lay two mushrooms; a person of medium height walking slowly with a curious lurching gait. Nobody she recognised, but at least this was not an agen. She relaxed. A little.

The figure approached. When only a few feet away, between the pitcher of water and the stove, it stopped. Muddy cloak behind, stretching out like the train of a gown. Still she saw no face beneath the floppy hood. Gloved hands.

The mushrooms were offered up. They were unique, exquisite. One was pale, with a pink cap and dense dark gills, its flesh scored with the finest lines, like corrugation. The other was darker, green tinted and shaggy, with a smaller number of chunky gills, white and slimy. The stems and bases of both were clean. Neither had grown in soil.

Psolilai chose the darker mushroom. It seemed wholesome.

The figure turned and lurched toward the gate, cloak dragging behind. Psolilai watched it pass through. The lane behind the wall followed a steep hill down, though the garden was level. Some yards to the right of the gate a hood popped up, to bounce a couple of times as it moved away, vanish, reappear as just a tip, then vanish for good.

She studied the mushroom. It smelled of hay in soft meadows. Of summer.

She ate the cap in one go, chewing long to savour the flavour, flowers, leaves, fruit, heady like wine. Ethereal music drifting from somewhere behind her: a choir underlying solo violins, and deep, deep bass notes like shock waves from the centre of Urbis Morpheos. She lay back, knowing a dream was close. Still she chewed.

Greenery around her faded, as nausea took her for a few seconds and her vision quivered. Her body seemed light. She felt cold, then warm again.

Her sight seemed to expand, as if she was flying . . .

The roof of the Church of the Parasol Cap was cold and damp. Bad fog billowed in the streets far below Gularvhen. Bad snow fell from low cloud. He pulled his cloak close. He saw a row of bird footprints, which he recognised as having been made by a raven; in the deliquescing stone they yet remained, at once a symbol of the mutable material and of its strength and longevity.

He turned to face east. The moontoo had not yet risen. But when, an hour later, it did, he was disappointed to see that it was yellow. He sighed.

Next night he waited solitary for the rising of the moontoo, but it emerged cornflower blue from heavy clouds.

On the third night the moontoo was green.

It sparkled like an emerald. He rose to his feet. For almost half the night he waited, until the moontoo was directly above him; and then he leaped. In that single motion was revealed the grandeur of Gularvhen, the power, and the wisdom. He was Morpheos, the dreamer, approaching his final struggle.

Then Psolilai awoke . . .

Music fading into the swish and sough of leaves in a breeze. Soon, nothing.

She struggled up from the cushions, now damp from ground moisture. Much of the day had passed. Visual disturbances faded as she walked towards the rear of the Church of the Parasol Cap. In the back hall she found Gularvhen. He stood silent, saturnine, staring at her. With a cry of joy she leaped forward, grabbed his hands and began to dance around him. A grin was his concession to levity as she skipped and leaped, and used him as a maypole.

"One final event remains for me," she said, "the funeral tomorrow of Karakushna. I can't miss it."

Smiling and happy, she returned to the rear door and looked out over the garden. The sky was smoky blue, winter sun low. High up, the moontoo shone like an emerald.

16

DREAM WAS THE METHOD

When psolilai, Metaxain and Cuanatola were called for unlinking duties it was for psolilai both an irritation and a distraction; and it would interfere with her sleep. Tonight's prowl through the local galleries would exhaust her.

But at least, as they worked, they suffered none of the attentions of Dezisserine's agents. Nevertheless psolilai found her tasks impossible to concentrate on. They were working a gallery of particularly thick soil, on one of the lower levels, where viniculture had been practised for centuries, and where the lowest layers of earth were dense with cabling and networked devices. But it was wrealities that were causing psolilai the worst problems. On nocturnal expeditions she collected wild wrealities, pulling them from decaying technology like puff-balls from pasture. In her room, as dawn broke through ragged cloud, she would with trembling hands take the wrealities and lick them as if they were sweets, experiencing a rush of meaningless visions, like meteors smashing into her brain from inner space. Meaningless, but addictive.

Today the underground wrealities seemed to sing to her.

Metaxain was in a world of his own, humming to himself as he worked, but Cuanatola watched her, and even remarked on the pallor of her skin. psolilai snapped back, "Let me get on with this, will you?" Whenever she could she put wrealities into her pockets, until, as the afternoon waned, every one contained half a dozen. The feel of them close to her skin made her sweat, her breath coming quick and short. Fatigue made her eyes feel dry and her limbs heavy, but the thought of the night's visions kept her going, sustaining her like caffeinated alcohol: the wreality rush.

Yet they were machines. She tried to forget what Dezisserine had told her.

She shivered, though it was not cold. Cuanatola stood at her side and asked, "Are you getting a fever?"

"I'm tired," psolilai replied. "Is it time to go home?"

Cuanatola indicated a pile of debris. "We only have to take that lot to the incinerator and the wrealities to the collection point. Half an hour, no more."

psolilai turned away. "Metaxain will do my bit for me."

A hand on her shoulder turning her around. She stared into Cuanatola's face. "You look ill, psolilai. Your pupils are dilated and your skin is white. You have been detecting the thinnest wires without glasses and you jump at noises we cannot hear. What is wrong?"

"Nothing. Tired."

"What is this?" Cuanatola gasped, feeling inside a pocket.

psolilai found herself looking at a wreality.

"Your pockets are full of them!"

Then Metaxain's voice. "What's going on here?"

"Wait," said psolilai. "I put them there to carry to the collection place."

"Leave her be," said Metaxain, pushing Cuanatola away. "I'll deal with this."

"You'll take her to the collection point," Cuanatola retorted. "I'll clear the rest of this debris. Better hurry, before your *girlfriend* has a fit."

Metaxain stopped any further exchanges by pulling psolilai into a corridor, where he leaned her against a wall. "You do look ill," he said.

psolilai felt dizzy. She dropped to her knees as the ground wobbled before her eyes. Then she felt a tightness about her chest, pain—sharp stabbing pain—and she regurgitated a scarlet pellet bigger than her fist. It dropped to the floor with a sound like pins on a tabletop. Blood on her lips. She fell back against the wall.

Metaxain looked in horror at the pellet. "Gularvhen said that you did this once before. What's happening to you?"

"Indigestible material," said psolilai, her voice a hoarse whisper.

Metaxain made no reply. His face expressed his shock. psolilai did not care. She had seen out the day and she carried at least twenty wrealities in her pockets.

"How grows the silver birch?" she asked.

"It's growing well," he replied. "Only a few days now and we'll be making our attempt on the Owl Palace."

psolilai grinned.

"Don't think you've distracted me from this," he added, indicating the pellet. "I'm taking you to the Teahouse. Tonight you stay indoors."

She let him take a few wrealities to the collection point, hid the rest for later, then followed him back to the Teahouse on shuffling feet. She decided to sleep half the night then go out. She refused food. She wanted to hunt her own.

The possibility of trouble at Dyeeth Boolin's inn led them to plan their assault on the Owl Palace from the Teahouse of Aurorean Eudemonia. The time was set. Their company would be five: psolilai, Gularvhen, Kirishnaghar and Metaxain, with Dyeeth Boolin for support and local knowledge. Ilyi Koomsy would stay behind.

One evening an hour after dusk they found themselves in the arrival gallery of the Complex Levels, silent balloons all around them. Each of them carried a backpack filled with every kind of equipment they could think of, except Dyeeth Boolin, who carried a small shoulder satchel and smoked tobacco like a dilettante. psolilai carried a rapier, Gularvhen a poignard. They were expecting trouble.

Half way up the Complex Levels, Kirishnaghar reached the limit of his knowledge. "Here," he said, "we must trust to luck and judgement. At least one hundred galleries lie above us, on ten levels. I have seen the external galleries and many of them contain buildings, one even a garden of moss and a pool. I have no doubt that agents of the Analyticate pass through the Complex Levels on their various tasks. People, I know not what sort, do live and work here."

"Assume the form of a wren," psolilai told him. "You must be our scout. Our presence here implies authority, but if we are questioned we will not mention you. Do not appear as a human to anyone you do not know."

"Very well," he agreed.

"Now lead on. We must go up."

A blue-eyed wren fluttered before her. For an hour they followed its lead, walking through galleries increasingly dark, as night fell outside and internal illumination was lost. Some tunnels glowed, others carried lamps, but more often they had to follow them with hands reaching out in the dark, twin blue dots ahead their only guide. Only once did they meet people. A group of women dressed in grey robes appeared without warning from a side tunnel, looked them over, then walked on. psolilai was right. It was assumed that only authorised persons climbed so high.

Then they met Dezisserine.

The agen dropped from a hole where the tunnel they followed met a cavern open to the outside air. For a few moments it stood in silence before them, studying them all, before pointing at Metaxain to say, "You I remember." It turned to Gularvhen. "You . . . are familiar." Then Dyeeth Boolin. "You of course are known to many on these levels." When it faced psolilai it hesitated the longest, before saying, "You I cannot quite . . . you are the one my men talk of, the source of my amnesia."

"Am I?" psolilai remarked innocently.

The agen returned to Metaxain. "What are you people doing here, dressed like journeymen, equipped as if for the mountains?"

"Is it your right to ask?" psolilai interjected.

"Yes it is, and I am asking him, not you."

Metaxain cleared his throat. "We're mountaineering," he said.

Dezisserine walked once around them as they stood still, ending up in front of Metaxain. "You are going to the top, no?"

Metaxain shrugged. "That's normally what mountaineers do."

psolilai smirked.

Dezisserine continued, "It is night, and you should be carousing. Instead you reach for the Sky Level, perhaps beyond. I am correct?"

"If you're not stopping us," Metaxain said, "we'll carry on."

"I will accompany you. I also wish to reach the Sky Level. I have never been there."

Metaxain hesitated, glancing at psolilai. Dezisserine pounced. Standing in front of her the agen said, "You are the leader here, as I suspected. What is your name?"

"Don't you know?"

"psolilai, that I do know."

psolilai looked away, as if bored.

"Do you know what lies at the boundary between the Complex Levels and the Sky Level?" the agen asked.

"Do you?"

"Gryphons. You know what I mean, don't you, Dyeeth Boolin?"

The felin's teeth clattered against the stem of his pipe. "Mmm, not sure," he answered, and he seemed disconcerted.

psolilai's attention was distracted by Gularvhen stepping forward. "I do not believe you have any authority over us," he said in studious tones. "To take just one example, you are an agen, barred from all natural havens. It would be the matter of a moment to report you to the Analyticate. Now, if you please, we have certain matters to attend to. We bid you good evening."

He walked away. Metaxain followed. psolilai was left looking into Dezisserine's cold eyes. "What do you want on the Sky Level?" she asked the agen.

For a moment Dezisserine stared at her, its eyes darting from left to right, as if caught in a dilemma. Then it replied, "I need to return the owl to the people."

psolilai knew at once that she had spoken these words. For one moment she hated the agen, knowing that it had recorded her speech: the next she wondered if it might be possible that they shared the same goal. Cynicism in the presence of the agen won over. She said, "So you've been listening to my conversations with Gularvhen and Kr—"

She stopped. Better not mention that name.

"What do you mean?" asked Dezisserine.

"That is what I intend doing—returning the owl to the people. It is symbolic of my task."

"Then let us join arms and walk on together."

Gularvhen returned. "Come along, psolilai," he said, "the night will not last forever."

psolilai was torn between dejection at the persistence of the agen and hope that it might be good, or at worst useful. She cursed under her breath then said, "Dezisserine will be accompanying us for the moment."

They walked on. But with the top level near, psolilai heard footsteps in the gallery behind her. She gave a hiss, then whispered, "People, four or five of them."

They listened. "I can't hear anything," said Metaxain.

"Nor I," Gularvhen agreed.

They were in a wide tunnel, a gallery at either end, nowhere to hide. "I believe I hear boots," said Dezisserine. "Remain with me and we will not be troubled."

A minute passed before the sound was definite. From the gallery a group of men appeared driving wheeled carts, four pushing, one leading, and it was the leader who hurried forward to investigate them. He was tall, old, ramrod straight, with a florid complexion and a moustache like two horizontal spikes; shiny boots and a grey uniform decorated with silver epaulettes. Striding up to Metaxain he said, "What are you doing here? This is a restricted route." He glared at Dezisserine, then turned back to Metaxain. "What are you doing up here with ol' Creepy?"

Metaxain said nothing.

"Got a tongue, lad?"

psolilai inched aside to peer into the carts. They were full of wrealities, tossed in with earth and debris like so many potatoes.

The uniformed man reached out to stop her. "Where you going, eh?"

psolilai tried to stare him out, but this made him lose his temper. "Ain't any of you people got tongues? Eh? A lot of lugworms, are you?"

Dezisserine took a step forward. "Captain Gironbiom, we are within our rights to walk any gallery in the Complex—"

"Not you, Creepy," the Captain interrupted. He pointed at Gularvhen. "You, beanpole. Whose authority are you under?"

Gularvhen blinked.

"There's that felin, Captain," said one of the men.

Dyeeth Boolin had been lurking ahead. When Captain Gironbiom saw the felin he frowned, then said, "Are these lot with you?"

"Yes," Dyeeth Boolin replied. "Dezisserine and I are exploring some of the older galleries. You know special authority is not required for research visits."

The Captain grumbled to himself, then said, "Right."

psolilai found herself asking a blunt question. "Where are you taking those wrealities?"

"Eh? Up top. Where else?"

"Who are they for?"

Captain Gironbiom looked at her as if confronting a lunatic. "Is that any of our business? It's how things is done. It's what the Elder Analyst wants."

psolilai contemplated what she hoped to do, then observed the energy weapons hanging from the belts of the drivers. "I may need one of those rifles," she said. "Give me one."

The silence that followed implied she had at least a small chance of success.

"Do you need five, Captain Gironbiom?" she continued. "In fact, why carry any at all? Who is there to fight?"

The Captain glanced at Dezisserine.

"Dyeeth Boolin," said psolilai, "make him give me—"

"Wait," Dezisserine interrupted. "Captain, why not give up one of your men's rifles? We may have need of it . . . if we happen across strangers in the galleries on the topmost level."

psolilai could tell that this was a ludicrous explanation, but nonetheless Captain Gironbiom clicked his fingers at the nearest driver, who with sullen expression strode over to psolilai and slapped the rifle in her outstretched hand. She tested its weight, then lowered it and aimed it at a wall. It felt good.

229

"There will be no need to destroy anything here," Dezisserine told her. "The rifle will work."

The men began pushing their carts away. Captain Gironbiom grimaced and said, "We'll be on our way, Creepy."

Dezisserine said nothing. The men departed, and soon the five interlopers stood in silence.

When Dyeeth Boolin turned to walk on, psolilai called out, "Slow down, felin. I want to know your position here. There's a lot you haven't explained—why Dezisserine calls you a regular here, why those men were deferential to you."

"Hmmm," said the felin, sucking at his pipe. "There is very little to explain, my dear. I have lived here for a long time and I am known on these levels. Though I am not a member of the Analyticate, I can wander here at will on account of my scholarly interest in the haven. This is not unorthodox. I know a dozen scoundrels who seduce women and get drunk every night who also come here to meditate on philosophy. Such is not unusual in the Haven of the Owl."

psolilai scowled. She was unhappy with this explanation, but its grace allowed her no room for a rejoinder. "We had better find these gryphons as soon as possible," she muttered. "Dezisserine, lead on."

She turned. Brief glimpse of a wren fluttering up ahead. For a moment she froze; and the agen noticed. It raised its chin as if to sniff, yet to her it seemed to be using some other, ineffable sense. Then the moment was gone. She fidgeted with the rifle, finding a hook on her belt from which to hang it, before returning her gaze to the agen.

It was staring at her. "Are we alone up here?" it asked.

psolilai made an attempt at frivolity. "Well, there's Gularvhen and Metaxain, Dyeeth Boolin . . . the Captain . . ."

The wren had vanished. Dezisserine stood silent for a while, then strode on. "The top levels are close," it said. "We will be there in an hour."

psolilai breathed a sigh of relief, and followed.

After half an hour they reached the level lying directly below the one hundred and twentieth level, halting at a broad gallery. It was large, gleaming in the light of a setting moon, in the centre a house, behind that a garden of potted plants and a pool. No lamps inside the house, suggesting no occupant. psolilai noticed fruit trees growing in pots around the front wall. She walked up and picked an apple, then a pear, which she bit into, savouring the flavours as she scanned the gallery for signs of danger. Nothing obvious.

Metaxain stood at her side. "Should you be eating that?" he asked nervously. "You don't know who it belongs to."

psolilai raised the rifle, holding it against her side so the muzzle pointed away from her. "I take what I need when I find it," she said. "It is like hunting." She threw the apple core aside. "There's something glinting around the pool. We had better check it."

Metaxain screwed his eyes up to look in the direction of the pool. "Glinting? I can't see anything. What like?"

psolilai did not answer. Instead she strode through the garden towards the pool, Metaxain and Gularvhen following, the other two watching. The sandy shingle around the pool was strewn with coiled shells. She picked one up and put it to her ear: a hiss and a swish, then a distant electric sigh gradually louder, louder, now distinct in her ear.

Gularvhen remarked, "The voice of the Constructor transmitted across Urbis Morpheos."

"How do you know?" she demanded.

Gularvhen shrugged.

"What are these shells?" Metaxain asked.

"Manufactured ears," Gularvhen said, "attuned to the vibrations of an artefact."

"You know this artefact?" asked Metaxain.

Again Gularvhen shrugged.

Cursing under her breath, psolilai turned to look away. She wondered now if the Constructor might help her conquer the Owl Palace, for if it was half as well defended as rumour suggested such power would be necessary. A tree and a toadstool might not be enough.

To Gularvhen she said, "What do you think of these shells?"

He answered, "I do not comprehend your question."

Deliberately vague! He knew something . . .

She turned to look out over the pool. An equivalence occurred to her. Mushrooms took her to natural information space, wrealities took her to artificial information space. If she was near the Constructor, as these shells suggested, then she should acquire information about this gallery, and the level above.

She came to a decision—after all, she was undisputed leader of this group. "I need to rest," she said, "this altitude is making me dizzy." An hour or two stood before the middle of the night. "At midnight we will continue," she added. "Dezisserine, ascend to the gryphon gallery and discover what state they are in. If you can find out how to reach the Sky Level, so much the better."

It looked at her in silence.

"Do I lead here or do I not?" she shouted.

The agen turned to leave.

"Gularvhen, explore the house. Metaxain, you and Dyeeth Boolin watch both gallery entrances in case somebody disturbs us. Try not to wake me."

Turning her back to them, she lay down and took one of the remaining vials from her pocket, the contents of which she swallowed without hesitation. In seconds she was . . .

Moving forward at speed . . .

Hurtling into oblivion . . .

Hanging in the bath of scintillating fragments . . .

Turning to face the deep ocean of numbers . . .

Then the glimpse of blackness as shifting veils parted to reveal lines of scarlet blobs, and pulsating ganglions lilac sheened . . .

So simple.

She fixed at the front of her mind the information she needed: coiled shells, the Constructor and the Transmuter, but most important, the power inherent in these artefacts. The power.

Like an owl she glided across the lines of ganglions, those scarlet blobs full to bursting with image-plates—a world of information that would allow her to explore the potential of the shells and the artefacts, and so reach her goal. With autistic intensity she analysed the plates, dipping here if she noticed a glint of gold, stalling there to investigate a group of symbols, flying on and on, until she found herself touring the edge of the network. Nothing leaped out at her. She saw gold, she saw agens, but nothing possessed that kernel of information she required. And time was passing, here and in the external world.

232

It struck her then that the birds—part of the system—enjoyed an advantage. They knew this network. They were an integral part, the means of transfer. She, on the other hand, was an outsider.

She needed a metawreality to help her understand this knowledge system.

She flew away from the network towards the great lilac owl, understanding that it too might be a source of information, and when after what seemed hours she arrived, she flew high, up to its head, where two orange eyes glared like twin suns.

She found that she could speak. "Do you hear me?"

Circular eyes staring, as if daring her to say more.

She did. "Do you hear me? The ganglions give me nothing that I want. I need information!"

Still no reply. She flew around the owl's head hoping to find some clue to its operation, wondering if in fact it was just some aspect of the environment. Then the head turned a half circle and she was hovering before one enormous eye. She saw a fluttering reflection. Wings, feathers, flat face.

A voice spoke, deep like a basso flute, all breathy, but with menace. "You require information concerning what?"

psolilai recovered her composure. "The Constructor, the Transmuter, I can hear their voices through the coiled shells, but I need the power of the Constructor itself, and I need it quick!"

"Seek those ganglions dealing with the melding of form and artefact. They lie in the centre of the network, part of the zone dealing with sculpture. Hover low and pluck out your plate with haste."

psolilai darted away, desperate to find the information plate before her trip finished. Soon she spotted plates dealing with architecture, then sculpture, and finally small plates filled with inscriptions that dealt with the merging of the living and the artificial. She plucked one at random. Knowledge flooded her brain, memories like a vista revealed behind fading mist. She linked this knowledge with what she already knew from her dreams, with Voaranazne in the copse of stone trees, with that same mallead in the garden of the Pool of Wrealities. But malleads were artificial beings. Could a melding take place between artefact and human being? In one sense, yes, for she had used the Constructor. But now she wanted a deeper link, one more permanent, though it would be deemed an abomination.

233

Again she hovered above the oscillating plates, waiting for that perfect one, her sight focussed on nothing but what lay below, ready like a bird of prey to pounce and to take. There! Corpus and artefact.

She dropped, plucked, flew high. Knowledge poured into her brain.

She lost touch with the network and the ocean . . .

Another reality imposing itself . . .

Exhausted, falling back . . .

Floating . . .

Ocean and network faded to be replaced by blurred vision and the smell of her sweaty clothes, and then, as her eyes focussed, by the sight of the pool, the house, and a distant starry sky. She licked her dry lips, rubbed her eyes. Metaxain and Gularvhen were watching the gallery exits. She sat up. Dyeeth Boolin knelt an arm's length away, his eyes fixed upon her.

She raised one arm to push back her hair. Her skin was lilac.

In shock she stared. Her forearm, elbow, and her fingers up to their middle joints were sheened lilac, texture granulated, like sugar on bread. Obviously metawrealities. To deny their presence she pulled her sleeve down, hid her hand behind her back, then glanced up at Dyeeth Boolin.

"Now the temptation becomes yearning," the felin said. "Your desires begin to take over your mind, you think about them all the time as you wonder what you will become."

Frightened, psolilai drew away, until her back hit the gallery wall. "You know this feeling?"

"Hmmm . . . I am familiar with the feeling."

"The potential to *do* things."

Dyeeth Boolin nodded. "We all want to do things, but only some of us can match our vision with our deeds."

psolilai quailed. A glimpse of what she faced confronted her, if only in the melancholy of the felin's voice. "You called me a visionary when we met," she said. "You knew even then what I wanted."

"My dear, there is a greater presence behind you." Dyeeth Boolin paused, sighed, then continued, "You see, I returned to Teewemeer to discover that you and Gularvhen had passed through the haven—that you had stood upon the ziggurat. Afterwards, the moontoo changed."

psolilai nodded.

"You face now your biggest obstacle, my dear. Already you are succumbing to the temptation of the power your situation brings."

"That is so."

"And I am here to help you, as I promised." He paused, glanced to where the men stood. "With me, it was scarlet skin. It burned me badly, but I was lucky, my fur grew back. You have gone farther than I. All I can do is help you."

"You have travelled to the wrealities?"

"My body . . . rejected the chemical complexes."

psolilai fell silent, and in the privacy of her mind she scorned Dyeeth Boolin. She knew now that she was close to penetrating the Owl Palace. Alongside Metaxain she would find success, where Dyeeth Boolin had found only failure. Her fear vanished and her mind turned cold. Now all she wanted to do was reach the Sky Level. So much lay within her grasp.

"Thank you for your advice," she said politely, "which I will bear in mind."

She sat upright, concealing her lilac hand by pulling on a pair of gloves. When Dyeeth Boolin glanced away, she put one of the coiled shells into her pocket.

Dezisserine had returned. She walked over, to ask the agen, "How are the gryphons?"

"There are five of them and they are awake," it replied. "Only they can carry us to the Sky Level. Follow me."

A tunnel cut with flights of steps took them to the highest gallery. They walked out of darkness into a cavern of fire.

The gryphons lay on bare substrate, their weight causing the ground to sag into depressions. Flames licked the edges of these bowls. The gryphons were as big as dirigibles, leonine of face, their beards plaited and their hair greased back, their eyes like smoking tar. Each gryphon had a pair of wings folded against its body. The nearest was coloured dun and green, its white teeth showing. Three others were red, the fifth yellow with grey stripes. Even psolilai flinched, her self-confidence battered into submission by the majesty of these beasts.

The nearer gryphon spoke in a voice that reverberated around the gallery. "You have come to be flown to the Sky Level?"

psolilai cleared her throat. "Yes," she answered. She sounded like a mouse in comparison.

"That is possible," said the gryphon. Its eyes widened, like a cat's spying prey. "But first you must pass our test."

"Test?"

"I will ask a riddle. Answer correctly and we will fly you to the Sky Level. Do you agree to this?"

psolilai glanced at the others, who, with the exception of Dezisserine, were staring dumbfounded at the gryphons. There was no chance of Kirishnaghar mimicking these beasts, she realised, for they were sentient.

"What happens if we fail?" she asked.

"That is an interesting question," said the gryphon. "It implies you entertain the possibility of failure, in which case, why are you here?"

Gularvhen stepped forward. "We accept your terms," he said. "Ask the riddle."

The gryphon nodded its head, and the flames below it were fanned. "What is it that dies when you darken its I?"

psolilai looked at Metaxain and Dezisserine, but their faces held no clues to an answer, while Dyeeth Boolin puffed at his pipe as if unconcerned by the situation. Gularvhen, his back to her, was a mystery. She asked herself, what is it that dies when you darken its I? She felt lost, very small. "It is difficult," she said, to nobody in particular.

"Patience, one and all, patience," said Gularvhen. He raised his voice to declare, "The answer is a suicidal man, for his I is already dark, and to darken it further is to have him kill himself."

Was it possible for gryphons to be amazed? Confused? For a few moments psolilai thought she detected human feelings on their faces, as they swayed their heads to look at one another—hardly the arrogant beasts of before.

The dun and green gryphon spoke. "That answer is correct," it said. "We will fly you to the Sky Level."

Gularvhen made a small bow in their direction. "Admirable," he said. Relief was plain in his voice.

The fires receded as the gryphons clambered out of their pits and stood tall, stretching, one yawning, before they leaned down to receive their passengers. psolilai clambered aboard to find a body warm but not uncomfortable, and within the minute all five gryphons were walking to the edge of the gallery, raising their wings and taking off. A swirling jumble of indigo sky and black landscape, rushing wind and terror, before mottled fields appeared, and they landed.

It was dawn. The gryphons departed without further word and they were left, the five of them, alone on the Sky Level.

17

Wisdom The Goal

C ome morning, Psolilai faced the funeral of Karakushna. She looked into her mirror then applied her disguise. Pale blotches caused by bad fog disfigured her forehead and both cheeks, and her lips were blanched; she used cosmetics to turn herself into the blandest worker from Rem. Leaving the Church of the Parasol Cap she walked alone down Baeocystin Lane, making for the Field of Gaia, to all the haven a solitary man with head bowed low. The air was bitter cold, daytime heat lost overnight. Thinking of Karakushna she returned again to dejection.

Who else would be at the Field of Gaia? The Rem lane community without doubt, all those old men and women, plus younger folk who might have grown up with Karakushna. None of Karakushna's family of course, because they did not know of her existence. Tightness now in Psolilai's throat. Two people here had paid a penalty, Karakushna and herself, one an innocent victim, the other a fool. And the guilt Psolilai felt would stick a long time in her gullet.

On the Field of Gaia she saw a crowd clustered around the Circle of Beak and Claw, and she recognised the two old men, other adults, a few crying children, and the officer of the Analytical Council who scorned the ceremony before striding off. She kept back, yet not so far away as to dissociate herself from the grieving. A few bystanders glanced at her, but none recognised her.

Tears rolled down her face. In her throat the guilt felt like a tumour, obstructing her breathing. She sobbed, put her hands in her pockets and stared at the ground, trying to forget the face of her cousin, then berating herself and remembering it again.

Down came the birds, fat vultures then hawks, and the aerial burial began in earnest. A few people wandered away. The sun rose to illuminate the stones, the field. So the day passed. In order to feel discomfort Psolilai stood silent, motionless, as the frozen ground leached the heat out of her. Noon, afternoon: come evening she stood alone, everybody gone, the corpse just bones and fat, and blood distributed far and wide.

She had arrived at the Field of Gaia with the sun a white disk rising through bad fog. Now it set, a white disk sinking into bad fog.

At length the cold forced her into motion. She walked away from the Circle of Beak and Claw, glad she was the last to leave, feeling the blood pumping again through her limbs. She breathed in deep: exhaled slow. It was over.

Halfway across the Field of Gaia she saw movement ahead. A single figure, in front of it snarling animals on leashes.

Snuffler pigs from Thee. And Ryoursh.

Psolilai realised she was in great danger. Where to run? If she made north along Baeocystin Lane she would be trapped at the Church of the Parasol Cap. Anywhere else and these pigs, trained to sniff out molecules of scent, would follow. Ryoursh was running towards her, the pigs on a long leash, their bodies bouncing, mud flying from under their feet. Psolilai turned and ran.

In too short a time she was climbing the wall at the bottom of the Field of Gaia and jumping into Tryptamine Lane, Ryoursh and the pigs catching up, but still distant. Bad fog was thick here; perhaps she could use it and the river to confuse the pursuit, water to wash away her scent, bad fog to vanish into. It was the only plan she could think of.

But the bad fog slowed her down. She heard guttural snarls, squeals, running boots. There was no stretch of water shallow enough for her to use. In desperation she decided to lose herself in a maze of passages, but soon she was herself lost, choking in the pall. Then back on Tryptamine Lane. Now she ran fast, trusting to luck that she would not launch herself into the river. She tripped, fell, got up and ran on. The pigs were closing. Bootsteps clunking. People staring at her.

Suddenly she found herself at the junction with Salvinorin Lane, close to the Feather Gate, and the option of leaving the haven presented itself.

Ryoursh's voice cried out. "Go get!"

There came a loud burst of squealing, tapping trotters, and then the sight of four grinning pigs galloping out of the bad fog, teeth glinting, making straight for her. She ran on, tried to find a high window in which to shelter, but it was too late. The lead pig snatched her ankle, bit, shook, and downed her. She screamed as the others crashed into her and into each other, eager to get her ankles and calves in their mouths. Stabbing pains from their teeth. They clung like dogs.

Guards appeared from the Feather Gate.

Ryoursh stepped in to cut off their approach. "Move away, old duffers," she said. The chill in her voice sent them running.

Psolilai tried to pull her feet free, but the pigs held firm. Cold did not reduce the pain. She tried to kick out. Her fear was deadened by the inevitability of capture; she felt a black dejection ready to smother her mind . . .

Capture! How could this be happening?

Ryoursh blew on a whistle and the pigs jumped back, assembling themselves behind her. "Nice moustache, sister," she said. "Couldn't you grow the beard?"

Psolilai said nothing.

"Get up!" Ryoursh shouted.

Psolilai held on to a lanthorn post. Her boots were torn, blood leaking from them. While her left leg was firm, she could put no weight on her right.

"Now walk where I say," Ryoursh said. "If you try to escape you'll be eaten alive."

"Where are you taking me?"

"To a temporary prison. You are an escapee. You are wanted." Ryoursh spat on the ground, then walked up and ripped off Psolilai's wig and moustache. "I changed my mind," she said. "I decided that death was too good for you. What you deserve is a lifetime of forced labour."

In other words, sent back to Tall Cliff Steel.

Ryoursh yelled, "Move!"

Psolilai limped along the lane. "You must overcome your jealousy," she gasped. "Aunt Sukhtaya told me what happened to you."

"All Aunt Sukhtaya did was convince me that returning you to prison for the rest of your life was preferable to killing you. For that insight, I thank her."

"My ankle—"

"Don't slow down. These Snuffler pigs are hungry."

Psolilai whimpered. She grasped that this was more than jealousy; her sister was a scion of Thee, a reactionary, opposed to free Ere. Ryoursh hated Aunt Sukhtaya too, since through sheer selfishness her aunt also stood in opposition to Thee.

At Analytical-Tendency House, Ryoursh spoke to a pair of guards. The men stared at Psolilai, then strode up to her and pushed her down onto a damp seat. Ryoursh strolled away, the pigs gamboling after her. The guards stood firm, silent, standing beside Psolilai. An hour passed. Both the cold and the pain began to exact their toll. Then Ryoursh reappeared. The guards saluted and Ryoursh indicated that Psolilai should walk into the building. Psolilai quailed, memories returning of the last time she had been here. It was happening again . . .

Her cell was sparsely furnished: one bed without a mattress, one ragged blanket, one bucket, one pitcher, one plate with bread crumbs still on it from the previous occupant. Silverfish sprang everywhere, and there were slugs coming in from the high barred window, a tracery of slime up and down the walls. One corner was flooded, filled with dead insects and food remains. Psolilai slumped on the bed. She had expected this. It was not the first time that she had been kept under lock and key in the dungeons of Analytical-Tendency House.

She did not know what would happen next, but she knew her sister was out to inflict the maximum amount of pain. That surely meant blinkers, a fate from which even she, courageous and lucky, could never hope to escape. Yet the return to Tall Cliff Steel would be by dirigible; and so, despite her terror, she began to plan.

With an open window, she quickly froze. The blanket helped, but her leathers grew cold; the Rem worker's clothes had been ripped from her back as she was thrown into the cell.

After a day she realised that while food might not be forthcoming, she could only last a couple of days without water, and the pitcher was empty. Some hours later, realisation came. The puddle in the corner was her water. She filtered it by pouring it through a kerchief in her pocket, determined to win even a tiny victory; but it tasted foul.

Another day passed, marked by the cycle of light and dark behind the window. Food was not forthcoming. Her rumbling stomach gave way to a more subtle hollow sensation in the belly. She covered the bucket with wood from the bed, but it still stank.

Third day, fourth day. On the fifth there came the sound of a key at her door. It rattled, then stopped. A voice said, "No, let's not."

Footsteps walking away.

By now Psolilai was feeling light-headed. She made a fungi search, but her captors were too cunning to miss that escape route. The walls were coated antifungal — that was where the sharp smell came from. It almost made her faint.

On the sixth day a rattling key did lead to the door opening, and then a masked warder bringing in a tray of food. Without word he departed, the door slammed shut. The food was edible, biscuits, dry bread, green cheese. But she knew what this meant. Her appearance, case and sentence were due, probably on the following day. They were feeding her so she would not faint and cause embarrassment. A few hours after dawn on the following day she was taken up winding stairs to a large, bright room filled with people sitting on benches. Decorations and furnishings had been consumed by bad fog, leaving a crusting of ochre. She sat alone on a bench.

Everybody was present. All five of the Analytical Council. Fenneoca the Analytic Logistician, swarthy lump of a man, hatted, wrinkled skin unshaven, smoking a neverending cheroot. The felin Kyoory Fye, tiny compared to Fenneoca, ginger complexion, red hair, blue eyes, and long, white whiskers. He was the Analytic Reificiary. Next to him Zethezdial, Analytic Justiciary, old, bald, caked with make-up to disguise his poxed skin. The powerful bulk of Analytic Serjeant Neogogg, also bald but with copper-tinted flesh, muscles rippling under his skin-tight grey plastic suit. And there, slightly apart, Amargoidara. Tall, lean, greybeard, slow movements but lightning-fast mind. He wore a mask that transmitted his state of mind, for it was not permitted that his inner self be revealed via his face to the ordinary citizens of the haven.

Here was the centre of political power in Theeremere, anti-nature all of them, anti-mushroom and pro-manufacturing, working in Rem but scorning the place to live in Thee, each man hazy behind rumour and whisper, which they encouraged to give their detractors

241

a harder task. What immorality they achieved was unknown, but it was assumed, even expected, Neogogg attacking women, Fenneoca the sadist gambler, Zethezdial in the pay of all four anti-fungal secret societies. Amargoidara naught but bile.

Psolilai stared at them, numb to their inhumanity, for in her mind she had long since cast them into the realm of the unnecessary.

There were others present, officials of the court, technicians, interpreters of the manufacturing ecosystem, also Aunt Sukhtaya, and Ryoursh sitting with dandies who must be Threadbreakers or Snufflers; and rows of people who just seemed to be an audience. Not a jury, that was certain.

Amargoidara stood up and walked towards a plinth, upon which lay an object beneath a cloth. He pulled the cloth away to reveal a scarlet globe a yard across—one of the three analytical-tendencies that formed the foundation of the triple-split haven. His voice hissed from behind the mask, which now showed an angry face. "This is one of three machines that tell us how to live," he declared. "It is a specialised wreality, assembling historical knowledge then giving us advice." The frown on the mask grew deeper. "It is not to be ignored. No other source of knowledge is superior since it accumulates human knowledge. But this analytical-tendency, and indeed the other two, have been ignored by one person."

Psolilai let her expression remain neutral, unsure of the purpose of this session. Best not to let them know what she was thinking.

Sad face on the mask. "It is always unfortunate when our moral sources are ignored, and, worse, when an alternative theory is put forward." Now Amargoidara turned so that the face mask gazed upon her. "Once before you defied the rule of the Analytical Council. We exist to transfer the immensity of human wisdom, accumulated in the analytical-tendencies over uncounted aeons, to you—for your benefit. Like a brat you ignored us. For that ill deed we exiled you from the hope of this haven, in a wilderness place cold and high."

Psolilai knew that her sentence was about to be pronounced.

Return of the angry face. "To Tall Cliff Steel you will be taken, there to become a blinkered one for the rest of your days. We estimate ten to fifteen thousand of those." He paused. "I believe you know what we mean?"

242

Blinkered ones: wooden flaps forcing the prisoner to look forwards, a punishment for those deemed too dangerous to enjoy even the smallest luxury. For the first time she felt she should speak. "I have seen the blinkered ones," she replied, her voice wavering.

"Do you have anything to say?"

Her mind went blank. Shock.

There was an official at her side. He slapped something white across her mouth. It stung. Psolilai lifted one arm, assuming that it would come off, but it did not because her fingernails could find no edge.

"Do you have anything to say?" Amargoidara repeated, his mask acquiring a leer.

The tape was stuck to her mouth. It was aerated, she noticed.

"Oh, yes," said Amargoidara, "you can breathe through it. You will be wearing it for some days."

Psolilai shook her head as two tears fell from the corners of her eyes. This was the time to change her future. This moment.

Snap!

Tiles dropped from the ceiling, crashing to the floor, raising a cloud of dust. A silent room, all faces upturned.

Then another tile fell. Two feet, legs, then a figure leaping through brittle plaster to the floor, a drop of four yards. Psolilai stared. The woman with the silver twined staff! She was old, yet she had dared a leap no youth would dare. She stood combative, her staff held like a weapon, her gaze darting around the room—and on some instinct born of hope alone Psolilai jumped over the bench before her and ran forward. The insane possibility of rescue beckoned.

Amargoidara's mask implied fury. "Seize them!" he ordered.

Two men armed with sabres moved forward, but their manner hardly inspired confidence; more like mice than soldiers, the threat of an unknown technology before them. Even Neogogg looked alarmed. The woman thrust her staff at the men and they jumped back. From her vantage point at the woman's side Psolilai saw a haze rise through the air, as if some mysterious energy had batted the guards away.

Then a neon blaze stabbed through the chamber, clearing a path to the nearest door, people bowled over, uninjured, but responding to a force. The old woman ran down this path, and Psolilai followed. Pandemonium ensued. Over shouts and screams Psolilai heard

243

Amargoidara yelling orders. Ducking, expecting some missile to obstruct her way, she followed her rescuer into a corridor then down to the front of Analytical-Tendency House. When she looked back, she saw pursuit. The old woman sent out another blast of neon to stop it.

Out in the lane. Fog drifted across them in waves of sepia.

Psolilai grabbed the woman's shoulder and pointed to the tape over her mouth. As if unconcerned, the woman touched the end of the staff to the tape, whereupon it fell off. The manufactured altering the manufactured, thought Psolilai, nanos at work, or something similar. Now a little suspicious, she reached out to touch the staff, saying, "What is this thing?"

"An object as ancient as the Pillar."

They hurried away. Psolilai heard noise from the building behind them as they ran along the street. Voices, the clang of metal on metal, then orders given in a harsh voice.

"Faster," said the woman, breaking into a run.

"Where to?"

The woman slowed to a trot, amazement on her face. "You don't know?"

"No. Where?"

In reply the woman ran faster, heading north along Indole Lane to the Emerald Bridge. To Thee.

Psolilai skidded to a halt. "Stop! I've got to get to the Church of the Parasol Cap."

"Now?"

Psolilai's mind span. "Why did you spring me from Tall Cliff Steel?"

The old woman turned to peer into the pall ahead, then, with one athletic gesture, she raised the staff and threw it at Psolilai, who caught it one-handed. "You'll need this," Psolilai was told.

With that, the woman ran on. Psolilai was left dazed in the lane, noise behind her, confusion ahead. Too much at once.

She turned around — no sign of pursuit — but she knew that her enemies were close, for although she could not see them she could hear them, the bad fog transmitting sound with fidelity. She had decided to head for the Church of the Parasol Cap because all her equipment was there, Gularvhen too. The quickest way would be to follow alleys to Serotonin Lane, then leap the gap in the Sundered Bridge to reach Ere.

Voices close, now. She darted into a passage. Although noon had just passed, the sky was grey with cloud, and bad fog filled the air. Shadows of houses and towers enfolded her, ochre fog surrounded her. She felt safe, concealed.

But she was not. Snuffler pigs were abroad. She heard their squeals, the mocking laughter of their handlers. She realised that even if she made it to the Church, to Gularvhen and to Hoss, there was no guarantee of fleeing the haven. She stopped, looking north to Thee.

She changed her mind. This was far too risky, not least because of her injured leg, which was beginning to hurt. She needed to be out of the way.

And she had grasped the symbolism of the old woman's staff.

They would expect her to make for the Emerald Bridge. No. She would run west, cross into Thee by means of the Possible Bridge, then make down Psilocybin Lane. And then . . .

This plan she followed. Sometimes her pursuers were close, more often they were distant, until as she neared the Pillar the noise of pursuit faded to nothing. Then the Pillar base emerged out of a brown pall. The riverside lane was empty, its lanthorns dimmed, or off.

Psolilai was twenty yards away from the entrance to the Pillar spiral when Ryoursh stepped out from a nearby doorway.

The shock Psolilai felt masked panic inside. She said, "So you think you can stop me?" It was all bravado, no thought.

Ryoursh produced an energy weapon that looked like the hand of a corpse. She pointed its fingers at her sister. "I'll stop you, criminal," she said. The fury she felt made her voice a snarl, as if she was bestialised by rage.

"You will not stop me," Psolilai answered.

Something dark, like liquid night, emerged from the end of the fingers, then hunched into globes and sprang out. Caught off guard, Psolilai was fortunate that the staff saved her. It produced light, blackness and neon merging into formless grey that thudded like mud to the ground.

Psolilai hardly knew what she was saying, so desperate was she to escape her sister, and the mob that would surely arrive soon. "Get out of my path!" she cried.

"Give me that staff. Surrender."

245

"No."

Ryoursh grimaced. The weapon produced more gouts of black energy, that rose, twisted like ropes, then fell, all in seconds—but the staff bucked in Psolilai's grip once again, and sent out a sheet of neon to neutralise the attack. Then more attacks and more defence. All Psolilai had to do was grip the staff. Her palms grew hot, as if the device was drawing energy from her.

Ryoursh threw her weapon into the river with a curse. Seeing her sister admit defeat, Psolilai relaxed, but then Ryoursh folded her arms, standing in silence. Black tendrils emerged from the bad fog hanging over the river, to grow, thicken, merge and form a cloud that, foot by foot, crept towards the Pillar. Psolilai moved away from it, but not wanting to distance herself from the Pillar she was forced towards Ryoursh.

Still no other people had arrived. Psolilai wondered if she ought to make a break for the Pillar.

Ryoursh forced her hand, leaping forwards, feinting, then when Psolilai retreated in confusion leaping again and grabbing the lower end of the staff. Now it was horizontal, both women grasping one end. Psolilai held tight but the fury of her sister proved the deciding factor, and suddenly she found herself sitting in a puddle, her hands burning, Ryoursh approaching out of the darkening pall with the staff raised above her head. Psolilai stood, and, bent over, ran towards the Pillar, but Ryoursh moved to block her, then tripped her so that she fell just yards from the spiral stair. She lay prone. Ryoursh swung the staff as a club.

No time for defence, or even for thought. The staff flew through the air.

And stopped over her chest, bouncing out of Ryoursh's grasp and clattering towards the Pillar. Something hot against Psolilai's breast. With Ryoursh staggering back in shock, screaming and shaking her hands, there were moments enough for Psolilai to stand, grab the staff and run onto the spiral. She clambered up a quarter turn, then stopped to glance back. A mob was forming, most of them guards and people from the court room. She glanced up at the stairs spiralling out of sight.

"Only one way for you to go now," Ryoursh said.

Up.

Psolilai continued up the stairs, round and around the double spiral until the pain in her leg forced her to stop.

She felt inside her shirt and drew out the scriber. It was still hot.

18

THE DREAMER—SEEKER

The Sky Level was no more than twenty acres, but to psolilai the density of packing made it seem larger. Much of this growth was artificial, leaves and boles too shiny, or twisted into unnatural shapes, but she also saw a variety of grasses, herbs and even bushes from the natural ecosystem. In the wind, these forms swayed and hissed. The centre was strewn high with rocks from which water ran, escaping off the edges in a number of waterfalls. Atop the rocks stood a stone horse. There was no sign of the hog, the owl, nor even of the Owl Palace.

Cold . . . and psolilai shivered, folding her arms across her chest. "The Palace must be over there, behind those boulders," she said. Really, she needed Kirishnaghar now. "Dezisserine, explore toward the centre. See if the building is on the other side."

The agen departed, forging a path through the grasses by bending forward to push them aside. Soon all she could see was its head bobbing up and down.

"Kirishnaghar!" she hissed.

"Here, psolilai," came a voice behind her. She turned, to see him leaning on his stick, a blind man, his white hair flapping in the breeze.

"Quiet," she whispered, "there is an agen about."

"I know."

"Be careful, I think it is suspicious of a mallead. Now, where is the Owl Palace?"

Kirishnaghar pointed to the centre of the Sky Level. "It lies behind those rocks. I have not yet had a chance to reconnoitre. Do you want me to?"

"Yes. I'll get rid of Dezisserine again one hour from now. Report back to me then."

Kirishnaghar made a small bow, then walked away.

psolilai turned to face Gularvhen and Dyeeth Boolin. She said, "Is it my imagination, or is everything turning yellow?"

"Gold," said Gularvhen.

psolilai looked where he looked. He was right. A golden sheen was enveloping the manufactured growth, and it had nothing to do with the gold mist of dawn because that had passed. Her mind turned to the Constructor, and for a moment—for a second, no more—her old fear returned, before it was smothered by confidence and she laughed out loud. Gold: the Sky Level recognised her.

"What do you find amusing?" Gularvhen asked.

"Nothing."

He grumbled under his breath.

"What did you say?" she asked.

"Nothing," he replied, using the same tone of voice she had. They glared at one another, but the moment was broken by Dezisserine swishing through the grasses and calling out, "I have found it."

psolilai walked over to meet the agen. "Where?"

It pointed to the pile of rocks. "It is large, made of white marble, with a flat roof on which many things grow."

Metaxain joined them. "Is my silver birch there?"

The agen nodded. "Quite safe, though swaying in every gust of wind."

"We will rest here," psolilai declared. "I need more sleep. Anyway, I prefer not to move too much under the light of the sun. Dezisserine, I want you to circumnavigate the level, observing as you go. Look out for routes to the Owl Palace, for dangers we may meet, and try to find the hog. Ascertain whether it is aggressive. Do not hurry, you have until dusk."

The agen hesitated, looked across the level, but then agreed. "I will do as you suggest," it said, glancing at the others.

psolilai settled herself against a clump of grasses. Kirishnaghar would arrive soon; afterward she could sleep, in preparation for the final assault.

Kirishnaghar's report was brief. "The Sky Level is as before," he said, "with the exception of a new gold veneer upon manufactured growth.

249

The scarlet owl sleeps in its roost, while the hog roots around in debris on the opposite edge."

psolilai nodded. "Good," she said. "The agen is on patrol. Keep watch over us, and come dusk we will make our move."

He agreed to this plan. But the sun had moved only a little before psolilai woke to find Kirishnaghar shaking her.

"psolilai?" he said, lowering himself to peer into her face.

She cursed. "I told you to let me rest," she grumbled. "I'm not a machine like you, I need sleep."

The tone of his voice hardened. "I woke you for a reason. Look yonder." He raised one arm to point north. "Do you see that speck in the sky? I think it is a dirigible flying this way."

In an instant psolilai was on her feet. Her vision both brightened and sharpened as her eyes accommodated the new view. She held her body rigid. It was more than just a dirigible, it was a dirigible with canvas slung low in which lay a number of bodies.

"Agens!" she exclaimed. "Ten of them lying beneath their dirigible. And I can see another two in the far distance."

"Another two dirigibles?" said Kirishnaghar. "Are they flying this way?"

"They are, and there may be more."

Kirishnaghar had turned to look in other directions. "Two more!" he said, pointing into the sun.

psolilai turned also, to see that he was correct. "They are coming for me," she said. "There are . . . fifteen more agens."

Gularvhen appeared from behind the mound against which he had lain. "What will you do?" he asked.

She mocked his fear. "They will only throw vile fluids again, or transforming objects. I *can* cope with that."

"And if they do not?"

At that moment Dezisserine ran from a clump of tall grass, hastening to psolilai's side. "Agens," it said. "They are coming this way."

Kirishnaghar was gone. She did not know if he had changed shape before Dezisserine saw him. She did not know what to say.

"Agens!" repeated Dezisserine.

"Are you frightened of your own kind?" psolilai asked in a scornful voice.

"They must not see me here."

psolilai detected a weakness. "Why not?" she asked, leaning towards the agen, hoping to intimidate it.

"Because I am cast out, no?"

"Neither assembler nor metamorphoser, you said. What kind of shaman are you?"

But Dezisserine ignored her question. "I will hide myself by the hill of boulders." And it was gone.

psolilai glanced at Gularvhen. "That gives us a hold over it," she said.

"Do you require such a hold?"

psolilai looked him up and down. "You are becoming a weakling, Gularvhen. Once you had backbone. I recommend that you rediscover it."

"We are aware that you are changing," Gularvhen replied, "but we are keeping silent."

psolilai felt anger surge within her. "Are you?" she said, her voice full of scorn. "*Are* you, Gularvhen?"

Without waiting for a reply she walked towards the northern edge of the Sky Level, where she stood beside Metaxain. "We will first observe what these agens do," she said. "If they interact with me again I will have to deal with them. Perhaps you could create a copse in which we can hide—there is soil here, of a sort. Most likely the agens will not stay once they have performed their bizarre ritual. We have nothing to fear."

"You sound very confident."

"You hear the voice of experience. Stay in my shadow and you will be safe."

Metaxain looked west. "Still more coming," he said, "from every quarter. You said they're attracted to you?"

"That is correct. To *me*. Now, prepare your copse."

An hour passed and the scale of the agen influx became clear. Thirty dirigibles had appeared, twenty wheeling above the haven like rotund vultures, the others closing fast, and psolilai, with her predator eyes, could see ten more dots above distant streets.

The skies would be full at sundown.

The sun set behind clouds of dusty orange and grey. Above the Sky Level a horde of dirigibles flew, circling in precise order so that there was no chance of a collision. When the sun vanished the agens began throwing stones, but psolilai had expected this. Metaxain's trees had grown tall, reified from seeds scattered by his entranced mind; a century of growth collapsed into hours.

The pair ran between the trees, and hid. The light began to fade. Crawling like a dog, Dezisserine approached them, glancing upwards then hiding beside the bole of a tree. It wailed, "This is terrible!"

"Why?" psolilai asked.

"They are worshipping you! Do you think they will just leave you alone?"

psolilai stared at the cowering agen. "Worshipping me?"

"Of course! What else?"

Again psolilai looked into the skies, watching dirigibles floating above the treetops. "Worshipping me," she murmured. Then louder, stronger: "Worshipping me!"

Gularvhen stood nearby. "As I suggested before," he said, "they do not threaten your life. This and all the other events happened because of your connection with the Constructor."

"They consider me a goddess because of that," psolilai mused. "If that is the case, I shall act like a goddess."

Dyeeth Boolin shook his head as psolilai prepared to leave the forest. "This is where drama becomes farce," he muttered.

psolilai strode out of the copse into a patch of land covered with low grass and bushes. Raising her head, she cried out, "Agens, listen to me! I do not possess the Constructor!"

In reply the agens began throwing gold coins, but where before they had dropped missiles at random, now they threw them with great force, and their intention was to hit. Gold coins began bouncing on the ground around her. One hit her cheek, and it hurt. She put her hand to her face. Blood.

She tried again. "Leave your goddess in peace! She wishes to be left alone!"

But they threw all the harder, cackling, sniggering. One coin hit the side of her kneecap, and after that she ran back to the copse, crouching low in an effort to reduce her profile.

"What are you doing?" Dyeeth Boolin asked.

In a rage psolilai snarled, "Let me be, felin! I take my own decisions."

Metaxain pointed in the direction from which she had run. "Look!"

psolilai turned to see golden objects scuttling through the grass. "What are they?" she asked.

As if offering the answer, Dezisserine ran away.

"They are heading for you," Metaxain said.

psolilai felt a touch of uncertainty. She had been sure that the agens would listen to her, but here was evidence that they followed their own design. She took a step towards Metaxain and linked arms with him.

"Make roots to stop them," she said, pointing at the approaching golden horde.

But the devices were hundreds strong, ducking and leaping over obstacles, scuttling like so many crabs towards her, a golden tide that she knew she could not stop. The nearest device was just yards away now. She tried to stamp on it, then shield herself behind Metaxain, but the device was like a rat, leaping up her cloak and clamping itself to her sleeve. Squealing, she tried to shake it off, then pull it off, but with a twitch the thing ripped her sleeve, extruded two claws and attached itself to her lilac arm.

Already others were crowding around her.

Gularvhen pulled Metaxain back, and the two men stood beside Dyeeth Boolin. psolilai realised they stood as one against her. Shaking her arm to dislodge the golden device, she cried, "You are plotting against me, all three of you!"

Sharp pain at her wrist dragged her attention away from their grim faces. The device was scraping metawrealities off her arm, skin and all, then with its palps stuffing the substance into its mouth. Another device sprang up and attached itself to her arm. She stared for a moment, then screamed and shook her arm, grabbing the device and trying to pull it off. Intense pain stopped her. Another device locked on. Now the weight caused her to let her arm drop; she sank to the floor and four more devices took the opportunity to grab free space.

She realised that the agens wanted knowledge. They wanted to know about her, and that was why their devices were eating the metawrealities. Horrified, she stopped struggling—wincing, screaming when the pain was too much. Eyes shut.

Then she felt the weight depart. She opened her eyes. The devices attached to her arm were changing from crustaceans to amorphous blobs, merging like mercury, and before she knew it the others were scuttling away and she held an orb of hot gold in her hand, that cooled, shrank, flattened.

She had acquired the Constructor.

Her mind was torn in two. She groaned, knowing that she possessed this artefact; but under the dread a stronger current ran, wondering if she might use it, wondering if it had come to her because in reality she was that golden goddess. She wept, and for a few moments lay curled up, her face hidden from the men so that they would not see her dilemma.

Then she sprang to her feet. "I will have both," she cried. "I will have my way and the Constructor's way."

Moments passed in which every single scuttling object stopped moving, and somehow turned, as if to look at her. Awaiting a decision.

Metaxain ran forward, concern on his face. "psolilai," he said, "are you all right?"

She waited until he was close, then slapped the Constructor in his hand. "You hold it for me," she said. "You can carry this load for me—"

"No!" he screamed.

Dyeeth Boolin leaped forward. "Not him," he urged. "You cannot palm off this responsibility. Either take it and use it, or reject it forever."

psolilai made her decision. "I do neither," she declared.

Metaxain gave a scream so loud it echoed through the copse. Writhing, he fell to the ground, the Constructor visible as sunlight inside his clenched fist, which he tried to open as in spasm his body was tossed across the ground. psolilai saw smoke, smelled burning flesh. Then she saw that Metaxain no longer had a hand. The Constructor was consuming his arm, leaving only ash. The man was in agony, rolling around oblivious to the real world. Dyeeth Boolin stood still, watching in silence. Gularvhen shut his eyes, his face buried in one hand.

psolilai looked down at Metaxain. She was torn. She did not want to hold this artefact and she saw nothing wrong with forcing another to carry it for her. Yet this was a man.

She had never seen a man behave like this. A man who, perhaps, loved her.

He had no elbow, now, just a stump: sunlight so strong she could not look at it.

She turned to Gularvhen. "What do I do now?"

Gularvhen ventured no reply.

She looked at Dyeeth Boolin, but he stomped away to stand by Gularvhen. Now Metaxain had lost his arm to the shoulder and his cries had acquired a hoarse whine so appalling she stepped forward to kneel beside him. Then fury took her. "All right, you coward!" she shouted. "I'll take it if you can't!" And with that she put her hand over his smoking stump and found the Constructor hot in her hand.

She turned her face to the sky, but the curse she formulated against the agens would not come. There came a brief vision of herself in thrall to their incomprehensible wishes, and she wept again. Afraid of appearing weak, she stopped her tears and ran away to the edge of the level, there to kneel down and consider what she had done.

She possessed the Constructor. Whether it was real or a manifestation of Mahandriana mattered not. She had called it and accepted it. She looked into the sky, to see that the agens were drifting away. They had won; their wish had come true. Stone cold fear entered her heart. She looked at the artefact, cursed again, then put it in her pocket. Was she a Gaian or was she not?

She knew one thing. She had to find out the truth of the Owl Palace as soon as possible.

255

Dyeeth Boolin was standing at her side, despair on his furry face. "Now you see the truth of it," he groaned. "Now you face a choice."

"I know that, felin. I know I have the choice."

"Hmmm, but did I not say you would be tempted? So far, as I expected, you have performed poorly. My fear is for the future, what might happen to your colleagues, what might happen to the people who, though they know it not, rely on you."

"You do not frighten me," psolilai replied. "It was you who suggested that my pure Gaian thought was unrealistic. I will never return nature to Urbis Morpheos, you told me. Would it not be better to accept a minimum level of manufacturing, you said. We could live with nature and still retain our required level of technology, or so you said. Those are your exact words. So do not force me into decisions I do not need to make, Dyeeth Boolin."

The felin knelt so that his snout almost touched her, and she smelled his smoky breath. "My dear," he whispered, "do you think it is easy for me to watch you making the same mistakes that I did? Do you think it was easy to watch Metaxain writhing in agony? I will say just this. Make your decisions, but make them quick."

psolilai withdrew the two remaining vials of wreality juice from her pocket. "These are two choices. Do you see?"

Dyeeth Boolin lashed out, and the vials fell to the floor, where one lost its stopper, its contents leaking into the ground. psolilai grabbed the other, cradling it to her chest. "You promised to help me," she said. "I don't call brazen attack a form of help."

Dyeeth Boolin stood up. "My dear, that was no attack. But you, perhaps, are not of a mind to accept my help." He took a deep breath. "You lead here. Tell us what we do next, before the night comes."

He walked away, leaving psolilai alone with her vial of fluid.

She decided to think awhile. She needed time away from them.

N ight. Cloud sweeping in from the west on damp, warm air, and the sparkling sky tarnished grey. The wind was risen again, hissing across the acres of grass, bringing with it the smell of rock and plastic, of rot and rust. No light of moon: all dark and dense, the cloudbase almost within reach. Yet there were hunting creatures about, black metal rats nibbling stone, a machine like a stoat, and from the natural ecosystem hairy moths fluttering from plant to plant.

psolilai surveyed the air, swaying from side to side, looking, listening. She was famished, her hunger intensified by the onset of night. Clear as day she saw the others, a few hundred yards away, sitting together by a tree and talking, but even she could not catch what they said, the wind blowing away their words.

There was something large gliding across the Sky Level, its wings outstretched and silent. psolilai tensed her legs and balanced her body. A moment before the shape passed overhead she leaped up and in one hand caught its talons. Pain stabbed through her fingers. She landed on her feet and dragged the squawking scarlet owl to the ground, smashing its head against a stone, spilling sticky juice. Breathing fast: examining her prey.

She ate the cold stuff like meat, taking strips and tearing them with hands and teeth, gobbling down the smaller pieces then setting upon the rest, until the front of her cloak was soaked scarlet and her face was sticky. Remains on the ground—cracked bones and scarlet morsels, the leftovers of her meal, already attracting interest from the black rats. She felt dizzy. Her crackling brain seemed to spin inside her skull, and she pushed hard on her temples in an attempt to stop the motion. A vague impression of three horrified faces staring at her, she knew not who they were.

This was strong stuff. Something more corrosive than neat alcohol entered her bloodstream, and her arteries burned. Her innards boiling.

Deep knowledge coming closer . . . closer . . . closer . . . coming:

Now:

Begin:

Subject the Owl Palace Mahandriana:

Historical analysis:

Skip:

Relevant analysis:

The Owl Palace a square marble structure one hundred and ten yards on a side on one level its roof flat four drainage channels internal grey matte floor slabs pristine white inner walls and ceiling polished to a glossy finish corridor following its outer edge two corridors leading off each side three rooms per corridor to inner corridor also square five rooms off each one inner chamber all interlinked no doors no windows foundations five yards thick:

Update:

Damage to north end caused by silver birch tree roots worsening twenty five microfaults in the marble to create three running fractures varying mean one sixteenth of an inch across the smallest eleven inches the middle twenty one inches the longest forty seven inches with mean width one tenth of an inch small amount of water erosion:

End:

Whirling knowledge subsiding in brain:

psolilai aware of herself in the real world, grey curtains before her, crossing left to right. Damp face. Voices talking at her side. She sat up, and at once sensed gravity. She had been lying flat on her back looking at the evening sky.

"psolilai?"

257

The spoken name brought her to her senses.

"psolilai?" Dyeeth Boolin. "Are you with us?"

"I hear you," she told the felin.

"Are you conscious? Are you yourself?"

"I hear you, Dyeeth Boolin. I know how to get into the Owl Palace. We were right. Slow and subtle does it, roots, the roots of a tree and the damage they do. Strike in the correct spot and the wall will split like so much slate. Come on!"

She stood up, wobbled, held on to Gularvhen. Metaxain, one-armed, stood apart, staring at her. "What are you looking at?" she asked him.

"Lead us to the Owl Palace," Gularvhen said, his voice sickly imploring, as if to forestall a fight.

psolilai pushed him away, sparing nothing when it came to force. He tottered, then regained his balance. "Leave me alone," she said. "I can stand upright."

"I beg your pardon?"

"Leave me alone! Do you think I am an invalid just because I tasted wreality flesh? It is that which gives me the strength to go on. Now follow me, all of you, before I lose my temper."

Cursing under her breath she led them towards the centre of the Sky Level, making a detour through thick grasses to avoid the boulders and the waterfalls, hacking away vegetation, jumping over rivulets, then pushing on through dense undergrowth until she got her first view of the Owl Palace. It chimed with her mental picture. The owl wreality had spoken true of what it resided upon.

The scarlet hog was rooting around the Palace, but it trotted off when it saw them, leaving psolilai to approach alone, with Gularvhen, Metaxain and Dyeeth Boolin behind, and Dezisserine following at some distance. She cursed them for their cowardice.

"Hurry!" she called, waving them on. When Metaxain came near she said, "Check the state of your silver birch, in particular the roots. If it is alive and stable, go into trance and use all your might to work open the fractures in the marble."

Metaxain replied, "I am quite weak from my ordeal—"

"Do as I say!"

He looked down to the ground, then gave a single nod.

"I will not tolerate disobedience. Does anybody else feel a little weak? No? Good. Then let us continue." She clicked her fingers in Metaxain's direction.

She allowed him ten minutes before beginning her own attack. Knowing the precise position of the three main fractures allowed her to sense their presence, settling her hands upon the cool marble to feel, through melded touch and hearing, those fault lines indicated by natural vibration. She opened her eyes. Now she needed a tool. To look around would interrupt her concentration, so she clicked her fingers over her shoulder and muttered, "Gularvhen."

Seconds later there was cold metal in her hand. She took a deep breath, turned the poignard so its hilt faced forward, summoned her strength, then struck. Once. Twice. Deep breath, then a third strike. There was a crack and dust fell to the ground. She paused, breathed in again, then struck once more. A section of wall to her right collapsed, falling as one block to the ground.

A hole wide enough for them to climb through. A sigh from Metaxain.

"We are in," she announced.

Darkness inside.

To herself she whispered, "Now, 3Machines, it is time to find out what manner of woman you are."

19

URBIS MORPHEOS—RUINED

With the noise from the mob at the bottom of the Pillar continuing, Psolilai had no choice but to ascend further, despite the pain in her injured leg. She did not know if pursuit would follow. The Analytical Council might post guards on the bottom step or they might set up an ascent team. Either way, she was trapped. Unable to put weight on her leg she resorted to crawling up the steps, until even that was too much, and she had to stop.

She took stock of her surroundings. She had ascended perhaps a hundred yards. The solid silver steps were icy cold, glimmering in dim afternoon light, to her left the column of emerald that supported the double spiral stairs, to her right a low railing also of silver over which she could glimpse the surrounding landscape. Theeremere was wreathed in bad fog. Far to the south, bad snow fell. She crawled to the edge and looked out across the haven, to see the triple loop marked in ochre, taller buildings rising up like rotting posts in mud. She shivered. Surviving the night would be difficult.

Perhaps she ought to return and give herself up. Better to live with even the faintest chance of escape than die of hypothermia.

She lay on her back, stretched out under the railing and looked up. To her amazement, she saw light.

All thought of surrender departed. She struggled on, until the neverending and indistinguishable spirals began to show wrinkles, then knots like metallic worm casts oxide-blackened. As evening approached she saw a glow in the silver above her. Then reflections. Then a galithien.

It leaned out over the railing, its roots criss-crossing, even boring into the steps, its gallium arsenide bark brown glazed grey, a thousand

pink and white lamps flickering up and down its bole. It was not tall;
gnarled like an apple tree. Its translucent leaves were broader than her
hands, pale blue in the half light. And she could talk to this creature
since it would sense the pressure waves created by her voice.

"I need help," she said. "Who are you?"

Poemona Fia Fiolo, who are you?

"Psolilai of Ere. Do you live here?"

Yes.

Psolilai saw a glimpse of hope. "I really do need help. I can't go back
down the steps because my enemies wait at the bottom. What lies
above us?"

More steps, through great vertical height.

"Is there anything at the top?"

*I believe so, and there are many other creatures of the manufacturing
ecosystem wandering up and down the Pillar.*

Psolilai said, "Do you know the old woman who recently came up
here?"

*I have sensed her motion, as I sensed yours. But to call her woman
implies she is of the natural ecosystem.*

This made Psolilai think. It had never occurred to her that her
rescuer might not be human. "How can I keep warm?" she asked.

*Fabrics lie a few turns upward. If you return, I can alter my metabo-
lism to provide you with a burst of heat energy.*

Psolilai crawled on to find a pile of clothes lying against the emerald
column, cottons, a heavy robe, even a hat and gloves; every garment
white. In the pockets were flasks of drink, high energy foods, nuts,
sugar, dried fatty meat. She realised at once that somebody was trying to
aid her survival, perhaps the old woman, who during their flight
through Rem had assumed that they would head for the Pillar. Psolilai
pulled on the clothes and returned to Poemona Fia Fiolo, who as
promised made its bark warm. She sat against the galithien, fatigue
overcoming her. But she must not sleep; her sister stood only a few
hundred yards below.

She woke. Night was old. Clouds drifting east. Stars and moon
visible through rents, the moontoo setting westward.

From her breast pocket she took the scriber. It had saved her life by
repelling the staff. Perhaps it knew who she was.

The sleep of a galithien lasted centuries, its life an aeon. Lights still flickered around her, reflected in the silver opposite like a gauzy and sequined fabric. Knowing Poemona Fia Fiolo would hear, she said, "Can I reach the top of the Pillar?"

A league and a half above the surface of the planet you will find breathing difficult.

True enough. She slept again.

Awake at dawn, she took her leave of the galithien to limp on up the spiral stair. Her leg, though sore, was at least useable, and the railing helped support her body. During frequent rests she gazed out over an expanding landscape—first foggy brown, then patchwork grey, then, after almost a day of effort, a hundred square leagues of slums and streets, squares and towers, metal and plastic, semiconductor and machine, with only flowing water any sign of nature, and that polluted. Leaning out over the rail she saw pinpricks of light through bad fog below.

The air was bitter cold, the Pillar no shelter except when she walked through its lee. Her new clothes were thick, but some cold got through. Her nose ran and her eyes ached.

She paused to make a mental calculation: the diameter of the Pillar was twenty yards, the gradient of its stair about one in ten. By the time she was in oxygen reduced zones she would have walked forty miles at least. If the Pillar reached an end at only two leagues she would have walked nearer sixty. But then she would be close to the ozonosphere. Therefore some days of travel lay ahead before she knew if she would have to turn back, and this small victory over the forces assembling below gladdened her.

Twilight, and time for rest. With no natural life on the Pillar she was forced to lie against the column itself, hard gemstone, unyielding metal below her. Night, and time at last for sleep. She was now above the lowest cloud base, though horsetail cirrus covered the sky from horizon to horizon. It grew colder, so that soon she was shivering. She knew what a good conductor of heat silver was.

Something peered at her from the spiral ahead, looking around the column . . . a furry head with a pointed nose. A bear. Psolilai remained motionless. The bear studied her, then settled against the column, closed its eyes and went to sleep, its nostrils exhaling a twin track of moisture that condensed upon the metal. Psolilai realised that this was no ordinary encounter. People—beings—on the Pillar knew of her, were somehow connected to her in a way as yet unknown. She had to get to the bottom of the mystery. Yet the innocent behaviour of the bear attracted her. It was warm. She crept up, and when it did not even open one eyelid she leaned against it, and later fell asleep.

In the morning when she woke it was gone. She felt torn. So obvious a deed annoyed her, more so than the clothes and provisions; she wanted nothing to do with those who dared manipulate her. Yet she was trapped. If she was going to stay on the Pillar for any length of time she would need help. She sighed. She might as well become used to that fact.

Her second full day on the Pillar; she climbed on. Motion warmed her. But with daylight departing a cloudless sky she knew the night was going to be the coldest yet, winter's full depth surrounding her. At dusk the bear appeared again, warming her, tugging her ever upward. She slept against it, as before.

She woke with dawn a hint in the eastern sky. The bear breathed soft.

She looked at it, and suddenly she railed against what it represented. She would not be pulled. Fury took her, rising up from the indignity she suffered, and she grabbed the staff, raised it, and brought it down with all her strength.

The bear shattered. There was a noise of breaking glass, fragments ricocheting off the column, bouncing down steps, an antiseptic odour mixed with the smell of burning. Before her lay the remains of the manufactured bear, red metal and black slime, from which in horror she recoiled.

She was the only natural life form on the Pillar.

When the sun rose she continued her ascent. On the silver railing she noticed the sticky fluff that suggested zri had floated by, perhaps decades, even centuries ago, for here there were few nanos to carry out the artificial processes of rotting. The material hung down like moss and the metal was black around it. As the day progressed the Pillar reverted to bare silver and emerald, marked by nothing and nobody.

With night came a new dilemma. The galithien had been friendly, the bear a creation of some other force. Tonight would be bitterly cold and without help she would suffer. She estimated her height as fifteen thousand feet.

But the forces tugging her up seemed to be aware of her position. There was no artificial animal awaiting her, rather a nuclear furnace similar to that with which she had escaped prison; yet another sign of the old woman. Frustrated, Psolilai embraced the furnace. The stress of not knowing her fate was eating into her. She wanted to hit out, but there was no victim to hand.

So the fourth day began. Now she was beginning to notice the effects of oxygen depletion. Her breath came short, and by noon she was too tired to continue. A rest helped, but only an hour later she had to give up again and sit down. The sky above her was cloudless indigo, the horizon showing the curvature of the planet. Again she leaned out under the railing and looked up, but she saw no structure marking the top, nor even any change in the Pillar itself. It just wound on. She pulled herself back onto the steps.

She saw a mushroom.

Stubby, a large scarlet cap with grey spots, white stem and the remains of a pale volva: a large fungus alone upon the silver. Its solitude amazed her.

She knelt down to examine it more closely, and so discovered that it smelled of meal. It looked real. From such a mushroom she could acquire knowledge.

She sat, fatigued, wondering what to do . . . no Gularvhen to advise her. Mushrooms were from nature, yet here she was separated from nature. There came a rattling sound, as of sticks striking one another, but she could not make out from where it came. But the mushroom: its colour was wrong, that was wreality colour. Angered once again she plucked it and threw it over the side with a screech, then watched it drop out of sight towards the clouds far below. She drew her scarlet-stained glove across her runny nose, then snorted up into the back of her throat what mucus remained. Swallowed.

Sudden dislocation of reality.

Rattling becomes melodic.

Eyes looking into squares.

Information jerking across her field of view. Jumping, not flowing.

Smell of meal in her nostrils.

Staggering across the step to the railing, holding on tight, looking down, feeling faint.

Holding on tight.

Being sick.

The ground below beckons as dizziness strikes. Head heavy, gravity pulling it down, cannot feel her body. Railing not supporting her.

She tried to shuffle back, found herself kneeling at the edge.

Had she almost fallen off?

The reality dislocation was too intense for her to know. Safety: she crawled across to the emerald wall and curled into a ball. The rattling noise sounded distant, then faded.

So they were not above experimenting with her, these nonhuman beings. She felt tears come to her eyes, felt them freeze; then anger yet again. She had almost acquired knowledge not meant for the human mind, but it had been rejected by her body, which knew better, the vomiting reflex saving her. Vague vision of hanging over the railing at twenty thousand feet . . .

Normal consciousness returned. She took out the furnace and set it operating. Here she would remain, for a while, recovering. She looked at the bland architecture around her: bare silver, featureless emerald. She realised that all she could do was continue: ascend, explore, think, react.

She got through the night with difficulty, the furnace struggling against winds that whipped around the Pillar. Striving for repose in the cocoon of her robes she found only fitful rest, dreamless, sleepless, somewhere between the two, and when dawn came she found that the anger within her remained close to the surface of her mind. Perhaps brought about by the thin atmosphere, perhaps by her circumstances, it irked her, goaded her. She remembered what she did to the bear and laughed out loud.

Oxygen depletion became her main problem. She found that she could walk no more than forty steps before a rest. Come noon, that was reduced to twenty, then, reluctantly, fifteen. Bad headache and blurred vision . . . but she urged her body on. Late afternoon, and she was resting between every ten steps. But she was high, the planet below her a grey and blue panorama, many districts merging into a curved surface; the sky dark, moon glowing white, moontoo yellow, with the ring system a gorgeous arc like a bow of scintillating pink dye.

She walked now in a zone of peril. Here, she would either find the top of the Pillar or the end of her road. She knew not which.

When the sun set in a wreath of russet streamers she stopped. She had gone too far, her body in pain, especially her injured leg and ankle. Not much food left, just scraps, and one flask of drink like spiced wine. She knew she was approaching the end of her path.

That night, as she shivered against the column, another bear appeared. She ignored it. Waking through the night she saw that it remained nearby, and she understood that it awaited tomorrow's effort. But she would not be humiliated.

With dawn, she ate her final food, emptied the final flask, then eyed the bear. She walked past it. Step left, step right, repeat. Ten repeats, then rest. Her lungs laboured, she felt alternately dizzy and ill. Altitude sickness, not enough oxygen to the brain. This could kill. The bear chose not to follow.

With the sun high in a cloudless sky, she collapsed, a brief faint, before struggling to her feet, wobbling, holding on to the rail.

Too weak to continue.

The staff began dragging her, wheezing like an engine. She resisted . . . then gave up resisting.

Progress was good. The staff was unaffected by the thin atmosphere and the cold. It clattered up the spiral, rhythmical as any machine, and in this shameful pose Psolilai was dragged along.

Lungs aching, brain slow.

Perceptions fluid, vision blurry. Sky above, ground far below; she knew that much.

A perpetual, chugging motion.

Upward.

Losing consciousness now, as the air changed; the bottom of the ozonosphere, a different chemistry, diatomic to triatomic and back in equilibrium. The possibility of brain damage.

She tried to cry out. She did not want her brain damaged.

Relentless, the staff dragged her ever up, up.

Then something different.

Soft, warm, perfumed air, no motion, no machine, a pale sky and a green land around her.

From dead slow to half human she returned to consciousness, drifting in and out of a faint, breathing better, the sensation of grass beneath her; she could smell soil, leaves, flower scent.

She sat up. Two people stood watching her, the old woman holding her staff, and a tall man dressed in a silvery robe, short sleeved and caught at his neck with a jasper owl; clean-shaven, young, yet with something of a leer in his expression.

The agen of her dreams was real here.

It spoke. "I am Dezisserine, and I am overjoyed that you are here. This is my lieutenant Ikhatarin."

"I know you are not human," Psolilai replied. "Who are you?" She waved her hand in front of her face to cut off any reply. "*What* are you?"

"Time for all that later. Are you recovered?"

Psolilai knew that she must put every obstacle possible before them. "No. I need to rest."

"That is good. Ikhatarin, bring suitable food and hot drink."

Ikhatarin turned and walked into the grove of orange bushes behind her.

Psolilai stood up, wobbled, held on to a sapling. "Ikhatarin sprang me from prison and rescued me from the court room. Why?"

"All your questions will be answered—"

"Why?"

"To ensure that you came here," Dezisserine replied, "and did not languish inside jail."

"And what exactly are you?"

"Later—"

"You said all my questions would be answered."

"So they will," it replied. "At the correct time."

Psolilai shook her head. "I will not be manipulated. I'm not a toy."

"True. That you are here is my sole interest."

"I could leave this minute."

It shook its head.

Psolilai was aware that she had blustered. She calmed, and fear returned. She felt lost. When Ikhatarin arrived with a tray of food and drink she picked and sipped at it, not wanting them to see her need. It tasted good, though.

Sarcastically, she said, "I can't wait to see my sleeping quarters."

"Ikhatarin will show you to them when you are ready."

"I'm quite ready now."

"Then follow us."

The land at the top of the Pillar was expansive. As they walked, Psolilai saw that it was a disk with an artificial dome atmosphere, plants at the edge, fruit trees towards the middle; also buildings, a tower three storeys high, and a large house, almost a mansion, built of red brick and black wood. Lawn and wild flowers everywhere.

"What is this place?" she asked.

"It has no name," Dezisserine replied.

"All places have a name."

No reply. Now Psolilai felt that asking certain questions would be dangerous, for she did not want them to guess what she already knew, what she suspected. She decided to cultivate silence.

Her quarters were set away from the mansion, a single storey house immaculate and warm, arranged with furniture and oddments in the Ere style, accommodating, even luxurious. From the front window she could see the mansion and its wild garden.

268

"You are free to move anywhere except into our abode," said Dezisserine, "which is, like this house, a private residence. If we want to see you, we will knock at your door."

"Are you saying I'm a prisoner here?"

"No."

"Then what? Can I leave?"

"Do you have the stamina?" came Dezisserine's reply.

The agen had the knack of knocking her back. She suppressed her anger, saving it for another time. "Then I shall explore this place," she said, striding outside.

They followed, then made for their mansion.

The disk measured a quarter of a league across, a green scented paradise, yet a prison, for she soon discovered that the only exit was the return step to the Pillar, and thus to the tropopause. The most curious feature was how artificial lifeforms imitated natural forms, as if mocking them. There were wrealities too, growing in clumps, or upon the detritus of manufactured life. She considered the possibility that all this was illusion, but she could touch and smell it; real enough.

Besides, the evidence of zri and galithien suggested that this place was real, despite Dezisserine's dream origin.

At the edge of the disk she encountered a grove of bladders each the size of a mammoth, gnarled and trailing root baskets underneath. Judging by their buoyancy they were filled with a gas lighter than air.

It was evening. She returned to her quarters to find plates of food and drink on her study table. Fine quality provisions, and she ate it all.

The next day she spent alone. Neither Dezisserine nor Ikhatarin departed the mansion, nor answered the front door when she knocked. So she took her evening meal, hot and tasty, as before.

On a side dish wobbled a red fruit jelly. As she decided whether or not to indulge herself she heard once again the rattling sound, but, listening with her head inclined this way and that, she was unable to determine its source. She took a portion of jelly and spooned a mouthful into—

Unconnected juddering sensations of: nausea: mesmeric squares of light: colour leached from world: looking down into own brain: hissing noise going deep into ears—

Dislocated—

Clattering, rattling symphonic sound—

Before her a new view—

Terrible fear—

Disconnected—

Figure leering at her approaching examining—

All perception judders—

Psolilai out of control—

More clattering in her ears, a sensation of flying, swooping, diving, and then Dezisserine appearing to take her by the hand and bring her gently to the ground, where, like a glider, they brushed across the lawn and came to a halt.

These visions were not meant for the human mind.

Psolilai opened her eyes to find herself lying on her bed, Dezisserine sitting beside her, the rattle fading to silence. "Can you hear me?" the agen asked her.

"Yes."

269

"What do you remember of your trip?"

"You tricked me," said Psolilai. "The jelly . . . a wreality. I should have realised . . . "

"Of course, we could not tell you. You would have refused."

Despite her confusion, Psolilai had the wit to reply, "I refuse you now."

Dezisserine's face took on an expression of anger. "And did you see a figure like me?" it asked in a cold voice.

"Yes, I did."

Dezisserine stood up and began wandering around the room. "I know what you seek. You sought it long before you were imprisoned for leaking secret information. You seek the owl, which is the symbol of the union of the natural and the manufactured—"

"No!" Psolilai cried. "I don't believe any more that there can be such a union! I seek purity, green, nature."

"If you reject the union of which I speak," Dezisserine said, "you reject Urbis Morpheos—and such rejection is impossible. Urbis Morpheos is a creation of time, of energy, of human beings. It is a city eternal, ever growing, like cancer. It cannot be rejected."

"It is perverted," Psolilai declared. "If it truly grows forever then it will eventually consume this entire planet! And then what?"

Dezisserine drew close, staring at her, clearly disconcerted by her words. "Who is the dreamer?" it hissed. "Is the dreamer the dreamer, or is the woman dreamed the dreamer? I put it to you that you will never know."

But Psolilai was not to be distracted from her small victory. "Then what?" she repeated.

Dezisserine leaned back. Eventually it replied, "There are other planets."

Psolilai felt cold. The agen was correct, but she also had spoken truth. She considered everything Dezisserine had said, then cast her thoughts back over her own experiences. "I will find out the truth," she said. "I am a truth seeker. Though I was a scribe to officialdom, I hated them all the time. And I have one ally untouchable by you."

"Who?"

It did not know! Psolilai looked away, hope in her heart.

"Who?" Dezisserine demanded.

Psolilai said nothing. She felt as insubstantial as a phantom, but triumph was hers, and the name of her triumph was knowledge.

"Theeremere will fall soon in battle," Dezisserine said. It paused, then said, "Theeremere will be taken in battle by the forces of artifice—and I will discover the identity of your ally. All this I promise you."

20

HOPE SYNTHESIZED FROM LEAVES

Psolilai gave them exact instructions. "Follow me in silence. Speak only if I speak to you, and then in a quiet voice. Be prepared for fighting and do not shirk from wounding or even killing—ready your weapons now. Do not attack unless attacked. Do not touch anything unless I say so. My goal is to locate 3Machines, capture and disable her, then interrogate her. Are there any questions?"

She expected none and there were none.

"Then follow me. Dyeeth Boolin, you come second, then Metaxain, then Dezisserine. Gularvhen, you are responsible for guarding our rear. Walk close, not in single file stretched out over yards and yards. Do not loiter, and never place yourself out of my sight."

She turned and clambered over the fallen slab, squeezing through the hole then examining what lay around her. The Palace was indeed marble, the stone itself sheened with luminous veins; floor of grey slabs, a corridor stretching out left and right, before her another corridor leading into the centre of the Palace. No sign of people. No dust, no algae, no damp, no sound of footfall nor even creak of stone against stone, just the wind moaning outside and the click-clack of the others clambering through the hole. Frowning, she turned, gesturing for silence.

When they were assembled she pointed to the right, then led them on. At the first corner she crouched and peered around, to see the next corridor empty and pale, stretching out to the opposite corner of the building. Again, nothing. This was not what she had expected. In her mind's eye she had seen patrolling guards, machines, wrealities, and of course 3Machines, the spider in the web. Cursing to herself, she led them down this second corridor.

The third stretched out as before, and the fourth. Twenty minutes passed and they were back at the hole in the wall. But there was an odour in the air, one half familiar.

She indicated that they would next explore the inner corridors, all of which had rooms leading off them. The corridors were empty, undecorated, but the rooms were stained scarlet and overflowing with debris, old and rotting, new and juicy, like so much red meat; and psolilai now recognised the smell.

"This is all wreality," she said.

"There will be a secret door," said Dyeeth Boolin, nodding to himself, "through which the wrealities from below are carted."

psolilai shook her head. "There is no door here. The Owl Palace is inviolate. The wrealities must grow *in* here, reacting to those brought up by the unlinking officers, or more likely to the information they contain." She examined some of the debris, to notice how easily they had been shredded, as if with a scalpel. "Are there any suggestions?" she asked.

They all shook their heads.

"Something lives here," she said, "that feasts on immense quantities of wreality."

She decided to make for the central room. Waving the others on she strode forward, assuming that they would follow—not checking—until she stood at an open doorway with the timid footsteps of her followers tip-tapping behind her.

She entered the central room, to see a bland marble chamber—and a figure.

Aunt Sukhtaya advanced, ready to fight, her guise that of a lilac owl.

psolilai stood motionless, shocked, and yet ready. *She* was the owl, not this woman!

She turned around to say, "This is a foe stronger than all of you put together. Flee now, before it is too late!" It sounded melodramatic, even to her ears, but she loved that sound. The Owl Palace appeared to shrink around her, and she felt powerful and ready to make combat, for the haven itself was augmenting her, preparing her for battle with this enemy by matching like against like.

She could not help laughing, because she wanted so much to win. But when, talons outstretched, Aunt Sukhtaya sprang forward and ripped a hole in her stomach, she stopped laughing. For a moment, shock. Then blood. Then she flew high in the air to avoid a second blow. She glimpsed the others, the little ones, scrambling to escape the chaos.

Wings flapping, Aunt Sukhtaya followed her, the orange fury in her eyes burning like flame. Aunt Sukhtaya opened her mouth and screamed as she made another attack, and it was all psolilai could do to avoid the talons and the hooked beak. In her panic she struck the ceiling, struggled to orientate herself and so took another blow, her flesh sliced—blood gushing. In a moment of surrender she saw how she had been tempted, how she had duped herself with the trappings of power, so that now, in single combat, she was losing. Stunned, she dropped to the ground, leaving a trail of downy feathers spattered crimson.

Then Aunt Sukhtaya was upon her. psolilai glanced down at her own body. Lilac skin leaking blood, but something shining through . . .

She took the Constructor and held it out. Aunt Sukhtaya hesitated.

Now the battle was more balanced. In the light of the golden artefact the wounds in psolilai's technological skin zipped themselves up, and she was pure again. She leaped forward and with her beak tore a hole in Aunt Sukhtaya's flesh, rending it from neck to belly, then jumping back to admire her handiwork. Aunt Sukhtaya opened her beak to screech, then extended her wings to rise, hover, then fall upon psolilai, covering her with its body, slicing with talons and beak, so that all psolilai could do was reply in kind, cut versus cut like a ballet of knives, until both of them were exhausted and the duel was paused. Panting, bloody faces. Then more, a flurry of claws glinting, feathers, dust, and dripping, spurting blood.

Again psolilai looked down at herself. Not much strength left. Blood everywhere, and she felt weak.

Another attack. Talons entering her flesh and slicing her vital organs. In retaliation she extended her neck and with her beak cut a strip across Aunt Sukhtaya's head so that fluids poured into her enemy's eyes and she was unable to see. But psolilai could not withdraw. They were locked as one, talons deep in flesh, not enough strength to pull them out, beaks opening and closing, now side by side, exhausted, opposed, feeble strikes with talons and beak rending each other, more like caresses than attacks.

So once again psolilai called upon the power of the Constructor; and her wounds were zipped.

And then, standing upright, she felt for the first time an attraction, a desire, pulling her conscious mind to a crossroads. Without thought she understood that this was a final call. She stood now on the junction between two modes, the past and the future, with victory over Aunt Sukhtaya offering manufactured power and the joys of the artificial world . . . that is, if she took Aunt Sukhtaya's place here in the Owl Palace.

Something else was becoming clear. Mahandriana knew about Aunt Sukhtaya's presence in the Owl Palace, of course it did. Mahandriana—with Dyeeth Boolin, perhaps even with Dezisserine—had been leading her along a path, one not of her devising, that she had followed without thought for any alternative. Mahandriana had created the woman she was today. So what was it to be? There was a crossing beneath her feet, and she had a choice.

Which ecosystem would it be?

She looked at the Constructor. She was too weak to contain its potential, or even to hold it. A furry shape moved in one corner of the chamber, so she bent down and handed over the artefact. Faintly a voice said: "Not me! You must make the decision yourself!"

But the voice was no more than a whisper and she did not want to listen.

She stood beside the spasming form of Aunt Sukhtaya and with a last effort bent over her. Slicing open Aunt Sukhtaya's head with her beak, she cut out her eyes and tore off her ears, then with one talon decapitated her.

Perceptions changing . . . the Owl Palace returning to its former size, large, white and noble.

The chamber in which psolilai lay was ruined, dust and marble debris everywhere, mixed scarlet with the remains of wrealities. The sodden form of Aunt Sukhtaya twitched in a final spasm. psolilai found herself lying on a pile of rubble, the walls of the Palace chamber shattered. Groaning, for her body was stiff and her skin covered with grazes and dried blood, she sat up and looked around. Nearby lay Dyeeth Boolin, his fur white with marble dust, eyes open, yet still. Dead, she supposed.

She clambered over the rubble and knelt at his side. "Dyeeth Boolin? Can you hear me?"

A flicker on his face, and his eyes moved to look at her. "Mmm, I hear you," he replied.

"Dyeeth Boolin . . . I gave you the Constructor. I'm sorry. I couldn't take the responsibility."

There was silence for a while as he summoned the energy necessary to speak. "I hope you have passed the test I failed," came his reply.

"Failed?" asked psolilai, unsure what he meant.

"You are not the first, my dear. Did you think you were? A long time ago, I was tempted by the lure of artifice, by the knowledge wrealities could offer. I surrendered. You see, I am more than half machine."

psolilai sat back, gasping for breath. "But how could you be?"

"When I first came here, so long ago, I was a felin. But now . . ." Dyeeth Boolin coughed blood. "I promised to help you," he murmured, "and that is what I did. You needed to come up here with a clear mind, if that was at all possible. You had strong friends, constant support."

Sudden understanding. Tears flooding her eyes, watery vision, choking throat. "I recognise you now," she whispered. "Oh, provident one, I recognise you, and I am sorry."

"That you are here is all that matters. My little part will perhaps be documented. I hope not to be forgotten."

"Provident one, you know you are remembered and loved. And I will never forget you."

Dyeeth Boolin closed his eyes, and died. From his charred hand the Constructor fell, to roll across the floor, spin, then settle, like a dull golden coin. For time unmarked psolilai sat weeping at the felin's side, as guilt consumed her. She knew she would have to leave the Owl Palace and confront the others, waiting outside, probably angry, in Metaxain's case perhaps beyond reach. She wept again for her stupid mistakes and her harsh words.

Time unmarked.

Dyeeth Boolin changing, fur darkening as if damp, body shrinking, desiccating perhaps, the eyes dull, the tongue protruding. Then the first hint of a sheen upon the corpse: scarlet veneer. Innumerable microscopic wrealities growing on the technology inside him, on the metal, the plastic, the genetically altered tissues, to inflate, become scarlet boils, acquire knowledge by spreading across the new terrain. Eyeballs popping, the body now just a skin bag of metal and plastic, covered from head to toe in scarlet.

psolilai stood up. Her vigil had left her exhausted, her limbs pale and heavy, circulation dead, flesh numb. She wandered across the rubble, through corridors at random, until she spotted blue sky and felt a breeze on her cheek. Then she clambered out into a sunny day.

Nature enfolded her: cold air and dew, the smell of trees, the sound of birds, sunlight in blue and green. The men sat clustered around the embers of a fire: Gularvhen cloaked and hatted, hands reaching forward for the warmth, Metaxain, one-armed, eyes closed; Dezisserine staring at the sky. In trepidation she approached. Sitting at the three corners of a square they had left the fourth space free, and she understood that it was for her. Perhaps they had forgiven her.

Gularvhen looked at her. "It took a great effort for us to hold back," he said.

psolilai nodded. She was cold. She put her hands out, palms forward, to glean what she could from the dying embers.

"A great effort," Gularvhen continued. "But for Dyeeth Boolin's immensely persuasive talk we would have stopped you and shaken the arrogance out of you. But he understood something of what was happening to you, and he counselled us to hold back."

"Dyeeth Boolin was persuasive," psolilai agreed.

"Was?"

"He is dead, of course," said Dezisserine.

Gularvhen grunted, as if commenting to himself on what he had already guessed. Returning his gaze to psolilai he said, "For the sake of Dyeeth Boolin I forgive you. He said you had to be tempted if you were to reject artifice beyond all possibility of succumbing. But you have tried us, psolilai, almost beyond endurance. We are imperfect. We respond to taunts, to violence, like ordinary folk. Because of Dyeeth Boolin we bit our tongues."

"I understand," said psolilai, "and I am grateful beyond words. Believe me."

Again Gularvhen grunted. "I do," he said, looking away.

"I also," said Dezisserine, "though in the company of these two men my suffering has been nothing."

Metaxain remained silent, his eyes still shut.

psolilai took him by the hand and led him away, out of earshot, until they stood, still hand in hand, by the boulders and the single waterfall there.

"Can you forgive me?" she asked.

"Time will tell."

"I want you to forgive me."

Metaxain looked at her, but only for a second, as if to say that more would have been too much, too quick. "No shaman is an ordinary man. We take what positions we are offered, letting life buoy us up or drag us down, as is. I can't forget what you've done to me."

Tears coursed down psolilai's cheeks. "I'm so sorry, Metaxain," she said, hugging him. He did not respond. "It was not me being harsh, it was a different psolilai, one from a different world, created by the aura of this haven. You have to see that."

"I heard what Dyeeth Boolin and Gularvhen said," came the reply, "and I understand. Perhaps I accept it. But . . . as Gularvhen put it, I'm imperfect. I hurt. I thought you were a good woman, but now I see you're not. You're like us all. That was a mistake on my part, I admit that. But you've not helped, these last few days. Perhaps you have a dark heart. Who knows?"

psolilai sobbed, "Don't say you made a mistake. It tears my heart."

"You do have a heart?"

"Of course I do!"

The ghost of a smile on his lips, departing in a moment. "Time will tell."

"Look at my face," psolilai implored. "I feel guilt. I know I've done wrong. I want to make it better."

Metaxain glanced down to where his arm had been, looked at her, then looked away. Silence.

She said, "Tell me what I can do to atone. Just tell me."

"As yet, I don't know. Perhaps nothing. Perhaps you don't need to do anything—"

"But I do! And I want to."

"I remain a shaman," he said. "I still have my trees."

psolilai choked. The simple sentences seemed like a slap in the face: rejection. He did not want her, he wanted his trees. She wept. He did nothing to comfort her.

They returned to the others, but not hand in hand.

psolilai sat in silence, then said, "How long was I there for?"

"Three days," Dezisserine replied. "We thought it best not to disturb you."

"We knew not what was happening," Gularvhen muttered.

psolilai wiped tears from her eyes. "It is over," she said. "Nature is all."

"Nature is all around us," Gularvhen said, "which is not the same thing."

She stood up. "I will be back shortly. I have one last thing to do."

She walked to the hole in the Palace wall and clambered through, then made towards the central chamber, where Dyeeth Boolin lay cold. She pulled him along the corridors, leaving a stain like new blood. At the hole she dragged him through.

And one last thing. She reached inside her clothes and took out the remaining vial. Her face twisted as she remembered the conflicting motives it had engendered.

There was no turning back.

True. She dropped the vial to the floor and stamped on it.

She felt the Constructor heavy inside her pocket.

It was the work of an hour to dig a hole and bury Dyeeth Boolin. She did not call the others. It was her own private ceremony, at which she wept once again. So much sobbing, exhausting her—atonement in itself.

When she returned to the others, Gularvhen pointed at a scarlet mound. "The hog is dead," he said.

It was. It lay on its side, collapsed and shrinking. "It is a sign marking the demise of the Analyticate," psolilai said. "I was right. Five scarlet wrealities, one in each section of the haven, designed to fool the curious."

"Now I see what I missed before," said Dezisserine. "I knew those wrealities were operational, but I did not see their operator."

psolilai nodded. "All part of Aunt Sukhtaya's plan to keep things constant, to act against change. Everybody who lives in this haven has fallen for the deception. And the fake rumours of her luxurious excesses — devious, so devious . . ."

"The political troubadour Ma will also be dead," Dezisserine continued, "the Brain of Han ruined, the Library of Dri burned, or disintegrated."

In silence they departed the Sky Level. The gryphons flew them back without asking questions.

The Inn of Twilight Ratiocination seemed cold without Dyeeth Boolin. Hoss welcomed them, Gularvhen especially, but even the obvious warmth between these two failed to raise psolilai's spirits. Alone in her room the tears she cried were more gentle than before, as she approached the end of her grief. Then a tap at the door and Gularvhen entered. "Ilyi Koomsy has departed the Teahouse of Aurorean Eudemonia," he said. "I thought you ought to know."

"I shall miss them both," psolilai said.

Gularvhen nodded. "I shall miss you," he said. He departed without further word.

21

FROM CREATURES

Psolilai understood that now she had rejected Dezisserine her future lay in her own hands, for the agen had vanished, and she was free to wander this strange land. She explored Dezisserine's mansion and found what she expected, a shell, nothing inside, the exterior arranged so that upon arrival she would experience a semblance of normality. Only her own quarters were solid, made so because she, a human being, would live in them.

She explored the manufactured garden. The verisimilitude was near perfect. Orange bushes smelled of orange blossom, or fruit if they were more advanced along their artificial cycle, butterflies were gauzy, as were the moths at night, the grass felt right, the bark of trees felt right, even the air was right, though contained by some technological force. She ranged further afield, walking through meadows, underneath trees. At the edge of the disk she found more bladders, rooted to the ground by crooked stalks.

Then she found the body.

Ikhatarin was no more. Unmarked, unburied, she lay with her clothes ripped and her staff by her side, her hair already falling out, eyeballs popped, skin blanched. Psolilai edged away from this gruesome discovery, before a scarlet stain on an exposed thigh made her return for a second look. Wrealities were beginning to grow on the body.

She must stop calling it a body. This was the remains of a machine, decomposing as the frameworks of the Shohnadwe shamen had decomposed. She picked up the staff, and left.

There was time enough now to recover from her ascent, and from the events preceding it. Balmy days passed by. Food that she could eat lay stored in her quarters, there was plenty of water, even clean linen, for Dezisserine had anticipated every outcome of his devious plan. Time passed, and she was healed; strong again. But she remained on a disk two leagues above the surface of the planet.

A t length, she returned to Ikhatarin, to find both legs covered with scarlet wrealities, some like mould, others like livid boils, what had been the head now a lump of waxy plastic, the hands pale upon the grass like cellophane gloves. She knelt to look at the new structures, and for the first time felt the germ of an idea in her mind.

Like so many others she had assumed that wrealities, the knowledge network of the manufacturing ecosystem, gave up their wealth only through abstract interfaces: diagram, hologram, speech. But recent experience suggested otherwise. Although the human mind was not designed to accept wreality knowledge as direct input—as it was for mushrooms—she had discovered through the agency of Dezisserine that some wrealities were orally active, albeit perilous in the extreme. It might therefore be possible to gain knowledge of Ikhatarin from this young scarlet growth.

282

She sat back on her heels to consider all this. The dangers were great, the benefits dubious, a notion for the courageous only.

Before giving the idea serious consideration she scoured the disk for more clues to the nature and origin of Ikhatarin and her master, but she found nothing new. She returned to the step leading down to the Pillar. A deoxygenated atmosphere awaited her, possible brain damage, even death. There must be something else. She returned to Ikhatarin. While she had been gone a new wreality had formed like a mole on one knee.

She fretted. Twice now she had experienced the disturbing potential of wreality knowledge. It was like dreaming an agen dream, a vision of pure and random machinery disconnected from anything Gaian. No wonder her body and mind rejected it through nausea and confusion. Yet short visions were possible; Dezisserine had shown that. If only Hoss were here to provide accompanying music. But she was alone, with only her thoughts for solace.

Next morning she was back with Ikhatarin, scraping off wrealities, transfering the scarlet gel to a wine glass, then returning to her quarters.

She steeled herself. The rattling noise began again. She noticed that the scarlet colour of the wrealities was mixed with lilac. Pouring a little water into the glass to make the gel flow, she brought it to her lips, took one deep breath, and swallowed.

Staring deep into concentric squares flowing to a point—
Sense of looking up—
Down—
Marvellous clattering music—
The possibility of wisdom from networks of wrealities—
Oscillating gravity—
Great emptiness at the heart of her mind—
The centre of her perceptions blank—
A symptom of the knowledge matrix of the manufacturing ecosystem—
Zero—

Lying on her back in musty air, a bitter taste in her mouth and a smashed wine glass on the floor. Taking the ceiling in, looking at imperfections in the plaster, counting them, then losing count.

Psolilai recovered consciousness. Part of her had wondered if she would come through this: part of her had known that she must. The rattling sound continued, scratching its way into her mind, and sensitised now to its noise she turned her head and saw the staff, to realise that it was the source. Music no longer: in a fury she swung her legs off the bed, reached out, stood, then smashed the staff against the floor, where it shattered into a thousand emerald shards and a length of twisted silver. Empty of emotion, she dropped it to the floor. Sitting on the bed again . . . lying down . . .

Some hours passed.

Why no knowledge? The wrealities should have imparted something of their host Ikhatarin, even if only the smallest fragment, some clue, a moment of image, or just a word.

Though she felt nauseous, she returned to Ikhatarin to examine the wrealities growing on her. They were scarlet, some with a lilac veneer; they looked normal. Yet all she had acquired was the knowledge that wrealities were a matrix of manufactured wisdom, a fact she already knew.

And then a flash of realisation. She bent down to study the lilac wrealities. They grew upon scarlet nodules. They were metawrealities.

Just as Gaia's ecosystem comprised one part studying itself, so did the manufacturing equivalent.

And then further inspiration. The staff had sounded on three occasions, when she had consumed the orally active constituent of a wreality. That sound must be music from the manufacturing ecosystem, produced for the same reason that Hoss sang—to create a facilitating ambience; to human ears a random din. But she had shattered the staff. If she was to consume these scarlet wrealities she would have to experience their bursts of knowledge without complimentary sound. It would be like deciding to orbit the planet without an oxygen supply.

The dilemma facing her could not be worse. To find out anything about Ikhatarin, Dezisserine or the Pillar on which she was confined she would have to expose her mind to a raw machine vision; no safety net. The chemicals in a wreality could seethe her brain like a rabbit in a pot.

No choice. All options were bad. Another day passed.

Dawn. With trembling hands she collected a sample of the scarlet wrealities growing on Ikhatarin's thigh, taking them indoors, moistening them as before, then sitting down and wondering if she was doing the right thing. Several times she raised the glass to chest height, then hesitated and let it fall so that it rested on her knee, until the dread of lifting it became the dread of what she might do to herself, and her arm was frozen solid. So she took the glass in both hands and raised it to her lips. Hesitated just one second. Closed her eyes, and drank.

Ikhatarin an agen.

Formerly a mallead, long since altered.

Become an old woman.

Cunning.

Psolilai exploding out of her own head like a dolphin out of water, leaving a trail of machine-tooled thoughts, fragments of unutterable wisdom from the depths of the mechanical. Flow of life departing, instead a series of pin-sharp interludes stitched together with no Gaian rationale.

She tried to find coherence, but saw only unrelated items of experience. A bed. A body. She a person, her head full of metal, broken bits of metal. Taste of shadows and death in her mouth. Lying back, head on pillow, to surrender to device life—

No!

She sat up. She understood that she was in a room, a room familiar to her. She recognised the clothes she was wearing, those boots, that mud, those grass stains.

She was Psolilai. She had returned from the infernal depths of manufacture. Returned alive. Elation took hold of her. She realised that she had won a victory, over what she was not certain, and how she did not know, but her desire for nature was undiminished, indeed stronger now that she saw the appalling vision offered by the manufacturing ecosystem. In joy she leaped from her bed and danced around the room, only to fall to her knees and vomit up bits of wreality like gouts of dark blood.

Smell of burning. She ran outside, to see smoke billowing out of the disk, where lay a hole: clear dark sky visible through it. Evening fell across the Pillar.

The disk of land was breaking up!

Psolilai ran as close to the fumes as she dared, to see the substrate of the disk already punctured in a dozen places, smoke spiralling out, wafting in clouds, making her cough. At this rate she would be burned alive in half an hour. She sprinted back to the mansion, hoping, though she knew it was in vain, that she would find some route to escape; but it remained empty. Her own quarters were useless. Back outside, she watched as the disk was consumed. She ran about, as if activity itself would lead to salvation. At the step down to the silver staircase she considered pushing back out into the tropopause, but she knew that way meant death, too long a journey before she returned to oxygenated zones.

No escape.

She recalled being dragged up by Ikhatarin's staff. That artifact she had smashed. She ran over to Ikhatarin's remains to find a wreality shroud, scarlet dotted lilac, with only the faintest hint of delicate machinery underneath.

Nothing, then.

Half the disk remained. The disintegration had begun near one edge. What survived was the centre ground and the further edge. She ran across to this lip and looked out. Through the force field containing the atmosphere she saw a faint arc, pastel blue; the edge of the planet.

Thirty thousand feet up; if the disk disintegrated she would fall. If she ran down the spiral she would die.

Panic very close.

Minutes remained. A strip of ground connected her to the centre of the disk. It could collapse at any moment. Tremors below her feet, shock waves, making the grass jump and trees sway. Nearby, her quarters were a shell of smoking fragments.

Another tremor, then a shock wave, and she almost fell over.

She looked again at the invisible wall behind her. The gas bladders too were moving, as their roots were disturbed or sundered. Some floated free. She ran towards the biggest bladder, thrust herself into the basket of roots below it, reached out, and with a gasp and a groan twisted the connector root until it split. Freed, the bladder rose.

Ground beneath her disintegrating, smoke billowing into her face.

Indigo sky above.

The disk gone, just a shining spiral of silver remaining.

As the bladder left the pressurised environment it swelled to twice its size, the creases flattening, a noise of creaking, hissing from vents dotted across its surface; stretched, and Psolilai thought it would burst. An icy wind in her face. Breathing fast, and no oxygen; clinging to the basket of roots.

Descent. Very fast.

Silver column a blur of light.

She closed her eyes as the bladder plummeted, opening them a fraction to see sky and moon and stars, then shutting them again. With no scale by which to tell her rate of descent she could only guess. Her ears popped. She was breathing in gulps like an athlete at the end of a race. Icy air flayed her skin. She could not see individual spirals on the column as she sped by, so fast was her descent.

Seconds passed. The Pillar stair changed from a blur to an oscillating spiral.

The bladder was not now so tight, as the pressures inside and out approached one another. Sky still dark.

The wind roared by.

The air was still so cold it made her throat raw, but at least she was not gasping to compensate for lack of oxygen. The sky above was paler, nearer the evening blue that she remembered, only the brighter stars visible. A pale blue moontoo rising in the east. The root basket held her secure. She began to think that she might survive.

Still the bladder descended. Though the land below remained a patchwork of grey and black, she began to consider landing. So far, the bladder had clung close to the Pillar, but winds lower down might blow it away from the haven. She looked up to see a few creases visible in gnarled hide. She looked down again, saw the first sign of terrestrial features, hills and escarpments, bad snow drifting in a river valley, and far away a volcano spewing magenta ash. The curvature of the planet was no longer apparent. Then at the foot of the Pillar she saw the first hints of Theeremere: streets, towers, squares, the Church of the Parasol Cap, the Pool of Wrealities.

She did not know where she would land. Either the bladder was a free lifeform of the manufacturing ecosystem growing high by accident, or it was part of a life cycle located in the haven, in which case it would land at a specific place. Her guess was the latter. But the descent was now more of a dawdle. The gas inside the bladder, lighter than air, was acting against gravity, and with vents hissing to release it she guessed the bladder followed a programmed plan. She suspected it would land close to the Pillar.

287

Now she was able to estimate her height, the Pillar rising into high cloud, the ground perhaps a thousand feet below. Still the bladder clung close to the Pillar. Below, the first lanthorns of evening were pinpoints of white and yellow.

When it came, touchdown was rough, gas escaping from vents in synchronised bursts, a drop, a stall, and then a bumpy landing in the Quartz Park. Psolilai rolled free. Looking back at the bladder she saw it enshroud a column of milky rock, melt, then release a hundred miniature bladders that attached themselves to over-wintering dirigibles or, if unsuccessful, disintegrated into puddles of components like soft clock parts. It was all over in minutes, dark splashes on the quartz where the bladder had landed, a dozen or so new lumps like warts on the local balloons.

Psolilai rested. Around her the haven was quiet, bad fog low over the river but not spreading far. Her breathing and heart rate calmed. A single light shone azure and clear, as the moontoo rose full above the eastern horizon.

Gularvhen approached, emerging from the bad fog as if he had known all along where she would land. For a few moments she watched as he approached, but then her mood turned angry, for it seemed to her that his mantis-like figure hid something far greater, and far darker, that was perhaps not of her world. She gestured for him to join her. In her gullet she could feel fury rising, like the plug in a volcano pushed up by magma.

"Are you returned to the Haven of the Three Machines?" he asked her.

"You . . ." Psolilai spluttered. "What are you doing here?"

He raised his eyebrows. "I would have thought you would be pleased to see me."

"You've got secrets and you're hiding them from me!"

He clicked his tongue against his teeth. "Patience, one and all, patience."

Psolilai found herself struck dumb, yet anger still animated her. She jabbed him in the belly, about to harangue him, but then she was struck by a sudden thought. She had heard him use that phrase before in one of her dreams: 'patience, one and all, patience.' He knew something about malleads, and he was hiding it!

She lost her temper. Her voice was shrill as she shouted, "You miserable wretch, you've known about malleads and agens all along!" With both hands she struck him as hard as she could, causing him to fall back.

He stared, dumbfounded.

And Psolilai understood. It was Gularvhen who had come forward with an answer to the riddle of the gryphons. What is it that dies when you darken its I? A suicidal man he had replied, and that was a correct answer, but now she saw that the real answer, the answer the gryphons were there to watch for, was mallead, for any being knowing the secret of such a transformation would be too dangerous to allow near the Owl Palace. Darkening the eye of a mallead changed it forever.

But Gularvhen just stared at her.

"Tardy wretch!" she yelled. "The gryphons were looking out for malleads, weren't they, because malleads can appear exactly like humans. And you knew that! So you gave another correct answer to get us through to the Sky Level." Again she struck him, causing his pointed

288

hat to fall to the ground. "How dare you keep secrets from me? How dare you, when I have the weight of Urbis Morpheos on my back? Are you so blind you cannot see that?"

Gularvhen took a deep breath. "Actually," he said, "it is I who have the weight of Urbis Morpheos on my back."

Then he turned away from her.

Psolilai began sobbing—not from grief, but from the effort of releasing her anger; chest heaving, throat hoarse, jaws clamped together.

Then came a sound that stopped their conversation dead.

It was the dull clank of a beater striking a rusty bell. But it was loud, a massive beater striking a bell as large as a mammoth. This sound echoed out across the haven, once, twice, three times. Then a gap, a deadly silence. Then three beats again.

Gularvhen leaped forward. "The ancient warning bell," he cried. Terror filled his face. "We have to escape!"

"Escape? Why?"

"Can't you hear it? That bell is warning of an imminent agen attack. They are coming here, they want control of our analytical-tendencies!"

"It's Dezisserine," Psolilai said. "You know Dezisserine?"

"Dezisserine does not know me," Gularvhen replied. He looked at the buildings surrounding them and added, "But we are trapped here."

Though Psolilai knew nothing of the ancient bell, she saw Gularvhen's terror and grasped the implications of what he said. She clutched him and whispered, "Save me!"

"I am the only one left who can save you," Gularvhen replied. "There will be no hope if we remain inside Theeremere. No—we must leave, flee to the north."

They hurried away. Gularvhen sheltered Psolilai by his side, winding one flap of his great cloak around her as if to conceal her from agen eyes, and she felt he would have picked her up if he had the strength. When they arrived at Psilocybin Lane they found acrid brown fog billowing between houses and along passages. They halted to get their bearings.

"We shall head for the Sighing Gate," Gularvhen said. "If we arrive there before the agens enter we can yet escape them."

"Where is Hoss?" Psolilai said.

"Somewhere safe."

Psolilai groaned, "But why does Dezisserine want our analytical-tendencies?"

"It is obsessed with purity and mixing. It wants both the purity of the manufacturing ecosystem and a bridge from it to us, to nature, mixing natural with artificial. But Dezisserine is a victim of its own fundamentalist thought."

Psolilai studied the urban decay surrounding her. "This is the beginning of the end of Urbis Morpheos," she said. "When all the havens have been destroyed, manufacturing will have triumphed."

"I have not reached that moment yet," Gularvhen replied.

They hurried along Psilocybin Lane, but at its end they saw flashes of light and movement, far off at the Sighing Gate. The agens were attacking, swarming over the high haven walls, crawling across roofs, smashing their way into homes. Some people were fleeing before them, carrying wailing brats and bags containing their valuables, while others drove beasts before them. Crows flew cawing across the streets; dogs barked. The moon rode high, full and bright, illuminating the chaos.

290

"What do we do now?" Psolilai asked. Dread of this phalanx of mechanical souls filled her, and she found that she was trembling.

Gularvhen considered, then replied, "I shall provide a diversion." He pointed along the street, adding, "Do you see that tower near the Sighing Gate? We shall shelter concealed in its garden, and when the diversion comes, we shall run."

Against the flow of the fleeing populace they made towards the tower, which stood a hundred yards from the Sighing Gate. Agens roamed the area, but as yet they had made no organised advance into the haven; they were securing the boundaries. The motion of the agens was like the dispersed fragments of a clock, at once incomprehensible yet familiar, and regular. Their cries were like the amplified noises of miniature machines. Many were covered in pieces of gold foil.

Psolilai watched all this with horror, until, with a sudden crack and then a musical wheeze, something darted through the Sighing Gate. She caught a glimpse of a four-legged glowing shape. The agens moved aside like a fluid, leaving a massive wake in the empty street, whereupon Gularvhen grabbed Psolilai's hand, guiding her towards the Sighing Gate while the agens' attention was captured. They hurried under the dripping stones, then shrank against the wall: out-haven.

There was a metallic skreek, then lights began playing over the ground before them.

Gularvhen cursed. Though they had been hidden by shadows, they had been spotted; he shook his fist at the sky. "They saw my pale face in the moonlight," he said.

They ran into the rubble-strewn streets that surrounded the Sighing Gate, a maze of deserted alleys and ruined buildings that stank of soot and rot. With a wheezing bray Hoss ran out of an alley. Gularvhen patted his horse, then lifted Psolilai onto Hoss' back. He jumped up to sit before her.

Psolilai looked over her shoulder to see a group of agens emerging from the Sighing Gate. "They're following us!" she gasped.

Gularvhen cursed again. Dark and so tall he seemed ennobled, gaunt yet powerful, his cloak and pointed hat making him a figure of majesty. "We can out-run them," he said, his voice wavering with the emotion of the moment. "We can flee north and west on Hoss, and with luck they will not find us in the shattered streets."

291

"Go!" Psolilai cried. The nearest agens were less than a hundred yards away.

With the sound of a blaring trumpet Hoss leaped forwards, but the horde of hissing, ticking agens followed. They ran like chess pieces on a board, independent yet somehow a gestalt entity, and the intensity on their faces terrified Psolilai. Yet Hoss—no ordinary horse—had a turn of speed that she had never witnessed before, and soon they were deep in the maze of soot-stained alleys, with no sign of the pursuit behind them. After an hour Hoss slowed to a walk.

Gularvhen said, "They will follow our spoor. But in this environment we can disguise our traces, and so escape. Do not worry. We can throw off the pursuit."

In a small voice Psolilai replied, "But what about Theeremere?"

"I suspect it will be taken over. The agens will go first to Analytical-Tendency House. Amargoidara will have escaped—"

"Alongside Aunt Sukhtaya!" Psolilai interrupted.

"More than likely," said Gularvhen, in a soft voice.

They rode on until the sun rose, then slept until noon, hidden in the cellars of a ruined skyscraper. They journeyed for the rest of the day, until, at sunset, they were so exhausted they decided to make camp and sleep again. There was no sign of any pursuit, but this did not mean they had shaken off the agens. Gularvhen seemed tense, tipping his head from side to side as if to improve his hearing, while Hoss' three ears flicked in all directions.

On the following day Gularvhen spotted an escarpment ahead, dark with paved streets and tumbledown houses. The wilderness around them was parched and cracked, sending up fumes to the sky, which in reply sent down soft trails of bad snow.

Gularvhen sighed. "I am tiring, but do not give up hope."

Psolilai shrugged. "Gaia will save us," she replied.

Hoss jerked up his head, then gave a musical bray.

"Agens!" Gularvhen hissed. "They have caught up already."

Before Psolilai could reply they were cantering along the street, a plume of dust and soot sent up behind them, heading for the escarpment. After five minutes of clattering up steps they were at its top.

Then Gularvhen pointed at the northern sky. "Hezoenfor!" he cried.

Psolilai saw the sparklehawk flying low across rows of terraced houses.

"He can lead us to a natural haven," Gularvhen said. "We must put our trust in him."

He urged Hoss on, until, a minute later, they were standing in a yard at the northern edge of the escarpment, a great plain spread out before them.

Psolilai gasped. Half a league away she saw immense fields of light, glittering despite the cloudy sky, magnifying what light was available. In a moment she realised where she was. She had seen this haven from the dirigible that had taken her to Vita-Hassa—specks glinting on the horizon, like gigantic mirrors; and Gularvhen had looked sad, and sighed. It was a plain of sunlight reflecting across the wilderness.

"We can hide there," he said.

Fifteen minutes later they arrived at the haven, where they dismounted. Psolilai had to shield her eyes against the light. It was not that it was too bright, rather that looking at it was like looking into an ocean of glittering shapes, constantly moving, like a school of mirrored fish in a sea current; a hallucinatory, mesmeric experience.

"If we are to escape the Vallevaess agens," Gularvhen said in a bitter voice, "then only here can we shelter. Alas that we have left the plain of Persellafaer. But this is a natural place, where Hezoenfor was born."

"How can we hide?" said Psolilai. "Where?"

Gularvhen did not answer. Instead he began hunting along the periphery of the mirror haven, until he returned with three bulging bladders, each reflecting a soft orange light. "Close your eyes," he said, "and pinch your nostrils closed with your fingers. Now take a deep breath and hold it for half a minute with your mouth shut."

Psolilai did as she was instructed. She heard a hissing sound as something cold was sprayed upon her skin. After a few moments she heard Gularvhen telling her it was safe to open her eyes, and she saw him crouched upon the ground, spraying a reflective gel over her boots. She lifted up her hands to see them shimmering with light.

"Now do the same for me," he said, handing over the second full bladder.

Psolilai sprayed him with gel, until he too was covered. Then Hoss was treated. The horse held three reflective helmets in his mouth, one of which Gularvhen put upon his head, demonstrating how it was worn. Then, covered from head to toe in reflective materials, they hurried into the outer mirrors, turned to face the dark yards outside, and waited.

Though Psolilai knew she was invisible, the sight of advancing agens made her shudder. "You can move," Gularvhen whispered, "and they will not see you in this hallucinatory light. But on no account make any noise."

A group of twenty agens approached, until they stood in loose formation a stone's throw from the edge of the haven. Psolilai heard their metallic voices, buzzing like bees over the paved yards that surrounded the mirror haven. For ten minutes the agens searched the yards, until, satisfied that their quarry was not present, they moved on. For another ten minutes Psolilai stood silent, until she noticed a moving column of light emerging from the haven, and recognised Gularvhen leading Hoss into the yards.

She followed him out.

"May we never be outcasts again," he said, gazing with one hand shielding his eyes along the street taken by the departing agens.

Psolilai sighed. "Nobody can be cast out of Gaia," she said.

Gularvhen took the book that he called *The Condition* from his pocket, and wrote in it with a graphite pencil. "Nobody . . . cast out . . . Gaia," he murmured.

Psolilai watched, but said nothing more.

Then Gularvhen's expression became sorrowful. "We will have to part soon," he said. "I shall miss you."

PART 3

AWAKE

22

From Gaia

I emerged in an empty chamber, Eastside, a place of walls painted the colour of leaves, of damp floorboards and steamy windows, of warm air that smelled of spearmint tea. I saw two empty cups on the floor.

I knew at once what I had to do. Yamajatha and psolilai had leaped into the heavens from the same place, but that had been Westside — in Teewemeer. In Theeremere I knew of an equivalent place.

I was standing below that place now.

I departed the chamber and headed for the nearest staircase. The registrar smiled at me as I began my ascent, saying, "Good night to you," as he passed on his way down. I nodded once at him and carried on upward, satisfied that my taciturnity would not upset him. At the top of the staircase I emerged onto a landing. There were no doors before me, but there was a single skylight leading up onto the roof. I was easily able to reach up and undo the catch, then pull myself out.

The roof was cold and damp. Bad fog billowed in the streets far below me, and bad snow fell from low cloud. I pulled my cloak close. Around me I saw a row of bird footprints, which I recognised as having been made by a raven; in the deliquescing stone they yet remained, at once a symbol of the mutable material and of its strength and longevity.

I turned to face east. The moontoo had not yet risen. But when, an hour later, it did, I was disappointed to see that it was yellow. I sighed, and thought of Voaranazne.

Next night I waited solitary for the rising of the moontoo, but it emerged cornflower blue from heavy clouds. Disappointed once again, I thought of Kirishnaghar.

On the third night the moontoo rose coloured green.

It sparkled like an emerald. I rose to my feet. For almost half the night I waited, until the moontoo was directly above me; and then I leaped. Like a man trying to escape a pool of dark water I scrambled up into the moontoo, crawling through the orb of green light, then dropping down on the other side.

I landed on the summit of the ziggurat, bending my knees to absorb the impact. All was dark and silent; it was midnight. Small piles of ash on the ground sent up an exotic scent, but there were no felins about. I stepped across the flat summit and entered my flyer.

Joy bubbled up inside me as I sat in a familiar bucket-seat and looked at familiar controls, arranged winking and glowing before me. I had been a long time away. It was the work of a few moments to activate the engine, deactivate the parking controls and then ascend. My seat creaked as it moved beneath me, ensuring that I was always in the most comfortable position. I looked around the cockpit to see that all was as I had left it—a chamber five yards in diameter, black metal, a thousand indicator lights. I touched a switch: the wall before me became transparent, and I was able to see the streets and squares below, as like a zephyr I rushed over them.

In due course I arrived in Theeremere, landing on the roof of the Sighing Gate. After securing my flyer I descended to the ground by one of the many internal staircases. Immediately, I turned left. The lane was narrow, wide enough for two and no more, the buildings to either side leaning like drunkards over a table. Stalactites hung down from eaves. Few people were abroad, those daring the weather dressed in woolly hats and masks, and great cloaks, sending not even a glance to their fellows in the lane. I approached the Emerald Bridge; half way across I paused, anxious, before carrying on.

So I stepped into Rem, and the single-file Indole Lane. Here I had to press myself into doorways when my way was blocked. With night fallen I navigated the shadow-strewn lane by light of window and methane lamp, until, at Analytical-Tendency House, the lane widened and new lanthorns threw off an ochre light. I stole on. At the place where Indole Lane became Salvinorin Lane, I saw the statue of Amargoidara, Steward Lord of the Analytical Council.

From the statue it was a quick step to the Wool Bridge and the path into Ere. I followed Tryptophane Lane along the river into the western quarter. At the end of the lane I hesitated, knowing that soon I would have to fight for what I believed in, but after a moment of contemplation I pushed my way through the gates and empty stalls of Isatin Lane, stopping only when I saw the Church of the Parasol Cap.

The Church of the Parasol Cap is my emotional home. I grew up there, a lad dressed in tabard and tights. I know the place from top to bottom. And yet, as I stood contemplating it, my long period of preparation complete, I grew nervous, for I knew who was waiting for me. With trepidation I strode forward, splashing through the puddles in the yards, until I stood before the front door and saw the registrar behind his great plastic desk. His presence reassured me.

"Is Sukhtaya here?" I asked as I walked in.

He nodded, then told me that she was in one of the meditation rooms adjoining the rear yard. I strode there, my anxiety making me hasty.

The room was bare of furniture, its walls pure white, one immense window—that could be opened when the weather was warm—taking up most of the western side. Sukhtaya leaned against this window, her pose relaxed, almost as if she was using the room for its proper purpose. She turned to face me as I walked in. I shut the door. Two small emerald-green lamps indicated that it had locked itself.

"Welcome back," she said.

I cast my gaze over her imposing bulk. She was dressed in her usual pale and loose clothes, a net drawn over her hair, silver bangles clinking on her wrists. I said, "I hope you will agree that I have had the best of our encounter. I have shown that artifice on its own cannot return nature to its rightful place. You hoped to use the Constructor and the Transmuter in the service of your own ideas, but you failed. In the end, Voaranazne was tempted, and almost ruined everything."

Sukhtaya's eyes narrowed. "There are two other malleads," she observed.

I knew that here I was on weak ground. With an air of nonchalance I replied, "Kirishnaghar converted to my side. Nothing speaks as eloquently as that deed."

For a moment Sukhtaya said nothing, and I wondered if she would concede defeat. But then she murmured, "There is yet Auzarshere . . . there is yet Auzarshere."

I nodded. He remained an enigma, though I knew his identity. "I will deal with Auzarshere later," I said.

Sukhtaya stared at me. "Will you? Will you?" She laughed, a sound devoid of any pleasure. "I think not. You believe you have won, but you have not yet."

I knew then that she was admitting defeat. She envisaged a later victory for those on the side of manufacturing, a victory in which she would play a minor, or even no role. I stood to my full height and wrapped my cloak around my body. "Then this part is over," I said. "Voaranazne, if no other, illustrates the inutility of your position — do we agree?"

It must have been the most difficult reply she ever made. Through a half sob she said, "Yes."

I did not want to twist a knife in her wound, but I could not restrain myself from saying, "We are not in a position to dictate to nature since we are part of it. You envisaged a world where thinking creatures ruled. I tell you that such a world is doomed to failure. The metaphor of nature is imprinted in our minds, and if we ignore it we commit suicide as a species."

With that, I departed the Church of the Parasol Cap.

Back in my flyer, I ascended into the sky and flew west. As I reflected on my conversation with Sukhtaya I realised that she was the weakest of my three opponents, since hers was the most extreme position. She envisaged a post-natural world and a post-natural humanity, a view that I had shown to be a dead end. Our conversation, however, had given me confidence.

I watched the land pass blurred and gloomy beneath me as I flew west. When the sun rose I saw ahead a pale finger stretching up into the heavens. I took manual control of the flyer and landed on Mahandriana's upper level, allowing the vehicle to rest in its usual position atop the water-strewn boulders. For a moment I stood outside the flyer, gazing out at the views surrounding me, before cold and the strong wind forced me down off the Sky Level to the nearest gryphon. It was not long before I stood outside the residence of my next opponent.

Dezisserine sat in one of its workshops, a long, narrow chamber with shiny walls and curved corners, set with windows on one side, where a corridor ran. Tables lay in chaotic rows, while shelves lined the walls.

On one shelf I saw a pair of emerald-green hand-torches. I leaped through one of the windows, and, hearing me, Dezisserine turned around and jumped to its feet.

"So, you have returned," the agen said.

I nodded. So human did it look, so natural, that I had to remind myself that here stood a machine, akin to Kirishnaghar, yet reduced in stature, because this being had shrugged off its shape-changing abilities to become a shaman agen: it had darkened its eye. But as I looked at it I knew what line my attack would take.

"You think you have illustrated your point, no?" Dezisserine said.

"Rather," I replied, "you have illustrated why your position is futile. You envisage a bridge between the natural and the manufactured, between life and artifice, but that bridge can never exist—"

"I say that it can!" Dezisserine interrupted. It made a gesture at the vials and scarlet wrealities that lay strewn over the tables of its workshop. "I have shown that it is possible for a human being to experience machine knowledge. I did that in various ways. The incidents on and atop the Pillar, and of course the work in the virtual spaces, where the souls of the agens were seen."

301

I scoffed at this. "You are a fool to believe in a universal concept of the soul," I said.

"And you the rational one, no?"

I drew a deep breath, then said, "There is no afterlife and human beings have no soul. Do you think I do not know the source of the ancient enmity between agen and mallead? It is because malleads created the Constructor and the Transmuter, and when those devices are used they destroy the immortal souls of agens. For agen souls are naught but raw material. Transfer Station Gold is no heaven."

Dezisserine made no reply. I knew that I had surprised it.

I continued, "Those four agen incidents were acts of worship, devised after Psolilai's first use of the Constructor in Theeremere. Truly, malleads fear agens because of what agens might do in revenge."

Dezisserine scowled. "All this talk of souls is a distraction," it said. I smiled, knowing that it was admitting defeat on the point. But then it said, "However, you have not answered my main point, which is that human beings can experience machine knowledge. I will have my bridge between the two ecosystems, no?"

"You will not," I replied, with some force. "All you showed was that human beings can experience disjointed knowledge emanating from artificial devices. No knowledge was passed the other way. No machine has ever understood mushroom meaning. And this is why a peripatetic mycologist, me. Why? Because right from the beginning I suspected that any bridge would be one way, that is, not a bridge at all. You have failed to show that wisdom mixing can occur between the two ecosystems. Even if Psolilai had understood anything, you would still have failed, for you never experimented upon your own kind. The so-called bridge was but a one-way torrent."

Dezisserine said nothing for some time. It paced up and down its workshop, on occasion glancing out of the windows, then returning its gaze to the wrealities on the tables. At last it said, "What then for you? You have not won yet."

"I never considered winning to be my goal," I said. "I seek merely to return nature to its proper place." I hesitated, my anxiety returning. "I know to what you are referring. One final opponent remains, and I do not know where he is."

Dezisserine shrugged. "Neither do I," it said.

302

I departed the chamber of the agen and returned to my flyer. In a few minutes I was relaxing in my bucket-seat, the comfortable and reassuring cockpit around me, dark land rushing below me. The sound of air hissing past the vehicle was music to my ears.

I suspected that my search would end in Theeremere, so in that direction I flew; but I was guessing. And despite my success with Sukhtaya and Dezisserine I knew that failure was still an option, for though I had shown the moral poverty of Sukhtaya's position and the logical confusion of Dezisserine's, I still did not understand enough about the manufacturing ecosystem to conclude my case. There remained mysteries yet to penetrate.

I had to conclude my case successfully if I was to take charge of the world around me and return nature to its rightful position. This I knew, more profoundly than anything else.

In Theeremere I returned to my personal chamber inside the Church of the Parasol Cap. It was a small room, brick and stone and fine cloth tapestries, one window only because the chamber was hidden in the maze of the fifth floor. Furnished with table, chair and desk, six neon strings following triangular panels down from the centre of the domed roof to provide omnidirectional light. Extremely thick carpet, so those on the floor below would not suspect my presence; an atmosphere of peace on the scent of old roses.

I sat alone, deep in thought. Of course I could not risk sleep. The irony of this fact did not escape me.

My final opponent embodied the dilemma that I faced. I recalled those prescient words spoken by wise Yamajatha at the Inn of Twilight Ratiocination: you will never return nature to sole occupancy, as you put it. There is always the question of sentience. Because we felins, like you humans, are conscious, we have the ability to manipulate our environment. We need tools. We need raw materials. Would it not be better to accept a minimum level of use? Given the opportunity to use sustainable resources, we could live with nature and still retain our required level of technology. And so I pondered the possibility of me advocating a similar line. But I could not decide. Something inside me, some emotion, some wisdom perhaps, told me that the manufacturing ecosystem was ultimately inhumane. What facts had I missed that would help me conclude my task?

I could think of nothing. My mind wandered to the situation I was in. I would have to watch out for motorcycles, balloons, blind birds, and all the rest . . . my opponent was cunning personified.

Next morning I found myself wandering through the evergreen garden behind the Church, where Psolilai had dreamed of me. It was dawn and I was alone. The sun rose behind the boughs of the evergreen plane, boughs that were lower and thicker than I remembered; and through the leaves it flickered green. I glanced at the laurel hedge, then the yew, then at the bed of old roses. Then I returned my gaze to the sun. It was still green.

I spoke, knowing that my opponent would hear me. "You are watching," I remarked.

"We two are duellists," came the reply.

I nodded, understanding what lay behind Auzarshere's statement. "Will a duel be the form of our struggle?" I asked.

"Sukhtaya and Dezisserine were no match for you. I am different."

303

"You were there?"

"Of course," Auzarshere replied. He opened his other eye, and there was a pair of green suns rising.

I recalled the two rooms in which I had spoken with Sukhtaya and Dezisserine. Then I said, "Let us begin our duel. I will represent nature, and you will represent . . ."

Auzarshere laughed at my uncertainty. "Do you know what I represent?" he asked. "I think not, for you were more akin to psolilai than to Psolilai."

He was right. Adopting a nonchalant tone I replied, "Tell me what you represent."

"Nature is not all. There will always be manufacturing, which will, inevitably, alter the landscape, and thus nature. But my manufacturing is not harsh and unsubtle. I am that manufacturing which mimics nature, for I understand that nature is design, honed over billions of years."

I nodded. Auzarshere was taking a position related to Yamajatha's. I stood in an awkward place. "Very well," I said. "We two will duel."

At dawn on the following morning I was taken by a drone to a street of shattered brick and sand. The ground was black-streaked, alive with worms and eels; all plastic. In a nearby lake lived a bank of kelzinzi, speaking to one another in their mournful voices. The drone departed, and I searched the street for Auzarshere.

As daylight became twilight I found a limestone mound set beside the lake, where I made a temporary camp, building a shelter from rusty iron poles and piles of plastic leaves. From a vantage point atop the mound I watched the sun dip through purple and grey clouds, to become a red disk upon the horizon.

"Here!" came a shout.

Auzarshere said nothing more as he approached me. He paused to glance at the kelzinzi in the lake, and I recalled that they were an artificial conscious species.

"I know what you are thinking," said Auzarshere. "You are wondering why I brought you to this lake."

I nodded.

"We have to go and see the kelzinzi," Auzarshere told me.

"Very well," I replied.

I rose to my feet and peered out over the lake. The water was dark, like oil, with a rainbow surface. I constructed a raft out of plastic leaves, tying them together into a thick bundle. The kelzinzi bobbed a few hundred yards out and it was easy enough to reach them. Like buoys of dark plastic they floated in the water, their immense weed-like bodies visible as an olive smudge underneath the water, their discharges pale like cream, their feet locked deep into the lake bed. Their upturned faces showed rudimentary eyes and ears, but it was their mouths and noses that took up space. In sad voices they spoke to one another, quiet as the raft approached, then silent.

"Greetings, kelzinzi," I said.

The kelzinzi did not understand me. I had expected this. But then the lake began to churn as the kelzinzi wriggled their bodies, forcing me to retreat. But it was no attack; debris, gas bubbles, and then fish, real, natural fish were brought to the surface, many of them dazed; an easy task to collect them. In ten minutes I was standing on the beach clutching my prize, some of which were still thrashing. I smacked their heads on a stone until every one was still.

"Do you understand?" Auzarshere said.

I turned to face him. I realised that I had lost, but I knew that I would still have to explain myself. "Yes," I said. "The kelzinzi mimic a natural form, but they are superior because they constitute external memory, that can be accessed from outside. Nature boasts no equivalent design." I sighed. "You win, Auzarshere."

"I win," the mallead repeated. I looked at him and realised that his existence alone was enough to win the duel, for he mimicked a human form, and yet he was superior.

But then a thought struck me. Mimicking was all very well... but was it enough? Did not the mimicking of nature constitute a degradation of nature? I had been persuaded by the extraordinary abilities of the kelzinzi, who had provided me with natural food despite my inability to talk their language. And yet there was another natural sentient species apart from human beings, that Auzarshere might not have accounted for: the felins.

I had to take a risk.

In a clear voice I said, "We will make it the best of three. This duel is not over."

Auzarshere's emerald eyes brightened. "What have I to gain from that?" he asked.

He had a point. After a pause for thought I replied, "We will make it the best of three, and if I lose I will return to the dream, to live there permanently." I gave a dramatic little chuckle, as if amused by my idea. "I would never bother you again."

For five silent minutes Auzarshere considered what I had said. I wondered what arcane processes illuminated his hyperdense brain. Then he said, "Very well."

And he vanished. I blinked, and for a moment received the impression of a crow flying away. Tired and apprehensive, I began the walk back to the Church of the Parasol Cap. At least the bird had not been an owl. Auzarshere was not claiming victory.

The felins, I knew, were the key to me winning the second phase of the duel. So I walked around Theeremere, observing it. I examined the changes made by bad snow and by bad fog. I studied the alterations made to the Church of the Parasol Cap. Then I spent a whole day at the Pool of Wrealities, observing the scarlet orbs there and recalling the forms of those most ancient. Then, when my case was complete, I called Auzarshere's name. Because the Pool of Wrealities was a public place he appeared as a blind old man leaning on a stick, wrinkled and pale, dressed in a long cloak and slippers.

"Observe the haven of Theeremere," I said. Confidence made my voice strong and clear. "Observe the alterations made by suites of artificial substances in snow and fog," I said. "There is meaning behind bad snow."

"Meaning?" Auzarshere queried. "There can be no meaning. Bad snow mimics snow, but it does not constitute a teleological form."

"You are incorrect," I said. "You pointed out that the kelzinzi, a sentient race, mimic nature, but I now point out to you that bad snow is returning Theeremere to the felins—as a gift, free and with no obligation. You see, Theeremere is a haven more ancient than you realise. Theeremere was built by the felins, which is why the holographic forms of the most ancient wrealities here are felins. Bad snow is shrinking the streets and reducing the heights of windows and doors so that the felins may be properly accommodated. And Teewemere, the felin haven situated Westside, is of course a topographic copy of

Theeremere." I paused, then added, "I understood as soon as I returned from the dream that the ziggurat and the Church of the Parasol Cap were conceptually equivalent structures."

Auzarshere said nothing. I caught a faint gleam of green light as he cast his gaze out over the steaming lake. Then he grunted, "The score alters to one each. The final part of the duel will be the decider."

To that, I agreed.

I spent the next day alone in my chamber. Although I had discovered the truth of the manufacturing ecosystem regarding the felins, I realised that Auzarshere and I both had a chance of proving our case to the other. I was missing one final fact that would illustrate the truth of my position, and so was he. We were, in fact, approaching similar conclusions from opposing directions. I knew that my original stance, that of a pure naturalist, was no longer viable—Auzarshere had illustrated that by means of the kelzinzi, and of course I had witnessed psolilai's failure, and subsequent recovery. But I had rebuffed his concept of the manufacturing ecosystem being a norm from which the natural ecosystem varied.

307

Psolilai and psolilai had acted, and their deeds had led me back to reality. Psolilai began mixed then became Gaian: psolilai began Gaian then grasped the necessity of a certain level of manufacture. From their deeds I could synthesize a truth, a new reality.

Hidden deep in the experience that I had gained lay the heart of the manufacturing ecosystem, but as yet I did not know it. I knew, however, that I was close to grasping that heart, which was the truth that would win me the duel.

That evening, Auzarshere and I went for a stroll along the river, beginning in Thee and ending in Ere. I listened carefully to what he said, alert for any sign that he was making his case, but I, with nothing to say, remained silent apart from a few noncommittal grunts. As we passed the boundary of the Field of Gaia I glanced aside to the hillocks that lay outside the haven wall, to see a menhir atop the tallest hill, in silhouette before a ruddy sunset. I paused to admire the scene. But what I had taken to be a stone object was revealed as two agens, moving apart then dancing away down opposite slopes. I recalled similar scenes that I had watched during my life, and as I did a revelation came to me.

It had long bothered me that Auzarshere and I might arrive at the same conclusion and be forced to work together. But now I knew that future could never be. He was at heart a manufacturer, and I . . . I was . . .

"You are deep in thought," Auzarshere observed.

"I claim victory in this duel," I said.

He uttered a choked laugh. "I do not think so!"

Ignoring his outburst I said, "At last I understand what Dezisserine was fumbling towards. And I understand the hotch-potch of concepts that Yamajatha was so close to refining . . . had he not been tempted. Of course! The answer is rejuvenation."

Auzarshere was alarmed by my joyous confidence. "Rejuvenation?" he said.

"I see now the deepest metaphor of the manufacturing ecosystem," I replied. "It is a metaphor that you have seen, yet which you have ignored as an answer because of your own desires, which, for you, still mask the truth. But I care only for the real world. I care not from whence ideas come. Yes, I was naive in my early years, taking the position of naturalist and denying everything manufactured. But sentience requires manufacturing."

"Then you are admitting defeat," Auzarshere said, "for such is my position."

"No!" I cried. The echo of my rebuttal bounced from building to building, dying at length amidst the hisses and groans of the haven. "The manufacturing ecosystem is not a monolithic entity. You understand this. It is composed of a constructing half and a rejuvenating half—what you might call a transmuting half."

Auzarshere was appalled at what he was hearing. Like a witless fool he murmured, "That cannot be . . . can not be!"

"The answer to the great question that we have pondered is rejuvenation. Transmutation! Recycling!"

"No!" Auzarshere shrieked. "We must construct!"

I let him calm down before continuing my declaration. "I saw two agens on that hill just now, locked in a sensuous embrace, and my realisation was that they exist in two genders, just as humans and felins are male and female. One gender is constructing, the other is transmuting.

There is a way to live with nature and yet manufacture. We must accept a minimum level of use of our resources. Then we must transmute, recycle. We must rejuvenate what we have without plundering irreplaceable natural resources. This is the future that I put forward, Auzarshere. You have lost. Construction is doomed. Transmutation is the way out of the nightmare that surrounds us. Dezisserine saw a ghost of this truth after he forsook mallead status and became an agen. There are two types of artificial shaman. One type assembles, that is, constructs, while the other type metamorphoses, that is, transmutes. But Dezisserine was envious of human wisdom and failed to understand the value of transmutation. He, of course, is an assembler."

Auzarshere stopped walking, and he bent over as if exhausted. I watched him, and to me he appeared to be shrinking. He knew that he had lost the duel.

"I am the master of all that is around me," I said. "I will take over from the Analytical Council in Theeremere, and I will head the Analyticate in Mahandriana. And when I have presided over the demise of those structures, new bodies will emerge that will bring the return of nature and the creation of a fully rejuvenating manufacturing."

Auzarshere sobbed.

One surprise yet awaited me. Two figures emerged from alleys to the side of the street in which we stood, that I saw were Voaranazne and Kirishnaghar. Voaranazne had forsaken mallead life and become an agen; his eyes were human, hazel, bright with knowledge. But Kirishnaghar's eyes were frosty blue and glowing like lanterns. As I watched he changed into a gryphon—I grasped the symbolism after a moment's thought. Auzarshere sobbed once more, sighed, and then the light of his emerald eyes was lost forever. He stood hunched, an ordinary agen: a constructing agen. Voaranazne was also of the constructing gender.

I turned to face Kirishnaghar. He stared at me then said, "I will remain a mallead, the last of my kind." A lop-sided grin appeared on his face. "You will admit that shape-changing is a kind of transmutation."

I nodded, and turned around to face the haven. Much work lay before me.

Astra Gaia.